MW00622423

ILLYADRA

KNOWLEDGE IS CURRENCY

ADRIEL

ADRIEL HOUSE
PUBLISHING

Illyadra

Copyright 2023 by Adriel Wallaker

This is a work of fiction. Names, characters, places, and incidents are products of the author's imagination or are used fictitiously and are not to be construed as real. Any resemblance to actual events, locales, organizations, or persons, living or dead, is coincidental.

All Rights Reserved. No part of *Illyadra* may be reproduced, stored in a retrieval system, or transmitted, in any form or by any means—by electronic, mechanical, photocopying, recording or otherwise—in any form without permission. Thank you for buying an authorized edition of this book and for complying with copyright laws.

Cover Design by George Downes
Interior Design by Printopya LLC
Illustrations by Rachel Ward & Grzegorz Wozniak
Copyediting by Adrienne Kisner
Developmental Editing by Peter Lundell

Published by Adriel House Publishing
644 Holly Springs rd
Unit 325
Holly Springs, NC 27540
adrielhousepublishing.com

Paperback ISBN: 978-1-961406-01-8
Hardcover ISBN: 978-1-961406-00-1
eISBN: 978-1-961406-02-5

First Edition

Printed in the United States.

To the intuitive.
To the fantasizer, the idealist, the daydreamer.
For the one whose thoughts persist beyond the boundaries
of the present world.
May you, when caught in the grips of a rich scent,
search ruthlessly for its source.
Amen.

PROLOGUE

The walls of the Graey Castle trembled; thin sheets of dust fell from the ceiling. King Ivan looked around in desperation. No wisdom would save him now.

"Ivan!" The yell of his name boomed with thunder, untamed by the thick stone surrounding him.

Only his strongest soldiers remained. The banister railing shook under their hands.

How has it come to this? He wished to muster up some speck of comfort for them, but the bitter truth remained. This would be the end.

"Ivan!" The monstrous voice shook him to the bone, but one thing kept the sword of Renovia fixed firmly in his hand.

It was the Age of Under. The next measurement, Kortaes, marked which of the nations was the current world-power. The most influential. Each Kortaes, during the current age, united all of Zoë under a common pillar of culture. A common language from the Illians, a world currency from the Masikonians, or a calendar from the Renovians.

The end of a Kortaes was seldom gradual, nearly always dramatic. But this time, it seemed, was bloodier than most.

"Alright," Ivan said, his voice weary from battle. "Let them in." In the past he would have given a speech—something to father the primitive instincts of men. But now even a hardy war-cry would be utterly inconsequential.

The Renovians released their spells that bound the thick oak courtyard doors. Enemy Sigu Nii soldiers burst through. Their boots clattered on the marble tile, and their guttural howls echoed down the castle halls. The remnants of Ivan's army gave no wait for their king's command. They liberated both arrows from bows and boulders from makeshift, indoor catapults.

The Sigu Nii shot shards of ice and balls of fire.

Ivan dispersed the primeval spells with the barest movement of his outstretched hand. Child's play. The danger was the sheer mass of men clambering through the doors, as well as the unimaginable force that led them.

"Ivan!" The yell mixed with a bit of chuckle at the end.

What evil have you handed yourself over to, Ash?

The castle quivered from the footsteps of the beastly king.

Ivan's gaze shifted back to his soldiers, where remnants of fear still clung, but overtaken by the relentless surge of battle.

He thought about waiting to gather a glimpse of how true the stories were, the rumors of Ash's monstrosity. But he knew it could be too late if he lingered. *I guess it's time then.* Every part of his body yelled at him to stay and fight. *Don't leave your people!* But this wasn't a matter of talent or skill of battle. It was a matter of preventing genocide. He turned toward the hallway behind him. Shooting a final glance down the castle stairwell, terror gripped him. A monstrous, infernal orb of black and white fire crashed through the thick stone wall above the courtyard doors. The spell was larger than the entirety of Ivan's remaining army. Shrill screams erupted from them, and they all reached extended arms—some flailing for safety, others wishing to magically dismiss their imminent destruction.

King Ivan's hand snapped their direction as well, but the ball of fire consumed his army in an unblinking instant.

The ball of fire sank deep into the castle, scattering stone and wood debris in every direction. The roof quaked and threatened collapse, and the shaking of the Graey Castle knocked Ivan to his knees. Dust and smoke stung his eyes so that he couldn't even see the stone wall closest to him. His eyes began to water, but not just from the polluted air. Tears rolled down his cheeks as he picked himself off the ground. A wretched wheeze insisted on clearing through his throat, but he forced it back down. If Ash so much as heard him *think*, he'd be there in an instant.

"Give me the crown, Ivan!"

He wanted the wooden sword of Renovia.

Ivan sprinted down the hallway. The light was dim, spears through the dust. He ran past familiar paintings and tapestries, past doors that previously housed welcomed guests and residential Aliyah. Thoughts of before the war filled Ivan's sight: servants and nobles bustling about. *Has anyone loved a king as much as they love me? Surely not!*

His hands slammed against the stone wall in front of him, and he thrust himself forward as he turned the corner.

The upcoming hallway was torn apart by Ash's power, leaving a gaping hole.

There's no time! He thrust his hand forward, drawing energy from the wooden sword. Broken stones flew up from all around to make hovering steps above the hole. Ivan sprinted across, not worrying whether they would hold his weight.

"There!" a throaty growl yelled below him.

Ivan glanced to make sure nothing was flying his way but otherwise paid the voice no attention. He arrived at his bedroom door and thrust it open. A startled scream came out, and a sword swung toward his face. Instinctively, he reached up and caught the blade with his bare hand, a slight sting pierced him due to his weariness.

7

"Are you trying to kill me, woman?" He forced a laugh despite the look of horror on his wife's face. He guided the sword down with his left and closed the door with his right. His room was filled with terrified servants and children. All of them looked to him for an answer, but no solution would save them. "It's time," Ivan whispered. Her face fell. "This isn't a battle to be won."

"What will happen to us?" One of the servants spoke up, her voice cracked. She clutched a small child in her hands.

It was not a day to spread hope. "The battle is lost."

The children began to cry. Ivan hushed them as footsteps trampled past the door.

"Is the king's son ready for a bath, then?" came a hoarse voice from an old man in the back of the room. His speech wobbled, resembling a clear itch to speak Old Vulgarhe instead. His hair was dirty white and patchy, with a bald spot in the middle, and a long beard to match.

Ivan straightened his back, preparing himself. El Neo Nii had approached him earlier in the season, when the port city Ryala had fallen in battle, and relayed that Renovia would indeed fall to the Sigu Nii. There, they devised a plan in place of defeat. They would send the crown into the future.

Life spans will be reduced to fractions, and perceived time—moments. All of Zoë will be susceptible to illness and disease, murder and war, even apathy and remorselessness. King Ivan's people will be barbarians amid civil courts. And though the crown of restoration would only be gone for a few short generations, as he understands them now, it will feel like dozens for his people.

"Yes," said Ivan confidentially. The atrocities to come are temporary. King Ash possessing the crown of Renovia would destroy a part of Zoë forevermore.

A sniffle came from Queen Epheriia, a sniffle that pierced through his projected strength. Tears erupted from his eyes as he drew his wife near. "I'm sorry," Ivan whispered.

The old man shuffled towards them, leaning on a dark bamboo walking stick while grumbling nonsense under his breath with every step.

Ivan took a small babe out of his wife's arms. Rocking her, he whispered words of love and remorse into his daughter's ear. He handed her to the old man and bent down to make eye contact with his young son. "Kairo," he paused. "You take care of Aterah. Your sister will need you to be strong. Can you do that for me?"

"I don't want to leave you, Daddy!" Kairo cried.

Queen Epheriia bent down and hugged her son with desperate regret beneath her closed eyes.

During the plan's inception, El cautioned that his children held pivotal roles in the unfolding future. The warning nearly dissuaded him, but now, he gratefully acknowledged their divine exemption from the impending doom that awaited the rest of them.

"You'll be a good king someday. Better than your father." Ivan took the boy's hand and led him to the old man.

"The Archeodon," the old man held the girl in one arm and embraced the boy while stretching out the bamboo walking stick with the other. Strange carvings of bright archaic runes covered the stick.

"What is going on?" a servant asked. No one answered.

Silver lined the edges of the wooden sword, with veins running along the flat surface that twisted and curled into the Silver Tree of Renovia. As Ivan handed the sword over, it transformed into an open-faced crown with seven troughs and peaks. He placed the crown around the bamboo staff. Power drained from him. His head throbbed and light danced across his vision.

"Another time then?" The old man nodded as a farewell.

The bedroom door shook and yells commanded it to be opened from the other side.

"Unlikely," Ivan said, turning toward the door, struggling to hold it in place with only his body. Wind swirled around the old man and the children, and with a crack of dusty black lightning, they were gone.

1

RESCUE

Twenty-eight generations later.

The squadron's eight swordsmen came around the first tent in the clearing. Mud covered the bottom edge of the off-white hide skins. They were sewn into a triangular tarp with a black tribal insignia painted on the side.

They crept past, wincing with each smack of their sandals in and out of the mud. Bright white lightning danced across the sky and thunder boomed through the valley.

Four bodies lay around the clearing. Mud spattered their arms and their mail, and arrows rose from their corpses like flags of surrender. Kairo kneeled and studied a crumpled Sigu Nii. The arrow had struck deep into his chest, and the heavy beads of the storm overhead sent his seeping blood into a chorus of lift-off droplets.

Kairo took note of the Sigu Nii's dull sword. His mail had scattered films of rust. His boots were parting at the soles.

Kairo strained quietly and turned the Sigu Nii body on its side. A black tribal tattoo partially covered his lower shoulder. A quarter of a circle shaped like a serpent's tail, with a down facing dagger beneath, and an inscription farther down that read, *Yutarah.*

The swordsmen lingered as Kairo stood and brushed himself. "The tribe is poor." He whispered. "Level-one grunt. The war chief is probably level-two."

Copt sighed with relief, Norly made a face of contempt, and Rouen nodded toward the dome in the middle of the camp. They continued. Kairo searched the tent entrances. He studied each one for the slightest of movements, anything that might signify a barbarian entering the rain.

With a bit of prayer, they reached the sizeable dome-shaped tent in the center of the clearing, ten reaches high and twenty steps across. They swept inside as Kairo held his sword tight in both hands, ready for Sigu Nii warriors. Or the war-tribe leader.

One man kneeled alone, his head slumped over unconscious, with hands tied behind the center pole.

Sticks and twine shaped the tarp together as it drummed with the rain. Norly's sword dropped to his side. "Where is everyone?"

"Maybe they don't know who it is they've captured." Copt shrugged.

Captain Rouen dropped to his knees before the slumped-over man. He seemed older, peppered hair, wrinkles creeping around the edges of his eyes and mouth. Splatters of dried blood covered his arms, his neck, and his tattered rebellion linens. "General," Rouen whispered, trying to shake him awake. "General Forst."

Kairo untied his hands from the center pole. The general fell against Rouen. He moaned. His head began to bob up and down as he passed in and out of consciousness. "Get—" He coughed and heaved for air. "Get me out of here, Captain." His voice was raspy and hoarse.

"Kairo, to me." Captain Rouen commanded with a sigh of strain as he lifted the general to his feet. Kairo rushed to the general's side and slung his arm around his shoulder.

He smelled rotten, Kairo noticed. A week with the Sigu Nii beasts and their stink already clung to him. A distinct sort of must, sweat, and grime that covered all of them.

Kairo looked to the south, through the clearing from which they had come. The ground was all dark-brown, sloshed mud, with drops splashing from the heavy rain. A dozen tents faced them as they walked.

Twelve steps to Kairo's left a tent flap fidgeted. A shockwave of adrenaline and pulsating terror coursed through him. He pointed with his free hand, and the Renovian soldiers turned to see. Their swords were up and ready, gripped tightly in their hands. One Sigu Nii holler and the whole camp would be in a frenzy.

The tent flap rose as a Sigu Nii walked out backward. He said a few final, playful words to the barbarian inside. But as the flap shut, the Sigu Nii soldier turned to see eight Renovian swordsmen walking out with his captive. His brows came in, the muscles in his arms and shoulders tensed. His mouth opened.

The tip of an arrow erupted out from the side of his neck. One moment, his mouth was opening; the next, blood dribbled down his chin. Another arrow hit him, right through the upper left shoulder. The Sigu Nii fell to his knees, and his eyes rolled up to face the sky as he splashed into the mud. Blood splattered the tent and washed its way down to the muddied bottom edge.

Kairo looked around. He looked to the tree line where he knew archers were stationed. He couldn't see them through the rain or through the shade of the trees, but in his mind, he thanked them.

Captain Rouen sighed in relief. He was a dark man. Several shades more than the average burnt-golden Renovian. Rouen was in his second-generation, making him a child during the Egress. Black fuzz, smaller than a knuckle's length, rounded his head and his chin. He slogged forward, and they continued to trudge toward the tree line.

Kairo had been a soldier under the command of Rouen for a little under a quarter-generation, or several dry-seasons. Though he could trust the soldiers around him with his life, most of whom had been under Rouen for much longer, Kairo loathed the slow pace under the general. A leech for Kairo's agility. He felt that because he couldn't move quickly, it was as if he couldn't think quickly. The heavy rain began to feel hot, and Kairo itched to be out of the clearing.

The swordsmen made it to the shelter of the trees, where even if a Sigu Nii left their tent, the squadron wouldn't be the first thing a barbarian laid their eyes on. Kairo and Rouen continued through the dense patch of tightly packed jungle, through jungle brush and towering trees, and back onto a small animal trail.

Captain Rouen nodded toward the trunk where their knapsacks rested. "Norly, Copt. Make a stretcher, and do it quickly."

"I would call that an easy mission success," Norly said. He and Copt hastily began to lace twine between two sticks.

"We're not home yet." Captain Rouen kept his gaze toward the camp. "There's no telling when a Sigu Nii will go to give the general a cup of water or a bite of bread. And when they do, the whole of them will be on our tail."

One by one, the archers returned from their positions around the clearing. Aterah brought up the rear, the last of them to arrive back on the trail. "We should leave," she suggested with a vain attempt at a steady voice.

"Already on it, OA." Rouen strapped on his knapsack.

Oracle Aterah. Kairo shook his head. Whatever this thing of hers was, it felt like it was getting worse. There were times when subtle jealousy would gnaw at him, for the strange role that Aterah had decided to play. A role that superseded all formal rebellion ranks. Soldier, second, captain, and all the superior forms of leadership. Aterah didn't just skip them; NeoDerii had to make up an entire rank specifically for her.

Her hair, muddy brown from the rainstorm, was tied back into a tight ponytail by a white wool string.

Once Aterah reached a generation old, NeoDerii had sought to send her east of the war and bear children. That's when this thing of hers started. And since then, it's gotten worse.

"Norly, Copt, take the first shift." Captain Rouen gestured to the incapacitated general. "Alright, let's head home."

With swords sheathed and knapsacks strapped on, the squadron marched out from the direction they came. They trudged east through flooded trails and rivulets in the storm.

Kairo watched the north side of the group. His eyes filtered out all the things that should be there—the jungle trees whose bark was dark and jagged, the waist-high brush on either side of the trail, and the bright red death berries that hung ever so tauntingly on them. He searched for movement. The tiniest ruffle of leaves, the cracking of a fallen branch, or the glint of Sigu Nii metal.

They stepped over traps hidden along the trail. Simple things, like a sharpened stick buried upright under person-sized leaves, with human dung slathered about the point. A wooden puncture might not remove a Sigu Nii, but infection would.

The squadron marched for hours. The storm gradually eased into a light shower as the sky squeezed herself of her last few drops. Not long after, a breath of fresh wind swept the sky, and bright blue patches appeared between the clouds, just glimpses through the canopy hundreds of reaches above the jungle floor.

With the storm gone, life returned. Monkeys cackled and jumped about the branches, following the lead of some unseen alpha. Birds soared and weaved between the trees while eyeing the ground for prey. Critters and rodents scurried along the trail ahead.

Captain Rouen had the soldiers rotate shifts carrying the general.

The roaring sound of the Maua filled the jungle as the squadron came upon it. A great southbound river rapid.

"If you took a boat and went that way," Copt pointed south down the river, "You would be at Raida in half a day."

Norly waved him off. "You're making that up."

"It's true, I seen the map in Command—"

"Hush." Captain Rouen snapped at them both. "We're almost to the river pass." They followed the Maua south and reached a small cliff, fifteen reaches high.

The river continued a dozen steps past the cliff's edge and disappeared in a clash of blue and white.

Rouen paused, leaning over the damp, rocky ridge, and peered both ways for Sigu Nii movement. The cliff cut alongside an old Renovian road from their Kortaes. A time when their people spread across the face of now-unknown plains and foreign waters. A road whose octangular bits of stone, clearly cut, molded, and laid by human hands, now only jutted occasionally from the broad, overgrown trail. Octagon bricks remained visible beneath globs of dirt, between root networks, or sliding off the sides of the road as the generations passed by.

The Renovians did well to stay off the old road. The Sigu Nii used it blatantly, leaving their trash and ash fire pits and moving their war tribes great distances without the slow trudge of weaving between trees.

Captain Rouen whistled, *clear*. And the squadron began down the cliffside.

To the right, the jungle canopy arched over the wide trail and extended down beyond eyesight. To the left lay the river pass, the only way across the Maua anywhere that Kairo knew of.

The road cut between the cliff and the waterfall. The cliff wall retained most of its original stone bricks. Only several were lying in pieces against a grey stone bridge partly covered in vibrant green patches of moss and vines. Two solid pillars of carved stone, intricately patterned with curves and etchings, held up the overhang where the Maua roared over the bridge.

The Old River Pass stirred Kairo's insides. A glance at any of the soldiers revealed that they felt similarly. The Old River Pass marked a different time in their history—a time when they could afford to build great and elaborate stone structures like an ornately patterned bridge, sixty steps long just to cross some water. A time before they were forced to quietly hide like prey of the jungle, before they were forced to live like animals in trees.

A heavy southern wind blew cold mist in waves across the bridge, sprinkling Kairo's face and arms from his right. The roar of the Maua echoed off the stone overhang. An archer named Tullia and a fresh recruit carried General Forst cautiously so as not to slip on the wet grey-green stone.

Birds screeched overhead, loud enough to overtake the crashing waterfall of the Maua.

Kairo turned. He strained his eyes down the trail. They were fleeing from something in the northwest. "Captain."

Rouen turned. "They're coming."

Second Copt's lone steps were loud on the stone bridge. Everyone else had frozen where they stood. "What are we going to. . ."

"Make for the trees," Tullia suggested, a slight quiver in her voice. "There's still time to tie off hammocks high above. They won't see us up there."

Norly grunted. "Cowards. Let's fight them. Every Sigu Nii still alive is a Sigu Nii able to hunt us later. If we deal with them now, that's a couple dozen less snakes in the outpost's vicinity."

"Have you seen any of this, OA?" Captain Rouen turned to Aterah.

Aterah shook her head. "I only dreamt of the clearing, the storm, and Forst."

As if awoken by his name, General Forst heaved and coughed up a wad of bloody phlegm. "Remember Graeynesh Law, Captain." Speaking seemed painful for him, and Kairo winced at the blood on his chin. "The sun is almost down. And if we're not in the trees by nightfall . . . we're all as good as dead anyway."

"We can't fight them!" Tullia shouted.

"You looked at their armor." Captain Rouen turned to Kairo. "What's your estimate on their tribe?"

"Poor." Kairo shook his head, unsure. "I counted twelve tents across the clearing. Each would house a single, low-level Sigu Nii. Minus two tents, the war chief's tent and his second's. That's ten Sigu Nii with the serpent's tail or no tattoo at all. Plus two Sigu Nii warriors who could have the first section of the torso or even the second."

"Do you think we can take them or not?" Copt asked.

Kairo looked to his Captain. He wasn't sure, especially with nightfall inbound. "If we take to the trees, our only advantage becomes hiding. If they were to see our dead trail, they would only need to glance upward. And if the act of hiding fails, we're dead."

Captain Rouen huffed. "The river pass has served another squadron before. It's wide. Wider than I would like. But it'll have to do." Once he decided, Captain Rouen went into full battle mode. He started pointing out places for them to take stands. He directed where to lay their knapsacks well out of the way of battle. He instructed Tullia and Norly to hoist Forst into the trees, out of sight.

A few swordsmen pulled out sharpened wooden stakes from their packs, quick traps to bury in front of the stone river pass. The archers positioned themselves beside the swordsmen. Rouen instructed that they would shoot at the approaching war-tribe and then retreat nearer to the middle of the bridge.

Kairo unsheathed his bronze sword. After two generations of use it was riddled with rust. He took a moment to read the names etched into the flat of the blade, the names of soldiers who wielded the blade before him. He silently wished for favor from the Korta Ellanii. On the other side of the sword was a faded insignia engraved during the crafting of the metal—a wide silver tree with crowding branches and roots on either side of the trunk—the Silver Tree of Renovia.

Twelve Sigu Nii against sixteen Renovians. And from the jittering in Kairo's hand and the urgency in Rouen's voice, they all felt the same. Terrified.

Movement brushed the corner of his eye. He snapped in its direction. Fifty steps down the old road, Sigu Nii started climbing down the cliff.

"They're here," Kairo said.

The Sigu Nii soldiers who reached the ground took off in the direction of the river pass. They didn't wait for the rest of their tribe to make the climb, they didn't wait to gather into a hard-pressed line, and they didn't hesitate to rush for Renovian blood.

The Sigu Nii wore loose fabrics, light and breezy for the jungle's heat. Metal plating equipped them in sporadic locations—a protected shoulder here, a helmet there. The black paint about the metal did well against the rust, but the pieces were old, and the rust showed through. Their skin tone was a sickly yellow, much unlike the dark sunset color of Renovians.

Aterah squeezed between Rouen and Norly, her bow strung and an arrow waiting near her right cheek. The other archers followed, pushing between each swordsman. They fired. Eight arrows flew from the river pass, through the old road, and each missed their target.

The handful of scattered, sprinting, bellowing Sigu Nii dodged. They sidestepped or ducked, and otherwise regained momentum.

"Again," said Aterah, fitting another arrow and releasing.

Three arrows caught the closest warrior in the chest.

"Inkless," reported Kairo, his eyes fixed on the enemy's upper left arm as the man dropped to his knees and cracked his head against a corner of the old brick road. Three arrows missed. And the final was caught by a hand gloved in fire. The approaching Sigu Nii whipped his hand up and snatched the stone-tipped, feather-stabilized sliver of wood straight from the air. It crumbled to charcoal, and he began his sprint toward the bridge again.

"Vuu," Kairo called out the mystical power and a wave of unease took the Renovians. He could feel it as each of them shifted weight, brushed hair from their eyes, or moaned dreadfully.

"Again." Aterah's voice wavered, jittery with urgency.

The beasts were drawing close. The nearest was several paces out from the buried wooden stakes at the edge of the bridge and the road. Five arrows exploded through his body, blood sprayed from his skull, his open mouth, and his gut. The other three arrows were swatted away by the Sigu Nii behind him.

"Level-one," called Kairo, observing the serpent's tail on the crashing soldier.

"Back!" commanded Captain Rouen. He held up his hand in front of Aterah and motioned the archers to retreat.

Three waves of arrows, and still ten snakes remained. Kairo swiveled his bronze blade in his hand. His stomach quivered.

He did not know why the Sigu Nii hunted them so. Every lump of dough the Renovians baked was eaten to resist the oncoming Sigu Nii. Every sandal scrapped from available hides east of the war was made for gaining ground and retreating quickly. Every baby born learned Graeynesh Law, swordplay, bowmanship, and some form of usefulness within an outpost's functions. Every baby was born so that they might fight later. This war waged generations.

Two Sigu Nii barbarians approached the river pass. Wooden stakes drove through their sandals, and they wailed as they collapsed to their knees.

Before Kairo could even celebrate the surprising usefulness of the trap, a charred set of hands reached between their shoulders and flung the incapacitated Sigu Nii to the sides of the road.

The animal stood groveling, staring hungrily at the swordsmen. He wore strips of loosely woven metal, much harder than anything the rebellion had been able to concoct. It decorated his body with even strips around his torso while leaving a cutout hole on his lower left shoulder. A tattoo celebrated the hole. Two pieces of a serpent's lower torso, with a down facing dagger beneath the first and a small flame beneath the second.

The sun sank behind the trees, lowering itself in the Mauan valley to the west, below the Delkop mountain range. They needed to prevail against the war-tribe quickly.

The rest of the tribe had gathered around the wooden stakes. There were eight of them. Norly had a clear view of their shoulders, standing nearest the waterfall, and spoke above the echoing of the Maua. "Four inkless, two level-ones, a level-two, and a level-three remaining."

Several Renovians cried aloud, "A level-three?"

Sigu Nii with the three-piece serpent were particularly rare, and they were so difficult to deal with that Graeynesh Law included a section that four Renovians were required to fight them simultaneously—otherwise, run.

Arrows whistled overhead. Most missed. It was a difficult angle to get the arrow above the swordsmen and drop it into the horde beyond.

The Sigu Nii stood close enough that Kairo could see the strings tied around their necks. Most were empty. The tribe was poor. But still, several brown-golden ears drooped with rapid accumulating rot. A testament to how many Renovians each had slain.

Two of the Sigu Nii let loose war chants. They pounded their chests like the primitive beasts they were and leapt over the wooden stakes. Their feet hit the grey-green moss, and their arms swung in wide arching motions in vain attempts to regain balance. Renovian swordsmen rushed up and plunged bronze blades deep into their guts.

Six remained.

The level-two Sigu Nii closed his eyes. Concentration took his face, his mouth quivered in a frown, his chin jutting up and down. He held his hands over the wooden stakes, and ice began to form around them. It grew until the ice was level with the bridge. His eyes shot open. His lips curled into a twisted smile, his teeth grotesque, many missing and many rotting.

The war-tribe charged.

Kairo's senses yelled from every direction. *Duck there. Swing here. Block there.* It felt like he were fighting three barbarians at the same time. It wasn't enough to avoid a fatal blow, Kairo had to charge his body to avoid even a nick. The smallest of broken skin could lead to deadly and incurable infection.

The level-two snapped his fingers over his blade, and neon-blue electric vuu rippled around his sword. He got Norly with the flat of his blade, and the Renovian soldier crumpled into a momentary spasm.

Kairo and Rouen ducked together. They propelled their blades to intercede at the sudden focus to kill off Norly.

Rouen blocked incoming thrusts when Kairo hadn't the speed, and Kairo quickly drove his sword deep between the strips of the second's mail.

As the last of his tribe fell to the ground, the war chief ascended the river pass. His nose was crooked, perhaps broken ages ago. His eyes squinted like seeds. He displayed the coiling three-piece serpent on his arm with certainty that it was greater than the eight present swordsmen.

Beasts wielding the level-three tattoo didn't just fight with vuu, they could kill. Easily.

The sun dipped behind the horizon. Twilight took the jungle. And throaty, growling, distant roars shook the ground.

The Renovians drew around the war chief. With well-practiced, choreographed swordplay, they thrust their swords inward simultaneously.

The chief threw his hands out and a blunt explosion tossed each incoming blade off target.

Distant vegetation parted as the four-pawed beast of night bounded through the jungle.

"Go!" Said Copt. "There isn't enough time. I will take him."

Rouen signaled the archers to climb the trees and hold tight for the night. They turned and scrambled.

The beast of night roared again, its growling thundered through the river pass.

"Go!" Copt yelled at the swordsmen.

"Vuuless filth," the war chief spat. He lowered into a fighting stance, facing Copt.

Rouen backed away and ran for the trees. The rest of the squadron chased after him.

The overhang pounded with the steps of the night beast, the *snagaeri*.

Kairo snatched up his knapsack and glanced back down the river pass. Copt stood still, his sword loose by his side, his eyes locked with the war chief.

Kairo climbed the closest tree he could find. Branch by branch, he heaved himself up into the canopy. He slowed around sixty reaches off the ground and tossed the strap of his pack around a broken limb. He rummaged through until his hands rubbed against the twine netting of his hammock. He tied each end to sturdy branches and looked around. He could see a dozen other twine hammocks around him, each containing a fear-filled Renovian soldier.

The snagaeri roared again and drowned out the fainter sound of human screaming.

2

AYRAH

The city's arena was a long oval determined by a loose ring of rocks around a pit of the same blood-red sand of the region that seemed to coat everything within the horizon. Even the slightest eastern ocean-front breeze would kick up fine dust, sending it up like red mountain fog.

Ayrah wiped her brow, ignoring the grime that covered her hands. Simula's red-clay buildings, squared off in shape, surrounded the arena like a perimeter of bleachers. Crowds gathered on rooftops all around watching a member of the Black Guard grash a member of their rival guild.

"Can't believe the guildhead didn't step in," said Boden. "That one down there must've messed up real bad." He stood with his right foot leaned against the vertical trim around the roof.

"Aye. Not often the Black Guard come after people like us," said Boden's older brother, Herk. The two were similar in more manners than their looks—dark oiled hair and sun-tanned leather jackets—they were both drunk with aspiring glory.

Their jackets were expertly crafted to pedestal their coiling black Nii-wa tattoos on their lower left shoulders. Four pieces of a serpent's body coiled around its own skeletal head, which wove the symbols of the Niiwa together: A dagger drove through its crown, it had a flame for an eye, a human skull entering its mouth, and blood dripped where the snake's skin peeled off its vertebrae.

An inscription beneath it all read, *Simula.*

The rooftop crowds roared as blows were exchanged on the pit. Gusts of flame reflected off of neon blue ice spikes ripping out of the ground, illuminating the evening sky.

Ayrah squinted. The grash was half concerning. The city Simula had settled into a peaceful power struggle between the guild class and the Black Guard. Boden suggested that perhaps this guild member had crossed the line in some way, but Ayrah wondered if the Guard grew hungry.

"Shadowa," Boden called her. Neither of them knew Ayrah's real name. "Y'ur eyes are keen on the grash. Scared?"

"Bug off." They wouldn't mess with her too much. They wouldn't dare.

"Let's hear you say that when I'm running this town," huffed Herk. Simula was divided by three guilds. And the brothers planned on lessening that number by two.

Ayrah rolled her eyes and spat over the edge. "No one knew your name before me."

Herk leapt to his feet, his fists balled. The veins visible above his jacket, the ones that ran up his neck and face, illuminated an aggressive orange hue. Vuu ignited within him. Herk shuffled sideways, advancing on Ayrah with his lower left shoulder in view.

Ayrah dragged her foot up from the clay ledge, fit it beneath her, and pushed herself to stand. She stopped Herk's advance abruptly with her nose in his face. "What?"

Simula was simply a point of interest for her, a rest stop on a grander mission. Fighting with them in the arena and on the streets assured her a bed at night, food during the day, and ale between.

Ayrah could smell Herk's sour breath. She could feel the warmth from the fire in his blood.

The evening crowd roared, louder this time.

Ayrah and Herk turned and watched a member of Simula's top gang collapse. The Black Guard drug his body to a large wooden X in the middle of the arena and fastened his hands to the beams. The Guard flexed his hands in a sweeping motion, and a blanket of the pit's sand soared into the air above them, funneled into a single, razor-sharp point, and crashed against the crown of the loser's head.

His skull ripped open, the tendons that held his eyes splattered, and his teeth shattered across the pit. His blood and the red sand mixed together. The grash was over. The Black Guard held his weary arms high, orchestrating loose cheers like music.

"If you want to take a dip in the sand, you say so." Ayrah whispered. "I'll meet you down there."

Herk breathed loudly, like waste heat from factory cogs. He was thinking. "Maybe . . . maybe you'd grash well enough to take me arm, or me leg. And my name can't be known if I'm lame."

"Aye," said Boden. "A good call, brother."

Ayrah leaned back. The man had decided. Though she knew she was capable of much more than taking just an arm or a leg. His blood was sewage compared to hers.

A man came running up the steps on the side of the building. The fine red sand clung to his face with patches of sweat, as if blood were dripping down his cheeks. "El," he called.

Herk and Boden turned to him. Their faces hardened, resembling a demeanor worthy of the title. "What is it?"

"It's Lord Mayor Gabya." He panted. "He's on his way to the Burnt Harem."

Ayrah winced. The brothers owned one of the finer brothels in the city. And they insisted on naming it the Burnt Harem. A semantic misfire. Herk and Boden knew nothing of Aylavuera's prettier speaking rules. The two could hardly read, as it were.

"What's 'is manners?" Boden asked.

"Pussy . . . hopefully."

"Is Taryn there?" Herk asked.

"Aye."

"And the Masikonian?" Boden asked.

"Nowhere to be found."

Boden glanced sideways at his brother and turned back to the errand boy, "Aye, run to the tavern, look for him there."

"Already checked."

"Well bloody find him!" Herk thundered.

Commoners standing on adjacent buildings yelped. They all had bad blood, reflected by their Niiwa rank, and didn't have the guts to be involved in governance, whether on the Warlord's side or the side of the people.

The errand boy shuddered. Ayrah watched his shoulder as he hurried to leave. Two coiling pieces of serpent, a down facing dagger beneath the first and a small flame beneath the second, that marked the winning of the Niiwa's second round.

"Shadowa, if you can sing even a note's worth of song, you'd better. . ."

Ayrah shook her head. "Like a rusty pipe, worse than a kettle."

The Burnt Harem's windows were mere holes in the clay formation, with thin purple curtains drawn on the inside so as not to make the day-porkers feel out of place. Painted across the front of the building was a bloomed pink-red flower sitting on an out-of-focus cactus. Fire surrounded it, turning the edges of its outer pedals to ash. Herk and Boden wore simple stitching of the flower as insignias across their leather jackets.

When Ayrah and the guildhead brothers strolled through, Taryn was already hard at work. She flung tapestries from the walls and instructed half-naked girls to fetch grander ones from the cellar. She straightened curtains and locks of hair alike. She shouted, her voice thundering as high as the second story of the brothel, "If I can smell you from here, then you didn't wash your arse as well as you washed your nose!"

Herk pounded along the floorboards of the hall, grabbed her by the neck, and planted his lips sloppily over hers. He stroked the deformed tissue on her neck, his hand stiff as it ran over the burn scar, across her hair, and down below her clothes.

Ayrah and Boden shared a glance. "Oi. It's like they think we're in a whorehouse," said Boden.

Ayrah chuckled at that.

The purple drapes on the windows cast a dark, atmospheric light throughout the brothel. Incense and candles and spices mingled aromas.

Their best showgirls lined up outside the foyer. They wore dresses made of their finest silk and cotton blends. The dresses clung to their shapely breasts, narrow torsos, wide hips, and fell in expertly needled strands past their feet. The strands of the dresses were the Masikonian's idea. He said it showed the most "give me more" amount of skin without going as modest as a pale skinned Illian.

"And for the bloodlust?" Boden asked.

Herk turned to Taryn.

"Aye," said Taryn. "Disposable girls are hidden away in each room El Gabya and his men might find."

Lord Mayor Gabya, thought Ayrah. *Just the man I've wanted to see.*

Herk and Boden knew nothing of why Ayrah was even in Simula.

It because of Gabya.

The doors slammed open. Everyone's breath stopped. The floorboards knocked with heavy boots. Two sets. Someone was panting. A hand drew past the foyer curtains and threw them aside. The errand boy stumbled into the brothel with the Masikonian in tow.

The whole brothel sighed in unison.

"What took you so long?" Herk asked.

"That—" a belch "—would be my bad." Slurred the Masikonian. The man swayed. His multi-colored ethnic skin showed in patches, dark over one eye, light over the other, splotches running down his arms and legs. His neck-length hair was much the same, an impossibly dyed mix of blonde and brunette, golden and murky.

"It's only evening," Taryn yelled. "How are you falling off your feet drunk already?"

"In my country . . . we dream—" a belch "—of seeing powerful Sigu Nii fight. Little did I know before I came, that's all you do. Even in t'is fine art, love-making estab'ishment, it's all just fighting. Over and over and over and—"

"Well, go bloody sing then!" Herk shouted. "Go! Get in your corner and *hum* if you're too drunk!"

"Oh no." He chuckled under his breath, drunkenly, "The fighting man is going to fight me." But deep in his throat, he began a hum; the rhythm and beat began to pound as he stepped across the dark varnished floorboards. His hum, as half-effort as it was, stirred Ayrah. The notes were high, they were low, they warped and whomped the whole brothel with Masikonian vuu. It took a creative type to let you hear a new thing and feel like you've known it all your life.

They waited. Many moments went by. Then they heard him, Lord Mayor Gabya. It was impossible to miss him and his whole host.

Armor clinked and clattered as they entered the building. Sunlight glinted black and gold through the curtains. Five men poured through in full hellinite armor, a dense black metal, with each edge and cuff trimmed in gold. Across each armored chest was the golden insignia of Warlord Lyta Tuio, shaped in the likeness of a hand with a bolt of lightning ripping up through the palm. Each upper left sleeve worn by these Black Guard held a hole, intentionally left during the crafting of the gear to show their fourth-round winning of the Niiwa. A four-piece serpent missing only the head that wound the middle symbols together. *Simula* was engraved on each of their arms just under the tattoo.

Typically, Herk and Boden would be El over them, since they have the complete tattoo. But a sixth man entered. His face was round and fat. He had thick black hair with sprinkles of grey. Wrinkles played at the corner of his eyes. Instead of armor he wore delicate silks of blue and green. His Niiwa tattoo engraved across his lower left shoulder was that of a clear victor. *Waike*, read the city inscription.

"El," greeted Herk, who knelt and bowed with his nose to the floor. Everyone did the same.

Ayrah lingered but decided to play the part.

When Gabya spoke, his words held the slightest mispronunciation. Several of his teeth were missing. "Rise, Herk. I've places to be and an itch that needs scratching." He didn't acknowledge or even seem to hear the Masikonian's tune at all. He passed the Black Guard and began inspecting each of the showgirls.

"O' course," said Taryn, who strained to wear her most inviting tone. "Pick your girls."

The showgirls all did a swivel at the waist, flinging the strands of their dresses outward.

"I've more appetite than sex," said Lord Mayor Gabya, flinging the last word from his lips as if it were off-brand ale.

"We prepared girls in your room, dark, so you don't have to see them. If it would please his El, they're replaceable."

"They'd better not be just any beetle from the outskirts of town. They grow diseases out there, you know."

Herk and Taryn shared a glance.

"How about this one?" Lord Mayor Gabya strode casually up to Taryn. He began to stroke her face with the backside of his hand. "She looks like she could put up a fight." He smiled, grotesque black spots on his gums where his teeth should've been.

Taryn winced away.

"El, she's not for—she's mine." Herk's powerful, grouchy voice lost its hue, turned mouse-like.

"Well," Lord Mayor Gabya flayed his hand across his chest, "That shouldn't be an issue." He snatched up Taryn's wrist, to her audible yelp, and stretched her arm across her chest to inspect her Niiwa tattoo. "Mmm." He hummed, "As she's under your employment, it seems you would grash on her behalf."

Words stuck in Herk's throat; his face reddened like the flower on his jacket.

Taryn ripped her wrist away from Gabya and took a step back. "I—"

Ice coated Gabya's hand like a crystal glove in an instant. He swatted Taryn across the cheek.

Taryn screamed in pain. Her hands flung up to hold her face, her eyes squinted with tears seeping through. Blood oozed between her fingers and dripped onto Gabya's approaching boots.

3

ATERAH

There was no trace of him. No torn cloth. No splatters of blood. Nothing to signify where a battle had taken place. Only charred claw prints—stained black soot on the grey-green stone marked where the snagaeri had approached.

Graeynesh Law VIII: The Renovian curfew is to rise and fall with the sun.

"Where is Copt's sword?" Aterah's brother asked. The Renovian soldiers wandered about the Old River Pass, searching for their fallen brother's blade. Norly even dove into the Maua hoping to find it.

Aterah felt a lump shove its way up her throat. *I could have saved him!* She averted her face and stole away from the group. Aterah leaned against a tree, a few steps off the trail. Her vision blurred through the collection of water on her eyes. Her back slid against the jagged bark until she sat in a crouch.

You're an abomination. No wonder they look at you the way they do. You can't save your friends. You can't save anyone. Aterah let her head fall to a slump. When she could fight the tears no longer, she threw her hands over her face.

"Hey, there you are." The voice was soft and solemn.

Aterah flinched. Captain Rouen stood over her. His eyes were pinched, the tendons in his neck tense, clear pain in his words.

Aterah looked away and hastily rubbed her wrist at the wet beneath her eyes. "It's my fault. I could have saved him. Why didn't I? I—I can still hear him screaming." She tried not to choke on her words.

Rouen crouched down, and his sword clinked against his belt. His hand rested gently on her shoulder. "You're upset about Copt because it's Copt that we lost. But he was a Renovian soldier, trained in the rebellion to put others before himself. Don't muck his sacrifice with your guilt, he saved *you*. And me. And Kairo. And all the others."

"But Rouen . . . I had a feeling. I knew it wasn't good, and I chose not to investigate it." Aterah stared at the ground beside her. She couldn't bring herself to look at him.

"You insult me. Aterah, who is this team's captain?"

"Y-you are."

"Then it sounds as if you learned a lesson, but the fault lies with me, and me alone." His face turned away, perhaps down the trail, at the rest of the squadron searching the River Pass.

A mantra rang in Aterah's mind, *Graeynesh Law VII.II: A level-three Sigu Nii requires at least four simultaneous Renovian soldiers.*

"Do you have any idea where our squadron would be without you? Let alone the outpost as a whole? NeoDerii has learned to lean on you and operate off your premonitions. Who knows where the lot of us would be? Oh, look." Captain Rouen bent over and rummaged through jungle brush beside them. "We even found his sword. Tonight, we'll immortalize him as we celebrate his passing into Yeshwin." He pushed himself to stand and held out his hand. "Come on. We have a general to deliver."

The squadron packed and marched home. East they trudged, towards their hidden outpost, NeoDerii.

Kairo walked up beside Aterah. "Did you know?" he whispered; his eyes were locked on the jungle beside them. Though they were past the Maua, the chance of running into a Sigu Nii war-tribe was still possible.

Half-a-reach taller, Aterah glared up at him. The question had pierced a chord. *"No.* I didn't know!" She meant for her voice to be flat, but it failed her. Though her voice was soft and small, it came out close to a growl.

She watched his face freeze. His dark brown eyebrows curved up, caught in surprise. His ear-length curly brown hair bounced as he walked. His bright green eyes darted between the jungle to his left and the soldiers that walked before them. "I'm sorry. I guess I still don't understand how this thing of yours works."

"And you think I do?" she huffed.

"No, I guess not." He said under his breath. "Did you see anything last night?"

Kairo's attempt to change the conversation was laughable. But she itched to humor it. "A little. I think Adakon is at the outpost."

"Adakon?" He turned toward her, eyes bright.

"I think. He wasn't quite how I imagined." She was excited to meet the famed general as well, but it felt small compared to the death of their second.

Adakon's name was known to every living Renovian. Adakon began the revolution, the rebellion against the Sigu Nii oppression. They celebrated him frequently at NeoDerii. Those old enough to remember told stories of his bravery and his leadership, how he freed Renovia from its exile, two generations ago.

In her dreams, she caught glimpses of a man laden with scars and filled with pride. He wanted to speak to their outpost. He wanted to speak to his rescued general. But most of all, he wanted to speak with her.

He's going to judge you. No one with powers like yours should be free to speak into the minds of man.

No, he's going to take you away. Your ability is wasted on the battlefield.

Aterah ached to be home. To climb into her hammock bunk and lather herself in safety and rest.

"I wonder if I'll get to meet him," Kairo said.

Aterah bit her lip and remained quiet. She marched onward, east for NeoDerii.

Incoming! Identify! The scouts overhead whistled like birds.

Aterah looked up, searching for the painted stations a few dozen reaches into the trees. She knew where they were but still could not see them. The scouts themselves were coated in full twine netting, with leaves and sticks of the jungle floor meshed in.

Captain Rouen of Edrei and his squadron! Rouen whistled back, his eyes searching through the trees.

Aterah wondered if he could see them. It would take a trained eye and a sensual awareness that Aterah didn't possess.

Lower the ladder! The bird calls traveled down the trees. A way down the trail, a twine-and-wooden rung ladder fell from the sky. It bounced and yanked before settling still as the squadron approached.

Platform! Injured! Rouen called above. An almost silent squeaking and cranking churned as ropes were lowered through the pulley system, and a five-step-wide wooden platform slowly lowered to the floor, connected above by four sturdy lines on each corner. The visible underside of the platform was painted and textured meticulously to match the Renovian jungle.

They laid General Forst on the platform, and back up it cranked.

Aterah let an exhaustive sigh escape her as she made for the ladder. *Finally, home at last.* She wondered about sneaking a nap in before evening supper. One hand behind the other, one foot after another, she climbed the rope ladder.

By the time she reached the last rung, her triceps were aching and burning. The stationed Renovian soldiers held hands out for her. "Welcome home, OA."

Aterah thanked them. She didn't know their names, and it was unsettling that they recognized her so swiftly. She shook herself of the thought and paced slow and steady onto the courtyard. She closed her eyes as her hands found the thin woolen white string that tied her hair back tight. She pulled gently and felt her mid-back-length-hair swish in the wind. She breathed deeply with the feeling of safety and peace washing over her.

The aroma of supper made her eager to taste what the Wheelhouse cooked up.

The West Deck was a grand wooden courtyard constructed amidst the trees all around them. Buildings and structures lined every edge of the deck except for the west. To the east, between the Locke and the Wheelhouse, several wood-and-rope bridges stretched to other courtyards.

"Six thousand steps, from one side to the other. Across all the levels, of course," Kairo had once said. He was into that kind of thing. The specific. Aterah wouldn't put it past him to have counted each step himself.

A golden people for a golden outpost. She watched the Renovians bustle this way and that. Their twilight-orange skin reflected the wood they walked on. Not one of them in sight stood idly.

A small group stood clustered around a tall pillar in the middle of the courtyard. Scrolls and writings were pinned to each side—upcoming passing ceremonies, squadron missions and orders, Chamber trials, Graeynesh lectures, incoming supply dates, and even recorded anticipation for the variation of sun fall.

They were nearing the end of the dry season. Another month, and the sun would sporadically decide against its previous routine.

"OA," a soldier called out, striding toward Aterah. Though she couldn't recall his name, she knew he was a member of NeoDerii Leadership. Only a few ranks beneath the Commander.

Graeynesh Law VI: Adhere to the process of rank.

Aterah brought her arms to her side. "Officer."

"I hope the journey went smoothly?"

"One casualty, sir. Otherwise, it's mission success." Aterah felt her voice twinge at the end, but he didn't seem to notice.

"Good, good." The officer peered behind her, watching the rest of her squadron slowly climb up the rope ladder to the West Deck. "Accompany your captain to Command immediately. A guest wishes to see General Forst."

"General Adakon, sir?"

The officer smiled and shook his head. "Of course. There isn't any surprising you, is there? Just don't tell your captain, Adakon has a liking for surprises."

Aterah nodded.

"If the casualty resulted in death, then I look forward to seeing you at his passing ceremony tonight." With that, the officer nodded and turned.

Aterah let a deep and exhaustive sigh escape her. *So much for a nap.*

Captain Rouen and Kairo slowly walked past her, with General Forst shouldered and limping between them.

"Captain." Aterah called as she caught up. "You and I are to take the general to Command. Right now."

"What?" Kairo's dark eyebrows slanted in, a scowl revealed his straight and stained yellow teeth. "He's in no condition for a briefing."

Aterah shrugged.

"I—I'm f-fine." The general coughed heavily, spitting up blood. His arms flinched and flexed inward reactively.

Kairo kept his scowl, his right eye straining closed as Forst seemed to slump back into unconsciousness.

Rouen nodded obediently toward the rope bridge east of them.

The bridges connected the various platforms, courtyards, and decks of NeoDerii. Most of them were surfaced with tightly tied planks about six steps wide, and they stretched anywhere from eight to thirty steps across.

Aterah could feel the movement of the rope beneath the planks as other soldiers went this way and that.

Aterah watched her brother tense, how he forced himself not to peer over the thin rope handrail, the only separation between them and the jungle floor a hundred reaches below, and how he eyed the soldiers passing them and wiped his brow clear of sweat when they reached the other side. He glared at the infirmary as they shuffled by.

The Command Deck was a bustle with officers of leadership hurrying across the courtyard, a trail of scribes and soldiers in tow.

Command sat on the north edge of the courtyard. A three-story building containing all NeoDerii's war information, meetings between Leadership, and the Commander's war room. Kairo and Rouen dragged the general up to its dark waxed doors and shiny bronze nails.

Captain Rouen stared at another building as they approached. Aterah followed his gaze. His eyes were set on the Chamber, a building on the east edge of the courtyard where elders held lectures on Graeynesh Law, trials for those who went against it, and assigned outpost bound occupations to the monthly young recruits.

Graeynesh Law X: Those found guilty of breaking Graeynesh Law shall be exiled.

They entered a lobby busy with scroll-bound scribes. Hallways ran out to either side of the building, leading off to archives and smaller meeting rooms. An older woman sat behind a desk at the back of the room, and she hastily directed them toward a staircase behind her.

By the time Kairo and Rouen reached the final stair, sweat drenched the spaces between their dried scrappy leather chest pieces.

"Who is this?" a guard asked. He was young, no older than Norly. His hand rested on the hilt of his bronze blade, and he stood before two large dark wooden doors together carved with an intricate pattern of the Silver Tree of Renovia. "Only you three were requested."

Captain Rouen glanced across Kairo. "He's my second."

"Only you three were requested."

"You wouldn't deny his seeing out his mission's end? To carry this general all the way from the Maua?"

"Only you three were requested."

Kairo scoffed as he heaved Forst's arm off his shoulder, and Rouen leaned hard against the wooden wall as he caught the rest of his weight.

Aterah squeezed past her irritated brother and tried to fill his place under the unconscious general. But her shoulder didn't even reach his slumped armpit.

The guard opened the dark doors.

Aterah had only been up there in the war room three times in her life, all of them within the last season. *"What have you seen in your dreams?"* they would ask her.

A thick, dark, and waxed table took up the center of the room. Aterah turned to the heaps of scrolls and war maps unfurled across its face. She briefly noted and absorbed the ridges of the Delkop mountain range, the valley in its middle, and the various hidden outposts spread out across the region.

Four people sat around the table, each with a small squadron of scribes and officials behind them.

The Commander, born of Ravid, sat closest to them. A stern-faced woman in her late second generation that oversaw all of NeoDerii's military functions.

Beside her sat the lead Chamberlain, born of Neltza, the eldest of the elders, with a full head of white stringy hair. He was in charge of the Chamber and all its Graeynesh and outpost-bound functions.

Across from the Chamberlain sat a hawk-faced general well into his third generation, his mouth perpetually pursed, and grey hair cut so close that it stood on end. Aterah guessed that this man was the famed General Adakon.

The fourth, a loud and gruff bear of a man, his curly brown hair and beard had sprinkles of grey. His eyes were pinched at the corners, as if he were smiling on the inside. He seemed a well-seasoned soldier. Perhaps bravery was enough to land him a seat in this room.

The Commander sighed. "There we are."

Aterah tried her best to help Rouen rest General Forst in the chair at the end of the large table.

"What happened?" The brown-haired bear leapt from his seat, his voice husky. He felt along Forst's forehead with the back of his hand. "Why wasn't he taken to the infirmary?"

"We were ordered to bring him here immediately, sir. . ." Captain Rouen gave a brief tug on his linen tunic, airing the visible patches of sweat.

"Adakon."

Rouen's mouth propped open. "Gen- Ad—" Nothing but stuttering letters seeped out, his eyes wide.

Aterah was surprised as well. This man felt widely different than what she remembered from her dream the previous night.

General Adakon roared with laughter, his head thrown back as he slapped the table. "It thoroughly amuses my soul to appear unsuspecting." He turned to the Commander. "All their lives they're told stories. They work up this image for who they think I am. You must find that funny, Commander."

"Yes, it's very funny, sir. But we . . ." Her face strained to appear casual.

General Forst coughed, his hands gripped around the edges of the table. "You can tell him, Commander. Ad-akon, I h-hate when you do that."

"You just spent the past two weeks in Sigu Nii captivity, being exposed to Kort-knows-what savageries, and that doesn't lift your spirits in the slightest?"

"It might." Forst groaned. "If the one you laughed at hadn't plainly broken Graeynesh Law."

The room froze. All eyes shifted to Captain Rouen.

"Is this true, Captain? And in the presence of a general?" the Commander asked.

"It is." Rouen's voice was stern, his chin high. "Article seven-point-two and eight. Circumstances provided less than ideal options, I did what I needed, and I fully understand the repercussion."

"The *repercussion*," Forst screeched, "is exile!" His elbows shook as he strained to turn in his chair to face Rouen.

"It's not his fault!" Aterah's voice cut through the room. All the eyes shifted to her. They waited for her to continue. But she found a sudden itching desire to crawl beneath the thick table and hide.

"OA," A whisper drifted from the hawk general in the back. "Unfortunately, Graeynesh Law is a very serious matter. And before we move on, I suspect we should remove the now compromised Captain Rouen. Perhaps relocating him to this outpost's holding facility."

"The Locke." The Chamberlain nodded, his body propped up by his elbow on the table. "We will hold a trial in the Chamber, tomorrow."

Captain Rouen nodded obediently. His shoulders fell.

The Commander called the soldier who guarded the door to the war room, "Escort Captain Rouen of Edrei to the Locke."

"Of Edrei?" Adakon asked. "Which half?"

Rouen turned back, halfway through the door. Something passed between the two. "South."

Adakon nodded and gestured to himself with his thumb. "North."

Aterah watched Rouen leave, her attention briefly leaving the world around her, and the wildly important people she stood before. Captain Rouen was as close a father figure as she'd been granted. For her and Kairo both.

Rouen found them a generation ago, wandering through the jungle as children. All of NeoDerii speculated, but the best answer anyone could come up with, is that they must have wandered away from an agricultural town east of the outpost. It was a day's climb through jungle climate, mountainous terrain, and snagaeri tormented nights. Some people had argued that this scenario was so unlikely, that Aterah and Kairo must have been captured by the Sigu Nii and released at NeoDerii as a hinderance.

But Rouen didn't raise them to be burdens. And he couldn't be exiled. He just couldn't.

No one survives exile. Every night the Renovian jungle belongs to the snagaeri.

Copt's hideous screaming, and its abrupt end still rang vividly in Aterah's ears.

"So, you're the famous Aterah?" Adakon sat on the edge of the table, to Forst's left, almost rendering him eye level with her.

"Famous?" Aterah asked.

"Oh yes." Adakon nodded, his brow arched. "They've been talking about the Oracle Aterah two, three outposts away. They say you've saved NeoDerii from discovery on more than one occasion." He glanced sideways at the Commander, "It's astonishing that General Baenek just found out about your presence recently. Almost *incidentally*."

The Commander turned away.

"Aterah," General Adakon called, his voice soft.

She turned from the doors. They were all watching her. Two of the most important people in NeoDerii, and three of the most important people in the entire rebellion. "You will exile my captain?" Aterah felt her nose burn hot, her ears turn red. "His only transgression was saving *your* general!"

"You know Graeynesh, don't you?" General Baenek asked. "I can tell you do. I can see you understand it better than most, and why it should be held dear."

"He hasn't been exiled yet," commented the Chamberlain. "His discretion could have been in the best interest of the rebellion."

Adakon shook his head. "I was beginning to think Oracles were a myth. Made grand from the passing of time. Twenty-eight generations have passed since we last saw your likeness. Queen Epheriia, the author of Graeynesh Law. What a different lot we were then."

"The truth is," Baenek continued, "You're the key to a door that we've been searching for all our lives. For generations, freedom from the Sigu Nii has been closed. But with you . . ."

"Aterah. We want you to think about coming with us. We've talked with our elders and they're certain your visions follow you. This means your talents are wasted on the battlefield. If you came with us, if we educated you in grand perspective, made you aware of all the moving parts—you could end this war."

"You would be treated like the King to Come. Everything we have, after a time, would be at your disposal. You could, after a time, even begin writing in Graeynesh Law again." Baenek shared a glance with Adakon.

Aterah froze stiff. The thought of crawling beneath the table felt well out of reach now.

"Does—does she actually have a choice, General?" the Chamberlain asked.

Adakon shared a glance with Baenek. Remorse flickered behind calloused eyes. "With all my being I wish we could accommodate your wishes." He rose from the table, approached, and set a hand on her shoulder. "But we do not have that luxury."

They spoke of doors opening, but she felt as if hers were slamming before her. They spoke of grand perspective, but they knew nothing of how she loathed attentive eyes on her. "You would exile my captain?" she repeated without thinking.

Confusion flickered across Adakon's face. A scrunched brow that made Aterah realize she hadn't made any sense.

"I have to go," she said.

Relief seemed to flood the generals. Adakon sighed, "Oh, thank the Korta Ella—"

Aterah was about to faint. "No. I have to *leave*." She spun on her heels and ran for the war room doors before anyone could speak another word.

The doors slammed shut behind her as she put as many stairs behind her as possible. She needed to be alone. She needed solitude, and there was only one place in NeoDerii that could allow her such a thing.

Aterah closed her eyes and turned her nose to the sky, letting the soft jungle breeze wash over her. *I told you, you would be plucked from here like a ripe melon in season.*

Aterah made across the deck, north, over bridges and other court-yards. She felt painfully aware of every soldier, worker, or leader who passed her. Her eyes were clearly wet and cheeks visibly red. They looked at her as if she were both a freak and a savior.

She came to the library of NeoDerii, a small building in the out-post. She entered and paused in the smells: ink, parchment, and leather. She hoped they would linger, that she wouldn't get used to them too soon.

The library had a limited number of volumes but was well used by the low and high of rank alike. The first few rows were stocked with interpretations, adaptations, and applications of Graeynesh Law. But she continued past those.

She went to the back of the room, where Renovian historians were prevalent, and people were scarce.

The library, a frequent fortress for her, contributed to her increasingly well-readness in ancient Kortaes-Renovia, when their people were at the top of the world. For some strange reason, Aterah felt as if she missed it. She missed when their laws, their wants and taboos, were the standard. When her people had children instead of bronze swords. When they lived in cities instead of outposts. When they were not hunted.

Aterah picked a history book that she had been making her way through and sought a corner with no chairs, out of sight, and sat against the wall with the book propped on her knees.

King Ivan Graeynesh's coronation was our downfall. He would be a great king for another nation. Any nation, really. But for Renovia, whose traditions, morals, and character are of such unique quality, King Ivan was our exile.

El Raeoh forbid Renovia from allowing tourism or immigration—

This sentence made no sense to Aterah. El was a title reserved for the Korta Ellanii, she did not know who Raeoh was, and she certainly did not recognize the word tourism.

We were to be a shelter for the world by traveling it, led by our great Aliyah. Our specific charge, where other missions might be different and good, was to till foreign land into fertility *rather* than inviting inhabitants of barren lands to our own.

But there is great success in tourism and immigration. And King Ivan failed to prevail against the persuasions of his court. And our people began to love wicked things. They listened to charisma more than honesty. They began to celebrate quarrel—

"Are you all right, darling?" a shaky old lady's voice asked her.

Aterah looked up, her eyes fogged with tears.

A wrinkly old lady, hunched over in a thin white linen shirt, found her way through the rows of books.

Aterah nodded and wiped at the wet of her eyes. "Just reading."

"I like history books too, but I don't think they've ever given me that strong of a reaction."

"It's—it's not the book."

"Well obviously, sweetheart." The lady lowered herself next to Aterah. "Tell me about it." Her voice sounded so genuine, so inviting, Aterah couldn't help but let loose.

Tears clouded Aterah's eyes. "The generals want to take me with them. To Edrei, or east, or who knows! They say I don't have any choice."

"Oh, well that doesn't sound too bad. No snagaeri threats every night, no Sigu Nii threats every day, no—"

"I don't want to go! My place is here. This is the only home I've ever known."

The old lady wore a sad smile. "I wasn't much older than you are now the first time I left the only home I'd ever known. Would you like to hear about it?"

Aterah shrugged.

The old lady's brows raised.

Aterah nodded.

"When I was still before my second generation, I lived in this great big city named Zetola. It had great big walls—"

"I know about the Egress."

"Don't interrupt, child. These great big walls, so high that you could only see the sun seven hours out of the day. The city was *horrible*. There was always trash everywhere. Drinking the water made you sick. The Sigu Nii killed whom they wanted for little-to-no reason. There were thousands of us, packed between these walls, with hardly the air to share between the lot of us. And one day, a young man came up to me. Younger than I was, he was. He started talking about all sorts of things I'd never heard of. Things as simple as *trees*, darling. I couldn't help but to listen to these wild stories of his. And by the time he started talking about freedom and escape, he had a crowd of us standing around listening. You know what I did next?" The lady's eyes met Aterah's.

"You joined him?"

"No. I threw trash at him. The closest things I could find. And so did every other person in that crowd. I didn't *want* to leave. Not because I was afraid of dying. Death would've been sweeter than continuing to live there. I didn't want to leave because I was used to my trash and water made of piss."

Aterah raised her eyebrows. She was taken aback by this old courteous lady. "But that doesn't make any sense. Why would you like living there?"

"I didn't I like it. It was awful. But I couldn't think any different. Can you imagine having never seen grass before, and then someone tries to describe to you what grass is?"

"I'm sure there's plenty of things out there that I haven't seen yet."

"Yet?"

"Well, I'm not going to stay here forever. . . ."

The old lady laughed.

Irritation crept in for a moment. But the old lady's laughter was contagious, and soon she found herself laughing too. "I see what you mean."

"This outpost certainly isn't made of trash. It's made of wood and bronze. But Aterah?"

Even this lady knew who she was. Aterah looked her in the eyes.

"If you're made of rubies, then wood and bronze are as good as trash around you. Only in the midst of other gems will you find yourself truly challenged."

Peace came over Aterah like none she had ever felt. She hadn't realized how scared she was of leaving. Listening to this old librarian, she wasn't so scared anymore.

Kairo came out from between the rows of books. "Hey, there you are." He looked sweaty, as if he had been running all over NeoDerii. "Didn't you hear the horn? It's dinner time." He reached out a hand to help Aterah off the ground.

"Don't worry about the book, sweetheart. I know where it goes."

"Thank you so, so much!" Aterah called to her as Kairo pulled her toward the courtyard.

All of NeoDerii shuffled to one building on the West Deck. Everyone that had been bustling about this way and that earlier, all fell into a crowd of back-to-back Renovians.

Aterah ran her fingers through her hair, wishing for the wind to reach her. She looked to Kairo. She knew how he hated moving slowly. How he took tiny baby steps as often as the feet in front of him would allow. How his curly brown hair shook as he looked either direction. How his hands moved from resting on the hilt of his blade, to wiping his chin, to brushing his shirt of dirt.

He doesn't know. Suddenly, all the apprehension and worry began to fill her again. *He doesn't know about Rouen. And he doesn't know about me.*

"*I want you to think about coming with us.*" General Adakon's voice echoed through her mind.

She glanced again at Kairo. *I must tell him.*

But what do I say?

Maybe. . . maybe now isn't the best time. Aterah let a deep sigh escape her. As they neared the West Deck, the aroma of sweaty Renovians around them slowly gave way to the roast and spice of the Wheelhouse.

The Wheelhouse, the largest building in NeoDerii, was filled end to end with wooden tables and benches on either side large enough to sit sixteen people each. Thousands of Renovians found seats with their squadrons.

Candles set before charred stone slate lined the wooden walls. Along the walls to either end of the room sat two elevated platforms and long, dark waxed tables. On the eastern side sat Chamberlains, and Leadership on the western.

Squadrons made their way to the back of the room, where a line of apprentice cooks dished out wooden ladles of stew and handed folded up leaves of bread. The aroma was heavenly. Meals after two-day field missions of munching on berries were a real feast.

"Where is Captain Rouen?" Kairo asked, after they all returned to the table.

"Maybe he was too tired to eat," Tullia answered. She sat on the other side of Kairo.

Norly huffed. "Too tired to eat? Never heard of it."

"He was sent to the Locke," Aterah heard herself answer. Her eyes went wide, and she could feel blood rush to her face as a dozen squadron eyes turned toward her.

"What?" Kairo asked, speaking much too loudly to be sitting right beside her.

Aterah's mouth opened. She stuttered for a moment, at a loss for words.

"Didn't see that coming." Norly chuckled at his own remark.

"General Forst accused him of breaking Graeynesh." She clenched her teeth. "He saw how close we were to the snagaeri last night. He saw how Rouen left Copt to face the war chief alone. The Chamber will be tomorrow."

"I'm sorry, you mean the general that *we* saved?" Norly spat.

"The general that Rouen saved!" Kairo's eyebrows were scrunched together, confused.

He's never been one to understand Graeynesh Law. But now, it's taking . . . it's taking our captain.

Norly's slurping and sloshing of his mouth and food were the only sounds across the table. They must've been the only squadron in the Wheelhouse to eat in silence. Several moments passed before Kairo resumed eating.

"Did Rouen assign a new second?" Norly asked.

Kairo hesitated. "Yeah. Just before I left him at Command, he gave it to me."

Norly scoffed. "Cheers to our new captain then." He lifted his bowl of stew to Kairo, an entirely mocking gesture. As he returned the bowl to the table, and began stuffing his mouth again, he said, "That must make you the youngest captain in the entire rebellion."

"He hasn't been exiled yet," said Kairo.

As everyone began to finish their stew, a single deep pounding of a drum rumbled through NeoDerii. Curfew would be in one hour.

A few candles around the Wheelhouse blew out, dimming the light. A unanimous shuffle filled the room as everyone turned toward the west wall.

An officer stood up on the platform and spread his arms wide. "I can truly feel it in my bones." He yelled out over the crowd of squadrons. "For two generations we have been fighting. Fighting for our lives, fighting for our laws, but most of all fighting for our freedom! But I can feel it in my bones, a change of wind is coming. Our time as Kortaes, the most powerful nation in the world, will be restored once again. It has been written! The Korta Ellanii will find favor in Renovia!" He brought his right arm up and faced a man walking onto the platform. "I give you General Adakon of Edrei!"

"Outpost NeoDerii!" Adakon yelled from atop the stage. The Wheelhouse shook with shouting and the stomping of feet. Most of them had never laid eyes upon the legendary hero.

Adakon raised a hand to silence them. "A great mission was completed today. With the help of OA, we rescued a general from the treacherous snakes that raid our jungle." A momentary shuffle of eyes darted to Aterah. Instinctively, she ducked her head down. "But my dear friend Forst was rescued at a cost. The night beast of fire and flame took their second, Copt."

"Captain Rouen of Edrei was kind enough to let me take his rightful place during the passing of the sword." Adakon held out his hand, and an officer gave him a bright bronze blade, Copt's sword.

The officer went to hand Adakon the ceremonial knife, but Adakon waved him off as he unsheathed his own dagger.

"Tonight, a Renovian is granted access into the gates of Yeshwin." Adakon chanted as he began to etch Copt's name into his blade. "Tonight, a Renovian is immortalized in the name of the rebellion." Another letter. "Tonight, two Renovians are made new by the passing of a sword." And as he finished etching Copt's name, he said, "Tomorrow, Renovia will be called Kortaes once again." A young man, fresh off the trails to NeoDerii, waited on his knees in front of the stage. Adakon lifted him, and the boy stretched out his arms. "What's your name son?"

"Reuel."

Adakon placed Copt's sword into the young man's arms. "Tomorrow, you will fulfill the work of those who have come before you."

A gut-wrenching feeling swept across Aterah. She curled over and grabbed her stomach in pain. A headache like none she'd ever felt seared through her mind. Her vision faded, and she nearly lost consciousness. But she heard herself speak, as if in a multitude of voices,

"He shall be called the Prince of Healing,
but he will bring destruction to our lands.
He is called Son of Graeynesh,
but he will bring life to the Law.
He was to be called King to Come,
but you will send him to his grave."

Slowly, Aterah felt her sight return to her. She looked up around her, and the entire room stared in horror. Aterah felt a lump push its way up her throat. An overwhelming urge to flee the room came over her. Kairo reached out a hand to place on her shoulder, but she was standing before he could touch her.

"A-Aterah?" she heard him ask. Kairo's voice sounded as scared as everyone looked. And suddenly the room broke out in whispers. "Aterah, your eyes—"

Aterah ran from the room as fast as her legs would move. This time, she didn't stop when she reached the courtyard. The sun was low, and curfew would send everyone to their beds at any moment. She ran across the rope bridge that led to the upper levels, and a bridge that led to the housing units of the outpost. Her legs didn't stop moving until she was in her nine-soldier barrack. Only then did she pause for breath. Three vertical hammocks lined each wall of the small barrack. Her mind raced with fear, and her heart wouldn't slow down. She felt like throwing up. Ignoring it, she climbed into the second hammock on the right wall and tried to fall asleep before her other barrack mates got there. But she ended up lying awake long after they settled.

4

NEODERII

"Did you see her eyes?" The question echoed a dozen times throughout the morning-lit Wheelhouse. For their squadron, it was uttered by Norly, who sat on the long wooden bench staring into his porridge.

"They were black," croaked an archer.

"But with little white lights running by, like taking a stroll through the stars." Tullia whispered from Kairo's left.

"Enough." Kairo didn't want to hear about Aterah any longer. He worried about her, and inclinations of searching for her swept his mind.

"Aye-aye, Captain." Norly belched and began devouring his meal despite others' hesitation.

Leadership probably came around and snatched Aterah at first light. Curiosity was certainly bursting their seams.

What was it she said? Something about the King to Come? In truth, the old Renovian prophecy meant little to him. Words spat by an old witch queen, dead for more generations than Kairo could comprehend. Mutterings to be feared and hoped for—far from day-to-day relevance.

"When is the trial?" Tullia asked.

"Noonday, today." Kairo grabbed his empty porridge bowl and pushed himself from the table. "Rouen will either be spared or exiled." He wove through the long squadron benches of gobbling Renovian soldiers, by the kitchen, and refilled his bowl.

He paused on the West Deck for a breath. It felt cool out on this day, which was unordinary for the jungle's dry season. Birds were cawing, ants were crawling, Kairo even saw a group of monkeys screaming at a snake a handful of trees away from the outpost. His lip curled up. What a foul creature. He'd scream too, if he was so close.

Porridge in hand, Kairo walked exactly forty-seven measured steps across the West Deck to the center pillar.

Typically, after Kairo returned from the warfront, leadership gave them a full day of rest. But every now and then, a day of rest couldn't be afforded, like today.

Kairo had two outpost bound occupations in NeoDerii. His first: carpentry. He and a team of eleven others would climb down to the jungle floor, walk a long way east, find a tree ripe for taking, cut it down, chop it up, haul the wood back to NeoDerii, let it dry, and fit the wood for upcoming projects. One jungle tree, as sky-bound as they were, was often enough for any project.

His second job: scout. A two-day trek lay between NeoDerii and the outpost to the south, Raida, and a day and a half to the outpost to the north, Edrei.

Although Edrei could hardly be called a mere outpost. Kairo had never seen it, but he knew Edrei was one of eleven cities that had imprisoned his people for twenty-six generations. It stood as the birthplace of Rouen and Adakon. As the first city to be freed from Sigu Nii control, Edrei now occupied a pivotal position, nestled among the hidden outposts, serving as the central hub between the warfront and Eastern Renovia.

Kairo searched the notice boards under scout calls and saw his name listed for the next day in the north sector, point thirty-four. Roughly a quarter-day's walk. If he wanted to get there in time and not be caught by the Renovian night, he would need to prepare supplies for a week and leave immediately after the trial.

From there, Kairo took another fifty measured steps to the far side of the courtyard. The slight discrepancy of distance between the Locke and the Wheelhouse to the center pillar was, to him, an insurmountable failure by the carpenters. If the engineering architect were still alive, Kairo would give him a near exile-worthy ear full. And Kairo knew he had not stepped with error, he had counted his steps between the center pillar numerous times, each occasion like a Sigu Nii's black steel ripping through his chest.

The Locke was dingy compared to the sandy-dirt colored wood of NeoDerii's finer structures. A mere hallway with three wooden cells against one wall and a single Renovian soldier shamefully slumped post-entrance. The hallway windows had wooden slats that could be oscillated to let in light.

"Breakfast for a prisoner," Kairo muttered loud enough to stir the drowsy fellow. He appeared just young enough to still be sent on war-bound missions.

A nod.

Kairo strode past an empty first cell, an occupied second, and paused outside the third, where a dark man sat with his legs out. His feet were unstrained, so that they laid in opposing directions. His shoulders were limp, and the whole left side of his head leaned against the wall behind him.

"Captain," Kairo called.

Rouen stirred. "Kairo." His face lit up, as if seeing his own child. His voice sounded dry.

Kairo fit the porridge, now cold, underneath the bottom crossbeam that held the wooden bars in place.

A moment passed. The only sound was the slurping of porridge.

"It's just not fair!" Kairo turned from the cell. "You shouldn't be here. You did what anyone would have done. And to count Copt's noble sacrifice as your loss? It's not right."

Rouen paused to wipe porridge from his chin. "Trust in Graeynesh. It'll be alright."

Kairo did. Or he wanted to. The thing was, if the Law were perfect, Rouen wouldn't be here in the first place. Kairo needed to trust the Chamberlains to properly interpret the Law's function and translate it to the current event.

The Chamber was the only domed building in NeoDerii. Kairo remembered it being built when he was a child—a full generation ago. He and Rouen watched the carpenters soak planks in water until they were pliable enough to be bent into a large-circumference frame.

Rouen squeezed Kairo's hand, and explained, "Making it a dome takes a lot of extra work. A lot of time, from a lot of different people. But it's worth it. To enter the Chamber is one of the few times that our people is broken into an 'us' and a 'them.' And the dome symbolizes fairness between all parties. The witnesses, the Chamberlains, and the accused."

It was not so big that all of NeoDerii could fit inside, like the Wheelhouse. Only a handful of different groups were permitted entry: their squadron, the Chamberlains, the visiting generals, the Commander and most of Leadership, and a number of other captains who called themselves friends of Rouen.

Three rows of benches surrounded the room, with four aisles cut through, leading to a raised circle platform where the five Chamberlains sat. Each of their seats were on different levels, marked by age, representing the power of having different perspectives on the forthcoming event.

Kairo sat in the front row of their section. Seats weren't assigned, but Norly enjoyed sitting in the row farthest away, Tullia closest, and others in between each of them. The other dozen members of their squadron fit within one of those three categories, which broke their group into a sort of squared-off section in the domed room. Aterah was still yet to be seen.

Kairo counted the moments until they began. The apprehension of the event was aided by his need for it to move along quickly, so that he wouldn't be caught by the Renovian night on his way to scout point thirty-four. *I should just leave,* he thought. But he wouldn't. No amount of snagaeri would cause him to miss this trial.

Tullia's nervous jittering was so much that Kairo had half a mind to switch seats, since he could feel every rapid bounce of her knee in the seat beneath him. She sat hurled over, her head darted from General Forst across the room, to the door where Rouen would come through.

He understood how she felt. He felt the same. Restless. Hopelessly hopeful. A tune of environmental awareness akin to that of battle preparation. Still, he laid a hand on her knee. She looked at him, suddenly still. Sparkless heartbeats of *us* thudded between their gaze as the Chamber doors flung open.

Rouen strolled in. He wore two soldiers on each arm. His head was hung as he passed down the aisle, but his steps were long, strut-like. He stopped in the ten-step moat between the Chamberlain's elevated landing and the viewer benches.

Kairo and Tullia both turned to *them.* The generals. Each wore a different face. Adakon's—inquisitive, Baenek's—calloused, and Forst's—smug.

The long-dead witch queen, Epheriia, prophesied that Renovia would lose their title of Kortaes as the most influential nation in the world, and enter a time of exile. As a people group, all of Renovia was powerless, hungry, and naked.

Adakon might have led the Egress out of exile, but here and now, Rouen faced the new exile. A fate that felt more merciful than death even though they went hand and hand. With the snagaeri polluting the jungle each night, and the war-tribes hunting relentlessly each day, no one survives long.

The elder Chamberlain quieted the room. "Please, begin recalling the events in question to the best of your ability."

Rouen took several moments to collect his thoughts. Finally, he began in NeoDerii. He described the briefing he received from several members of Leadership. How they were to trek two days out west—the direction that the Sigu Nii were coming from, and therefore denser. But that it was necessary because the rescue target was General Forst. One of the big three. The original three. A member of the rebellion who led beside Adakon during the Egress.

Rouen recalled aloud that he asked Leadership how they came to find out Forst's location. They replied with two sources: News come directly from Edrei, and Aterah, who had dreamed the mission in its entirety the night before. "So, we were prepared." Offered Rouen. "We knew the conditions of the weather, we knew the layout of our soldiers, we knew that the mission would be successful. And we escaped without alarm." Rouen paused. "But I had my soldiers rotate shifts carrying General Forst's stretcher to save their arms in case of an upcoming fight. It took them most of the day, but Sigu Nii did eventually catch up."

Kairo played out the vivid memories as they were described. He wondered if it would have been more advantageous to turn and wait for the Sigu Nii war-tribe earlier. That way, they wouldn't have been pinched by the sun. But the Old River Pass was one of the most defensible locations that Kairo knew of, out in the wilderness.

"By the time the battle ended, it was twilight and snagaeri were spawning throughout the valley. I know that Graeynesh states our curfew prior to the sun's set, but what could I have done? Leave the fight between swings?"

The Chamberlain nodded impartially. "Continue."

"The war-chief remained. A level-three. The snagaeri was inbound. We had to finish him quickly and retreat to the trees before he had aid beyond any of our ability. I organized my squadron in consecutive attack sequences, but the war-chief resisted each. Finally, with the beast of night a moment away, my second, Copt, sacrificed himself by holding back the warrior while the rest of us escaped.

"So, you see, elders, there was nothing I could do. If I didn't let Copt play this part, we all would have died that night. And honestly," Captain Rouen's voice grinded with accusation, "If breaking Graeynesh Law is *ever* a better course of action than not, well then, it's not exactly 'law' then, is it?"

The room broke out into mutterings from Rouen's closing sentence. Most audibly from the Chamberlains on their pedestal with hoarse whispers of "Blaspheme!" And from the generals, whose scoffing sounded more insulted than disbelieving.

The elder took some effort to silence the Chamber. "General Forst, do you have a response?"

"I do."

"Rise and speak."

General Forst made his way to the open space between the audience and the Chamberlains. In the handful of moments between his rising and his speaking, while he collected his thoughts, it began to rain. It was a light evening, jungle shower. The dense canopy overhead would collect most of the blanket into heavy beads. They drummed unevenly on the wooden dome of the Chamber.

Kairo scratched his neck. He thought about standing up and leaving. He still needed to gather his belongings into a knapsack. It probably neared dinner time, right?

"It's true, I am General Forst of Zetola. My city was freed soon after Edrei, and I fought beside Adakon to rescue the rest of you." He faced the audience with his shrewd, bird-like voice. He turned to Rouen, "Do you despise our Queen Epheriia? Her prophecies have foretold our future for dozens of generations." Even a carefully armed sentence sounded like a shriek. "To think you were raising the next Oracle. Not anymore."

What did he mean by that? Kairo's brows caved in suspicious disbelief. Forst was chuckling under his breath.

"Or what about the great Adakon? Do you despise him? He has been diligent to experience each component of the rebellion, and you suppose to have more wisdom? We go to bed at nighttime," Forst spoke as if he were speaking to a child, "Because that's when the monsters come out. It's not that hard. And we don't fight Sigu Nii with more tattoos on their arm than we have soldiers because they're just stronger. It's not that deep."

Forst paced around the room, his wording and speaking in beat with one another. Then he stopped in front of Rouen and began to circle him. "What you don't understand is this—you think you saved fifteen at the cost of one—but certainly Copt lost to the war chief, right? You said even a correct number of you could not beat him. So, you hoped one would do the trick? How do we know that this sole Sigu Nii did not trail you back here? He's probably gathering up an army against us as we speak. You think you saved fifteen. . .you've endangered us all."

Captain Rouen was sweating.

Tullia's knee began to bounce again.

Kairo didn't understand. The main accusation was imaginary—a what-if. Certainly not means for exile. Right?

He didn't hear her enter. She snuck in, opening and closing the Chamber doors without creaking. But Norly and several others in the back row did. "Aye, there she is."

Granted, it was a normal volume. But Norly's normal volume was louder than the average Renovian, and the Chamber—a quieter room than the average room. So, in a matter of a heartbeat, every head in the building whipped to Aterah. She looked helplessly defeated. She gulped and fumbled for the nearest seat.

Kairo attempted again and again to keep from turning round and surveying Aterah with a glance, but each attempt was without success. He had to know how she felt. Had anything like the prophecy last night ever happened before? Was she scared? All surveys through the crowd between them relayed that she was distracted from the trial. She wasn't looking in the direction of Forst or Rouen whatsoever. It appeared as if she were thinking of something else entirely.

Kairo wondered. . ..

The general turned to the raised platform and nodded, "Thank you." And returned to his bench.

"We will take a moment to discuss the verdict," said the head Chamberlain.

Kairo patted Tullia on the knee, not to shush her, but as a goodbye. He pushed himself to stand and huddle-walked to the aisle.

"Where've you been hiding?" He asked as he sat beside her.

"Where do you think?"

The library. Kairo nodded with a frown.

"I have something—"

"Forst said something—"

"You first," she said.

"Forst said something weird. He said Rouen's been raising the next Queen Epheriia, but not anymore. I suppose that he just means Rouen is about to be exiled, so not anymore. But. . ."

Aterah began to nod, slowly. "They're taking me," she said at last.

It was as he feared. He turned back to look at Rouen. They shared a look. Rouen's eyes asked, *any sign of trouble?* Which was typically reserved for the depths of the jungle. Seeing that look here made Kairo feel uneasy. *Yes.* He responded.

Kairo took in air to reply to Aterah. The slight hesitation—an infection of distraught. It spread through his chest. It perspired on his palms.

"The Chamber has come to a conclusion," said a subordinate Chamberlain. The room hushed. Kairo's intake fizzled out through his nose.

Rouen straightened up. He held his hands behind his back. They were trembling.

"The Chamber finds Captain Rouen of Edrei guilty, worthy of exile immediately."

The mourning to follow was silent. Like the gloom of curfew on the turn of a generation. Kairo felt the turmoil build up in his chest and a sharp pain crawl up his throat. A distant ache to wail echoed in his mind, but he hushed it. Not for manliness' sake. But to be quiet. Out in the jungle, where any beast with vuu has ears, you can't cry when you want to. Even if its deserved.

The company of congregants marched with silhouette tears toward the West Deck. Most of the walk was dry, covered by layers of courtyards high above and carefully sown tarps laid on top of the jungle canopy to collect water.

"Why?" he asked eventually. Days' worth of unease accumulated into that one, single-word question, and it sliced into Aterah.

"They say I dream of battles when I can dream of wars." Her voice shook. She was crying. He hadn't known.

"Are you going to go?" he asked, much softer.

"Don't have any choice."

"They're just stealing you?"

She nodded.

"Just like they're stealing Rouen."

She shrugged.

They reached the West Deck. The western most courtyard. Heavy, canopy collected rain drops crashed against the congregants in a splotchy pattern. Four soldiers with hands on hilts cornered Rouen. "Strip," they demanded.

Rouen's fingers trembled as they loosened the sheath belted around his hip. He undid his pants. Took off his shirt. His eyes flickered in the rain. The shame worn on Rouen's face made Kairo sick.

Rouen's hands wrapped around the backs of his arms while his knee hovered over the other to block sight of his part. He shivered even though it was the end of the dry season.

The forced disrobing of his father figure had Kairo bent over, queasy.

"You are not to take a single step further east than your current position. You are now regarded as an enemy threat," said the Commander.

The elder Chamberlain flicked his hand in a backward motion, shooing Rouen. "May the Korta Ellanii spare your soul and grant you access to Yeshwin where we have not."

The group of them standing on the West Deck watched their captain descend the ladder down to the jungle floor. Kairo hung over the railing. Rouen gave a sweeping glance around and sprinted off south. Exile was naked.

Aterah whimpered. The rest of the squadron was crying as well.

The outpost horn blasted. It was time for dinner.

Kairo cursed in sudden remembrance—he had scout duty tonight. "When do you leave?" he asked Aterah in a hurry.

"Tomorrow morning."

Kairo dragged her in by the shoulders and embraced her. He wouldn't be back to NeoDerii for a week. "Promise you'll come visit."

She nodded. "I promise."

With that, Kairo ended the hug and took off toward the Barrack Decks. He had to get back to his barrack unit, throw together a pack of supplies, and head north as quickly as possible. Any more time wasted, and he would get caught by the Renovian night.

He grabbed his knapsack, a hide skin with cotton patch compartments for smaller items, and strings from which to hang water pouches and jungle rodents. He untied his twine hammock from the wall and stuffed it into a tight little ball. He grabbed twine and bronze hooks to set up snares for animals, extra clothes, and flint to start a fire. He draped a thick mesh suit of sticks and leaves over the top of the knapsack.

He would be out, far away from his home with little to do besides keep watch for approaching Sigu Nii war tribes. The only rest from that would be occasional trips to snares, relieving himself along the jungle floor, and locating the nearest creek.

When he returned to NeoDerii, Kairo supposed it wouldn't feel like home. Sure, he would be captain of his own squadron, possibly even the youngest in the entire rebellion. But for why? Aterah would be gone, and Rouen would be gone. He stuck his tongue out at the thought of looking over Norly for the rest of his days.

Kairo's triceps had a faint burn by the time he felt soft, brown jungle dirt beneath his sandals. He turned and began a jog north to scout point thirty-four.

A while passed. The sun departed behind the western Delkop mountains. Twilight took the jungle. Each step he took was within eyesight of the scouts above him, those lucky enough to be stationed nearest to their hidden outpost. He still had an hour left. The jog turned to a sprint, but he couldn't keep that up for long.

Finally, he realized: He wasn't going to make it. Not in time.

Incoming! Someone chirped in the language of birds.

Kairo puckered his lips, ready to clear himself.

Sigu Nii!

He looked around, *have they mistaken me?*

Multiple tribes!

Kairo's heart skipped a beat. Out west, tiny glimpses between the obstruction of trees, fires burned. Enough to be mistaken for a forest fire. They moved southeast.

They're headed for NeoDerii. Kairo stopped in his tracks. His heart plunged through his stomach. They *had* been followed. Forst was right.

Uncertainty boiled in his mind, whether to continue his path for scout point thirty-four. *They're many.* It seemed the indistinguishable moving mass had no end. Turn and return to NeoDerii? If he ran, he would make it before them.

A stick cracked behind Kairo, and he felt a sudden warmth on his back. He turned, slowly. A snagaeri stepped out from behind a tree, not a dozen steps from him.

Kairo froze in petrified horror.

The beast was an intangible torrent of blazing vuu. A bonfire on legs. Two swirling coals of pitch squinted with animalistic thirst. Rain hissed against the demon.

No one had ever come face to face with the beast of night and still lived.

Incoming! Sigu Nii! Multiple tribes! Kairo listened as another scout repeated the bird-chirp call down the line. Although they did their duties, their eyes were undoubtedly turned to the horror beneath them.

The snagaeri's hind legs rose slowly. The heat of its torso stung Kairo's eyes. He whipped his bronze blade from his hip, it felt as useless as a waxed twine string in his hands.

And then something changed.

The air between Kairo and the beast fizzled. Tiny black sparks cracked and hummed before they erupted with ground-shaking thunders of dusty black lightning.

And then, there was a man.

5

EIDHIN

The skies were a blanket of grey illumination. Eidhin stood with one hand in the other, the tips of his sandals just over the edge between moist grass and dirt garden. He watched his father, Eidhinr, bend down in a patch of onions, whose tubular green leaves snapped in the rolling east wind.

Eidhin and Eidhinr.

He wondered if his father regretted passing down their generational name to him. His older brother, Illao, was set to inherit the family farm, he would've been the obvious choice. It was the Yaerta Generation. The last in a cluster. When Eidhin had children, he would give them their own names to shorten and pass along.

"See, this one here," Eidhinr addressed Illao. He took out a short pocketknife and used it to straighten a rotting leaf. "Now, nothing drastic will change, nothing too bad will become of our onion if we don't prune it. It will continue to grow, and we will still be able to eat it, come the end of the season. But it won't be as sweet. It won't be as big. It won't find its potential, as much an onion can have potential." He gave a weak smile.

"What does this brown leaf have anything to do with the rest of it?" older brother Illao asked. He knelt in the dirt, a pace between Eidhin and his father. He was tall, his arms were shapen, dirt clung to his clothes.

"I'm not completely sure." Their father, Eidhinr, pondered. "Though it might be that the onion is still sending some bit of attention to the parts of it that are dead. Some bit of energy, water and whatnots. But if we remove the dead part, it can focus fully on its healthy self. Might be that a human touch is what an onion wants. Here." Eidhinr handed Illao the pocketknife. "Go 'round and prune the patch. Time you're done, breakfast will be ready." He sighed as he pushed himself into a stand and rested a hand on Eidhin as he passed. "Watch your brother closely now."

"Y-y-yes, d-d-dad." Eidhin watched his older brother, a half-generation in age between them, as he walked around the garden and inspected each onion carefully, with an occasional *swsk* of the knife.

Eidhin reached through the pocket of his trousers and took out a faint yellow parchment paper, a thin rock, and a finger-sized stick with both ends charred. *14, 15, 16. . ..* He counted each onion Illao inspected. The parchment had three horizontal columns that read, *"Potatoes—87 plants. Corn—53 stalks. Apples—3 trees."* When Illao finished pruning the onions and tossing the cut branches out of the garden, Eidhin made a new column on the paper and wrote, *"Onions—47."*

Illao brushed sweat from his brow as he stepped out of the garden. "Thanks for your help."

"I-I-I wa-was wr-wr-i-i-i—"

"It's all right. Let's go inside and wash before breakfast." They climbed to their small farmhouse atop a hill. Smoke puffed softly from the brick chimney.

Eidhin followed his brother inside. Bread was toasting and eggs were frying. Eidhinr sat at their thin wooden dining table, a cup of steaming tea set before him, and a half-blank book beside it. He had cracked spectacles over his nose and a quill in hand. He was dressed in a white button-up stained by sweat and dirt. A brown jacket with patches hung over the chair behind him. "Go dress," he said. "We'll leave right after breakfast."

"Wh-where's my-my jam?" asked grandpa Eidhinro. He was old. Near-ly four generations. His head buzzed as he turned round the table, and his eyes lagged, like he was following a really fast fruit fly.

If the calendar was perfect, grandpa would drop dead the moment Illao had a child. They were in a cluster of generations called De'lm. It was a great-granddad-to-great-grandkid type of moment. It was a lifetime.

Eidhin and Illao turned and pattered up the staircase to the second story, the wood creaking under each step. They turned down a small loft-styled hallway and into their bedroom. Three twin-sized straw beds spread with woolen blankets sat in each corner across from the door.

Eidhin dug through his wooden dresser and pulled out a frayed mustard yellow sweater with leather patches on the elbows. He tossed off his chore clothes and dressed himself in slacks, his sweater, and his sandals.

Illao was dressed in slacks, sandals, and a dark brown button-up with the cuffs cut off and rolled up to hide the frays.

Fried eggs were still steaming on pottery plates when Eidhin and Illao joined the table. Half a loaf of toasted bread lay sliced in the middle, beside a small dab of berry jam that grandpa Eidhinro was quickly taking the lion's share of.

Mother puffed down her thick, frilly, stained dress as she squeezed between the legs of the table. Her long blonde hair curled heavily once it passed her shoulders. Eidhin's sister reached for a slice of toast. Mother swatted her hand away. "Ahht." She scolded. "Pray." She shot a glance at Eidhinr.

"I-I-I c-c-can d-do i-i—"

Eidhinr cleared his throat. "I'll cover it this time, son." He bent his head. "El Hwaerta, please use your quadratic attention, of infinite lengths, to hear my prayer. If three others are praying to you more articulately than I, then I understand. Rai is the logic that weaves and maintains the shape of our whole world. Please spare some of it for us farmer folk. Might you see fit to shed the crumbs from your robes, that we may understand?" He cleared his throat again and looked around the table. "Okay. Indeed. Dig in."

After breakfast, the six of Eidhin's family met outside. Illao packed a small wooden wagon, no more than six paces long. He loaded hefty bags of potatoes and corn, as well as a single cleaned potato sack packed with a change of clothes for each of them. Eidhinr strapped a pair of their best oxen to the front hitch and gestured everyone to get aboard.

Fall's crisp breeze scratched at Eidhin's face, but he endured it to continue peering across Gehni's rolling hills. Far to the southwest, Mount Gehnson could be seen peeking over the horizon. A long since dead volcano.

Eidhin emerged himself from time by letting his mind wander. He daydreamed. Sometimes they were present things, like a little man running and jumping between the branches of passing evergreen trees. The little man would fall behind, or sprint ahead, but always managed to stay somewhat parallel to Eidhin. Other times Eidhin would daydream of other places, like a great stone schoolhouse with children running around, eager to learn. And instructors who wanted nothing more than to pour themselves and their thoughts, their thoughts on other people's thoughts, out onto eager Eidhin. Sometimes Eidhin pictured himself playing in the Aylan games. A series of debates to the death. There, in his mind, his tongue had no summersaults, no handicaps. He spoke as quickly and articulately as he could think. He never lost the Aylan. He was all but immortal there.

The blanket light across the sky had dimmed slightly by the time they reached Snowstock, a small-town northeast of their farm, a connection point for farmers and village folk a half day's journey in every direction.

Snowstock was a wooden town, with a tight visible perimeter of evergreen trees parted only by dirt roads hand-cleared of stumps and trunks.

The wooden plank buildings were all two stories high, with thin half logs supporting thatch roofs.

Eidhinr pulled the wagon up by a stable with a dozen other horses and oxen grazing in troughs. Eidhin and Illao unhitched the oxen to let them eat and rest.

"Help with the offering." Eidhinr gestured to Illao. "Eidhin and I will handle the rest."

Illao heaved the great sack of potatoes out of the cart and slung it over his shoulder. He followed his mother, sister, and grandad across the dirt road.

Eidhinr heaved the sack of corn over his shoulder and began down the street. Eidhin grabbed the bag of clothes and hurried after him.

The people of Snowstock were all dressed in common fall wear, thin brown woolen clothes, with leather-strapped boots. There was an eagerness about them, almost anxious like.

Eidhin followed his father into a building that seemed to stretch long ways into the parting evergreens. But when they entered, it was a mere ten-pace wooden foyer. There stood a desk and a sharply dressed lady with a shiny silver pair of spectacles over her nose.

"Selling corn, today," said Eidhinr.

The lady placed the sack on a brass plate, strung up with counterweights. Satisfied, she rattled through a pouch under the desk and placed five silver pieces and seven copper pieces before Eidhinr.

He scooped them up, the pieces clinking into his hands before gesturing Eidhin toward the door. "Two more harvests, son."

Eidhin looked up at his father.

"Another two harvests, and I'll afford to put you through school." Eidhinr sighed. "It won't be anything expensive. But it'll be school."

They walked up to a large wooden building on the corner of a dirt street. Its porch wrapped around, populated by rocking chairs, tables, and pottery ashtrays. Thick pillars supported the second story overhang.

The inside of the building had wooden tables and chairs scattered about the lower level, and a waxed countertop in front of great barrels and spouts. Stairs led to a second story loft with a thin rail in front of a dozen doors around the building. A man in the middle of the room pushed chairs this way and that while sweeping under tables.

A loud bell began to clang outside—long continuous beats that vibrated the legs of the tables.

The sweeper looked up.

"One room for five." Eidhinr said.

The sweeper glanced toward the door. Eidhin could tell he was eager to get past them. "Can't this wait till after?"

"You'll be full after. It'll be quick, I promise." Eidhinr's pockets jingled as he began pulling out coins.

"Alright, two silvers for the night."

Eidhinr tsk'd his lips. "My family and I have been coming here for—"

"Fine. One silver." He stretched out his hand.

Eidhinr put the coin in the man's hand. He grabbed the sack of clothes from Eidhin, set the sack down in the corner behind the door and placed a hand on Eidhin's upper back, leading him out of the building.

The whole of Snowstock was in motion. Like streams flowing into a creek, farmers and townsfolk poured out from every building, every crevice of the town. There was a briskness to their orderly walk, with hands placed on the backs of children to keep them from straying, and a hat blowing downwind.

Eidhin and his father fell in with the flowing crowd. They turned the street and onto another until they found themselves close to the center of town. Before them stood a great building made of slate, cobblestone, and blue stained-glass windows.

Eidhin took the first two steps at once. He could feel his heart pick up in pace, all sorts of pleasurable thoughts pouring into his mind.

"Slow down!" Eidhinr snapped under his breath and glanced at the villagers beside them.

The waxed doors to the building had carvings of scrolls and books and runes in a language Eidhin couldn't read. A man stood holding one open while he greeted each family who entered. He was well seasoned, with streaks of white in his blonde hair. His gold-colored robe was clean and crisp and fell past his ankles with intricate blue silk on the seams. Eidhin recognized him at once. The Teacher.

"Good evening, Eidhinr." The Teacher smiled, revealing clean white teeth.

"Good evening, El," Father replied, returning the smile.

"And young Eidhin?"

"I—I—"

"I received your offering. The gesture is greatly appreciated. Please, enjoy the service."

Eidhinr nodded and they continued through the doors.

Long wooden pews stretched in two dozen rows between the door and a center podium. Stone slabs carved with old words lined the curved corner between walls and ceiling. Beneath that, great windows of assorted shades of blue let in stained light on the collecting crowd.

"*Ahht!*"

Eidhin glanced back toward the doors. El Teacher shooed someone. His voice was too quiet to hear, but his tone felt like a spear. The other man was older, not far from El's own age. Soot shaded his face, and dirt covered his torn and tattered clothes.

"There we are." Eidhinr guided Eidhin down the aisle and sat him between him and his mother.

Eidhin tried to peer behind him, to see what became of the dirty man. But his mother scolded him for staring across several rows of people.

The Teacher allowed their family to pay their fair share with harvest. A few potatoes. It was not expensive. This dirty man, shooed away, must have had absolutely nothing to offer. Air darted out of Eidhin's nose, amused that this dirty man would convince himself that he had a right to thirst for knowing, when he had no doing.

The room was loud as farmers and their children mingled and caught up with one another.

Eidhin sat, his hands on his knees, his knees bouncing, staring at the podium where El would soon be.

The doors creaked shut.

Delicate clacking began to echo through the building as the congregation gradually quieted, and the Teacher pattered down the tiled aisle. He reached the front of the room, took the single stair up, and wrapped his long pale fingers around the edges of the podium. "Good evening!" He smiled.

"Good evening!" Everyone said in unison.

Eidhin remained quiet.

"It might be best to begin with some announcements. First, come this winter, I will be retiring."

A hundred gasps filled the room, along with a single whimpered, "No!"

"I know, I know." El gestured his hands for calmness. "But this has been coming for some time."

"To where?" someone yelled.

"Not here, that's for certain." El teased.

The congregation laughed with loose hesitation.

"I'll be moving close to Mount Gehnson. There is a small gathering of retired teachers there. Just a bunch of old people rasping nonsense at one another." He smiled, but continued without time for reaction, "And I've met my replacement. You will enjoy him splendidly. A brilliant young man, fresh from Rai's own school.

"Second, I'll require a few of you to volunteer tomorrow morning. The slate of our building is loosening, and unless we enjoy the multitask of bathing while learning, we will be needing to fix it.

"What else? Ah. Some of you mentioned a fallen tree along the western path. Perhaps a few of you might gather to see about that. And that just about brings us into our lesson, today. Okay, all at once now—"

A unified intake of air filled the room. "The Church of Rai—that is, the house of truth, in all its relations—is the congregation of knowledge from all other houses of thought. We apply as they study. We do as they talk. We recognize El Hwaerta as the teacher of all, and mankind as the student of some."

Eidhin closed his eyes, letting his ears fill with the collective mantra. He used to join. Or try to, at least. That was many seasons ago, now. It's alright, listening was enough.

"We have a guest today." Teacher gestured at a man rising from his seat in the front pew. "I hope you might welcome him and his words more than my own. He comes directly from Gehni, the capital of our isle, on authority from Rai's provincial instructor. Good evening, El Penoa."

"Good evening," replied a man dressed in velvet black robes, with a small deep blue sigil of Rai sewn across his chest. His hair was dark above a sea of golden heads, and his voice sounded strange. A crisp accent, with clear annunciation that rolled off his tongue with care and ease. He gripped the podium with one hand, while his other flung around as he spoke, "We live in strange times, these days? Do we not?"

The congregation gave scattered approval.

"How different were the days of our fathers, and fathers' fathers?"

The farmers nodded. "Different."

"I'll tell you now, through avid devotion of my time and effort, I have discovered the root of these differences. And to spare you all the prologue, all the lines of thought it has taken me to arrive at such a conclusion, I give you the boiled down statement: They were uncomfortable with contentment.

"For example, Snowstock is not an old town. Three generations have these buildings laid in their location, maximum. Tell me, what must take place for a town to begin its creation?" He paused as he looked around the room. "Discontentment! Someone, or a small community of someones, must have come from a city, Gehni perhaps, and said, 'We don't like how we are. Let's change it!' So they traveled some four days southwest of Gehni and chose this spot to lay roots. Tell me now, have you accomplished their dreams? Or do you find yourselves content?

"Perhaps you say, 'Ah, but El, they sacrifice contentment so that I might find some.' But to this I say no! How great and mighty are Masikus and Sigu Nii? Their shadows envelope us consistently, so that the lowest and highest of us can feel their influence. No matter a man's own education, or vuu, an introspective one will notice his craving for change and glory. Do you think either of these mighty nations stand tall because they are content? To this I say no! They want not because they take. I tell you now, find it within yourselves to *want*. And take it."

El Penoa paused for breath as he looked around the room. "But some of you have found it already, I can sense it. Some of you are already restless, hungry, tired of pulling the same crop while the young grow old. Some of you are so committed to the Church of Rai that you might give up your life for her. To these people, meet me at the inn tonight. I wish to speak with you directly."

6

CAPTURE

Black afterimages of lightning faded from Kairo's eyes.

The man stood chest out, facing Kairo, hardly an arm's length away. Despite the man's sunset shaded skin, he radiated the presence of Sigu Nii. He towered over Kairo, his build was tree-like. His eyes were a shimmering purple and his hair a dreadlock mop with decorative wooden and metal beads. His face was scruffy, clean shaven perhaps three days prior.

The strangest part of this man was his arms. They were covered in tattoos, box shapes, like that of a maze. Except they came *out* of his skin by a knuckle's width. They looked like solid grey stone.

The snagaeri roared as his opponent was replaced with this other, mid-pounce. The fiery demon crashed into the back of the man-with-stone-tattoos. He hollered in pain. They tumbled to the ground, groveling a few steps from Kairo. The smell of sizzling human flesh filled his nose.

Kairo hacked his rusty bronze sword at the back of the beast. It felt like chopping a jungle tree with a sandal. What good was it anyway? Both men were dead already. No one had come face to face with a snagaeri and lived.

The man-with-stone-tattoos shoved the beast from atop him with a forceful kick. Kairo couldn't be sure, but it almost felt as if a breeze had accompanied the kick. The man jumped to his feet and slid a silver blade out from a sheath on his back.

CAPTURE

The two eyed each other for half a moment, a thing that Kairo had never witnessed. Not that he had spent much time with the beasts of night, but from all information gathered, it seemed the snagaeri were totally without the instinctual impulse of the animal world. They had no predators. Their only prey: Renovian blood, which they did not feed on. They were as sentient as a stormy sky, doing only what it does. So, to watch one *hesitate* added to the uncertain events continuing to berate Kairo this day.

The snagaeri pounced once again, it's finger-long talons stretched, its open mouth held a hundred teeth like licks of flame as white as the visible sun.

The man stepped back and shifted his wide footed stance. As his hand found the pommel of his sword, he shoved the silver blade clear through the racing chest of the beast. It penetrated all the way to the hilt, sizzling louder than the rain. The snagaeri screeched in pain.

The man cursed and yanked his sword free. "I killed it." His purple eyes turned down to Kairo. "Run!"

Kairo stood in disbelief, still clutching his own rusty blade.

The man snatched Kairo by the collar and took off.

"Run!" He repeated and released Kairo.

Kairo forced his legs to move. Mud kicked up behind each sure-footed step.

The sizzling of the snagaeri's wound grew louder, squealing like a hundred mice. An explosion thundered throughout the jungle. The hot blast slammed Kairo to the ground. He felt his nose and brow scrape against rock and root. And heard the faint sound of human screaming up in the trees.

Kairo slowly picked himself off the jungle floor. He wiped dirt from his eyes and hair while he let his heart wrench for the fallen tree scout caught in the crossfire.

He turned his attention to the man-with-stone-tattoos. "Who are you?" he wondered, *Some Sigu Nii sent to trick me?*

"Arden." The man's voice rumbled deep. A would-be powerful tone, if it weren't for the drowsy, sloshy, almost uncarefully placed words. Like he had just woken from a long slumber. "Show me to your outpost, boy. There is a host of Sigu Nii moving against you." He pointed to the distant mass marching through the jungle.

"I can see them."

"Not like me." He growled. "Truly, it is a stormy day in hell."

Kairo didn't know where this hell was, it rained here, in the jungle.

The man had saved his life. That was sure. And this Arden had the color of Renovian ethnicity. Then why did Kairo feel so hesitant? Was it Arden's entirely foreign nature? His stone tattoos? His vuu-shattering entrance? His incomparable height and build?

Arden grabbed Kairo by the collar. "Quickly boy!" His breath reeked of something sour and unfamiliar, and he swayed as he stood still.

"Alright." Kairo pulled his collar from Arden's grip. He turned south and glanced at the scouts stationed along the way. What did they think? Surely, they wouldn't speak aloud. Silent watchers they were.

"Do you have any concept of urgency?" Arden scoffed. "I know they teach you little in this bark-eating rebellion of yours."

"Alright." He began to jog.

Kairo kept the host of war tribes in view. They were moving quickly despite so many of them. He counted the fires he could see, he estimated how long their mass might be and compared it to how far away they seemed. Five. Maybe six full tribes. That was too many. Between war chiefs, seconds, and grunt soldiers, that was too many. Kairo prayed silently to the Korta Ellanii that NeoDerii was already fast preparing for an all-outpost war.

It was terrifying running along the jungle floor at night. He jumped over fallen branches, ran along boulders, ascended and descended the uneven terrain with practiced instinct. But it appeared so different. It was dark. About as expected, Kairo had experienced darkness often, like lying in his hammock trying to fall asleep while snagaeri roars fill the valley or keeping watch out here in the dead of night for Sigu Nii war tribes. But the lack of illumination made Kairo's senses feel crazy. Not only did the environment provide less information than normal, but he swore, he saw things that weren't there.

A shadow that wasn't there. Or something flying in the corner of his eye.

They reached NeoDerii. A small road passed underneath the painted and textured courtyards of the outpost. Scouts were stationed all around them, so that they had ample time to prepare in case a war-tribe was coming this exact direction—which there was.

Incoming! Identify! Their secret bird chirps sounded off. Shaky. They understood that battle was imminent.

Renovian! Captain Kairo! Kairo responded. *Lower the ladder!*

He waited a moment. There was no response.

"Quickly boy. . . ." Arden hummed.

The host was nearly upon them. Kairo could feel the march of their many in the soil beneath him. *Lower the ladder!* Kairo chirped again. The first of the Sigu Nii rounded the trees and turned onto the trail. Kairo and Arden stood in full view.

"They won't," Kairo croaked. "The Sigu Nii're too close. We're stuck down here." His eyes swept the jungle around them as his mind raced for alternate plans. Hide? No. Climb up the trees, themselves? No, all the mid-way branches around NeoDerii had been removed. Take out as many Sigu Nii as they could? Yeah. That was the only option.

Kairo turned toward the host and ripped his bronze blade from his hip.

The first handful hollered at them. Their voices growled with blood-lust. That's what they lived for, as far as Kairo was concerned. This was the sentience of their species. They had found a Renovian outpost, and they ached to destroy it.

Arden's throat rumbled, a scratchy irritated grunt. "Hold on to me." He spat.

"What?" Kairo was preparing his gut for blades. Swatting them, striking them, and eventually harboring them.

Arden snatched Kairo's forearm and closed his eyes. His face contorted. The air vibrated. Wind swirled around them. Arden's eyes shot open. The screaming Sigu Nii were a moment away. Thunder blasted through the jungle and black lightning cracked around them.

The next thing Kairo knew, he stood on the West Deck of NeoDerii. Thunder and black sparks were still ringing. "How did you—" He stopped short as he peered around the courtyard.

The West Deck drummed softly in the rain. Three dozen archers kneeled along the twine rope railing, aiming their arrow-fitted bows at a single point on the trail below. They waited with breaths held for the command of a pacing Leadership officer.

Fire! Fire now! What were they waiting for? Did they still hold out hope that the host was searching? The Sigu Nii were piling against NeoDerii. *Fire! Fire! Fire now!*

Kairo waited breathlessly. The Sigu Nii horde continued beneath them. Their march shook the soil, which shook the trees, which shook the wooden planks. Full moments passed.

"Make no mistake, Kairo," Captain Rouen had said, two seasons ago. *"The locational secrecy of NeoDerii is our only advantage."*

A day's trek lay between NeoDerii and the closest town east. If the barbarian-host happened to not see NeoDerii above and continue through, then the outpost could maintain its secrecy, send for aid from neighboring outposts, and confront the Sigu Nii tribes on more advantageous ground.

And then, just like that, the last of the horde passed under the West Deck. A chorus of sighs rang out, so unified that they could have shifted the breeze.

Kairo crept across the West Deck, to the rope bridge by the Wheelhouse. A few soldiers followed him, all of them peeked over the edge.

Kairo made eye contact with peering beasts on the ground. They seemed to just be standing there, staring up at the painted bottom of NeoDerii. Kairo flinched away from the edge, his hand clutched around the rope railing. He shared confused glances with the soldiers beside him.

"What are they doing?" one of them whispered.

Then came the snagaeri roars.

"The snagaeri," Kairo gasped. "They're—" A tree in the gap between courtyards began to shake. He glanced down in horror as a fiery demon clawed its way up. Its snarly roar thudded and crackled. "Get back!" Kairo yelled. His voice was the sole sound in NeoDerii. Hundreds of Renovian faces turned to him. He had broken the silence.

Kairo turned and ran from the ledge, not half a moment before the snagaeri bounded onto the wooden courtyard. It's orange-fire head writhed as it snarled. A strange collar encircled the beast's neck. A black metal thing, growing white-hot along the edges. A metal rope was attached to it, strands of flimsy metal wrapped together, like twine, that extended past the railing from which the snagaeri came.

The Renovian soldier who had whispered to Kairo slipped as he tried to scramble from the edge. The West Deck watched, frozen with fear, as the snagaeri's jaw clasped around him. Fire set to his clothes, his hair, his skin. He shrieked the way Copt did two nights earlier. High and desperate for death. His voice stopped abruptly, his legs and arms fell loose against the courtyard, blood-puss dripped from his already cauterized limbs.

Kairo looked around for the man-with-stone-tattoos, the only one Kairo had ever seen or heard of who had bested the fire beast of night. But Arden was nowhere in sight.

The archers posted on the far railing turned and were instructed by the officer to fire at will. Arrows whistled overhead and caught flame before even touching the snagaeri's torso. The beast growled, a mere irritation.

The snagaeri slipped, and its head smacked against the deck. The archers cheered, thinking they had caused some noticeable damage. But Kairo saw otherwise. The beast's paws and its sharpened ember talons were so hot that they were burning holes through the wet wood. And the holes were widening.

It picked itself up, writhed its head, and glared hungrily at the archers. It pounced toward them, clearing the full thirty-eight step courtyard in just two bounds. The snagaeri's metal rope snapped through the edge of the courtyard, sending splinters of wood flying.

"Find the Witch!" A throaty growl, thick with a Sigu Nii accent erupted behind him.

Kairo turned, the animal-horde was crawling up through the hole the snagaeri had made. His heart pounded. Somehow, some way, he knew the snake spoke of Aterah.

Two, three, four . . . The enemy soldiers were climbing onto his courtyard like ants from an anthill. He didn't know what to do about the snagaeri, but these soldiers demanded immediate attention.

Kairo sprinted to the hole, it's edges black and glowing with charred embers. The dark-grey smoke emitting from the embers gave off a sweet aroma; a taste like honeyed leather dried the inside of his mouth. He planted the bottom of his sandal on the face of one pulling himself up and shoved him back down the hole. The savage soldier screamed the whole way down, past the snagaeri's metal rope and dozens of soldiers climbing upward.

Something exploded in the distance. East. Then another snagaeri's roar. Other battles had started as well.

He stood in the most crucial position, the entry point where the Sigu Nii were squeezed together. Thinning them there was of utmost importance. Even though the Renovians would outnumber them by hundreds, it would only take a handful of high-level Sigu Nii to rip NeoDerii out of the sky.

And some would slip by. That's just how it happened. Kairo couldn't be responsible for guarding the hole and preventing each and every Sigu Nii from entering. And he couldn't shake the nagging feeling in his gut that those who slipped by would search ruthlessly for Aterah. He had to decide.

Find her first? Kairo shoved the tip of his bronze blade through an enemy's hand clutching the wooden hole. Find her first.

He left the hole, moving as fast as his legs would take him. He paused hesitantly over the rope bridge. Fire licked the hinges. With gritted teeth, and prayers lifted to the Korta Ellanii, he sprinted over.

The Barracks Deck looked worse than the West. Sigu Nii soldiers were everywhere. Swords flying, bronze and steel clashed together—a musical pause to Sigu Nii ears, covering the softer, sweeter sounds of flesh tearing and humans wailing.

Then there were those who didn't fight with blades—the wicked animals whose upper arms portrayed black tribal engravings. The tail of a serpent here, a torso there, even a soldier whose grease-covered-build rivaled that of Arden's. A full circle snake, missing only the head. A level-four vuu-caster. A beast of a man, whom Graeynesh Law's instruction insisted to "run from at all costs."

This level-four monster hurled swirling balls of fire into entire groups of fleeing Renovians. All of them were engulfed in gusts of flame and swept from their feet.

He wore no shirt. Scars covered his back, and black tattoos intricately pointed eyes toward his left shoulder. He grabbed dead and wounded Renovians by their ankles, cast a layer of ice over their bodies, and spun them in a circle to release them in a deathly flight to oblivion.

As heart wrenching as it was, Kairo was careful to step clear, well out of eyesight. He knew the man could kill him with the slightest flick of his finger. Kairo ran past groups of fighting soldiers and his own barrack unit, which was completely on fire.

Across another bridge, and he was on the Command Deck, whose critical state was similar to the West—bad and quickly growing worse. He passed them all, friends and enemies alike. He turned into Lezyne's Command building.

Kairo watched Arden's unmistakable stone arms pass around the corner up the staircase. Kairo chased after him.

"You weren't requ-estahh-ke." The guard at the top cut short as Arden's large, calloused hands fit around his face, and hurled him down the stairs. The soldier toppled back-side up past Kairo.

Kairo and Arden entered the war room together.

"You're all hiding in here?" The words escaped Kairo's mouth before he realized he'd said them.

A dozen faces turned his direction. Commander Lezyne, with a handful of high-ranking soldiers and officers huffing over her shoulder, all of the Chamberlains, General Adakon, General Forst, and General Baenek all leaned over a dark-lacquered wooden table, spread with war maps of NeoDerii and the surrounding region.

"Kairo." Commander Lezyne remembered his name. She glanced him up and down, disregarding his accusation. "Where is your sister?"

Kairo's eyes swept the room. Dark-grey smoke seeped through the wood all around them. "I hoped she would be here." He began backing toward the door. If she wasn't here, then here isn't where he wanted to be. The back of his sandal stopped short, he looked down and saw Arden's massive boots standing still behind him.

"Who are you?" Lezyne asked, turning to Arden. Fear seemed to seep into the corners of her squinting eyes.

"Wait." Adakon huffed. He slapped the wooden table with the palm of his hand and straightened his back. "Al—Alaku Arden?"

"It's Alakuel." Arden corrected. "And not anymore. Just Arden now."

"We don't use that word for mere men," chimed in a Chamberlain.

"My." Adakon shook his head. Clear disbelief across his face. "A generation has passed since the last time I saw you."

"Back when the snagaeri first polluted our jungle." Baenek nodded.

Adakon held his arms out and smiled. "How do you like what we've done with the place?"

"It's on fire," said Arden quietly.

"Is it coincidental that you return on such a dark evening?" Baenek asked.

"I'm here for the Oracle."

Everyone halted. Even soldiers who were previously occupied turned at the mention of Aterah.

General Forst's head shook rapidly, his face turned crimson. "How have you learned of her existence?"

"It's why *they're* here." Kairo's voice was hoarse. "I overheard one of the Sigu Nii mention her."

"Aye." Arden agreed. "Best we find her before they do."

"How do we even know we can trust you?" General Forst asked, looking at Arden. "You could have led the host here, for all we know!"

Adakon frowned. "General, you told us that Captain Rouen led them here."

"Well . . ." Forst's voice shook as he yelled. "They couldn't have just stumbled across NeoDerii with full-fledged *level-fours!*" It was clear to Kairo that he still had not recovered from his time captured by the barbarians.

Explosions boomed outside, followed by screams.

Kairo turned from the most important people in the rebellion and heaved the doors open. Back down the stairs he chased. It was confirmed. They were here for her.

Kairo was met with eye-stinging smoke on the Command Deck. The carefully measured wooden planks now reeked of char and burning ember.

The Renovians were dwindling. The ground they walked was fragile. The wickedness of Sigu Nii vuu was too much.

Why do you abandon us so, El? Kairo asked with his face lifted. An outpost-wide storm of sparks and ash rose toward the canopy. It would be pretty if the circumstance were different. He watched a bead of rain form between nailed-together planks on a courtyard higher up, drop, and collide with a meandering, air-borne ember.

The drip won. But it remained ashy. It splattered beside him.

He forced his legs to move, careful to avoid brittle planks. He searched all of NeoDerii, filtering out every face that was not Aterah's. He climbed burning rope bridges with no second thought to whether they would hold his weight. He searched the Training Pavilion, an entire deck located nearest to the canopy that now held mostly injured or dying Renovians. He searched other barracks, decks, and wooden courtyards above the West Deck.

Finally, he thought he saw her. He was searching so rapidly across so many faces, between fires and explosions, battling squadrons and hordes, that he had to go back to where his eyes sensed some recognition.

Aterah was being dragged toward the west edge of the Upper Decks. A single hand clasped the back of her collar. It seemed as if the snake was about to hurl her off the outpost.

Kairo took off in her direction. He dipped and slid between straying blades, friendly and hostile alike. He leapt over burning wood and widening charred holes. He passed Norly, who was caught in a two-on-one battle with, by the look of their tattoos, a pair of level-two Sigu Nii.

"Captain!" Norly shouted with relief. He was near out of breath. "You've decided to join us!"

Kairo paused. A rich moment of doubtful hesitation. He hummed with irritation and drew his bronze sword. It was amazing that Norly was still alive at all. "They're here for Aterah." Kairo clanged his sword against an incoming blade and pointed toward her.

Norly nodded. "Help me off these two."

One of the Sigu Nii laughed. "Aye, do I not have yer full attention?" Bright neon ice covered his hand like a glove, and he caught Kairo's next swing by the edge.

The other growled, a rumble in his throat as if he spoke snagaeri. His black sword turned ablaze with a flex of his biceps.

Kairo leaned back as if to pull his sword, shifted his weight to one foot, stomped the soldier in the chest, then yanked his bronze sword free. "We don't have time for this!"

Aterah was nearing the edge of the Upper Deck.

A bright-hot sword flew past Kairo's face. A swing that would have ended his life had Kairo's knees not instinctively buckled.

They exchanged a few more blows and swings, the Sigu Nii alternating gusts of ice or fire vuu. Each moment Aterah neared the west edge of the deck. Their battle might have gone on forever, destined to discover the rate of weariness between muscle and soul-damning-vuu, had a golden brother not approached the opponents from behind and slashed his sword across their backs. They coughed blood. Kairo and Norly, as if choreographed, shoved their blades into the heaving chests of each level-two Sigu Nii.

Norly heaved for air and wiped his brow dry.

Kairo exploded into a sprint toward Aterah. She was moments from being thrown over the edge, or so it seemed.

As he neared Aterah and the beast dragging her, he could hear her cries for help and see the redness of her cheeks, even the slivers of tears illuminated by NeoDerii's fires. The Sigu Nii bent at the knees, Aterah in one hand, as if he were about to leap off the deck and kill them both.

Kairo threw his hands around the savage's neck and tore him back onto the courtyard. They groveled for a moment, rolling against wood and bronze-nail.

"Aterah, *run!*" Kairo yelled as the two of them scrambled to stand.

Aterah pushed herself to her feet and took one quick step before tentacles of ice clasped her ankles. She toppled back to the ground.

Kairo and the barbarian stood still, eyeing each other. His hair was pitch-black. His eyes were dark and strangely speckled with blue. He wore no armor over his baggy brown clothes. His left sleeve attempted vainly to cover his lower shoulder, but Kairo could see that this Sigu Nii bore no ink.

"Oh." Norly puffed in amusement as he and the other Renovian strolled up. "We just fought four-times worth this man."

Kairo wasn't so sure. He glanced back at Aterah. The bright ice around her ankles suggested this inkless man had at least a little vuu.

The man closed his eyes in concentration.

Before this snake could conjure up any wickedness, the Renovian soldier charged him with a jab. The sword darted out, aiming under the Sigu Nii's right collar bone.

His eyes shot open, making eye contact with the soldier. His right hand exploded upward, trails of fire streaming beneath it, forcing it up faster than muscle could move. With the back of his hand, he smacked the jab away by the flat of the blade. The rusted bronze sword shattered loudly into dozens of shards that tore through the Renovian.

The Renovian stood there, arm still outstretched. There had been names on that blade. Fellow Renovians immortalized by the passing of that sword. Gone. And another taken with them. Gone. He collapsed to the deck, blood pooling around him.

The man's lips curled in grotesque delight. His teeth yellow and crooked.

Kairo and Norly both took a hesitant step back. Neither of them had ever seen a Sigu Nii do something like that.

"Your shoulder lies," Norly spat.

"Aye." His voice was calm and cold, unlike the regular grouchy growl of Sigu Nii accent. It was clear, fluent, almost proper sounding. His eyes closed again in concentration.

Norly and Kairo stepped back again.

Dark mist blasted from his fingertips. Kairo could only describe it vaguely as Darkness. It swirled around the soldier, then settled neatly in the shape of a sword in his hands.

The Sigu Nii twirled it a moment and swung at Norly, who lifted his sword to block the swing. But the black blade swept straight through it. Half of Norly's blade fell to the ground, the cleanest cut Kairo had ever seen. The swing continued through Norly's neck. His head rolled. Blood gushed from both ends.

Kairo turned to run for his life, but his eyes met Aterah's. She was shivering with fear.

Everything in Kairo screamed *run*. All his instincts. His Graeynesh teachings. He feigned another step out, hard and heavy.

He thrust his sword behind him as strong and fast as his muscles could muster, praying to the Korta Ellanii that the tip of his blade would meet flesh.

Again came the sound of shattering bronze. And a shard burst through his own lower left leg. Aterah's widening eyes were splattered with his blood.

He fell to the deck and looked at the warrior that had bested him.

The Sigu Nii grabbed Aterah by her ice-bound ankles.

Her mouth opened in a scream that Kairo couldn't hear.

He felt his temple hit the courtyard, but he didn't hear its heavy knock. His vision faded to black as the barbarian leapt off the west edge, Aterah in hand.

7

FORST

Forst, Baenek, and Adakon stood atop the Wheelhouse, surveying the battles on the West Deck. The charred, ember edges of the hole in the courtyard had grown to consume the notice board, which now lay in splinters on the jungle floor.

Forst looked upon the battle between the rain and fire and compared it to the Renovian and the Sigu Nii. The battle was close, but Forst could spot the winner.

"Let us retreat," he pleaded.

These were the highest-ranking men in the resistance. Should they fall, so would Renovia. It's culture. It's people. It's land.

The prophesied King to Come would lead Renovia out of exile and restore them to Kortaes—if one believed in such things. That's why even the great Adakon held the title of just a general. Despite leading the Egress, he was only a man.

"There is an underground barracks, an hour east," said General Baenek in his typical solemn voice.

Adakon stood before them, his feet at the edge of the roof. He remained quiet. His dark-brown hair ruffled in the crosswinds. Airborne embers flew upwards in front of him.

Then the world snapped.

Thunder erupted between Forst's own two ears. His vision fogged, and his temple throbbed. Everything took hues of blue and gold. Forst knew the whiteman had entered his mind.

"Adakon remains." The crisp, proper-accented voice of the whiteman crawled, relaying its disapproval with tone. It squirmed like a snake weaving through his brain tissue. Forst squinted and massaged his head, the dissonance of desires tore his attention like ground herbs. *"I will not have him slain before I can squeeze out your full use."*

"We outnumber them," said Forst, lifting his voice. "But we are falling. Please, Adakon, let us retreat."

"Your convincing is lamer than a man with no mouth, ears, or eyes!"

News of bronze stashed in the valley had spread through Edrei, three weeks earlier. A supply of swords, nails, axes, hoes, and the like. Forst had led the expedition, though he retained doubt that the rumors were true. Their mysterious benefactor had gone silent a half-generation prior, leaving their existing tools to be the last in circulation. They had already begun returning to stone.

Perhaps they would be able to discover the formula for the strong, shiny material themselves, but the Sigu Nii would not let up. Ninety percent of their population was spread across the warfront. Devoting people to more occupations prompted a management of resources that they simply didn't have.

Instead of civilization-saving tools, it was an ambush. High-level Sigu Nii warriors overtook him and his squadron, whose vuu was remarkably more powerful than their meshed jungle wear, their knowledge of every fallen-stick and unturned-stone in the jungle, and superior bowmanship and swordplay. And when they fell captive, it was a whiteman who led the interrogation.

His methods: hardly any more than a pale palm wrapping around Forst's forehead. His perception had remained compromised ever since, unable to fight the unknown vuu, unable to combat the flow of information for his location within the jungle, and unable to plead with his peers to just toss him off the roof and nod at his crumpled bones.

"They're retreating," observed General Baenek, his voice still solemn. It was true, the Sigu Nii warriors raced for the holes and metal ropes or flung themselves from the courtyard and broke their fall with vuu.

Adakon spun on his heels, his hands held behind his back. "Then the Oracle has fallen," A shaky breath escaped him. "Carry the *injured* to the Wheelhouse and signal curfew."

Where the fires around NeoDerii were previously outpacing the rain, now the steady drum of the overhead shower outplayed the roaring and crackling. A steady rain is better than a short downpour. Trees, plants, and the wood around NeoDerii can only soak in water so quickly. But now the fires were having a hard time finding new food.

General Forst was among the top three ranked soldiers in the Renovian rebellion. He did not show remorse. He did not show uncertainty. And certainly, he did not cry. But with every body he heaved by the arms, avoiding eye contact with the soldiers of NeoDerii, he could feel his upper-cheeks pinch over his eyes and a knife crawl up his throat. He was responsible. Him and the Whiteman that peered through his own eyes.

Morning came.

Soldiers lined up at the marked trees on the outskirts of NeoDerii, whose wooden courtyards weaved around for their inclusion. Hide-skin tarps were laid at the canopy of these trees, collecting and funneling rainwater down the hollowed-out trunks. Soldiers filled buckets at the spigots and brought them for the injured and dying in the Wheelhouse.

The canopy was dense enough that it often obscured the sky from the jungle floor. A handful of sewn tarps sporadically laid at the top were entirely invisible. Forst nodded in approval at this outpost's assembly of infrastructure.

"I spoke with the brother," said General Adakon when they next convened. "It's true. They took the Oracle."

Baenek paced. "I will tell Lezyne to gather her best and send a team after her."

"And should this team discern that they are incapable?" Adakon asked.

Baenek wiped his narrow, bony face. "Then they will do what needs to be done. An Oracle in the wrong hands would be the end of us."

Adakon nodded and sighed a grim and grouchy breath. "This location and its construction was proven to be among the best." Adakon was frustrated, "I picked it. When I first escaped Edrei, it was here that I wandered. And when I arrived, a Renovian grandfather and his children lived among these very trees. They survived three generations hidden from the Sigu Nii. Why have they found us now?"

"Do not tell my own story as if it is yours," General Baenek hissed.

Forst could feel sweat seep onto his brow. *It was me!* He screamed in his mind. *I told the Sigu Nii where we are; that we have an Oracle.* He wanted to cry. To wail aloud. But the Whiteman was in control of his body. In fact, the Whiteman felt more in control of his body, while not even present, than it would if it remained under Forst's supervision. He tried to contort his face into something strange, he tried to raise his hand and punch Adakon, anything to indicate that he was not on their side.

A sound like two rocks clapping against both of his ears rang inside of his mind. His head throbbed. The generals took on colors of blue and gold.

"I suppose it was righteous that Rouen got exiled, after all. Not that I ever had any doubt, but it's nice to see the fruit of your reasoning come so quickly," said Forst.

In honesty, he marveled at the Whiteman's power. His tone of voice, inflection, and pitch were all slightly different than he would have used.

But the thought processes and vocabulary? All his, rearranged ever so slightly. And the Whiteman's vuu provoked his mouth to utter them.

For being one of the most in charge people in the entire rebellion, Forst was effectively not in control of anything at all.

When Forst first arrived at NeoDerii, delivered by the Oracle's own squadron, he thought that the Whiteman would have him pull out a blade and plunge it into Adakon right then and there. The Whiteman scolded him for such narrow thinking. Forst would convince Adakon to lead the rebellion in a direction more suitable to the Whiteman's wishes.

It was then that he realized the desolate hopelessness that this war deserved. If the Whiteman wanted, he could use Forst to collapse the entire infrastructure, practically overnight. So, why didn't he?

Forst discovered the Oracle's existence *after* he was rescued. To have extracted so much use out of an asset in its first couple of days was remarkably dismal. What could possibly be of more value than her?

"*Your entire species is like a field of crops to me,*" the Whiteman replied. His voice was like the slow creaking of large castle doors. "*And although we've discovered an Oracle, there is still a grander harvest that I await hopefully.*"

There was something more valuable than the Oracle, then. And even though the Whiteman compared him and his people to a farm, he could not discern any visible resource that they were being extracted for. Sure, some soldiers were taken captive as prisoners of war, but that happened far too infrequently for it to be the primary drive.

"*You would not understand it, even if I told it to you.*"

Forst despaired. He wished for death. The event playing out surpassed torture, it was the rotting of his life's work. No, more. It was the discovering that all their lives, all of Renovia, toiled for nothing.

8

AYRAH

Ayrah backed away slowly, letting the purple curtains melt around her. She stood with her fists clenched around her belt. The Masikonian's hum continued, unhalted by Taryn's wailing and stumbling and dragging. Though she was his woman, Herk did not try to save her from Lord Mayor Gabya's violent lust.

The rich purple drapes blew gently in a breeze belonging to summer's end. Ayrah listened as the Black Guard laughed, throaty and growly. They snatched up each of their own girls and dragged them to the Burnt Harem's various bedrooms. The show girls, now suspecting that sex would not be the only thing to happen, began whimpering and resisting. Smacks and bludgeoning sounds echoed through the brothel.

"I—I—" Herk's stammering trailed off.

"Aye." Whispered Boden. "You'll find another woman." He patted Herk on the shoulder.

The building began to shake. A rocking sort of shake that rumbled the walls and floorboards and curtains alike. Soft moaning drifted through the two-story brothel, followed by the second most desperate screaming Ayrah had ever heard. Lord Mayor Gabya and his men had chosen bloodlust—a service the Burnt Harem provided for the crueler of their customers. And then, just like that, the screaming began to cease, room by room, as each of their girls were torn from this world.

"I loved her." Herk's voice caught in his throat. "I'll take him in a grash!" He took two stomps through the small lobby before Boden caught him by the shoulder.

"Not a good call, brother. Lord Mayor Gabya's stronger 'han he looks."

Ayrah stepped lightly along the curtain, behind the brothers. She stepped around velvet couches and pillows sprawled along the floor. Through the brothel she walked until she found the master bedroom. Ayrah twisted the brass knob as quietly as she could, opened the wooden door, and crept inside.

The room smelled like bloody arse.

A man stood facing the opposite direction, his green and blue silk robe hung around his ankles.

"Gabya," said Ayrah.

Gabya whipped around. His eyebrows arched in surprise. "Oh!" His face softened when he saw her. "Did they send me another?" His lips lifted, showing his black spotted gums.

"Do you miss your younger days?" Ayrah asked.

"What?"

"When you were an Officer over the whole Gya province." Ayrah snickered. "I'll bet it makes your insides melt, knowing that your glory slips by the day."

Gabya's eyes squinted. "You recognize me." He shrugged. "Then step carefully, girl."

"Now you just watch over this barren town. How low you've become."

Gabya let a single strained laugh escape him. "This one is feisty." He kicked the silks from his ankles and faced her. Blood and bits of Taryn were smeared across him. "Show me your tattoo."

Ayrah hesitated, and turned slowly, so that her left shoulder faced him.

Gabya's eyes widened. He stared her in the eyes, turned his head up, clasped his belly with both his hands, and ripped laughter from as deep he could. "Too feisty. Much, much too feisty. You're vuuless, girl!" He glanced around, "Certainly this establishment is not worth its prestige, if they let just any rat crawl in here."

Ayrah stepped closer toward him.

"Get back. Don't touch me." His voice held genuine disgust.

Ayrah held out her left hand in a flat line before her chest. The temperature of the room noticeably dropped. Specks of frost began to coat her arms and condensed on the palm of her hand. Ayrah brought up her right hand, held in front of her flat left, and reached just past where the skin of her palm should've been. She felt the sharp cold of her vuu stinging her own body as she drew out a sword of black ice.

Ayrah gripped the sword with her right hand and swung it in a circle. It was rigid and crooked. Neon blue vapors fell as the ice mingled with summer's end.

"So, you're not vuuless," huffed Gabya. "How old are you, girl?"

Ayrah didn't respond.

"You've not even taken the Niiwa for the Dagger? If you don't take it soon, you'll be too old, and stuck a rankless coward your whole life."

Ayrah spat. "Grash me."

Gabya laughed. "Over what?" He shook his head. "I've decreed all grashes in Simula must be held at preordained arena locations." He gestured to the dimly lit wooden walls around them, "To keep from destroying buildings and businesses."

"Over what?" Ayrah asked with gritted teeth. Her stomach burned and she strained from charging Gabya in the instant. "Over the arrest of my father."

"Oh, bloody El." Gabya wiped his face, accidentally leaving streaks of blood across his forehead. "Another one dead-set on vengeance. Who, child? I've signed the arrest of more—"

"Nahkon Veligreen."

Gabya froze.

Ayrah stepped forward.

"You're . . . You're Ayrah Veligreen?"

Ayrah nodded slowly. "Why was he arrested? Why did his own men turn against him?"

Gabya's hand flickered. Bright orange sparks fluttered around his fists. Sweat condensed on his brow. Gabya's veins illuminated all over his body, a deep sunset red. His eyes turned desperate. And in the flash of a moment, he shot his hands together, and a ball of fire exploded toward Ayrah.

Having seen the buildup of vuu, Ayrah side-stepped quickly. The fireball crashed against the wooden door.

"To me!" Gabya screamed, straining his voice to reach through the atrocities that his soldiers were committing across the brothel.

Heavy metal bootsteps slammed around the wooden floor overhead.

Ayrah sighed and brought her ice blade up.

His eyes were darting, trying to take in as much instinctual information as possible.

Ayrah jabbed her rigid ice blade forward.

Gabya's right hand exploded upward, neon blue ice coated his knuckles and traced down to his wrist. He smacked Ayrah's attack away by the flat and punched with his left. Smoke and sparks trailed behind his balled first.

Ayrah twisted her sword, swinging its momentum down after being smacked away. Her biceps burned as she forced it to move between her and Gabya.

Flesh tearing from bone met both their ears. They looked down at Ayrah's black ice blade. It had penetrated Gabya's middle two knuckles. Dark frost traced from her sword to his hand, and his hand turned black.

Blood froze mid-drip. Gabya screamed in pain and clutched his cut-in-half hand in the other.

"You've grown old," said Ayrah.

Fire crackled as it caught from the door to the ceiling to the drapes by the entrance of the room. Ayrah felt its warmth growing steadily on the back of her neck.

"El!" yelled a throaty man.

Ayrah listened to the clanking of five Black Guard soldiers descending to the first story of the brothel. With a flex of her arms, she shed frost onto the fire and jumped through the shredded and charred doorway. The wooden staircase was to her left, and all five of the guards were in a half circle around her.

Ayrah's feet slid into a wide stance. Her knees bent and her sword raised. She glanced at Herk and Boden, wearing grim faces near the foyer. Ayrah called to them, "Help me!"

Boden held back his brother and shook his head. "You'd have all of Gya and Warlord Tuio storm our doorstep."

Ayrah itched to run past the soldiers in front of her, and punch Boden straight across the jaw. Two Niiwa victors and herself against five round-four-winners? The Guard would stand no chance.

The five soldiers each wore loose items of their hellinite armor. Streaks of lipstick traced their faces, their belts were poorly tied, one was missing a shoe. None of them seemed to care. The armor was primarily for show anyway. Oceans part for those who wear recognizable insignias.

Vuu, channeled and manifested to look like material weapons, filled each of their hands one by one. A burning orange sword. Two single-hand axes of neon-blue ice. Two short daggers of lightning bolts. A murky green mist shaped like a spear, which Ayrah knew would expand to a poisonous cloud on impact. The last one held his hands out flat, and the floorboards of the brothel screeched, bended, and shattered into a thousand razor splinters. The wooden bits flew up around the Guard's hands, hovering and rotating as he crouched into a fighting stance.

The Masikonian's tune continued through it all. Faltering neither for curiosity nor fear.

Ayrah looked each Guard in the eyes. They were confident, as fighting any rankless commoner would. As having survived the fourth round of the Niiwa would. And as being accepted in Warlord Tuio's Black Guard would.

The fire-blade swung low. Ayrah jumped over it, watching the flame brush her boots.

The axes arced toward her head. Ayrah's black-ice-blade met them in the air, frost clashed and fell lightly around them.

The dark green spear shot past Ayrah's hip, and murky mist exploded, seeking to fill Ayrah's lungs, sting her calves, her neck, crawl into her clothes, and itch her to pieces.

Ayrah threw her hands out wide and flexed her arms and wind blasted through the east windows, the drapes flew up against the ceiling, and the green mist pressed against the west wall until it dried like paint.

The orange fire-sword swung again, arching for her torso.

The Guard with the bits of floorboards hesitated and asked, "Who are you?"

"She's Ayrah Veligreen!" Bellowed Lord Mayor Gabya, roughly three steps behind her. "Kill her!"

Weapons and vuu halted. The Masikonian's tune ceased. The eyes of each Black Guard widened and mouths propped open.

They did not know her. But they knew of her father. Every boy and girl child who could talk a half-generation ago, knew the name Nahkon Veligreen. Suddenly, the room knew who they were dealing with—and how hopelessly outclassed they were.

"Sh-Shadowa?" Boden's voice squeaked like a pubescent boy.

Ayrah reached down in her aching gut to the stormy oceans that churned there. Rage and wrath, battling each other like unseen gods.

Ayrah's veins turned black. All over her body, just beneath her skin, they illuminated. She could feel her eyes strain, as if darkness were pumping into them.

"What are you doing?" Gabya yelled at the Black Guard. "Kill her *now!*"

Weapons hit the floor. Hesitant steps were taken in retreat.

Ayrah screamed. Out of her churning stomach, her bellowing voice released a shadow. She fell to her knees, her vision foggy and her stomach empty of feeling. She watched as the misty darkness devoured each guard whole. They flailed at the black mist, but their hands were severed from wrists and arms from shoulders. They tried to run but it tore leg from groin and groin from torso.

One by one, the horrid screaming of the Black Guard was cut short by death. And still the shadow surged forth.

Ayrah watched, rather helpless, as Boden and Herk's hands flew up in plea. She was drained. Her vuu-muscles had burned to failure. And the guildhead brothers were no more.

The mist-like darkness slowed. It swirled around and around near the foyer. It funneled itself into a little ball, no larger than a marble. Warm firelight glared off its side, and it dropped to the floorboard with a bounceless thud.

The dark-glowing veins in her hands gradually faded. She breathed hard and needed to collect herself. She pushed herself to stand and strained with all her might to keep from swaying. Gabya stood behind her, the fire from his vuu was setting the entire brothel ablaze, illuminating his horrified face.

"Why did you arrest my father?" Ayrah asked, trying to make her voice sound more powerful than she currently felt.

"It wasn't me! It wasn't me!" Gabya held his hands over his face and turned toward Ayrah like a helpless child. "It was King Ash. He signed the charge and handed it to Warlord Tuio to carry out. Treason! Treason is all I know."

"You signed the papers. I saw your signature," said Ayrah. "I've been raiding the Warlord's Office here in Simula for an entire summer. You keep very good records."

"Yes. Yes. I can see that was you now," he cried. "I was only in charge of hiring the people powerful enough to complete the job."

"Who?"

"The Tamagai! Yes! They would know more than me."

"You hired the Tamagai to arrest my father?"

"Well, they were the champions of the national Kaeselwa. They're in Pratuel. Go ask them and let me live."

Ayrah huffed. "All of this, and you still dare to offer commands?"

"I'm sorry! El! El!" He gestured to the floor with an open palm, momentarily ceasing the caressing of his cut-in-half-hand. Fire and sparks and ash were raining from the ceiling around them. Gabya bent down and put his nose against the floorboards. "El," he said.

Ayrah nodded. The Officer had submitted. She turned and put the Burnt Harem behind her. That guild had not even been the most powerful guild in Simula. *The Tamagai, in Pratuel.* They were one of the strongest guilds in all of Gya. Perhaps even Sigu Nii.

9

EIDHIN

Mugs clonked on tables. Chairs squeaked. Chatter filled the inn. Eidhin stood in the far corner, rubbing one hand with the other.

He counted six of them. The oldest was well into his third generation, with greying hair and wrinkling skin. The youngest was only half a generation. All of them waited breathlessly.

Eidhin tilted sideways and squeezed between the small group. *When he spoke, it was as if he were speaking right to me.*

On the other side, El Penoa sat, legs crossed, with his right elbow resting on a table. "Alright now." He gestured forward with his hand. "Come, come. One by one."

Everyone turned to one another. A shared hesitation. The child took the first step, but someone put a hand on his chest. A young man gestured to the seat across from El Penoa and looked at the old man. "It's yours."

"Hurry, hurry. No need for such civility."

The older man nodded in appreciation and took his seat.

"Describe yourself."

"Well . . . I've lived in Snowstock for the better half of Generation Lotra. . . ."

Eidhin turned from the table. *A man's business is his own.* He meandered across the room.

"And you're sure about this?" Eidhinr asked Eidhin. A half-full mug of wine sat between him and mother. Eidhin's sister sat across from both of them, tapping her finger on the table. Grandad and Illao were off to bed already. "I just—I didn't know you felt that way. Another two harvests, son, and I'd be able to put you through a decent school."

"I—I—I—"

"I think it's wonderful." Eidhin's mother shrugged. "You heard El Penoa. It's good that little Eidhin is feeling restless. And the church has done well for us."

Eidhinr frowned. "Restless? Maybe. But discontentment?" He hummed in thought and reached through his coat pocket, then pulled out a small wooden pipe and pushed himself from his seat. "I need to think."

Eidhin turned back to the corner of the inn. He watched as a younger man, close to his early second generation old, sat down with El Penoa.

"Who knows, maybe if you did well enough, you could even become like Teach—" mother cut herself short and glanced at Eidhin.

She did that often. She forgot that he couldn't speak right. Each time briefly filling Eidhin with a proud hope—she recognizes that he's special. Then it rips away. Disillusionment fills her face. And a dreaded disgust replaces him in her eyes.

Eidhin took a seat and stared at the corner of the inn. *One.* He counted. *Two. Three. Four. Five.* He counted and counted. *Fourteen. Fifteen.* He had a vague idea of what he was counting. *Sixty-three. Sixty-four.* Something between time passing and the length of his attention. *One-hundred-twenty-seven. One-hundred-twenty-eight.* An exercise for special moments of anxious boredom. *Two-hundred-eleven. Two-hundred-twelve—* A stretching of not how many numbers he knew, but how long he could remain counting them. *Three-hundred-ninety—*

"Come, come." The numbers ceased as El Penoa's crisp accent drifted through the chatter-filled inn. The voice commanded Eidhin's attention. He quickly rose from his seat, knocking his chair against the table.

Eidhin stumbled and squeezed through groups of people talking and drinking and hurried to Penoa. Not a second to spare. *El's time is not to be wasted.*

Eidhin took his seat.

"Describe yourself." Penoa's velvet black robes were perfectly clean and fell past his ankles. The deep blue insignia of Rai was sewn delicately across his right chest. His greying-brown hair kept a well-washed shine. His hands looked soft, like ones that only knew the toil of a quill, not a plough.

"I—I—I—" Eidhin had never described himself before. *What do I say? I knew this question would come. Why didn't I plan ahead?* "L-l-li-k-ke t-t-to c-cou-cou-count."

A moment passed. El Penoa's brown eyes felt cold.

I like to count? That's all you could think of?

Penoa raised a hand. "May I?"

Eidhin frowned and nodded.

The crest of Penoa's palm reached over the table and touched the round of Eidhin's forehead.

Something snapped. Loud, almost thunder-like. The world around Eidhin blurred with soft blue and gold colors.

"Is this better?" Penoa's distinct, unmistakable voice rang through Eidhin's head.

You're in my head! Eidhin's eyes went wide.

El Penoa removed his hand from Eidhin's forehead and leaned back in his seat. He smiled, revealing bright white teeth. *"I am."*

But—But how?

El Penoa shrugged. *"There are many things to know. But tell me, what is it you know? Of what things are you certain?"*

Eidhin frowned. It was a vague question. He repeated it in his mind while he thought. *I know that plants should be pruned. Whether they enjoy a human touch, or. . . or maybe a human touch is supremely influential.* He disliked the vague nature of his response, so he added quickly, *I like to count!*

"Hmmm."

I know how to read and write.

"Oh? Have you read many books?"

Eidhin shook his head. *No, but* . . . He reached through his trouser pocket and pulled out his faint yellow parchment paper. *I keep track of my father's crops.*

Penoa took a quick glance at the paper before handing it back. *"You do like to count."* He noted. *"Continue."*

I know that you say restlessness is good, and I know that I am quite restless.

"Why do you find yourself so? What is it you hope I am offering?"

Eidhin paused. *I . . . I want to be one of the greats. One of the people who discovers something about the world and never leaves it the same again. The type of person whose thoughts are taught and discussed and implemented and . . . I never want to be forgotten.*

El Penoa laughed. Audibly. *"Ambitious."* He shook his head. *"You come with me, and maybe you just might. I run a small program in Gehni called the Freedom Encryption. If you come with me, and find yourself well, you will become a student to one of the greats. I see something in you, Eidhin. You're smarter than you could possibly let on. Unfortunate for you that articulation is half the game. But you will get there when you get there."*

Wait. Does—Does that mean I made it?

Penoa nodded. *"Yes. I grant you the honor of being invited."*

"Oh! Oh!" Eidhin jumped from his seat. *Please, El. You must come tell my father!* Eidhin ran through the inn, weaving between stumbling drunkards, dodging overflowing mugs. He rested a second at his mother's table and glanced back at El Penoa.

"Hello, love. What's the—"

Eidhin took off again, around tables and chairs, and out the doors into the brisk night. The intense candlelight of the inn spilled halfway into the dirt street. The stars were shining bright, only a quarter of them hidden by rolling clouds.

Eidhinr sat alone along the eastern wall of the inn. He rocked gently as he tipped his pipe against the pottery ashtray beside him. "Eidhin? Son, what's wrong?"

Eidhin stood there catching his breath, aided by a calm breeze. He opened his mouth to speak, but the gentle steps of a figure filled the space behind him.

"You must be Eidhin's father." El Penoa walked toward him and stretched his hand.

"Eidhinr." He answered, pushing himself from his seat and shaking Penoa's hand. He laughed uncomfortably. "I tell you, El, Eidhin sure is set on this Rai thing. I'm sorry if he's been any trouble."

"No, not at all!" El Penoa gestured to the rocking chair on the other side of the ashtray. Eidhinr nodded, and they both sat. "Actually, I think your son is exactly what we're looking for."

"Mmm? And what's that?"

Eidhin found the wooden ledge between the wrap-around porch and the grass beside the inn and sat on it. He noted the strange difference of accent between his father and El.

"You might not know, but your son is quite intelligent. More so than he can articulate, obviously. It seems there are wheels turning behind his lame lips. He also has *no* other education besides the Church of Rai, and whatever you may have passed onto him. This is a very valuable spot to be in, for a large variety of people."

Eidhinr made a *tsk* noise. "To whom?"

"A large variety of people." El repeated bluntly. "To have a high rate of comprehension, but not many things yet clouding... worldview. It is valuable."

"Valuable." Eidhinr let the word roll off his tongue. He sat for a moment, the ashtray beside him emitting a sliver of smoke from burning tobacco. "Valuable?" His brows came in. "What game are you playing, El? You scheme. You . . . You . . . Eidhin, leave us." Eidhinr stood from his rocking chair, holding El Penoa in the grips of his glare.

Eidhin hesitated. "B-b-b-but—"

"Now!"

Eidhin pushed himself from the wooden porch step and wandered back to the inn entrance. He glanced once more at his father and El.

With his eyes on his feet, and his right hand rubbing his other, Eidhin slowly weaved his way through the inn. His stomach burned. *Why is father so flustered? Can't he see? El wants me.* He found his way to his mother's table.

"Oh! Eidhin. How was it? Are they speaking now?" His mother swayed partially.

"Y-y-ye—"

"Oh, I hope it is well." She sighed.

Eidhin stared at her. His stomach burned. He picked his hands off the table and noticed the sheen of sweat he had left there. His brows came in as he wiped them off. *Why can't father just be proud of me? I get that he wants to send me to school, but why does he* have *to be the one to do it? I have made this of my own accord. Be proud of me!*

Eidhin sat. After a moment, he let his mind wander. *Anywhere but here,* he pleaded with his daydreams.

Eidhin's father stormed inside. His ears were red, his fists clenched.

"Wh-what-t-t hap—"

"Do not go outside. Do you hear me?" Eidhinr stuck a finger in his son's face. "Do *not* go and see him."

"Y-y-e—"

"Good."

Eidhin's father marched to the bar in the back.

Then something changed. Like a worm wiggling its way through his mind. Eidhin turned back to the inn doors.

"Eidhin," A whisper echoed in his head. *"Eidhin, come here."* El Penoa's eyes peeked over the double swinging doors.

I can't. My father said I—

"Your father wants to keep you. He sees your value as much as I do. He fights to keep you from leaving. That is no way to learn. Come to me, now. I have something for you."

Eidhin felt his knees twitch. They straightened as he stood, his chair squeaking as the wooden legs rubbed against the wooden floorboards. His eyes were fixed on Penoa's.

"Eidhin? Didn't . . . Oh—" Mother held a hand up to her head. "I think, uhm. I think it's bedtime."

"Quickly, child."

Eidhin made his way through the stumbling crowd. He stepped past the double swinging inn doors. Penoa stood with his eyes boring into him. "How much do you wish to see more than this?" He gestured to the streets and buildings around them.

Eidhin thought for a moment, and he nodded. *I'll do whatever it takes, El.*

"Good," Penoa said as he reached through a pocket in his robes. A dark matte metal filled his hand, the size of *his* forearm, with a glinting shiny edge on one side. "Take this."

Eidhin's eyes widened. He felt his breath quicken. "I—I—Ah—" *I can't take that! That—*

"Hush. You said you would do what needed to be done. They will fear you. Take it." Penoa softly nudged the dark wooden handle of the dagger into Eidhin's hands.

Eidhin stared at it. It looked dirty, like it had been dropped in the mud. *Where did you get this? How was this not visible from your robes?*

"From another man down on his hopes. Now go inside."

Eidhin felt his knees twitch, his feet turned toward the inn doors. He could feel his own sweat collecting between his palm and the handle of the blade. His eyes darted around. He began to carefully stuff it beneath his mustard sweater.

"Ahht. Keep it out."

Eidhin felt his knuckles twitch. Suddenly, he was rethinking everything. *I—I—I don't think I want this. I don't think I want this.*

"You want it. We must take measures to secure fruition."

With his free hand, he pushed the inn doors open. The black metal knife hung awkwardly in front of his torso in his other hand. Eidhin could feel his face contorting as he began past the wooden tables and drunkards whose eyes slowly found their way toward him.

Slowly, Eidhin put one foot in front of the other, continuing through the inn. People started rising from their seats. Eidhin tried not to look at them, but he did. *Their eyes . . . they look terrified.*

Someone screamed. A woman wailing with a finger flopping about Eidhin's direction. "Knife!" Her voice found language. After that the whole inn was in a frenzy.

Wooden chairs toppled and knocked as people leapt from their seats, hurrying in fear to find the edge of the room or run for the doors.

Eidhin stopped in the middle of the room as he looked around. His grip tightened around the dagger, but it felt clunky in his hands. *What do I do now?*

"Eidhin?" His father's voice drifted through the wailing. He stood pressed up against the counter, even *his* eyes looked afraid. "Eidhin, put that down, *now!*"

Eidhin felt his fingers flicker. An itch to throw the knife down as hard as he could. But he couldn't. He stood there, shaking, his eyes started to water.

"Eidhin?" Another voice drifted through the wailing.

Eidhin looked up. People were beginning to come out of the inn rooms on the second floor. They peered down across the wooden tables, across the people screaming and running. At Eidhin standing there with a knife in his hand.

"Eidhin, what's— What are you doing?" Illao asked. He rubbed his head and his eyes, as if he didn't quite believe what he saw.

"You there!" A crisp, heavily accented voice thundered through the building. Eidhin shuffled his feet and looked toward the doors. El Penoa stood there, chin high.

"E-E-El—"

"Do you hear me, child? Unhand the weaponry!"

Eidhin winced at his voice. He began to cower. *"El?"*

"I am assistant proctor for the Church of Rai on Gehni Isle. You *will* do as I say." Penoa turned about the room and gestured for calm. "Is anyone injured? It seems I returned in time." He straightened his back and walked slowly toward Eidhin.

Eidhin looked around. He looked at El Penoa carefully stepping toward him. *As if I would actually hurt anyone! El!*

Eidhin turned toward his father, whose eyes were burning toward Penoa. Illao's cheeks seemed wet, a sliver of shine caught by the candlelight.

El Penoa stood before him. "You have violated the king's law, listed under 'tools of deviance.' As the ranking citizen present, I take it upon myself to deal with you." Penoa's long pale fingers wrapped around Eidhin's, and slowly, he took the knife from him.

10

CHASE

Kairo slowly regained his senses in a dimly lit Wheelhouse; a groggy wail escaped his mouth, echoed by a hundred others lying about.

His eyes opened with some difficulty, and he winced as he raised a hand to brush away the dried crust of blood, sweat, and ash around his eyes. His left leg seared sharp and hot while his head throbbed with dull beats.

Piss, dung, and rotting wounds made the air dense. Like the noonday jungle during rainy season, but instead of moisture in the Wheelhouse air, it was death.

He remembered a vague state of waking previously. Did he talk to Adakon, or was that a dream?

"Captain. Captain! He's awake." It was a girl's voice.

Kairo nearly mistook the voice to be Aterah's. But Aterah was gone.

The archer Tullia came around with a bucket of water and bent by his side, a NeoDerii physician in tow. She lifted a ladle to his mouth. The slightest sitting up and straining of his neck to reach the sip caused his whole thigh to light up in a burning flare. He drank. Water streamed down the sides of his neck.

A rushing urge to wretch came over him. Tullia must have seen it on his face, because she brought up an empty wooden bucket just in time.

A damp hemp blanket ripped off him, leaving his body cold and shivering. The physician knelt over him and soaked his bandages with water to remove them without reopening the wounds. First, the cloth tied tight around his head, then the one around his left thigh.

The physician hummed with grim speculation.

"What? What's wrong?" Tullia asked.

"The cut is probably infected. There's no way to tell."

"What can we do?"

"Now? Nothing. Twenty-eight generations ago, when our people had healing powers, I could do something."

Kairo ignored the myth. Vuu had placed him here; it would not save him. And he had seen the infection on fellow soldiers before. They arch up and down and seize with full body muscle cramps violent enough to break bones. It looked a worse death than one during battle by far.

"If your jaw locks up then you have less than a month to live," said the physician. "Until then . . . pray." He stood up and began searching around the Wheelhouse for his next victim.

Kairo tore his elbows out from beneath him, falling back to the blanket with some degree of drama.

"Captain." Tullia's tone contained notes of inquiry, but she asked nothing.

He clenched and unclenched his jaw, testing for stiffness. Nothing yet. Maybe he would be blessed. Given favor and mercy. He eyed the wooden rafters above as he fell back asleep.

The outpost horn boomed. Kairo awoke with a start. Pain rushed back through his body.

The outpost was being raided again—his first instinct. Kairo laid fear-frozen until the grogginess passed, and he realized it was only dinner.

A walking stick had been laid next to him. He eyed it with disdain.

His face scrunched into a permissible wince as he pushed himself to stand. He wobbled. His knees knocked together. He curled around the walking stick like a rope dangling over the jungle floor. He scraped one foot ahead, the other rushed back to fit beneath him, then he scraped his foot ahead again.

More than a hundred others were also injured—Yeshwin's doorstepped soldiers laying and crying around the Wheelhouse. They were plopped up on the long tables and benches, and they took up the width of the floor between. No dinner here. His nose filled with rotting gore. Kairo shuffled around them toward the doors and pushed them open.

The West Deck was infected by some black, wooden plague. Charr was everywhere. Soot coated every surface.

Volunteer carpenters sawed and dispatched the charred wood from the salvageable as they worked around the hole in the West Deck. It had consumed the notice board. He guessed the hole must have been twenty-steps wide in each direction.

"Wh-where are you going?" Kairo forced the wheezing syllables from his mouth.

One of the carpenters passing by with twine-tied wood slung over his shoulder stopped. "We're preparing for relocation," he said and continued on his way.

"Relocation," Kairo mumbled. He wobbled backwards and fell against the exterior Wheelhouse wall. He sat there. His fingers scratched mindlessly at the infected wood beneath him.

NeoDerii would no longer be home.

He wondered what was becoming of Aterah at that moment. He thought of the barbarians, their subhuman, primitive monstrosity. He shuddered. Did their vuu torment her? Did their hands wander across her?

Kairo clasped his hands over his eyes. His sobs struck pain down into his torso.

His muscles quivered. Blood rushed to his face, his ears were hot, and his nose burned. He beat his curled fist against the West Deck. He hit again. And again. And clawed back up the walking stick into a stand.

Rouen was gone. Certainly, slain by the beasts of the night.

Norly was gone. He could still see his headless torso smashing bloodily into the courtyard as the Sigu Nii chuckled.

Aterah was alive. Gone. But alive.

A stray knapsack lay near the Wheelhouse doors. Kairo snatched it up and emptied its contents onto the deck.

His wounds were infected. Probably. He was nearly certain. And he would not spend his likely last month alive wasting away in foreign territory. NeoDerii was no longer home. But if he could reach Aterah before the turn of the generation and escort her return, it would have been a worthy final month.

He ducked into the kitchen hallway and snuck past the curtains that separated the sweaty cooks from their materials. He was in a large storeroom. Shelves lined every wall holding flour and grain, herbs and spices, vegetables, and salted meats.

A man stood near the back, ruffling through ingredients on the top shelf. "Where are you going, boy?" The man did not turn to look. But his voice carried with a low, rumbling octave.

Kairo stepped quietly around the shelves.

The man's tattoos were like stone. His hair was a mop of dreadlocks, littered with wooden and metal beads. Arden. He turned and made contact with his purple eyes.

"I—I'm leaving."

Arden scoffed, amused. "To where?"

Kairo turned his back on the man. He began sweeping vegetables and salted meats into his open knapsack. "I'm going after my sister."

"The Oracle." Arden nodded. "And how do you plan to make it past the snagaeri?" He stared derisively at Kairo.

"With a hammock."

Arden laughed. "Aye. And the war-guilds?"

"With a hammock."

"You're going to die." His mop ruffled as he shook his head. "Tell you what, *boy*, I have business in Vasara. I can get you past the warfront."

"Vasara?" He had only ever heard the city's name uttered by Aterah, who was well-read in Renovia's past. She called it the City of Old, a command center for their kingdom, back when they used to be one. She used words like throne, gathering, holy, secure, and a ladle for the world. She likened the place to Yeshwin. Kairo did not even put together that Vasara was a real place that still existed.

"Aye." Arden sighed. "If the Oracle is dragged west, she'll be moving through Vasara."

Kairo had trouble finding words. In truth, he still did not trust this man with stone tattoos. Though he had saved Kairo, he radiated savagery. More than his strange accent, his far larger build than even a big Renovian, or the foreign look about him: it was the vuu. Renovians were simply not wicked enough to conjure vuu. So, this one was?

"Meet me on the jungle floor." Arden brushed past. "Bring enough food and drink for the coming forecast."

"The what?"

Arden tsk'd. "The approaching weather in hell, boy."

Kairo grit his teeth in frustrated wonder. What's the worst that could happen? Arden kills him. Well, Kairo decided that he was nearly just about dead anyways. He would trust this beast with stone tattoos.

The cooks and their apprentices formed a shoulder-to-shoulder line along the interior Wheelhouse doors. Carts filled with large leaf-plates of buttered breads and wooden-cauldrons of stews stood between them. The fragrance of food mixed with the soiled pants of dying soldiers.

Renovians entered the Wheelhouse, grabbed their food, and rotated out on the last door to their left. Kairo limped along, his knapsack strapped over his shoulders, and mingled into the exiting crowd.

"We have suffered a great loss, make no mistake," a pain-ridden voice called across the courtyard.

Kairo looked around for its source and saw Adakon standing on the Wheelhouse roof.

"But they too have made a mistake! They did not crush us. They did not finish us off, so that we have no hope of beginning again."

Kairo glanced around the courtyard, making sure he had not captured attention, and tossed the rope ladder over the edge. He climbed down. Each rung felt like a thousand. His leg spasmed and flared and seared tears into the corners of his eyes. After half a dozen positions, he opted for hopping down one rung at a time, so that he would not have to bend his injured leg. Finally, he reached the bottom.

"I just pissed there," Arden laughed from the evening shade beneath the West Deck.

"We'll have to sneak past the scouts," Kairo said, his voice cracked from the settling pain. He eyed their locations, making out the meshed jungle suits and the meticulously painted and textured wooden platforms high in the trees surrounding NeoDerii.

"Why?" Arden asked lazily. He strode out from under the courtyard.

Kairo followed with his head bent, hoping that the scouts would not recognize him and call him coward or defector. He tried to step lightly. To avoid the crunch of a twig or leaf with practiced care, but his left foot flopped short. It seared with pain each step and his weight rushed to the walking stick.

Incoming! Identify! the scout whistled.

"Fuck off," Arden grumbled, as one who couldn't care less whether they heard him.

And strange enough to Kairo, the scouts silenced.

The sun ducked behind the western Delkop Mountain Range. Kairo shivered. Shadows moved out of the corner of his eye, ceasing upon direct inspection. Terror crept through his bones. Here he was again, traversing the jungle in the dead of night for the second time in his life. Bloodthirsty snagaeri roars filled the valley in every direction.

Arden slowed to a halt. "Drink." He said, his hand outstretched.

Kairo fumbled around his belt and hastily handed him the canteen.

Arden drank and spat. "Is this water?" he growled, his voice harmonizing with another snagaeri roar. He tossed the skin back and knelt. He scooped his hands into the dirt, bent over.

Kairo did not take him to be a praying man.

The dirt began to bubble. It swirled and puffed and gave off steam as if it had been heated to a boil. And slowly, drips of a clear, sour-smelling liquid seeped between his fingers. Arden slurped until he had only to lick his hands.

What was he doing? Did he brew some snagaeri slaying-elixir?

Arden belched and sighed, "That's the stuff."

11

ATERAH

Ffft. A subtle sound, followed quickly by a thud. Aterah looked around, though it was daytime, the edges of her reality were blurry and dark. *I'm dreaming.* Even in her dream state, her wrists felt raw, with a sharp pain every time the twine rope twisted or pulled. A roll of cloth propped her teeth apart, and drool constantly seeped down the corners of her mouth. Spots of her head throbbed, where the beasts around her had torn her hair from her scalp.

Ffft. Aterah looked around and stumbled over a tree root. *There it is again.* The twine rope that restrained her wrists tugged forward, causing her to wince and trod to keep up with her Sigu Nii captors. She tried to look at them, the beasts, but they were silhouetted, clouded by her dream. *Who then?* She asked herself.

Ffft. The tip of an arrow erupted through her shoulder. "Ghhh!" Blood flowed from the wound and soaked into her clothes. Pain seared hot and static through her body. She tried to scream, but the cloth gag kept her muffled.

Aterah's knees buckled and hit the dirt. The silhouetted beasts around her turned, ferocious in posture. They shouted, but their words were incomprehensible.

With all her might, she forced herself to turn and see from where the arrow had come. Her shoulder felt as if molten glass were burning a hole through her.

Then she saw them as they crept from the edges of the jungle.

Ffft. Ffft. Ffft. Arrows flew by her and over her and thudded into the trees around them. People she knew, soldiers she recognized as friends, emerged with painted faces and strung bows. Renovian soldiers, protectors of NeoDerii, protectors of her people, came out of the jungle.

Aterah tried to scream at them. She wanted to tell them to run for their lives. But they weren't aiming at her monstrous captors, they were aiming at *her*.

They strung up another set of arrows. *Ffft.*

"Up." Hard calloused hands took hold of her. "Up, Renovian witch, up!" Muffled noises of terror escaped her as she woke. Aterah expected to see the stone of an arrowhead poking from her left shoulder. But her shoulder was bare and unscratched. A man kneeled over her. His cheeks bore the beginnings of wrinkles, and there was a thirst in his eyes as he shook Aterah awake. "Up." He said softly as he fidgeted with the damp cloth in her mouth.

Aterah shook her head, trying to push his hand away with the only mobile part of her body. *No*, she tried to say, but it came out mumbled. The Sigu Nii, older than the others, left her as she wiggled into a sitting position.

She was with four Sigu Nii beasts. They had slept a little way off the Old Road. Trees surrounded them, and jungle brush scratched the edges of their small camp. A firepit, whose flames had long since died in the night, sat at the center, sending up grey whisps of smoke. A short and stocky Sigu Nii with buzz-cut hair tended the fire and was trying to use his vuu to ignite the branches.

Across the pit sat a woman, probably in her late second generation. Burn scars in the shape of large animal claws ran up her neck from beneath her shirt. She leaned against a tree, peeling away the skin of a rodent with a knife, and when her hands were full, she used her teeth to tear the fur skin away.

And then there was Verano, the one who had taken her from NeoD-erii. His hair was short, almost like spikes, pitch black with the tiniest streaks of red. He was the strangest of the group. The other Sigu Nii were hot headed; Verano was cold. The other Sigu Nii wore studded leather fur boots. Verano wore a loose black cloth shirt and dark brown trousers, both tattered and dirty. The other Sigu Nii had tattoos, shiny and bold, where even the birds of the forest could see them. Verano, when his sleeves didn't cover his shoulder, had no ink.

"Hurry with my breakfast," the wrinkled Sigu Nii grumbled as he stuffed his fur pelt bedding into his knapsack.

"Quiet, old man. You'll have your dish when I'm ready with your dish." The woman's voice was muffled between bits of furry skin, her neck straining as she tore the flesh and meat apart.

Aterah shifted. Her hands were still bound, and her mouth still gagged.

"Yutarah is still five days away, inkless," the short one said as he got the fire lit. He looked up at Verano. "So, stop wishing for it to come closer."

Verano turned and looked at him with steady eyes. "What do you mean?"

"That's why you're staring off west, right?" he asked. "You're tired of this." His burly arms gestured to the jungle around them.

"No." Verano turned away. "This is the last Niiwa season that I can participate in."

"You were born in Lotra?" The one by the fire chuckled. "Coward—"

"Who cares?" the older Sigu Nii growled. "The reward for bringing her to the Warlord's Office will be enough to retire on a nice plot of land, somewhere outside of Vasara."

The woman chuckled in amusement as she handed the skinned rodent to the fire. "I got more appetite than a bit 'o gold." She smiled and looked at Aterah. "Whoever she is, the Warlord's Office is moving her somewhere.

And I mean to be part of the crew that do it. The reward on the late end of that deal will be way more than anything Yutarah could scrape up."

Two days had passed of their making quick pace west through the jungle. The Delkop Peak, when the canopy didn't cover it, could be seen looming over all.

The first night stuck in Aterah's mind like a thorn, the night Verano had torn her from NeoDerii. With her in his grasp, he jumped a from the Barracks Deck to the jungle floor. Aterah screamed the whole way down, thinking the inkless warrior had killed them both. With a kick of wind and flame, their momentum broke, and they rolled across the dirt.

In that instant Aterah leapt up and tried to sprint in the first direction she looked. But a hand snatched through the air, grabbing the first thing it could, her hair. A fistful of her hair ripped from her scalp as her neck and back slammed backwards into the ground. Aterah gasped for air, but it wouldn't come, her eyes fogged with perspiration. Verano bent down and grabbed more of her hair. She pried at his hand, hit and kicked at him, and screamed as he dragged her west across the jungle floor.

Holding on to his wrist and pulling herself closer was all she could do to prevent another fistful of her bloody scalp from tearing apart. The dirt began to rub her back raw before she tried to stand while trying to keep pace with her violent, silent captor.

At first a few Sigu Nii emerged from the jungle beside them, moving in the same direction. Then it was a dozen. Finally, a clearing hosted a hundred tents and hundreds more Sigu Nii.

They chanted and bellowed, they laughed and shouted for all the night jungle to hear, with no fear of snagaeri hunting them down. Her captor dragged her through the camp, with each group of Sigu Nii screaming in her face. Spit and blood covered her before Verano hurled her into a tent of his own.

The cream hide tent reeked of Sigu Nii must and sweat, and damp fur pelts covered the ground. Verano stood, just in the threshold of the tent, and looked at her with blank and icy eyes. Aterah shifted, she touched the back of her head and felt the wet stickiness that covered her hair, and a small bald spot where her hair was no longer. She looked at her captor, the inkless warrior. She wanted to scream, she wanted to cry, she wanted to be back in NeoDerii.

I'll go with you, Adakon. She had decided. She *had* decided.

In a sweeping motion, Verano turned from the tent. And a tall, older Sigu Nii took his place. His cheeks were just beginning to show wrinkles, and a thirst was in his eyes. "No." Aterah shook her head. "No!" Aterah screamed as the Sigu Nii crept in.

Aterah had no dreams that night. Nothing to tell her of the days to come.

That was two nights ago. Four of them sat around the camp. Four beasts of Sigu Nii. The short and stocky one had divided the breakfast rodent into several bites and handed some to each. They tore into the scrawny, juicy-looking flesh. Aterah fumbled with the white cloth tied tight between her teeth, wincing at the rubbing of her wrists on the twine rope. Drool tickled her jawline, and the sight of food wasn't helping.

She also felt a pinch-like twinge in the top of her gut. An uneasiness. It was subtle, and oftentimes Aterah forgot about it completely. The feelings of the present were well enough to drown out the cries of a little *twinge.* But it was there and never went away. At first it was small, almost unnoticeable. Aterah felt it first the night of the day she had met Adakon. It had first appeared while she lay awake in the top row of hammocks in her barrack.

It was hardly anything then, just a discomfort among a day of discomforts. Though she forgot about it or was distracted from it, not once had the feeling gone away. The pinch-like twinge loosely resembled the feeling of hidden eyes. As if deep in the jungle around her, someone sat perched, watching her.

Aterah looked around, remembering the vivid dream of her Renovian *saviors.* Though she couldn't see them, she wondered if they were there. *Maybe. Maybe not yet.* Aterah looked down at her shoulder, softly rubbing the spot where the stone head of an arrow would soon be.

12

AYRAH

"Lick it." Ayrah commanded. The bottom of her boot kept the face of a baker pinned to the ground.

"Er wahtn adk!"

"Shut up. I can't understand you at all." Ayrah moved her boot from his face and touched her black ice sword to his neck. "Where did you get this?" She held up a hand-drawn picture of her face, with words big enough to read from afar:

Wanted dead or alive:

Shadowa

Dead reward: 150 weight in silver

Live reward: Praise from Warlord Lyta Tuio

Gya's most wanted #11

She wasn't sure if the baker could read, but when she had entered through the back-alley door of his shop in search of food, he recognized her.

"The Black Guard will find you."

Ayrah pushed the rigid tip further into his neck, just before puncture. "Where?"

"Aye!" His plea held more anger than yelp. "They're all over town. Travelers come in, talking rumors that you offed someone important. They say you possess the power of Shadowa."

Ayrah Veligreen shoved her sword forward, through his flesh, through his throat, nicking bones until it pierced the floor. The man's neck turned black, and a thick frost spread over his upper torso. Small spikes of black ice sprouted from his skin, coated in splatters of frozen blood. Ayrah bent to her knees and channeled into existence a small ice blade into her hand. She cut a strip of cloth from his dark brown shirt and tied it around her lower left shoulder. An inkless arm would be noticed in Pratuel.

Ayrah peered at the shelves around her. Sackcloth bags of flower and grain, sugars and spices. Her stomach growled just looking at the raw ingredients.

She had saved up a little coin from her time in Simula. But between the horse and the long ride to Pratuel, it was practically squandered.

Ayrah cautiously let the backroom door of the bakery swing open. The front of the shop's brick tile shined with wax and lacquer. Little wooden tables with twisting iron legs held up teas and breads for various well-dressed customers. Bakers bustled back and forth behind a glass counter, attending whistling kettles and big stone ovens.

A rack of cooling bread with honey butter freshly melting over the slices sat just within arm's reach. Ayrah didn't think twice as her hand darted out and grabbed several.

She stepped past the dead baker and slipped out the back door.

Horse-drawn carriages passed each other down Pratuel's wide streets, paved over with multi-colored cobblestone of black and white, orange, red, and hues of blue. The buildings on either side were all laid foundationally from brick, with a Pratuelian wood that uniquely sparkled. Veins of thin iron held sections of glass that covered nearly entire walls of shops along the street. Ayrah peered through as she passed by, glittering suits of armor and swords, fine silks, and restaurants with crowds of people.

A breeding ground for the glory slaves. Ayrah frowned as she peered through the pedestrian masses. The three-piece serpent tattoo was common here, the one that reached the Skull.

Ayrah turned her eyes to the west, a low mountain range lined the edge of the city. The closest part of it was a perilous cliff whose ledge rose two hundred reaches from the ground below, and atop it: the Tamagai Castle. Its red shingles glistened in the midday sun.

I should wait for the night. Ayrah decided. The Kaeselwa fighting guild was no joke, five winners of Niiwa, and a well-seasoned guildhead.

Ayrah continued north down the Pratuelian road, parallel to the mountain range and the castle, adjusting the strip of brown fabric hiding her upper left arm. She decided to see what wonders the city had to offer.

A parchment paper caught her eye, nailed to the glittering wood of a shop. It was a hand-drawn picture of her face, with the same wanted and reward inscriptions big enough to read at first glance.

Ayrah snatched the paper from the wall and crumbled it between her fists. She looked around, watching, wondering if anyone had seen her. A spark ignited in her palm, and she continued walking, letting the soon-to-be-ash parchment fall to the stone.

The street opened into a square. Shops, stores, taverns, and inns made a walled perimeter, with a few narrow allies between them. Vendors formed an inner circle between the shops with a statue fountain at its center. Scents of charred meat and well-spiced noodles filled the air. Vendors called out strange names of trinkets and potions, anything to help a man in a fight.

Ayrah's eyes wandered across the statue standing over the water. A man whose blood and ferocity took his name into recognition, not just wide across Sigu Nii, but immortally, even after his death. Ayrah shrugged at the dead, stone, fountain man, and carried on.

Beyond the vendors, blackstone walls soared up forty reaches.

"Public grashing! Public grashing!" A man called.

Ayrah knew the building as soon as she came up on it. It was the city's Niiwa arena. *They must use it to hold grashings when it's out of season.*

Two men in full, black-coated armor manned the entrance, a half-circle corridor of dark carved stone. Each of their chests were decorated with Tuio's insignia, the gold hand pierced by lighting. The left sleeve on their armor had a gaping hole, well-crafted to lead the eye to the golden-tanned skin that lay beneath. Each of them wore the fourth rank. With *Pratuel* as the lower inscription. Ayrah stayed in the middle of the crowd in hope to go unnoticed. Things would be a lot more difficult if she were recognized.

The corridor opened to a stadium big enough to fit a few thousand people, though the crowd was sparse. Ayrah stood frozen as she looked around. The stadium's large stone bench seating continued for rows above her and rows below her. In front of the bottom row, a wall dropped seven reaches to the hard dirt field. The field was huge, a hundred steps in radius, much bigger than Simula's. An impressive, dusty square for the dead.

Two men dressed in their finest metals, well suited for a low-rank battle, fought to the death. It must have been toward the end of the match since the two were groveling all over the ground, spitting up dust and blood.

Ayrah walked up the rows and took her seat amid the predominantly empty stadium. Ayrah turned and noticed a boy near her age quickly look away, a row above and to the right. Ayrah couldn't help but take note of his arms. Scrawny. The feeble attempt at facial hair came out as a thinly grown moustache at most. His dark brown hair was nice, though. Well kept.

He avoided eye contact.

"What are they grashing for?" Ayrah heard herself ask.

The young man leapt from his seat and began toward her.

Oh El. What did you do? she thought.

He sat beside her. "Apparently *that* man," he pointed to one of the two rolling in the dirt. "Slept with *that* man's woman. So, they're grashing for her."

Ayrah let out an exaggerated *hmmm* sound.

"Say, wasn't that Niiwa insane?" He bumped his fists on his knees, his eyes were glued to the dirt field. "I can't stop thinking about it."

"I—ahm, I'm from out of town. Must've missed it."

He turned to her, jaw dropped. "Oh, man. It was like the god-king came down and blessed the battle himself."

"Hmm. Who ended up winning?"

He laughed a bit. "Kizmaldi Tuio." He turned to her, smiling ear to ear.

Ayrah's heart skipped a beat. "As in Warlord . . ."

"Lyta Tuio's son? Yes. The very same."

Ayrah turned her gaze back to the pit. "Huh." Images of what the battle might have looked like passed by her eyes. Explosions and fury, she imagined.

"He even joined my guild."

"*What?*" Ayrah snapped in the boy's direction. "What guild?"

"Oh," He waved a hand. "Just the Tamagai."

"*You're* in the Tamagai?" She couldn't believe her ears. No chance this punk wimp kid was in one of the strongest Kaeselwa guilds across all of Sigu Nii. Her eyes glanced instinctively toward his shoulder, but his shirt hid his tattoo.

He nodded the affirmative.

Maybe I could sneak in another way. She wondered—and felt her cheeks burn at the thought. "So." She coughed and cleared her throat. "What's your name anyways?"

"Ryan."

"That's an odd name," she mocked. *Flirt you idiot!* "But it's—it's cute, though." Her voice sounded painfully bland.

"You know what's even cuter than my name?" Suddenly, confidence seemed to fill him.

"What?"

"My bedroom. In the Tamagai Castle."

Bloody El. "I—I would love to see it." Ayrah practically slapped her forehead with tone.

The stadium's small midday crowd gasped and followed up with throaty cheers. Ayrah turned to see what had become of the two. The accuser's head lay severed and in vertical halves, with nothing between the two but a red pool and swirling dust.

"What's wrong?" The boy's voice was like a screeching hawk.

Ayrah shook herself out of it. She hadn't even felt her attention faulter. Her gaze was fixed on the split head, just lying there. Memories stabbed at her, memories that wanted to be sheltered and locked away. Ayrah felt moisture threaten her eyes. But in an instant it was replaced with anger. An anger that wanted to become tangible, to come out of her. To see the light of day and then consume it.

"Nothing." Ayrah stood from the bench.

Ryan laughed light-heartedly to ease the tension. "Grashing can be a gruesome—"

"I said I'm fine." She took a long breath. "Take me to your bed, castle boy."

If Ryan were any older and Ayrah any luckier, he would've been a member of the Tamagai for the past half-generation, near her father's execution. But she could tell by the way he walked, by the way he talked, the way his shirt covered his shoulder, no chance was he anything more than a castle gardener. Not Tamagai material. If he had been, she could've skipped the guild entirely and just captured, interrogated, and tortured him.

Ayrah began back down the rows. The winner of the grash unleashed his skin sword and urinated between the loser's eyes. The small crowd hollered in excitement, they screamed for more.

Ayrah could feel blood rush to her face and her stomach grew queasy. She turned toward the stadium entrance. Ryan followed behind her, but she could feel his attention still drawn to the victor on the field.

"Stick around for the next two!" An official of the city's arena called across the stadium. "The next grashing is an affair of duty and property! One man owns a tavern, the other wants it from him! Who will hold the deed in the end? Who will find themselves grashed?"

Ayrah ran through the trickle of people walking toward her through the corridor. She burst back out onto the square, hard of breath. An itch to bend over and rest her hands on her knees pricked at her. Ayrah made toward the fountain, through the ring of vendors.

An extravagant mosaic spread beneath the water of the statue fountain, deep in color and glistening under the flowing water. She remembered the courtyard of her childhood home, her brother helping her train, and her father's constructive scolding.

"There you are." Ryan's voice sounded like a morning bird, plucking her mind from where it was. She shivered with annoyance.

"Ready?" she asked. Ryan took her by the hand and began to lead her south, back through the streets of Pratuel. The Tamagai mountain stood foreboding in the distance.

"So, what's your name?"

"Shadowa." Ayrah answered without thinking. She winced. Had he seen the posters all over the city?

Ryan turned to her. His murky green eyes searched her face. He shrugged, probably presuming it to be a nickname. *Surly she doesn't actually possess the power of shadowa,* Ayrah guessed his thoughts.

Their road began a gradual incline as Ryan led her up the cliff's foot-hill. The sparkly wood of Pratuel's shops gave way to pine as they neared the western outskirts of the city. Brick foundations turned to cobblestone. Pedestrians' clothes turned to rough linens and sandals, Niiwa tattoos no longer on display.

Ayrah ascended the worn stone switchbacks beyond the slums. Her dreadlocks blew in the breeze. "Do you ever think about Nakhon Veli-green, and whatever happened to his kids?" she asked.

Ryan shrugged. "I hear rumors every now and then."

"Like what?"

"Well, some say the older, Verano Veligreen, fled Sigu Nii entirely. Changed his name and resides in Masikus. Others say he had face changes, and fights in the Kaeselwa unknown to anyone. Still, others say he fled to the Ryalan colonies and joined the war against Renovia." He chuckled, "But that would be a waste of his blood."

Ayrah nodded. She knew he joined the squabble against the caramel-colored bark-eaters, back when he still wrote her letters. She wondered if he was even still alive. "And his sister?"

Ryan breathed hard and shook his head. "I used to listen to the her-alds, back when it first happened. They talked of bounties and hunters. But it's been a long time since anyone heard anything."

"Were you there during the coup? The day the Pikemaster took over as Warlord of the Ryvl province?"

Ryan wheezed a laugh, and talked breathfully, not wanting to waste any. "No, no. I've only been with the Tamagai this past season. Only Errta remains of that generation. The rest have retired to the Warlord's Office or died in the Kaeselwa."

By now Ryan was pushing his hands off his knees with each heave upward.

The sun began down its evening course, radiant spears of light filtered through a mountain-top forest on Ayrah's left.

The stairs finally ended. To her right, Pratuel spread out through the region. She could see the blackstone Niiwa in the north and a grand triangular tower of the Warlord's Office in the south. Tavern and brothel lanterns began illuminating city streets.

Before them stood Castle Tamagai. The blackstone structure seemed to loom dangerously above the cliff. It amazed Ayrah that mudslides had not yet taken out sections of the castle. Various interpretations of the Sigu Nii god were carved straight into the walls. Demonic faces, whose eyes seemed to mock as she neared. Some had lightly shaved heads, others were completely bald with bloody horns erupting from skin. Some had serpents coiling around necks or slithering from pitted eyes. And some had fang-like teeth with smoke dripping from the corners of twisted smiles.

Ayrah's stomach churned. She was ashamed to admit to herself that she felt a degree of nervousness. It wouldn't be her first time in a castle, though it had been half a generation. It wouldn't be her first time in the presence of powerful men, though it was a while since they tried to kill her.

The brick-paved path led to two dark red doors. Hellinite studs, slightly bigger than the palm of her hand, jutted out from the door. And hellinite rings, too thick to touch forefinger and thumb around, made for door handles.

Ryan swung his arms and strutted as if he owned the place. But he looked very small when he grasped a hellinite ring with both hands, braced his feet, his veins bulging under the skin of his arms, and strained to crack the door. "There you are." He gestured for Ayrah to enter.

Ayrah restrained herself from laughing and mustered everything within her to politely tip her head at him.

Two shirtless men were wrestling and tossing across the floor. A sweat-drenched back even rolled over the tip of her boots. They smacked their fists into already-bruised tissue. One of the men had dark, shadowa-colored skin. Like the night. A Razite. Ayrah stared at him as he tussled with the Sigu Nii. She tried to place a memory of ever meeting a Razite, but none came up. The man was slenderly cut, his head shaved near bald, with defined muscles that Ayrah didn't know existed.

Suddenly, Ayrah was worried. She did not think the Tamagai would have a Razite. She squeezed behind Ryan, hoping his dung-blood vuu would mask her own.

"They're *always* fighting," Ryan tried to comfort her.

Exhausted sighs escaped both men, and they parted to lie on the stone floor. The Sigu Nii was a shorter man, hairy, and something close to two generations old. His arms and thighs were like trees.

Ayrah's eyes went wide when they wandered the common room. A fantastic living area, with leather couches and in-ground fire pits. The far wall was made of all glass, connected by stone pillars and a set of double doors that led out to a dark stone courtyard. The blackstone walls on all other sides held up dozens of crude and vulgar paintings. Naked women. Naked men. One even had a man putting out his cigar on the rear of a woman. Portraits of past Tamagai members were sprinkled between, with them doing just as fun things.

Hallways spanned out to either side of Ayrah, leading as far as the castle was big. The left side of the common room had a wrap-around bar that stocked barrels of ale and a hundred liquors.

"So, who won, boys?" called a girl from behind the bar. She wore clothing that exhibited more skin than cloth. She had the painting-perfect sandy-golden Sigu Nii tan.

"Who do you think?" The Razite stood up and made his way toward her. "This Sigu Nii compares nothing to the black deserts of Ra'che, or the beasts that reside there."

Ayrah gave a little sigh, relieved that he did not seem to notice the presence of her power.

"Well, your drink and kiss are waiting for you," she cooed.

"Oh, shut up, Tagon." the other grumbled. "Fight me with vuu next time, and I'll show you what death looks like." But he spoke with hardly hurt pride.

Ayrah caught a better glimpse of the ink that ingrained his shoulder. A victor tattoo, four pieces of serpent with symbols in the middle that decorated a viper's head. *Pratuel*, was the city inscription.

He gazed at Ayrah. "Ryan, did you bring *another* girl up here?"

"Errta, shut up." There was a strain in Ryan's voice. "Please, just this one time, shut up."

The woman laughed from behind the bar, which interrupted the kiss that she and the dark man shared. "You poor girl."

"Please."

"Ryan said he was in the Tamagai," Ayrah acted surprised. "Is he not?" If she was about to be kicked out, it would make sneaking back in during the night a bit more difficult. Especially with the Razite among them, able to sense idle vuu.

"Oh, he's in the Tamagai alright," Errta answered. "He's our bookie. Our accountant. He tracks how favorable we are among the commoners of Sigu Nii." Then he laughed. "Sorry kid, but we don't even let him use a knife at dinner."

Ayrah felt her fist raise instinctively, and she punched Ryan on the shoulder with force enough to prompt a squeal.

Errta raised his brows. "Good punch." He walked her way. "It's fair if you want to turn back now. But those stairs are something else. Stay for a drink?"

"Aye," she shrugged, and followed Errta to the bar. Ayrah sat down beside him. His shirtless body was a hot red, which seemed to be darkening into bruises.

"What wouldja like, sweetheart?" the pretty woman asked. Ayrah had to keep herself from staring at the vast amount of flesh between sparse cloth.

"Do you have any of Ryvl's cinnamon ale?"

Errta chuckled. "Ryvl girl, huh? Good stuff, we get that delivered by the barrel full. You should see the little couriers lug that thing all the way up here each forecast."

Another man sat at the bar. His skin was pale, almost bright white. He wore fine white robes that fell past his ankles, trimmed with gold and blue. A strange set of glasses sat on the bridge of his nose. "Tagon could quite simply, easily even, engage the slightest bit of his vuu. Summon some beast from the depths to help them." His voice was silky but higher pitched. He spoke smart, too many words to say too little.

"And I specifically tell him not to." Errta nodded. "They gotta make a living somehow. What praise would they be worthy of if Tagon did it each time? None by my book." Errta picked up a half-smoked cigar from the counter. He lit it with his finger and tucked it between his teeth.

The woman set a mug of Ayrah's ale before her, then poured Errta a glass of bourbon.

"I guess we could make Ryan do it." Errta erupted with laughter.

Ryan tried to speak and protest from the seat on the other side of Ayrah. But Ayrah made sure not to look his direction, to give him the permission of attention to speak.

"So, how long have you guys been in the Tamagai?" Ayrah asked, hoping her voice sounded amiable.

"Pfft. Most these wimps here aren't technically Tamagai, or Kaeselwaworthy anyhow. Tagon is Razite, but I'm sure his skin gives that away. Ecanaes here," he pointed to the scrawny whiteman with glasses, "is from Aylavuera. The two of 'em are just here for missions prescribed by Warlord Tuio, or sometimes the king for that matter. Only Urota, this beautiful chunk of woman you see there, and myself are actually Tamagai. She been here, what, close on three seasons now?"

The woman nodded and smiled before turning back to talk with Tagon. Ayrah eyed her for a moment, briefly letting her eyes wander to her shoulder. Another Pratuelian victor.

"And I been here since . . . the middle of Generation Yaerta. Fresh ink back then."

Perfect. I'll have to steal him away somehow. Ayrah stopped her thought in its tracks. "Illian, huh?" she asked, trying to sound conversational. She looked at Ecanaes. "So does that mean you can read my mind and stuff?"

A black man that can sense vuu—of which she had plenty, and a white man that could sense thinking. How in the world would she make it any farther in the conversation than this? Certainly, between the two they would realize she was here with ill intent.

He chuckled, a geeky little chuckle. "No, I studied combat analytics in one of the Mathematics' most prestigious schools. Though a sprinkle of captivation for Philosophy resulted in my admiration for Warlord El Rai Ezs, and his . . . groundbreaking sociological systems of value. I do admit this interest, along with my ethnicity's natural inclination toward body language and other sorts of intrapersonal awareness, possesses me some aptitude as to observing where your heart lies."

Ayrah's heart crawled up into her throat. If she were outed by a slimy pale skinned . . . She forced a half-smile. "Oh? And what do you see?"

"Bloody El, girl!" Errta shot her a glare. "Don't ask him *another* question. He'll keep talking nonsense all night!"

Ecanaes glanced between her and Errta. A smile crept into the corner of his lips, and he winked.

He thinks I like him. That's . . . I guess that's better. But Ayrah could feel her cheeks turn red. Errta's arms did look big.

"There's a long line for that one. But I guess you might be in front of me at least." Ecanaes' glasses fogged up as he let out a sigh.

"I hate lines." Errta grumbled. "I always skip them. And if anyone gets his sword in a bunch, I'll just rip it off him."

"Shadowa," Ryan whined. "I was supposed to show you my bedroom."

"Ryan, you sound Renovian." Errta mocked.

That tickled Ayrah mid-gulp, and she coughed up some of her cinnamon ale. "Alright. Let's see it then," she said, disdain evident in her voice. The common room grew dim, so that Urota had to pull a few candles from underneath the bar.

"Finally!" Ryan jumped from his seat and grabbed her by the arm. Ayrah sloppily chugged the rest of her drink before Ryan pulled her from the room. He dragged her down a hallway beside the bar. They passed door after door as well as other hallways that branched off. More crude paintings and shiny weapons decorated the walls. Eventually Ryan paused in front of a door. They walked into a bedroom, hardly ten steps each way.

Ryan lifted a hand to stroke her hair.

"Actually, Ryan, could I bathe first?"

"Absolutely."

He didn't need to agree so resoundingly. She frowned.

He led her back into the hallway. Ryan opened a wooden door across from his room and showed her through. "I'll fetch a servant to draw your water."

The bathroom was large and tiled, with a ceramic tub, big enough to submerge even Errta. Another wall was entirely covered with mirrors. Ayrah twisted back and forth, looking at the full length of her body. The front-left side of her previously red hair was beginning to form dreadlocks. She hadn't brushed in seasons. She frowned. It was turning black, lock by lock, and she wasn't sure why.

Ayrah stepped closer. Her eyes were bright blue along the edges of the white, gradually darkening in color until they mixed seamlessly with her pupil. Waves and trenches ran perpendicular to the fade to black. Dark bags lined the bottom of her eyes, she rubbed at them in a vain attempt to brush them away.

Ryan returned with a stout little lady. She wore a black shirt with sleeves that went down to her elbow. She smiled at Ayrah politely before drawing water from a pump near the back. The lady lit coals beneath the ceramic tub with a brief spark from her palm.

Even their servants have vuu, Ayrah awed.

"It'll be ready shortly," said the servant as she slipped out of the room. Ayrah turned longingly to the bath. It felt like ages since she had taken a hot bath, but sadly it would have to wait a bit longer.

Ayrah peeked into the hallway. Sure that it was empty, she darted out and made her way back toward the common room. Ayrah paused around the corner, out of sight. Two distinct voices reached her.

"He's new. The Niiwa has given him a big head. He'll warm up to us eventually," Errta said.

"Kizmaldi Tuio won't be one to *warm* up. He's shooting for his mother's spot as Warlord." The voice that responded was deep and raspy. It was aged and flushed of emotion.

"El Malik, it won't be a problem. He'll fall in line soon enough."

Malik. It was the Tamagai guildhead. A seasoned warrior who played in the Kaeselwa games in his younger days. *Not one to be messed with.* Vuu wearies with age, so Ayrah figured she could take him, but to have survived Sigu Nii for so long, and without avoiding combat, it was best to leave his glory undisturbed.

"He'd better. Now that he's here, it's not likely we'll be able to get rid of him. If anything happens to that boy, the whole province will be storming our door."

"Well, with him on our team, at least Warlord Tuio will give us the Vulgarhe training pavilion you requested." Errta responded. Ayrah heard him grab a bottle from the bar.

"I wouldn't be so sure. She's not one to show favorites. We'll be under more scrutiny with that boy here." Malik sighed. "Training at first light. Wake up the children, I'll be waiting in the courtyard."

"Yes, El." Errta mumbled. Ayrah tucked further away from the corner as Errta strode to the castle door. He carried an unlit cigar in his mouth and a bottle of bourbon in his hands. Malik began for the hallway, his footsteps echoed off the walls.

He's coming down the hall. Ayrah peered around, there was nowhere to hide. She'd been eavesdropping for some time. She darted out from the hallway, her eyes on the castle door, trying to wear an innocent face.

"And who are you?" His voice ripped through the air. Ayrah jumped, attempting to look startled.

"Oh," She laughed shyly. "Uhm, Ryan thinks that I'm in the bath. But . . ."

The guildhead laughed and patted her on the shoulder. "No harm done. The kid needs a bit of meat on his bones." His face had grey stubble, and his hair was messy. His clothes looked old and worn, fashioned in a previous generation.

Malik started down the hallway, a slight limp in his step. Ayrah watched him walk away, her heart pounding in her chest. The common room was dark, lit only by a few candles around the room. Ayrah turned and made for the castle doors.

The city spanned out past the edge of the cliff like a sea of fireflies. Lights were turning off as the working class of Pratuel went to bed.

Errta disappeared into the woods opposite the cliff. Ayrah quickly followed him but kept her steps quiet. Most of the moon became blocked by the shade of the forest. The angle that Errta walked put the castle farther and farther away.

"Who are you really?" A cigar ignited from the shadows.

Ayrah flinched, but mustered command into her voice. "Tell me about the arrest of Nahkon Veligreen," A sharp cold struck through her left hand, and a sword soon followed.

Ayrah could hear the faint sound of bourbon swishing and Errta drinking. "That's been sealed by the king. I couldn't talk about it to anyone outside of Tamagai, even if I wanted to."

"I'll grash for it."

Errta chuckled dismissively. "You know my Niiwa rank. But you've had that pretty little brown bandage on all day. Show me." Errta dropped the bottle to the ground but kept the cigar between his teeth. He flexed his muscles inward, above his abdomen. Veins of fire and molten lava burned out of his skin, casting a warm light on his wicked, calm face. He stared Ayrah down.

Explosions of fire and wood echoed through the forest. All in unison, twelve bonfires ignited in a perfect circle around the two of them. The fire began catching the trees.

Ayrah smiled. The trees crackled ablaze, and burnt leaves scattered around them. She slowly unwrapped the cloth strip that covered her shoulder.

Errta's eyes fell on her bare shoulder. His face remained blank. "You're the daughter, aren't you? Ayrah. Ayrah Veligreen. I knew there were something familiar with those eyes. The dark auburn hair."

"Why did you arrest Nahkon?"

"Tell me, girl. Do you still dream of your father's death?"

Ayrah charged him, her black sword held out. Errta stepped gracefully, his hands moved toward her like water. Sparks of fire and lightning erupted around his hands, and a storm of fire blasted through the forest.

Ayrah thrust her sword into the ground, and it exploded into a spiked wall of black ice.

Errta's fire blew around her like a river parting around a rock.

Her wall shook and cracked.

"You're not giving up already, are you?" His voice was light and unconcerned. "Come on, show me what the blood of a Warlord tastes like."

Ayrah hurtled over her black ice cover, already drawing another sword from her palm. Her father had instructed her mostly in the art of close quarters combat. They hadn't made it much farther.

Close the gap! screamed Ayrah's instincts.

Errta's molten veins beat rhythmically with illumination. He punched and stomped the ground, and entire burning trees came crashing toward Ayrah. Like thunder ripping around them, trunks were torn from roots.

Ayrah leapt through the air, her feet braced the trees as they fell, from one to the next, as she darted toward her attacker.

Dirt and leaves and sticks rose from the ground around Errta. They swirled around him in a tight ball, and with a flex of his muscles, they shot toward Ayrah.

The leaves crunched on impact, doing little else. But the sand and sticks pelted through her shoulder and splattered out the other side. Ayrah screamed in pain. She grabbed her arm and rode the tree crashing into the ground. She clawed her hands inward, and a black dome of ice exploded out of the ground around her.

Ayrah sat clutching her shoulder for a moment. Anger boiled within her—a rapturing, soul-ripping anger. She grabbed her stomach, a wretched dry heave gagged her throat. Again and again until a shadow began to seep from her mouth. It widened and deepened. The mist of night. The black mist hovered around her. She suddenly felt empty of feeling, as if she had a need to be angry but an incapacity to feel it.

Errta laughed.

Ayrah let down her cover and nodded her head.

Errta's eyes changed tint. "Shadowa." His veins changed from molten red to a soft glowing white. "Just like your father was. I prepared for that the day I took him down." His hands caught fire as white as the visible sun. The shadow swarmed around him. For a moment, Ayrah thought she accidentally killed him. Her only chance at finding out why her father was arrested, gone.

He blasted white fire through the mist. But the hole was quickly filled. Several more came, rapid shots of white fire soared into the forest. The remaining mist funneled itself into a little ball, no larger than a marble, and dropped to the ground by Errta's feet.

Errta's forehead glistened in the warm light of the forest fire, but he remained upright.

"One of the fires of El. It's enough to send your shadow to its knees. It takes a lot out of a man." He coughed. The circle of bonfires that began the battle had shrunk to little more than licks from a candle, even though the forest still raged ablaze around them.

Ayrah felt similar to how he looked. Drained. Sore. Though she had blood dripping down her shoulder, breasts, and back. She rolled to her side, ready to jump to her feet, but a sword pinched her neck.

"You've got good blood." He said. "A lot of raw power."

"Why did you arrest him? On what charge?" Ayrah breathed heavy and stared up at him.

"I told you, girl. I can't say even if I wanted to. The king put an Il-lian spell on my mind, I'll kill *myself* if I utter a word to anyone outside of Tamagai." Errta brushed the ashen sweat from his brow. "But. . . you fought well. A little more training, and we could make something of you. Join the Tamagai, fight with us in the Kaeselwa, and then I could tell you." The sword point left her neck.

"You would invite a girl with no Niiwa into the Tamagai?"

"You're the daughter of a Warlord. I'm sure Malik could make an exception."

13

TERRITORY

The jungle leaves gently danced in the light afternoon shower. High above, the canopy played the song of a hundred thousand leaves singing in the wind. Kairo limped with his walking stick clutched dear as he passed over root networks, their dirt long washed away by the violent crashing River Maua beside them.

Line of sight in the jungle was never more than the width of the West Deck. Every tree Kairo passed on his right or left was met with a brief, lingering pause, a quick search for movement along the floor, or the glint of Sigu Nii metal.

When Arden paused, it was always a fumbling around his belt for the canteen that Kairo had given him the previous day. He had since replaced the water with that clear, sour smelling liquid. Long, audible gulps would emanate from his throat before he would continue again.

Kairo willed forth each step with a grimace. His eyes frequently snapped shut. His teeth ground together. But he would not stop. He couldn't. He had to catch up to his captured sister. He had to free her, not just for her sake but also for his people. If Aterah's Oracle capabilities were grand enough to place her at Adakon's side, the Sigu Nii could use her to such advantage that the entire rebellion would certainly fall. Every law would be known to them. Every outpost location known, each possible route of surviving a battle gone—all because Aterah would have seen it already and been prodded and tortured by the snakes to tell them.

So, they pressed through the jungle.

Arden's tunic sat halfway across his shoulders. The knuckle-width, stone tattoos gated rainwater rivulets from his neck down his back. His twine-roped mop of silver-streaked, beaded dreadlocks sat heavily in the rain.

With every step forward, Kairo watched him more cautiously. His gruff voice was similar to the Sigu Nii accent. The stoneman had said he had matters to attend to in Vasara. So, was his guiding through hostile lands a mere coincidence? A manner of convenience that they both meant to head the same direction. Or something else?

Kairo mulled it over. He thought about Arden's vuu-empowered entrance. The black lightning. He had never seen a Sigu Nii able to do that. And if Arden wanted to go to Vasara, why did he not just teleport there, if he were so capable? No. Arden wanted to go to NeoDerii first. He knew about Aterah. And he knew that the Sigu Nii were after her.

Kairo walked behind the stoneman. He wouldn't see Kairo reach for the bronze blade on his hip. Kairo's fingers brushed his belt and the surrounding linens. *Stupid.* His sword had been shattered during the raid. A moment surprising to forget, since with every breath, step, and stretch of his arm, he could feel where his sword had gone.

Arden's boots dragged. They brushed dirt and rock and stick against one another as he halted along the trail. "You think loudly, boy."

Kairo's heart crawled up his throat. Could this stone-man hear his thoughts? Or was his hearing so defined that the reaching for his belt was telling? Kairo swatted the thoughts from his mind, and demanded, "What interest do you have in my sister?" Kairo stopped eight steps away.

Arden turned. His vibrant purple eyes could not hide his disdain. "All of Zoë is in a cold war. A battle for believed things. Without Aterah, that war will turn very violent. I aim to stop it."

Kairo had no idea who Zoë was. But Arden's words reinforced his worries. Kairo bent at the knees, dropped his walking stick, and held his fists up to guard his face. This stoneman was not Renovian or Sigu Nii, Kairo reasoned. He was some unknown third party, whose allegiances varied in his own self preserving way.

Arden laughed. His chuckles rumbled out of his throat in the most patronizing way. He clasped his belly each time his eyes fell upon Kairo's preparation.

Kairo rushed him. He charged. Every other step felt as if he were about to faceplant. But he reached Arden, whose dying, puffing snickers ended when he swatted away the silver blade coming out of Arden's scabbard.

"Aye," said Arden with a nod, a smile still staining the corners of his lips. A fire ignited in his eyes, overtaking the purple glint in a dark red. The veins in his body illuminated in a molten glow. A tattoo rose from his lower left shoulder—a full level-five serpent.

Dread shot through Kairo as if he had stumbled into a den of snagaeri. The type of limb-freezing fear that only seemed to occur in dreams. He had never seen the full tattoo. The serpent's head was drawn in a skeletal style, and it wove the other four symbols together. It had a dagger embedded in its head, a flame for eyes, a human skull entering its mouth, and on the fourth section—flesh tore from spine in a bloody mess.

The tattoo hovered above his skin. And it was colorless. Not black, white, or grey. Colorless. Light shimmered around the tattoo like heat radiating in the middle of summer.

An inscription beneath it all read, *Sehlya*.

Fire exploded from Arden's mouth. A hundred rain droplets screamed their sizzling demise.

Kairo's knees buckled. He fell to the ground with his hands flailing above his face. A wail escaped him. He cried aloud from the pain that shot through his slashed leg.

Arden stood over him. "Vuu is influence, and everyone, in their own manner, is fighting for more of it. The ability to see the future has vast influential capabilities."

Kairo leapt to stand, using his good leg, and whirled a punch at Arden's gut. His knuckles met stone. Kairo stifled a scream while he flung his hand back and forth, and clutched it, inspecting whether his knuckles had shattered. "Vuu is evil." He protested. "It turns an otherwise regular human into an animal."

Arden sighed as one would when tired of a game. "If you were able to do a handstand, I would certainly perish. It is my mortal weakness."

Kairo flung his way from Arden, and coiled up onto his hands, shooting his legs high above him. He could feel his face bulge under the blood pressure.

Arden, who surprisingly stood still and fine, said, "If it were the kingdom of Aylavuera that you were pushed up against, you would think vuu to be persuasive. Their vuu is a power over beliefs. A false teaching is a scrape in your skin. And the country is filled with false schools—you can't walk down the street without a knife coming at your throat. But it's a different sort of blade, boy. Then, since it is Sigu Nii that haunts your doors, you see vuu as devouring. This is influence."

"The Sigu Nii are persuasive," Kairo croaked, and sank to the ground. His left leg felt wet, not just the light rain shower sort of wet, but a sticky, warm wet. Blood seeped through his trousers.

Arden chuckled lightly. "Aye. Vuu determines how *in charge* you are, each in their own manner. Without it, ya'll are just a bunch of monkeys throwing dung in the jungle."

Kairo went to sit up, but his neck stiffened. He tried to turn it in either direction, but it wouldn't. Even when he began to protest audibly it came out as a closed-throat groan. His jaw was locked shut. At first, he thought Arden had played some trick of vuu against him. But realization flooded him. He had been given his death sentence.

His wound had the infection.

He laid there absent-eyed. From this moment, he had less than a month to live. He resumed trying to pry his lips apart.

Arden stood halfway over him. "You look like an amused monkey, with your lips like that."

Finally, he managed to groan, "Heal me."

"I can't. Not without the crown—the Renovian Archeodon," said Arden. He peered pitifully at injured Kairo. "Without the crown, no one can be in charge of the building block. No one can intervene or intercede in the way that Zoë has otherwise been set up. Only time can heal. Or in your case. . . ." Arden dropped to one knee and scooped two hands through the loose jungle dirt.

"For now," said Kairo, his jaw eventually loosening, "you speak of the King to Come." It was Queen Epheriia's fourth entry in Graeynesh Law. "The Prince of Healing." That's what Aterah called him when her eyes went black several nights prior.

Arden pressed the dirt firm in his hands and brought them over Kairo. He snickered, "You people cling to prophecy the way a rodent clings to the last nuts of winter. How long must pass before its deemed a miss? A whole generation? A cluster? You people have been waiting for twenty-eight generations on this King to Come." He mocked. A clear, sour-smelling liquid seeped out between his fingers.

The droplets hit Kairo's thigh and burned. He grimaced. "What— What is this?"

"Alcohol. From right-handed Masikonian vuu. But . . . aye." He paused. "That's what King Ash wants. He wants the crown that you don't even have. He's ended entire societies before, and he'll do it again." He brought the last few droplets to his mouth and licked his hands.

Arden's proactive dealing with snagaeri was so varied and contra-dictory that Kairo found it difficult to emulate his practices in any way whatsoever. Some nights Arden would trample through the jungle, and stumble over rock and root and catch himself on a tree trunk with a huffing breath. Other nights he would freeze completely, as if a mouse's crawl would stir the demonic beasts.

On the sixth night, they reached the base of the Delkop range. The mountains overlooked the Renovian jungle, everything within Kairo's understanding—and more. As they neared the Mauan valley, Kairo realized he was in foreign, uncharted lands. The trees were still his, their sky bound height, and their broad, head-sized leaves. But he had not seen these particular ones before. He did not know where each was placed. Which fallen branches were new and which were old.

A soft, rhythmic drumming drifted through the jungle. Singing and tribal chanting followed. And when the warm firelight reached Kairo's sandals in broken slivers by the trees, he trembled.

"Aye." Arden grabbed Kairo by the arm. "You'll need to see the Sigu Nii through their own eyes."

"I've been on infiltration missions before," Kairo replied, his voice a shaky whisper. "A war-tribe passed us on our southern borders—"

"Not like that." Arden wiped his face and laid a hand on Kairo's head. "Don't scream."

"What—" A convulsion interrupted Kairo. He dropped his walking stick and hunched over to grab his stomach. He watched his hands in the warm light, bubbles grew on his skin, and when they popped, a steam seeped out like the smell of an extinguished candle. It seared, and to keep from yelling aloud, he fell to his face. He pressed his nose and forehead deep into the dirt as he writhed. His skull cracked and shifted. Even though his eyes were shut, yellow swirls danced across his vision. He felt his eyes move farther apart and slant inward.

Slowly everything settled. When he picked himself up and peered at his hands, he saw the yellow skin tone of Sigu Nii. He leapt backwards, flinging himself away from the light in a furious crabwalk. "What did you do to me?" He asked, his voice high pitched.

"That be the left-handed Masikonian vuu, boy."

Kairo looked up at the stoneman as he flexed his arms inwards. Bubbles covered his skin between the tattoos. They swept over his person in the blink of an eye, from bottom to top. His hair turned black. His eyes slanted inward. Kairo figured it must have hurt as badly for Arden as well, but the spell took place in a quarter of the time, and Arden's expression did not change.

14

EIDHIN

Four days Eidhin sat with his back pressed against the cushions of the stagecoach. Four days he felt the bump of every rock and pebble along the dirt road. Four days with nothing to do or say other than watch the evergreens pass by.

Eidhin's knee bobbed subconsciously. He yawned and stretched his hands to touch the opposite lacquered wood walls.

"Ease yourself," Penoa El felt the need to say every then and again, his crisp, eloquent Gehni accent rolling from the back of his mouth to the front. His eyes seldom came up from a thick, word-dense book, the sort with fine paper and a leather binding.

Eidhin took a breath. His arms and legs settled. He rested the temple of his head against the side of the open window. El Penoa's words typically had this effect. Not many people could say relax and stir its desired outcome.

"C-c-ca-n I-I-I r-r-rea-d-d?" Eidhin tilted his head from the window to point at El's book.

Penoa laughed. A contained, restrained, polite little laugh that teetered a tad too close to a snicker. "No. No, no, no." El shook his head the tiniest degree to either side. "This is why I am here, and you are there. Next you might ask, 'Can I teach *you* what the text means?'" He snickered again.

Eidhin sighed and steered his attention outside. He caught a brief parting in the dense evergreen trees. A perpendicular road with the same dark dirt. On the corner, with little sprouts of grass and flowers along the post, a sign pointed each way. Kort Gehni, read the wood that guided their current trajectory. Though the words were written in the Common Tongue, Eidhin vaguely recognized the first to derive from Old Vulgarhe.

"Wh-wh-at-t d-d-does K-k-k-kor-t-t—"

"The meaning of Kort?" El looked up from his book.

Eidhin nodded.

El Penoa glanced around. Briefly letting his eyes gaze out his window, searching the inside of the stagecoach, then resting on Eidhin's window. "Kort Gehni." He nodded. "Kort leans heavily on context. And culture." El Penoa tilted his head at the second statement, his brown eyebrows raising a moment. "In this way, Kort Gehni means the pinnacle of Gehni Isle, or in this context, the City of Gehni. The city of Gehni is the king of Gehni Isle—I don't know how else to describe it, child."

Eidhin nodded.

"You might be honored that I give you teachings so readily. Gratitude especially for insights of Vulgarhe, so few percent have any understanding. Though, 'Kort' is common enough to be bleeding into the Common Tongue, you needn't work yourself too much."

Eidhin sat for a moment. "Will y-you t-t-teach th-thi-ngs lik-ke th-that?"

El Penoa breathed deeply and held his breath so that it seeped from his throat at an audible pace. "Some. Perhaps. Though the Freedom Encryption program is being more rigorous than 'What d-d-does this mean?'" Penoa's voice deepened and slowed, like one from Snowstock. "It's a painful process, child. A process that adds and subtracts from the ways your thinking has been taught." El waved his hand, his eyes upturned. "Add more empathy yet remove suggestibility. Add speed of speech yet remove speed of thought." El glanced in Eidhin's direction. "A mind too quick is a mind deviating from the common way. And no El will pay for a deviating sla—scribe." El tapped his knee. "Remove question. For sure the child asks too many questions." El shrugged and looked Eidhin up and down. "Just from the tips of my thoughts, your ways of thinking will be fully dissected from the insides by our El of Medicines. Just to tease, I perceive you to be primarily intuitive, though a liking for counting adds a level of dichotomy." Penoa El nodded, sure of himself.

"M-med-d-d-d—"

"Yes. The Medicines."

"Are th-they sm-m-art-t-t-ter th-an y-y-ou?"

El Penoa paused for a moment and looked Eidhin in the eyes.

Eidhin felt the prick of his stare. His lips were thin, though not moving one way or the other. He just stared.

"I am beginning to be amazed that I had to throw a stunt to take you from your parents." He sighed, turning his gaze to the stagecoach wood. "No, they are not more vertically knowledgeable than me. Actually, I wonder, does philosophy require a depth of thought, or a wider range of cohesive—"

El cut short as the stagecoach hit a sizable rock. The wagon shook and jittered continuously. Eidhin thought maybe a wheel had sprung loose or had broken. A common enough problem. He stuck his head out the window but saw that the wheel was fine. They were riding over many rocks, seemingly hand placed, like the walls of the church in Snowstock. As they continued, the rocks began to smooth out. They grew larger sideways, and the stagecoach settled into more of a glide over the ground.

Eidhin turned his eyes to the north. Between the stagecoach horses and the evergreens, he could see gleaming stone buildings.

Kort Gehni had no walls. There were no armed guards. No moats. No defensible castles. Not one shape in the city was crafted with primitive savageries in mind.

Their carriage reached the first of these buildings. Eidhin held his head out the window, his eyes bright with awe. Their stone was like goat's milk, shining nearly white, even in the overcast. Houses with white pillars, dark spruce walls, and slate roofs.

The cobble-paved street was well used as various other carriages passed on perpendicular roads. Tall, straight-postured men on horseback passed by with tight-buttoned vests and frilly shirts.

Black metal posts stood along the cobble street above the pedestrians and rose taller even than the men on horseback. On top of each one was a glass-protected oil-wick lantern.

The carriage crossed a star of cobble roads. A square of streets, with five points of lantern posts between them. More whitestone buildings rose tall behind the paved walkways, with iris flowers and vines hanging from second and third story balconies.

Faint yelling drifted through the breeze. Eidhin searched for its source. A man stood on a two-stretch high brick wall around a raised grassed, flowered, and treed square. A garden-park, with various sections of crowding headstones. He called to the crowd, but no one seemed to pay him any attention. Eidhin strained his ears, curious to hear what the man taught.

"Truly, I tell you! For what purpose do you have eyes if you cannot see? What good does a scrub behind your ears do if you do not use them? Your El misleads you. The Rai they possess is not the Rai they hand over. You are the pillars of this brilliant nation, for without you, whom are they El over? Oppression taints! You count yourselves not among those forced in the quarries. Yet truly I tell you: You are!" He wore a silver-buttoned vest over a white long-sleeve shirt. Black leather boots covered the bottom of his pants.

"Are you listening to him?" El Penoa asked.

Eidhin turned to him and nodded.

"Best not. A conspiracist is an unsustainable vocation. He will not remain where he stands, come the next phase of the moon. Sure, you say Rai is relative, but the spectrum of his words will fall on the . . . short-lasting end.

"Maybe you wonder: How is it legal? Why mightn't we intercede and remove the man, be it his words so sharp? Easy. The king doesn't need to. Gehni doesn't need to. An untrue thing fades into the fog." El Penoa moved his hand like a wave, demonstrating the instability of falsehood.

The stagecoach rolled on, unaware of Eidhin's interest in the man. *Unsustainable.* He repeated in his head. *Then why was he dressed so fancy?* Then again, looking down at his own fraying mustard sweater, he knew little of fashion in the city. His eyes squinted at the dark, well-waxed stagecoach wood. *If the whole Isle of Gehni were an onion, there seem to be a few brown leaves.* The dirt-adorned man crossed his mind, the one that had pleaded to be let into the Church of Rai. And then this "conspiracist," as El put it. They seemed to Eidhin to be standing behind a similar line, despite the two being so drastically different. *What is the line? Attention? Who will pay attention to these decaying leaves?*

Eidhin wasn't completely faithful that he had found root. He sat for a moment, mulling it over. *Attention.* But after a few moments, he decided it was best to pay gratuity to El Hwaerta, the father of Rai and teacher of all, of all the things to be thankful for, the fact that Eidhin was not among these brown leaves was *Kort*—the apex, the pinnacle, the greatest of all such things.

A building passed them by, on El's side of the carriage. Eidhin a glanced at it and then did a double take. The building was so large, it took several moments to pass. It held the same unifying whitestone, along with flowery, swirling, blue gem trimming. It was covered by a gargantuan half-domed roof, open toward the road, with rows and rows of stage seating in a larger half-circle around it.

El Penoa shifted, feeling Eidhin's stare across his lap. He turned to see what caught the child's eye. "Ahh yes." Penoa smiled. "The Amphitheater of Gehni. A battle wages there, as old as time. To be profound—or entertaining. Surely, you find it within yourself that profound is the more interesting, the more attentive of the two. But I admit, when entertainment wanders into the profound, a harmony is created from which no one can withhold a tear." Penoa held the tips of his fingers together and kissed his lips. "We'll take the whole church to see Sonte's Masikonian Orchestra." Penoa's voice became matter-of-fact. "But of course, Sonte himself is Illian. A brilliant composition, each time his hand touches paper. And to make use of the superior Masikonian voice? Well, it's practically his birthright."

By the time the stagecoach rolled to a stop, the light had drained from the sky. Eidhin watched men dressed in pale brown clothes climb ladders to the tops of the metal street posts and hold matchsticks to the oil wicks inside the glass.

Penoa grabbed a shiny black leather suitcase from a small aft compartment.

Eidhin exited the stagecoach, breathing deep and moving slowly, stretching each of his journey-rusted ligaments. He held his hands on his knees as El fiddled with his suitcase. Eidhin rubbed the back of his arms and his elbows. It was chillier here than in Snowstock. And the wind felt snappier. He wondered if they were closer to the ocean.

Eidhin's eyes rolled over the front compartment of the stagecoach. A draw of fascination that he had discovered along the trip: No one led the horses. There was a wooden bench attached to the front side of the cabin, but no one had taken its seat in the past four days.

"The human brain is the trickiest of all known organisms," Penoa had said four days earlier, when Eidhin's jaw first dropped at the leaderless animals. *"It takes a great deal of effort to make it think in one way, and a greater*

deal more to make it think another way. But a horse? A quick hand to the fore-head from any vuu-capable person is enough to infiltrate influence."

There were four horses, two on each side, with brown leather reins tying each of them. Their eyes looked blank, a glaze over them as if they were all daydreaming of things beyond their immediate surroundings.

"Alright. Prepared to see your new home?" Penoa El asked. He began a stroll north from the stagecoach. He kept on the walkway, the cobble-street on their left.

"Y-ye—"

"A nod should suffice."

Eidhin nodded. He stole a glance back at the horses, feeling strange that El just left them and the stagecoach to sit there. He wondered if they would be among Gehni's rotting brown leaves. Or were they part of the already pruned onion? Either way, Eidhin assumed someone lesser than El Penoa would be by to take care of them.

"Well, there we are." Penoa El held out both arms, his black suitcase dangling in his right as he gestured to the buildings on either side of them.

To Eidhin's right, a two-block-wide park area. Foreign-looking trees with opaque blue leaves grew branches as wide as they were tall. Walkways weaved through meticulously kept grass. The light draining from the sky was replaced by the warm light of the street posts all around them.

All of this led to a palace of a building. Seven stories tall and a width that took up the entire distance between two streets. This must have been Gehni's Church of Rai. Windows wrapped the building in triangular lines, stained to paint scenes of discovery: sailing and map charting, agricultural advancements, and vuu. The architecture of the building, what with all the structural beams and aesthetic curves, gave off a rather dooming presence. The stone was dark, which stuck out among the white buildings of Gehni. Eidhin had never seen so many curves and edges on one building before.

With a bit of effort, Eidhin tore his eyes from the church and steered them across the cobble street to the other building El gestured to. A rather regular square building. The stone was white like most of the city, with irises planted around the outside. Four stories high, which was taller than normal but small compared to the church. Light green vines grew around the square building, broken only by balconies wrapped in the same black metal as the streetlamp posts.

Instinctively, Eidhin began to stroll toward the church. His heart thudded, and he clenched his jaw. *How long will I be here? Who else is here? I don't have any change of clothes! I wonder if father is all right. Will he be able to count the potatoes without me?*

El *tsk*'ed his lips. "Do you see the illuminated streets?"

Eidhin turned back to Penoa, who stood in the same spot. Eidhin nodded.

"What illuminates them?"

Eidhin pointed at the lamps. He could still see the men lighting them on the far side of the park.

"Right. So, in other observable words, it's late. This way, child." Penoa walked slow, he stretched his knees with each step toward the particularly regular building.

Eidhin had never seen glass doors before. He stared at the little wires that connected each circle of glass to the wood-framed door. Penoa swung it open. Eidhin hurried in after him, as if he might be forgotten out in the growing cold.

Eidhin ran a hand through his short blonde hair. The smell of burning tobacco wafted through the air. A calm fire flickered in a stone pit in the middle of the room, casting warm light and shadows across the pinewood walls. A square whitestone chimney, grimed with layers of smoke scars, hung down from the ceiling.

Three men dressed in identical black velvet robes, with the small blue insignia of Rai sewn across the chest, sat chatting around the fire. They all seemed about El's age except an older one who had thick grey hair pulled tight against his head. Each of them held a long wooden pipe, smoke drifting softly from the bowl to the chimney canopy above. The three of them turned in their wooden rocking chairs, swaying gently with the push of their own weight. "Penoa!" The younger two called.

Behind the firepit, a set of dark wooden stairs laid in a cut-out square. The stairs were worn, dusty, the lacquer peeling in the middle where feet most frequently fell.

"The children are all upstairs already?" Penoa asked, setting his briefcase down on a four-step square of varnished floorboard surrounding the inside of the door, a miniature foyer of sorts.

"In their chambers, studying their day's lessons," one with dark hair answered. His gaze briefly scraped past Penoa to connect with Eidhin. "I trust your journey to the village went well. I see you've returned almost empty-handed."

Penoa El inhaled sharply and glanced at Eidhin, who stood awkwardly rubbing his hands. "Snowstock was a heap of dung. I doubt their teacher would pass the first story of the Aylan. Anyone who seemed remotely worth conversing with were either too old or too content." Penoa waved a hand at Eidhin, gesturing for him to come near. As Eidhin approached, El briskly grabbed hold of his shoulders and held him out on display. "Even this one has a cost. The boy's lips are lame."

"And you've brought him?" asked one with golden hair. His voice sounded cold. But like the others he wore a perfectly blank face. "I know they don't do much talking once they reach their El. Even so, who would pay for him, knowing there was a chance at having to listen to such a thing?"

"Even so. I await your examination enthusiastically. I sense the boy's intuitive processor to be . . . rather remarkable. But . . . on the chance I had sipped their ale too long, we could just as easily sell him to the quarries."

"The Dajo family is always in need of scrapped parts."

"And the harbor always needs barnacles scrubbed."

Eidhin watched a frown slip its way across the older fellow. "Yes, yes." His old voice sounded permanently grouchy. "We all understand the slaving class. Best keep from it, children. A different caliber of blank-eyed blokes come from here."

Eidhin blinked repeatedly. He heard each word uttered and understood it. But unless they were speaking to him, none of the words would translate into intelligible thought. He shook his head and wondered if it was some trick of vuu.

The dark haired El hummed. "Alright. Well, on with it then." He pushed himself from his rocking chair and gestured to a table set in the corner of the room.

The dark-haired El, Eidhin, and Penoa approached the table, on which sat a round wooden board and six carved-wood pieces on small offset circles. Penoa guided Eidhin into a chair set in front of the table, and the dark hair El rested his fingers around the backrest.

"Wh-what-t i-is th-thi—"

"Oh El, make it stop," the dark haired El scowled. "Hwaerta surely has laid obstacles on you."

"It's a game," Penoa said to Eidhin. "No need to take it too seriously. It only helps Sor'al here determine the functions of your thinking, your brain's strengths and weaknesses, the blood-bound physical traits you've received from your ancestors, and the vuu you've inherited from your corner's micro-culture."

"Essentially." Sor'al nodded.

"Y-you c-c-can d-d-do all th-tha-t?"

Sor'al scoffed a chuckle. "I will see your mind here in a moment. Penoa speaks highly of my insight, though really the information he seeks is easier sought from the niche I specialize in. The game here simply removes subjectivity." His voice turned a snarky, proud tone, "Since the mind is full of how *you* perceive things, and adding my mind is not enough to counter that equation, engaging in a cerebrally straining game is adequate enough to synthesize a control."

"H-how-w d-d-do I-I-I p-p-play?" Eidhin gulped. He felt weary of speaking at all. By the way these El spoke, and things they spoke of, he could tell that any one of them had more vuu than the entire combination of Snowstock.

"Pick your piece. There's one for each school of thought. The Medicines, Philosophy, Hi—"

"Wh-what's—"

"Eidhin!" Penoa thundered. "Do not interrupt!"

"The child." Sor'al shook his head. "The six pieces: The Medicines; Philosophy; History; Biology; the Mathematics; and finally, the newest of the schools, the Church of Rai—represented by his nobility: High Priest Grandon Delshau."

Penoa gave a smug nod at the mention of the Church.

"So, you'll pick your piece now. Take note that there is a mixture of wisdom between picking one you're most comfortable with versus picking one you find most interesting." Sor'al lifted his fingers from the backrest of Eidhin's chair. He walked around and pulled out a chair across the table.

Eidhin stared at the board. It was difficult to pick. He did not know how to play. Most of the pieces he had no knowledge of. Like biology— *What in the world is that?* It showed him how much he did not know. His hand pricked up, beginning to hover over the circular board.

Sor'al stood up and held his left hand out over the table. "Stand up. Shake my hand with your left and touch my forehead with your right."

Eidhin did so. He felt the brief bob of a clammy finger softly poke the middle of his forehead at the same time he touched Sor'al.

BOOM! Like a trumpet, something sounded off in Eidhin's ears. The world shook. Everything turned a strange golden-blue hue, as if there were no other colors in the world. Eidhin struggled to regain his balance, his hand searched frantically for the chair beneath him, before collapsing into it.

"*Pick your piece, child.*" Sor'al's unmistakable accent drifted like a whisper inside Eidhin's own head.

Eidhin looked down. The board and all its pieces looked different. Each of the six wooden pieces, carved to resemble the aura that each of the schools of thought carried, sat an equal six circle spaces away from each other, and six spaces from the middle.

Eidhin's hand moved over the carved piece that he inexplicably knew to be Biology but continued as quickly as he came. The Medicines was next, Eidhin found the subject to *sound* interesting, but realistically, he was already playing against an El of that school. His hand hovered over the Mathematics. *I do like to count.* He fidgeted, a brief little twitch that made his hand look as if *it* wanted to pick that piece. But Eidhin willed it to continue. The Church of Rai? Surely, that option would make the most sense. He had spent his entire life soaking in their teachings; he'd even gone as far as to give his life away in order to be with them to a higher degree. History? He found himself fascinated by the idea of history. So few people in Snowstock knew anything about their village's history, or even their own family's. As if someone was going 'round and guarding time's memory. And last, Philosophy. Eidhin did not know much of philosophy. In truth, he couldn't tell what sort of thought could even be classified as "philosophical." But still, he felt his entire body linger around that carved wooden piece. As if it sucked him in.

"*Pick the piece, child.*"

Eidhin let his hands close around Philosophy. He looked to Penoa El, to see if his face would mark the wellness of his decision. But El looked off. He swayed as if in slow motion, his chest rose and fell from his breathing, his shoulders shifting from the journey's unrest. Slowly. Eidhin glanced at the fire, full around him, and noticed that his body felt like molasses. *What is this?*

"Your thoughts are faster than the world around you. It's common enough."

Are we in my thoughts? Eidhin asked, driving his body to spin back to Sor'al.

"Not in their own realm. But, I admit, we are closer to them than the perceivable. Perhaps that explains the golden-blue around you." Sor'al lifted his hand and moved it over the wooden board. His hand instinctively reached for the Medicines and paused. His eyes glanced up to meet Eidhin's.

It was terrifyingly strange. Eidhin could *feel* this El's thoughts and decisions. The sort of intimacy that a marriage could only dream of. Eidhin knew, just from this moment, that patterns of thinking could be devised from and to either one of them. Given Sor'al's vast experience in this space, Eidhin knew he was more vulnerable than he had ever been in his life.

Sor'al wavered. A fleeting shift of his consciousness suggested he was impressed. *"You play well,"* he noted.

Eidhin did a mental double-take. *But . . . we haven't even begun.*

"We began as soon as our minds met one another. As soon as we rid ourselves of the profound-nagging-hindering-art-form that is 'communication.'" Sor'al's hand closed around the wooden piece carved in the likeness of Biology.

You've picked a piece that I know nothing *about.* Eidhin noted.

15

GATHERING

"El!" Sigu Nii gasped and pushed their noses through the dirt, their hands spread out.

The sky-bound trees were sparse among their camp. Nearly a clearing. Three dozen cream-colored tents lined the perimeter. Kairo made out three different tribal insignia sewn into the sides. It was a gathering of multiple tribes.

A bonfire roared at the center of the camp. Its highest flames licked the forest's lowest branches. But the Sigu Nii didn't care. They wouldn't mind if the whole jungle blew ablaze.

Some sat a comfortable distance away from the fire, beating on hide skin drums; others danced shirtless, and hands raised, chanting nondescript sounds.

Arden strode through the camp. His serpent tattoo hovered on his left shoulder, colorless and light distorting. Sigu Nii eyes widened upon recognition of the symbol.

"Wh-what—" One stammered.

"A-are you doing out all this way, El?"

"His—His tattoos are *stone!*"

"Aye, all the better for blocking stray steel, or breaking vuu," replied Arden. "Fetch me a drink."

Kairo cowered behind Arden. He had never walked so blatantly into a Sigu Nii den. And their response of fear and awe made Kairo feel like a helpless infant. Who was this stoneman? He provoked emotion from the beasts Kairo previously thought incapable.

A Sigu Nii handed Arden his own hide skin canteen. And another handed his to Kairo. Arden gulped and opaque red liquid streamed down his neck. Kairo sniffed tentatively, sipped cautiously, and spit the sour taste from his mouth. It burned. Did they drink poison for fun?

The near quarter of the den laughed. "Is it not 'uitable for 'is El's standards?" Their eyes wandered to Kairo's upper left arm. "Oh! The boy is vuuless!"

Arden tossed the empty hide skin back to the Sigu Nii. "He is not." His voice was harsh and casual at the same time. "He sneaks among the bark-eaters and provides information."

The Sigu Nii blinked repeatedly. One of them began, "Cowar—"

Arden clasped his tunic collar, hoisted him with one hand so that his feet dangled, "Finish that word."

"S-sorry, El."

Arden tossed the barbarian to the ground. "More drink."

The spectacle was attracting more eyes around the gathering. More and more of them wandered over, saw Arden's tattoo, and collapsed to bow. The drums ceased. The dancing halted. And Kairo crept further behind Arden with each new Sigu Nii around them.

"Will you stay for the fight?" asked one.

"What is the event?" asked Arden.

"A snagaeri grash."

Arden nodded and waved a hand to say, *make it happen.*

The Sigu Nii brought out fur pelts, large skins, whose topside was fluffier than a hundred twine hammocks. They laid them at Arden and Kairo's feet and gestured them to sit. Most of the barbarians around them sat on thin, dirt and sweat-stained linens.

The drumming resumed with a modified rhythm. Slow and steady. *Da dum. Da dum. Da dum.* A Sigu Nii came round the bonfire. His triceps were strained, his bare feet dug into the dirt, and he was heaving on a thin metal rope.

A snagaeri came into the clearing, resisting every step. The fire demon roared. It writhed its head and snapped at the air.

Kairo leaned close to Arden. "I thought snagaeri only went after Renovians."

He whispered back, "Typically, aye. But if you poke 'em and hit 'em enough, get 'em real angry, they'll attack whoever."

The Sigu Nii holding the metal rope reached a stick to unlatch a pin on the snagaeri's red-hot collar. With a few attempts, the large, rusted piece thudded in the dirt beside them. He snapped his fingers, channeling icy vuu and sending it in sheets across the beast. The snagaeri growled and snapped at the Sigu Nii. He rolled out of the way, and the fight had begun.

"Say, El," began another of the Sigu Nii around them. "Are you excited for Yutarah's Niiwa? I hear there's a prize this season."

"Aye?" asked Arden. "A bit o' gold?"

The Sigu Nii waved his hand dismissively. "Some Renovian witch captured at the hive raid." Then he said with awe, "She's to be escorted to the Warlord."

Aterah. Kairo froze. He did not understand what a Niiwa was, but his stomach stirred, thinking that she would be its prize. A Sigu Nii game could not be a good one.

A spear of bright blue ice filled the fighter's hand, held over his shoulder, then hurled into the beast. The snagaeri writhed in pain, its fiery flesh sizzled like squealing mice. It leapt toward him, gnashing its white teeth. The fighter sprinted and slid between its legs, clear under its torso. Ice formed in the dirt on the other side and caught his foot, sending him upright into a fighting stance.

The crowd roared, and the beast of the night turned slowly.

Kairo gradually became aware of the frown staining his lips. Utter disgust polluted his chest. His ears and nose were hot. The snagaeri were terrifying. His people had come up with laws for curfew, hammocks to keep off the jungle floor, whole outposts and protocols to avoid these demons. To watch this savage fight one for fun stirred a new sort of dread.

Kairo glanced at Arden, expecting him to show similar sentiments. But his eyes glinted. He watched with excitement. Taking hefty sips of the sour red liquid between attacks or defenses.

With the fighter on the right side of the bonfire, and the snagaeri approaching from the left, Kairo could see his tattoo. He was a level-three. At least the demons were tough, and it took a tough Sigu Nii to fight them.

Then the fight changed. The snagaeri rose to its hind legs, swatted aimlessly in the air, then quickly crouched and pounced. The snagaeri landed his giant paw on the Sigu Nii's chest. He fell to the ground, and the paw pressed in harder. He screamed, his tunic caught fire, and his chest melted. The smell of burning flesh filled the clearing.

Kairo lurched to his feet. And without thinking, his jungle-born instinct moved him forward to help.

Murmurs and confused whispers echoed behind him. He stopped just beside the face-stinging heat of the beast's torso. What was he doing?

Put others first. That's what the rebellion taught. And to see someone in desperate need of aid—it stirred Kairo to act instinctively. But these weren't people. They were primitive, beast-like, less than human barbarians. Why would he stand to help one of them?

The snagaeri sniffed the air, repeatedly, and raised his paw off the fighter. The demon peered around, sniffing, until its pitch-coal eyes landed on Kairo.

The snagaeri had found a Renovian.

The snagaeri crept closer. One paw in front of the other. Each step gained was like an oven-opening blast of heat. The snagaeri growled and lowered into a cat-like pounce.

"Alright." The word came out in a harsh, grumbled sigh. "That's it for tonight."

Kairo's eyes were still locked with the beast when something unimaginable happened. It turned to stone. Much the same color and density as Arden's tattoos. The vuu crept up its hind legs, encompassed its tail and torso and front legs, and the beast roared one last breath as its head turned solid. The curvatures and carvings of the beast were so ornate, Kairo would have mistaken it for an ancient statue, come from back when Renovia was a mighty kingdom.

"It didn't explode," said Kairo.

"Masikonian vuu." The whisper echoed a dozen times around the camp.

Another whisper quickly followed. "He ain't provoked it."

Kairo spun around as each war-tribe rose to their feet and unsheathed blades. One called out above the rest, "He's Masikonian! 'Is tattoos are fake!"

"Aye!" yelled another, "And the little one is Renovian!"

"Idiot," growled Arden.

Kairo's stomach turned in knots. His heart pounded. At least thirty Sigu Nii crept toward them, lowering into fighting stances, with vuu igniting in their open hands.

He fumbled for his sword and brushed against his empty scabbard. He cursed.

Arden unsheathed his silver blade, glinting harsh against the bonfire behind them, and handed it to Kairo hilt first. "Don't lose this, boy."

Kairo gripped it desperately and nodded a thank you.

Arden pointed at the closest of them approaching, and said, "You there. Your boots are too loose. You might misstep." Despite the natural growl in his voice, when he spoke this time, his voice took on a silky accent.

The Sigu Nii peered down at his boots and watched as his own left boot buckle caught onto his right. He tripped forward, landing face first on the edge of his tilted blade.

Arden thrust his hands out and clenched. The flex traced all the way up his neck. And before Kairo's eyes, the dirt in a five-step circle around them turned to a sour-smelling mud moat. The first wave of approaching snakes flailed their arms as they struggled to stay upright in the mud.

Arden turned to the bonfire and kicked a supporting log. The whole thing came crashing down. Blazing trunks came rolling around their moat, and upon contact, the mud ignited. Nearly a dozen Sigu Nii caught fire and screamed and swatted their own searing flesh.

Kairo's skin flickered. A small wave of bubbles passed over him repeatedly, alternating Sigu Nii and Renovian skin tones. His body burned with each wave. He cried aloud as his skull cracked and shifted back into its original position. He looked Renovian again.

Neon blue ice flashed against the fire on one side. A beast with a three-piece serpent stood tall on the other side of the ring. His leather armor was painted and studded. Tattoos rose up his neck and decorated his face. He took three steps back, sprinted forward, and leapt clear across the moat.

Fire ignited behind Arden's elbow, and with inhuman speed he punched the man in the face the instant his feet touched their ground. The war-chief's eyes and nose blew out the backside of his skull.

The remaining Sigu Nii saw this and yelped. They backed away slowly, turned heel, and began racing for the tree line.

Arden's breath trembled.

The mud-moat turned back to solid ground, its fire ceasing simultaneously.

A shadow passed over Arden's eyes. "No survivors." He picked up a sizable rock and broke it with his hand into a dozen little pebbles. They began to float above his palm in a spinning circle, then Arden waved his hand forward as if hurling them. Each of them blasted forth and embedded themselves deep into the backs of the fleeing Sigu Nii.

Breath heavy, he said, "I'll be needing my sword back."

16

AYRAH

Soft morning rays crept in. Ayrah rolled restlessly in the fine linen sheets. She extended her hand to Errta's side, intending to rest her arm on his chest, but her hand fell on the down-stuffed-mattress.

Ayrah sat up. He was gone.

The four-poster bed frame had its silk curtains drawn back. The rubies and emeralds engraved into the posts reflected a hundred little dots of light across the bedroom.

She slid her feet off the bed and recoiled briefly at the cold stone tile. Ayrah had entirely forgotten the feeling of raised beds.

She walked to the window. Pratuel stretched out halfway toward the horizon, and mist lingered at the city's edges along the hills in the north.

An explosion went off. The castle shook. Ayrah spun around, placing the origin west, inside the castle, toward the common room. *We're under attack.* She ran to the corner of the room and threw on clothes. Her heart thumped in her chest.

Another explosion.

Then another. Dust sprinkled down from the high-ceiling hallway rafters.

Ayrah bounded around the corner into the common room, frost pinched her hand as her black ice sword formed in her palm. Fire blasted in a circular manner around the full glass wall, leaving scorch marks like tint. She hurtled over soft leather skinned couches and the in-ground stone fire pit and slammed through the courtyard doors.

A dozen eyes turned her direction. "Well, that's an entrance."

The high servants stood to her left, Ryan, Ecanaes, and Tagon. The Kaeselwa fighters on her right, Errta and Urota. Malik stood with his back to Ayrah, facing the blackstone courtyard, where two other Pratuelian victors stood in fighting stances toward each other.

The blackstone courtyard was a polished circle twenty steps in diameter within a square of four glass walls. Five-step-wide walkways led to a walkway along each surrounding glass wall. The corner areas were luscious gardens of grass, flowers, and miniature trees.

On the far wall, across from the common room, a gold and hellinite statue stood opposite the double doors. The statue was of the Sigu Nii god, with blood-coated horns erupting from a bald head. The skin of the beast was crafted rough, with intentional cracks flaking away like a man being cremated during battle. A serpent coiled around the god's neck and fit in his extended hand. A bronze basin sat at the feet of his fighting stance, and Ayrah knew offerings of food and milk would be rotting inside.

Some worshiped the Sigu Nii king-god. Ash. Rahktavah. Others— their ancestors. They thank their parents, and parents' parents for being strong, because that means they're strong too.

Ayrah's black ice blade fell to her side. "I . . . I thought we were under attack."

Several snickers responded to her.

Errta went to put a hand on her shoulder. "By who?" he asked, with amusement in his voice.

Ayrah shouldered him off.

"You." Malik spun on his heel. His grey, stubble-filled face grimaced as he pointed and strode toward her. "You get out of my castle."

"Aye," said the dark-skinned man, Tagon. "De girl ez not who she zays she ez. I can feel her power."

"Yeah, we've been over it." Errta waved a dismissive hand. He stepped in front of his approaching guildhead and said, "Malik."

"No. The answer is no. Look at her, look at her shoulder. I will not have an inexperienced *child* bringing shame to us in the Kaeselwa."

"She nearly beat me in a fair fight!" Errta argued. "She's got the blood of a Warlord. The tiniest of training would make her as good as Kizmaldi!"

"Training—" Began the pale skinned, Ecanaes, as if he was prepared to give an entire speech on the word.

"I don't care who's bloody kid it is. Without the grit of the Niiwa, she'll be the mockery of the kingdom."

"And you'd have these Renovians in her place?" Errta gestured to the two Pratuelian victors standing awkwardly behind Malik. "They couldn't beat a drunken fisherman! You know why she hasn't taken it yet. She was probably in Gryyn when her father challenged the king."

"Aye. And just my point. She'll see just as gruesome things in the Kaeselwa." Malik leaned around Errta. "Get out!"

"We've seen nothing like Gryyn."

Ayrah could feel her blood beginning to ignite. She glanced down at her hands and saw the color in her veins delluminating. "I just want to know why!" She screamed.

Dark-black ice shot out across the courtyard. Frost covered everyone's boots and sandals.

"Why did you arrest him?" She asked.

Malik peered down, appearing unimpressed. He sighed as he kicked frost from his boots. "There's still one Niiwa left."

"One . . .?" Errta squinted at him.

"The last one before the Oscillation," said Malik, a grimness enveloped his voice.

"You can't expect her to compete in *that* one."

"Ayrah Veligreen, if you're to join the Tamagai, you'll compete in the Niiwa of Sehlya." Malik peered down at her, over his stuck-out chin. "Til then, you can eat and piss here." he swung back around to the fighters.

"Which of us is she gonna replace, El?" asked one Pratuelian.

"Aye!" Protested the other with folded arms.

"Whichever of you is the weaker." Malik acknowledged them and passed by. The guildhead favored his left leg heavily as he strode to the west walkway.

"Breakfast is ready," said Ecanaes suddenly, as if receiving information from some unseen source. With that, everyone followed Malik.

Ayrah stood frozen. She had just been handed an order for her own execution. *The Niiwa of Sehlya.* That was the king's Niiwa. The event that marked the end of a generation for all of Zoë. *The Niiwa of Sehlya.* This generation though, was the last in a cluster of three named Th'lm. And Th'lm was the last cluster of the current Age.

It was no joke, and Malik knew what he suggested. There would be Warlords and their children, kids who grew up studying the various arts of Sigu Nii vuu since birth. There would be Wardens and Coryndal, nobles' students from other kingdoms, who think themselves powerful enough to compete among the best of Sigu Nii. There'll be kings and queens, and their El-tier relatives taking the Niiwa of Sehlya for the highest of glories.

If there were any other contests left, then maybe she'd consider competing in one of those. Air funneled out of her nose as she imagined what the Niiwa of Simula would look like. Easy. Or what, like, what about the Niiwa from the war-camps east of the colonies? Yutarah or whatever. That would be like stomping a few bugs.

So, not only was the king's Niiwa the hardest contest to fight in across the world, but *this* one specifically marked the end of a very, very long time. The celebrations in the city would historical. And the fighters attracted to the event would be godly.

"Piss off." Ayrah tossed her black ice sword to the ground, underhand, in a this-nonsense-is-beneath-me manner.

"Ayrah," Errta huffed. "I know you're scared—"

She shot him a look that made him choke those words down.

He rephrased, "No one has ever seen anything like what happened in Gryyn. That won't happen to you, Ayrah."

Ayrah stormed back through the common room. Unsolicited images of her father flashed in her mind. She stood there a moment, breathing heavily.

Her eyes swept across all the gorgeously vulgar paintings, the wraparound bar, the fancy leather couches, and stone fire pit. These people lived like kings. Ayrah watched the servants and guessed even they had the tail of the serpent.

Ayrah pondered all those unlucky enough to be born with weak blood. Those who, no matter how much they trained or refined their capabilities and movements, could not defeat someone of a higher Niiwa. You could find these people on the outskirts of any city, out of sight down alleyways, bundled up in tattering wools, where hygiene had become the least of one's concerns. Though Ayrah was not one of them, she'd found herself sleeping among them for more nights the past half-generation than places like the Tamagai Castle. All because of her empty shoulder.

"What a waste," said Errta, who had been standing quietly behind her.

"Aye." Ayrah nodded.

"You can beat them." Errta shook his head. "Malik didn't see the way you moved last night. However you've been spending your days, they've been good on you."

Ayrah remained quiet.

"You've grown comfortable with specific arts. Which is good, that's what most do. But you rely on them. Your shadowa will not make you sovereign."

Ayrah laughed absently, "That's a big word for you."

Errta shrugged. "The Lord Mayor of Pratuel is my mother." He waved a dismissive hand. "You'll stay. I know you will. And when you decide that I'll help you train. The Niiwa of Sehlya is at the end of the current forecast." He turned and bounded through the courtyard threshold, "Breakfast!"

All these Niiwa Ayrah had survived without the ink. All these moments she'd called herself "Shadowa" and run from Warlord Pikemaster's bounty hunters. All these seasons she'd tracked down leads, tortured and interrogated in-the-know Black Guard officers, just to reach this moment. *The Niiwa of Sehlya.* Was it worth finding out why her father was executed?

Was it worth the glory?

Was fear—or not taking the Niiwa—worth the humiliation that would follow her, for the rest of her life?

"Ahht." Ayrah sighed with grit teeth and chased after him. She would do it. She would compete in the hardest fight to the death in the world. She was the daughter of a Warlord, after all.

The Tamagai dining hall was a narrow room, with a dark wooden table long enough to fit a couple dozen people. The room felt wilder than a tavern after new guild ownership. Servants and fighters clambered over top one another, fighting to get the better seats. Errta and Urota shot finger flicks of bladed needles at each other, while Ecanaes spoke with his silver tongue, convincing Ryan to crawl under the table and eat down there. Malik grumbled under his breath as he shuffled to sit at the head, uninterrupted.

Ayrah took her seat toward the foot of the table, where seats were less fought over. After everyone was settled, a double swinging door popped open, and a line of Masikonian women walked in carrying silver platters.

The girls were gorgeous. With skin like silk, made to look the most fashionable golden shade of Sigu Nii. Their flowing hair shimmered with gemstones, moving in ways as if they were submerged in water. Their breasts, hips, and rear-ends were unanimously bubble-like. Crafted and shaped with keen Masikonian vuu. Ayrah couldn't help but think how much coin Herk and Boden would've paid for any one of them. *More than they could afford,* she decided, even though they were Niiwa victors.

When the girls lifted the lids of the serving dishes, the room took on a captivating sensation of salts and spices, honeys and jams, coated steaming biscuits, omelets, and even an entire leg of pork. Cattle tongues sat in a dish, baked in a casserole like fat snakes.

No one waited or hesitated. Hands darted out from one plate to the next. Ayrah could easily tell which hands dashing before her had seen battle. Some of them were soft and pale, others tan and calloused.

Malik spoke out, between mouthfuls of food, just as Ayrah was losing herself in the best meal she'd eaten in a long time. "Ecanaes, I'd hear your report now."

The pale-skinned Illian was delicately cutting his food into perfectly bite-sized pieces. He set down his cutlery at the mention of his name and pulled out a parchment scroll from under the table. He pulled a small red ribbon tying it, unrolled it, and began to read. "We fight the Waterdome tomorrow, in their arena. This is the championship for the Gya Games. Whoever wins this goes on to fight the other victorious guilds around Sigu Nii—the national Kaeselwa.

"It has been three seasons since we have made it to the Kaeselwa, but with our new training regiment, and bringing myself aboard as an oppositional analyst, I am confident we can place nationally. Perhaps even go on to win the Kaeselwa itself.

"For the past season, I have personally attended all of Waterdome's matches. Here, I have written portfolios on the team as whole, their most used and least used plays, their ability to defend (instead of evading), and their favored style of Sigu Nii vuu. Then within this study, you will find specific and detailed accounts of each player." Ecanaes handed the scroll to Urota on his left. Without a glance she handed the scroll to Malik. "Everything from positions that each player dominates, their competency in each style of vuu, positions within the pit that they subconsciously move toward, any standing injuries that hinder their full movement capacity. . ."

The grand dining hall doors slammed open with a thunderous sound. "Who let the Illian talk?" A young man strode in. His eyes were red like the evening sun on special nights. His arms, which had several deep and bleeding cuts, seemed to be chiseled out of stone. They weren't as large as Errta's, but they had unparalleled definition. His hair was ear length, pitch black, and it hung heavy with a clear shine of sweat.

Kizmaldi. Ayrah's stomach churned. *This is the heir to Warlord Lyta Tuio?* It was the sort of odd feeling you get when you meet someone who shares your name. The subtle, irrational feeling that they might be a better version of you. Ayrah opened her mouth, wanting to speak up. She wanted to introduce herself, to tell him that she was the daughter of Warlord Nakhon Veligreen. But as she watched him, how the room quieted at his entrance, how he didn't look at anyone, how he plopped down and stuck his face in his plate of food, she decided against it. The urge turned into a desire to fight him. To see just how strong this heir was. A tattoo of a crowned serpent coiled around his shoulder and seemed to look straight at her, as if to remind her how she was both inkless and about to take the strongest Niiwa in all of Zoë.

"I did," Malik barked. "I gave him permission to speak." He was livid. He gripped the edges of the oak table and glared at this boy who sat stuffing his face. "You missed our training this morning."

"I trained myself. See the blood on my arms?" Kizmaldi held his sweat-drenched, blood-smeared arms over the table. "I don't see anyone else sweating. This is the problem with you Tamagai. You think bringing in an Illian will help you return to glory. It won't." His eyes turned back to his food, and he tore off a bite of ham from its bone. "Ferocity will help you. Raw vuu and power will help you. Follow me, not—not *this*." He gestured to Ecanaes.

Ecanaes' face remained unchanged. He peered at Kizmaldi over the rim of his spectacles, and neither his mouth nor his brow contorted to anger or rage. He simply resumed the cutting of his food. "Power?" He chuckled, geeky and high pitched. "To know someone is to have power over them."

Kizmaldi scoffed.

Malik breathed out deep through his nose. His rage was clear, though he said nothing.

He's at a loss. Ayrah's lips curled up, amused at how drama wove between El-tier nobility as well. He looked as if he was weighing a grash in his mind. But even if he won, against better blood and age, Warlord Tuio and every Black Guard across the province would be here in the instant.

The rest of the meal continued rather quickly and quietly. Malik finished his food and stormed out. Gradually, Urota and Errta, Tagon and Ecanaes, and the rest of the servants cleared the hall. Kizmaldi remained, piling his plate with seconds and thirds. Ayrah remained, well after the room had cleared of the Tamagai. Only the Masikonian girls stayed, carrying away finished platters of food.

Ayrah held her gaze as Kizmaldi eventually caught her eyes. "What?" he snapped, and chewed pinches of food flew from his mouth.

Without moving her eyes from his, Ayrah dug a small note of parchment from her trouser pockets and slid it across the table. "What do you know of this?"

Kizmaldi's deep and bright red eyes darted to the paper. He wiped his left hand clear of grease on his shirt before opening the parchment.

"Your mother helped organize the arrest of my father. What do you know of it?" Ayrah watched him as his eyes swept across the lines of the note.

He squinted at her. "You're Ayrah Veligreen?" He paused as he let the note fall softly onto the table. He looked her up and down. Ayrah imagined he felt the same when she first laid eyes on him. He was sizing her up. "You're a wanted girl." A brief chuckle escaped him. "It's a smart game, I admit. Seeking out an El-ranked Kaeselwa guild for refuge. But if you don't perform well here, don't think Malik will hesitate to throw you out for the Black Guard to devour."

Ayrah's brows came together. "I didn't come here for refuge. I came here to find out what happened to my father."

Kizmaldi shrugged. "He was a traitor. What more do you want?" He turned toward her, propping himself up with his elbows on the table. "Are you really upset that you had to grow up without parents? You're naive. Most Sigu Nii are orphans. Kids' parents get grashed *daily*. My father was killed by my mother. They grashed over me when they decided their familiarity was no longer reason to live under one roof." Kizmaldi shrugged again. "You're not special."

Ayrah leaned back in her seat. "I understand."

"I guess . . ." Kizmaldi turned from her and peered at his unfinished third plate of breakfast. His voice softened to something ponderous. "I guess the only thing you really missed was training. The resources I had available to me, forced upon me, were vast. I had handfuls of elemental vuu trainers, battle vuu trainers, I even had the pale likes of Ecanaes over me, teaching me about history and the difference between the economics of Masikonian coin and Niiwa-fueled glory." He paused as he looked at her, red and blue eyes meeting together. "I don't know anything about your father's arrest. I remember hearing about it, and how the lot of Ryvl fought itself to replace him. But I don't know why." He took a few more bites. "Do you want to see something?"

Ayrah tilted her head. This was something Ayrah had never experienced before. Ayrah had been running, hiding in caves and alley streets, not letting anyone know who she was or where she came from. Now here she was, one child of a Warlord to another. This felt . . . *good.* Ayrah nodded her head.

Kizmaldi stood up from his chair and unsheathed a short, bright steel blade from his hip. Just for a moment, Ayrah thought they were about to fight. But Kizmaldi walked over to her and handed her the sword. "Your father and my mother were friends. They made this sword together."

Ayrah stared at him, eyes wide. She grasped the milky-white hilt, wondering if it was made from some type of bone. A blue gem decorated the pommel, glowing a sort of rhythmic beat. Burned into the silver blade were large runes, letters that Ayrah couldn't read. "They made this together? But then why—"

"Look at these runes too." Kizmaldi felt the etching of the letters. "This is Old Vulgarhe. Not many still know it, how to read it, how to write it. My mother studied it. She devoted her entire life to understanding these etchings. With the help of some old Illian, they discovered a new vuu. If you write incredibly specific patterns of Vulgarhe and devote vuu into the writings, you can create a sort of channel. You can create an item that uses vuu independent of human muscle."

Ayrah felt the writing with the tip of her finger. The blade felt as smooth as water spilling over her fingers. But the runes felt like burn marks, rough and black among the flat of the blade. "What does it do?"

"Not much." Kizmaldi frowned. "It was a prototype of sorts. The first experiment that led to my mother creating the Tuidiia." He reached to take the sword back.

"Can—can I keep it? I don't have anything left of my—"

"Don't be ridiculous. Of course you can't keep it." Kizmaldi snatched it back.

"Close-quarters is good," Errta said with a strain in his voice that suggested close-quarters was not good. "But you're limiting what vuu *is*."

"You've been hanging around Ecanaes too long. You're getting all philosophical." Ayrah teased. They stood in Castle Tamagai's center courtyard. And though they were alone, Ayrah couldn't help but continuously check the window walls surrounding them. What if Malik saw her make a mistake? Or Kizmaldi, for that matter. She even offered a sneer to the little god-king statue, Rahktavah.

Errta forced a small laugh. "But think about it though. An Illian writing a book, filled with deceptions, so that his vuu enters your mind, doesn't need to be around you at all. He can be halfway across the world! And their six Warlords, or whatever they're called, are in charge of types of thinking. *Our* Warlords are in charge of provinces. Do you see the connection?

"Sigu Nii vuu is for dominating an area, as much as it is for dominating people. For you to stick with, 'I'm good at close-quarters,'" He mocked, "It limits your ability, and it'll be your death. You'll face people in the Niiwa of Sehlya that can possess vuu across the entire arena, let alone *this*." He gestured to the small courtyard.

"Aye, I get it." Ayrah ground her teeth. She didn't like this—someone demonstrating superiority over her, whether it was in battle, conversation, knowledge—whatever. "My. . . father and I never made it that far."

"Aye, I'll help—"

"Yes, Daddy," she teased.

Errta spat across the stone. He was growing frustrated.

Ayrah laughed. She liked seeing him all worked up. The vuu in his veins began to illuminate a soft red hue, just from her being such a poor student.

"If you ever sit and watch the grashes down at the arena, you'll notice that Skull-ranks often blow through their power in moments. They'll kill everyone in the pit as soon as the battle starts, but if anyone dodges, ope, well now they don't have any more vuu, they're too tired. But if you watch the Blood-ranks, they make the opposite mistake. They sit there all scared, holding a weapon made out of vuu, like your black ice sword, waiting for other people to make a mistake."

Ayrah realized what he was getting at. Even though she has plenty raw power, she fights like someone with less. Like a Blood-rank. "Are you going to tell me what the victors do, then?"

"Victors don't make mistakes. They're precise with their vuu when they need to be precise, and they cover the whole building with fire when the whole building needs to be covered in fire."

Ayrah scoffed. "Oh, well if that's all."

Errta lowered into a fighting stance, "Lucky for you, and don't ever get Ecanaes started, he'll go on about it 'till you die, good blood goes much farther than good training. And you've got plenty of that."

Ayrah nodded and reciprocated his motion.

17

YUTARAH

Kairo stood hunched over, resting his hands on his knees. He didn't understand how the infection in his thigh made it feel like he had just received a right-hook across the jaw. He stood up straight, arched his neck over his back, and massaged his neck with his hands. If he could just turn his head to either side, then they'd continue on their way. What an annoying way to die.

At least he would die doing something important. If he would have stayed in NeoDerii, he probably would've been sawing planks apart and belaying them down to the jungle floor. Rescuing his sister, the OA, was far grander.

The Delkop range lay two days' walk behind them. Its rocky cliffs and ragged bluffs were awe worthy. Kairo frequently gawked at its majestic foreign face.

Even though it was the source of his infection, Kairo's left leg felt a great deal better. He kept his walking stick on him, but only leaned on it heavily when they came across elevated terrain.

The trees here grew differently. They were a hundred reaches shorter, more twisted, and brighter in bark. They were sparser, with lush grass covering the ground as often as not.

Kairo and Arden were splattered with blood. They had found a creek earlier, and Arden had instructed Kairo not to clean off too well.

A bit of blood about their persons could do some good in the coming den. Here, Arden reapplied Kairo's Sigu Nii ethnicity. Though it wearied him visibly.

They adorned Sigu Nii black leather, taken freely from those slain the previous day. Kairo subconsciously fingered the hole in his lower left abdomen, where Arden shot a pebble through the previous wearer.

His new boots felt like blocks on his feet. They were suffocating. And thick. He would hit the inner sides against one another every dozen steps or so, and it was becoming increasingly frustrating.

"You said that the crown, this Archeodon, is what gives humans vuu. The crown of Sigu Nii gives them the vuu of destruction, the crown of Ala-Ayal—"

"Aylavuera."

"Aylavuera, gives them power over beliefs. But you seem to have all of these. How?"

"It's a transformation of the soul, an ancient art called Ohaer. A handful of people ever master their racial bound vuu. Fewer still have room to spare." Arden spoke short and breathed heavy.

"You're really strong then. That's why you were able to teleport us with the black lightning onto the West Deck during the raid."

"Aye." Huffed Arden. "There are some art styles only available to the Ohaer. And I'd bet any number of coins that there be less than a hundred of us around Zoë."

"'Coin?' What is *coin?*"

"Oh bloody El. That's a talk for another day." Arden shook his head. "But I'm nothing compared to my younger days."

Kairo wondered aloud, "Graeynesh Law says that a level-three Sigu Nii requires four Renovian soldiers. But to run from a level-four at all costs. You're a five. And you effortlessly took out thirty barbarians! Inkless, level-ones, level-twos, and even level-threes!" It was difficult to avoid feeling excited when so much power aligned with your side. But Kairo didn't forget that vuu carried a wicked nature.

"Aye. I know more now; I have a wider equipment of vuu. But my wits are dulling, and so is my energy. You say I took on thirty, but I didn't fight long. I used to be able to cast vuu for *days* at a time."

A few hours passed before the twisted trees began to grow sparse and gave way to shrubs and more grass. The air took on a smell that reeked of Sigu Nii. Sweat, must, charr, spice, blood, and most of all, ash. Kairo switched between breathing through his nose and his mouth, unsure whether the overwhelming smell or the slight taste of these things was worse.

Kairo and Arden broke through the tree line. A small hill declined before them and stretched into flat lands with ankle high, yellow-green grass.

As far as the eye could see, nothing but grass.

It was unsettling to see so much empty space. So much air, nothing to block line of sight. No mountains, no trees, just . . . grass. Kairo scanned left and right. It's only a clearing. . .. A really, really big one.

He had half a mind to turn back and run for the cover of the forest.

A wall of smoke covered the horizon ahead. Kairo could make out a sporadic row of tents on the edge. The smoke billowed up and slanted with the breeze into the sky, like a massive grey banner.

Each step they took had the cloud of smoke growing thicker, stronger, and smellier. Twinges of burnt hair began to mix in with the unruly smell of the Sigu Nii.

"Aterah will be here," Kairo said, looking at the size of the den. "Right?"

"Aye." Arden nodded. "She'll have to move through here."

"*Through?* What do you mean through?"

"Yutarah isn't the end of Sigu Nii, boy." Arden gestured to the hide skin tents. "No more than NeoDerii is the end of your rebellion. There's no Adakon here."

"How long do we have to find her?" Kairo asked between gritted teeth.

"A day." Arden shrugged. "Maybe two."

They reached the first rows of tents, which stretched in a wide circle farther than he could see through the smoke.

The rows were made of tight circles of tents, with burning fire pits in the middle, and assorted insignias painted or sewn into the sides. Sigu Nii were everywhere. Shoulder to shoulder they walked along the small unwritten pathways between the circled tents. Others stood or sat inside their make-shift camps, sharpening blades or cooking scaly reptiles. Others still were in-side the hundreds of tents around them, some laughing, some talking, some grunting and moaning loudly for the world to hear. Children wove between the crowds, laughing and flinging flicks of vuu at one another.

"They're so. . . public." Kairo winced, gesturing at one of the tents with soft moaning drifting out.

"Aye. Where else?" He shrugged, looking around at Yutarah.

"Sure, but—"

"And with all the fightin' and dyin' they do, I don't think they can afford to be too prudish about it."

"What about the prize?" Kairo asked. "One of the barbarians men-tioned Aterah being a prize for something."

"Aye, the Niiwa." Arden nodded. "Might be best we find her before then."

"What's the Nii—"

"At tutahtat tah." Arden's hand snatched up and grabbed Kairo by the mouth. Kairo flinched and threw his gross hand off, spitting and wiping his mouth of grime.

Guess it was a fundamental thing. Something so basic that unrecogni-tion would display their true identity in the instant.

Kairo wiped his eyes. The smoke stung at them constantly so that he held them closed in slits. They took a main path, and shuffled, bumped and nudged past hundreds of sweaty, greasy barbarians. Every ten steps or so, the unwritten path would wind or weave a bit to accommodate some tent that failed to keep off.

Dread crept through Kairo. Each step forward showed just how many Sigu Nii inhabited this den. Thousands. And only seven days' march from NeoDerii. He wondered if Commander Lezyne knew they were here. Or Adakon, for that matter.

They came to rows of little wooden structures with cloth strewn over them. Scrawny, inkless Sigu Nii sat behind wooden shelves, under the ragged, stained, and fraying colored cloth. They shouted, loud and high pitched, holding up their goods. Some held up strips of salted pork or beef, others held shiny metal decorations that they demonstrated by putting on their fingers and necks, and others still held daggers and swords.

Arden stopped off to the side of the pathway. He bent down and scooped up a handful of dirt. He spit on it, and with two hands, he pressed against the dirt hard. When his hand opened, just enough for him to glimpse inside, Kairo saw the yellow glint of shiny metal.

They went up to a screeching man. Lines of twine held up dozens of skinny charred legs of meat. "Three legs." Arden pointed to a bundle of meat.

The Sigu Nii was all bones, despite being surrounded by food. His eyes were deep, dark little sockets, and his elbows were pointed. He did a quick glance and shuffle of his head as he looked at their shoulders. "Vuuless!" he screeched. "Coin?" he asked, in a softer voice. Arden put down a little flat piece of shiny yellow metal. It was circular in shape, but seemingly cut in half. "Gold?" He asked with wide eyes, before they narrowed into a squint. "Where are the engravings?" With vulture-like hands, he snatched up the half coin and bit it. "Hmm. It's real." He pulled out a blade and cut a twine rope holding three legs of seared pork.

"What was that?" Kairo asked as they walked away from the stand.

"Gold. It's a form of trading, one thing for another." Arden answered in a flat tone. The two of them walked back onto the clustered pathway, heading deeper into the heart of Yutarah.

"Why're those up there, then?" Kairo pointed to some of the gold beads decorating Arden's dreadlocks.

Arden growled in contemplation, and eventually replied, "Having a lot of gold is fashionable."

Kairo had half a mind to ask what this new word was. *Fashionable.* But he was still mulling over the previous. *Trading.* Arden handed him a pork leg and tore into it. It was cooked a bit more than he liked, but it felt good to have something solid in his stomach. "What else can we get with it?"

Arden chuckled. "Not much. I have to maintain its shape and I'm still weary. If I let go it would turn back to dirt and then we would be in trouble." Kairo could still hear Arden's breathing, even in the crowd. "There's something worth far more: glory. With my Niiwa rank, these common wenches would practically throw their goods and services upon us, but a tattoo that shiny would stick out here like a king in a farm field."

Kairo didn't like the sound of that. Blending in with the Sigu Nii was already unnerving; sticking out in a manner worthy of praise seemed dangerous. Especially since their whole purpose of being there was to steal back Aterah.

They walked past more tents, stands, and ragged wooden buildings, and reached a small square of hardened dirt. To the north of the square, shaded wooden platforms were built overlooking a pit.

"That, boy, is the Niiwa arena." Arden pointed. "That there is the Warlord's Office of Yutarah." Arden gestured across the square to a ragged black building. It was a story tall and eerie with the wood painted so dark. Its only decoration was the same shiny material as Arden's coin—a gold insignia of an eye with swirls coming to a point in the middle. Soldiers stood at the entrance, with arms folded and in black and gold leather armor.

"And that, dear Kairo, is a tavern." Arden gestured to the west side of the square.

"I have no idea what any of these things are. Why are you showing—"

"I'm glad you asked." Arden patted him on the back with hard calloused hands. "I'll show you." He strode toward what he called the tavern.

The building had holes cut through the middle of it, like windows. But a clear material filled the space. Kairo poked it. It's sound was distinct. Sigu Nii beasts stared at him from the other side.

Arden drug him in by the collar.

Wooden tables and chairs were spread out inside, all of them filled with monsters. Most were burly, hairy, and wore regular cloth without any leather. Kairo's eyes darted from shoulder to shoulder, it seemed every arm in the room was decorated by some level of ink. In the back of the room stood a counter with wooden mugs filled with sloshing and foaming liquid and behind that several huge barrels laid on their side.

"Oh no. Not this again," Kairo complained. But Arden grinned. He strode to the counter, pulling Kairo in tow.

"A room for the night." Arden placed the other half of the golden disc on the counter. "And as many mugs of Zya's Rum Soured Ale as this'll get."

The man behind the counter was the largest in the room. "Gold's gold. You just took up the last room. Seems Yutarah's Niiwa has people all over the Delkop coming our way. Should be a decent show tomorrow night." He turned and filled two mugs under the counter.

"Shame," Arden muttered. "One or two more hits against the Renovian hive and they woulda' been wrecked for good."

The bartender chuckled. "Aye, guess they have a break. But now we know where that outpost is." He turned and glanced Kairo up and down. "Say, are you going to be taking the Niiwa? How old are you?"

"No, no," Arden huffed before Kairo could answer. "He's younger 'han he looks. Maybe look out for us next season. Boy said he's sure he'll take it then." Arden picked up the two mugs and searched the room for an empty table. They strolled over to a corner beside the counter.

They had the table to themselves, and Arden slid one of the mugs to Kairo. He shook his head. "I don't like the taste of it."

"This one's different."

Kairo rolled his eyes, grabbed the mug by the handle, and sipped foam.

"Keep going."

Eventually a real liquid reached his lips. It was spicy! Not in a peppery way. In like a . . . stormy sort of way. It burned too, like the red one from the gathering. Kairo winced and tried not spit it out. He slid the mug decidedly back to the middle of the table.

Arden shrugged and chugged it empty.

"So, what is it?" Kairo asked emphatically. He leaned in over the table, his elbows propping him up. "What *is* the Niiwa?"

"It's a game. The name comes from *Watta dae Nii*, it's a bit of Old Vulgarhe and Sigu Nii's language before the common Aylan Tongue. It means 'fight for your life.'"

"That's it? It's a fight?" Kairo leaned back in his wooden chair. "But they're always fighting. What makes the Niiwa special?"

"It only takes place near the Oscillation—the final days of the season. It's a fight for glory and status." Arden paused as he gulped. "Every town across Sigu Nii with a name celebrates the Niiwa. But this one's special. It's the end of a generation, the end of a cluster, and the end of the Age of Under." Another long gulp and Arden returned to the counter for more ale.

Kairo ignored Arden's funny talking of time. But it seemed like "glory and status" might be like captains or leadership at NeoDerii. Instead of picking who was most suited for these positions, or who had earned them through time and diligence, the Sigu Nii just sparred for them. For titles of importance.

"Okay, well that's not so bad," Kairo thought out loud when Arden came back with two more mugs, and a third one of water for him. "The level system under Graeynesh Law makes so much more sense now. The reason Sigu Nii with more levels to their tattoos are harder to fight, is because they've proven themselves in the Niiwa."

"You're not making any sense, boy," Arden mumbled and drained a mug clean. "The Niiwa don't define how much vuu a Sigu Nii has. They got the same since birth. Rich vuu breed with rich vuu, and poor of vuu breed with the poor of vuu. The Niiwa is only a means of glory. It's to tell everyone who is worth messing with and who isn't." Arden jabbed a finger in Kairo's shoulder.

"Ow!" Kairo hollered. "Quit that!"

Arden chuckled. "Or what?"

Kairo rubbed his shoulder but got Arden's point. "And Renovia is worth messing with because we don't have vuu?"

"Aye." Arden finished off his fourth mug and left to get another.

So, with the glory and status, Aterah is going to be awarded to the winner of tomorrow's Niiwa. Kairo shook his head. The thought of Aterah belonging to a level-five Sigu Nii made him shudder. He gripped his hands tight and swore that he wouldn't let that happen. "Where do you think she'll be then?"

"Boy." Arden grumbled, taking his seat with more mugs. "It is just question after question with you." His voice was beginning to take on its regular hue, sloshed, words uncarefully placed, with just the hint of complete exhaustion. "Here try this." He slid one of the mugs over to him.

"I said I don't want it." Kairo's brows came in. "And I don't think I like you when you have it either. This *ale*."

Arden chuckled, slow, but then louder. Several moments he bellowed with amusement. "You'll come to change your mind." Kairo opened his mouth in protest, but Arden quickly changed the subject. "You mean the Renovian witch? She'll be in the Warlord's Office, no doubt 'bout that."

"The Warlord's Office?" Kairo whispered. "The black building next door?" His fists were shaking. "Well, let's go then!"

"Aye, calm, calm." Arden wiped his face with his hands. "Best we wait till dusk, boy. That ain't a place to just stroll into. It ain't like a war guild, with muck for blood."

Kairo eased back in his seat. "Why?"

"Well, you get how the 'iiwa is means of finding the bes' vuu in a town now, right?"

Kairo nodded.

"Well, the Warlord is one of six. One of the six *strongest* most *powerful* people in all Sigu Nii. Each of 'em got total control of a province. They do what they want with it. Total control. The Black Guard, those mean lookin' black-painted soldiers you saw outside, is the Warlord's means of enforcing themselves in each town throughout their province. That means, they're tough buggers, not just some trash lickin' barbarian as you call 'em."

"Okay," Kairo said. slowly. "So, we find her tonight."

"Aye." Arden began his sixth drink. "And if we don', we risk her getting escor'ed to the Warlord of Ryala by the winner of 'morrow's Niiwa. Undoubt-edaly, he's the smartest of the six, Warlord El Rai Ezs."

Kairo's tightening neck woke him. His teeth were locked in a clenched position. He strained his eyes shut in a violent wince, praying his teeth would not shatter.

His bed was little more than a folded rectangle of blankets on the floor, perpendicular to the foot of Arden's bed. It was a few hours before daylight.

The tension passed. Kairo breathed heavily and rolled his jaw in a roundabout motion.

"Come on, wake up." He shook the sleeping mass of stone and skin. Arden was face down against the straw bed, dreadlocks like a frayed mop across the pillow. Their room was smaller than the barracks of NeoDerii. A window on the north wall overlooked the Niiwa arena and the droves of tents beyond it.

Kairo felt strange being awake before the sun, an unnerving feeling that kept his movements quiet and his voice low as he whispered at Arden. "It's time. We have to look for Aterah."

The beast of a man moaned and rolled so that Kairo was in the corner of his right eye. "Go on without me." His voice was hoarse. "Two people sneaking about the Warlord's Office makes for a crowd." He rolled back over and closed his eyes.

"I can't believe it. What's wrong with you?"

Arden breathed heavily, something close to a snore.

Kairo sighed. He squeezed his hands in and out. He put on the studded leather chest plate, his black baggy cloth trousers, his clunky boots, and the dark Sigu Nii blade around his hip. All taken from the slain gathering. Sweat rolled down his temple. He took one last glance at Arden before slipping out of the bedroom doors.

Kairo quietly made his way down the catwalk loft above the tavern. Snores grew loud and faint as he passed other bedroom doors.

All of Yutarah was quiet. There wasn't so much as the flicker of a candle to be seen. Yutarah's blanket of smoke was mostly dispersed, only faded opaque wisps of it lingered throughout the dirt trails. Kairo wondered if all the smoke had floated up into the sky, because dark clouds hid even the brightest of stars.

The Warlord's Office of Yutarah blended in with the darkness. Somehow, the swirling eye of gold kept its glint, even in the night. Kairo felt like the swirling gold insignia of Warlord Rai Ezs watched him creep around.

No guards were posted on the outside of the building. Kairo wondered if he could just creep through the front door. Cautiously, he eased his ear to the wood. Silence. He tried the brass handle, but it was locked.

He made his way around the side and then the back of the building, hoping for another entrance, a door, a window, anything. But his hands clenched as he saw that the far wall of the building was completely flush. The front doors were the only entrance.

Then a curious idea came to him. He crept back to the front of the square and looked at the roof of the building. It seemed that the walls were a bit higher than the roof, and there might be a walkway up there.

The roof extended on support beams a few steps over the front door. Kairo wrapped his hands around one, and with the quick, agile strength Renovians were trained for, he swept up the beam with ease. When the wall turned flush, he dug his fingers into the tiny spaces between wooden planks. Once he wrapped a hand around the top edge, he climbed up the rest of the wall.

The roof of the Warlord's Office was littered with rusting swords and spears, bows and quivers empty of arrows, and glass bottles with long dried-up liquids. Behind that, a wooden latch. Kairo offered a celebratory sigh.

With two firm hands, he eased the wooden latch up and winced as it squeaked from old bolts and rusty hinges. The snores that roared out caused Kairo to tense up, thinking for a brief moment that they kept snagaeri inside. He stepped down the top rungs of a ladder. Wooden beams nailed together made up two platforms, with straw beds on each end, like the bunks from NeoDerii, except with a straw cushion instead of a twine hammock.

As quietly as he could, his feet found the floor. The room was long and narrow with six bunks on each wall. The ladder was nailed to the far end from the doorway.

Kairo used the corners of his eyes to navigate the mess strewn across the floor and emerged into some sort of hallway. He looked each way.

He roamed around the building and found an armory filled with an assortment of blades. Then a kitchen, with pots and pans, cast iron skillets and strung-up salted pork. Then he found a stairway leading down under the ground.

A row of metal bars made up several cages on the left wall. A single unlit lantern hung on the right.

"Kairo," a parched girlish whisper reached out through the dark.

"Aterah?" he whispered back, his heart picking up in pace.

"Over here." It came from the far cell.

She sat leaning against the wood, hugging her knees. She was covered in splotches of dried blood.

"Kairo," she whispered with a quivering voice, as if fighting back a blanket of tears.

"I'll get you out of here." He looked around but saw no keys.

"No." She shook her head. "You won't." Her hair was tangled and straggly, almost bald looking in some places. Her right eye was black and swollen. And a dark, moldy cloth wrapped around her left shoulder.

Kairo's heart fell. "You've seen me here, haven't you? In your dreams." He grabbed the metal bars between them. It explained why she didn't react to his Sigu Nii skin tone.

"Kairo, listen to me. There's a man coming here now, so you need to think of a reason why you're here."

He looked behind him. The stairs were empty.

"Kairo, *listen.* They're going to fight in the upcoming night. They called it a Niiwa. And I'll be awarded to the winner. But this man, he's the one who took me from NeoDerii. He says he doesn't want to fight in their Niiwa. So he's going to challenge the winner to a duel. You have to wait until *after* that. Kairo, tell me you'll wait until after."

"I'll wait."

Aterah didn't look convinced. "I'm so scared, Kairo. There's something watching me. Even now I can feel its eyes upon me, searching my mind. Sometimes . . . sometimes I can hear its voice, like whispers in the depths, just beneath my attention."

"Aterah, it'll be okay. I'm going to get you out of here." A muffled sound came behind him. He turned and saw a shadowy figure coming down the stairs. He tried to think rapidly. He cursed himself.

The figure paused as soon as Kairo was in his line of sight. The dark was too thick to see his face or his clothes, just the outline of his shape, a Sigu Nii with short hair that stood on end. There was no scabbard on his belt, and no hilt over his shoulder.

"What are you doing with my prisoner?" He asked far too loudly for the dead of night.

"Verano." Aterah whimpered. "I—I was thirsty."

"Aye." Kairo nodded. "She woke me in my sleep. Wouldn't shut up about it."

The figure took a few steps forward. "Then where is your cup, soldier?"

"What?" Kairo asked. He followed up quickly, "Look, I don't know who you think you are." He stood up and placed a hand on his hilt. "But I am a soldier of the Black Guard. If you challenge me, it'll be the wrath of the Warlord's Office against you."

He thought that was pretty good convincing.

The figure stepped closer. With the snap of a finger, a little white flame popped up in front of Kairo. No larger than a candle's light, and yet it was dreadfully hot and bright.

At once he could see the figure's face. His jawline was cut and angular, coming to a point. His eyes were slanted, black, and speckled blue. His hair was black and spikey.

A flashback filled Kairo's eyes. The night of the raid. It was *him*, the same inkless Sigu Nii who wielded the blade of darkness. The sword that had consumed his brother in arms, and his power that had shattered Kairo's own sword across his thigh. Dread shot through Kairo. It took everything in him not to show it. This was the man who had killed him. Sweat lined his brow.

"Where is your Niiwa, soldier?" Verano asked. "I've never seen a member of the Black Guard with so little achievement." His face made no inclination of recognizing Kairo.

"Where is yours?" Kairo asked in return, gesturing to his shoulder and hoping he himself looked calm.

"I am the son of Warlord Nahkon Veligreen." He took another step forward. "This witch is *my* prisoner. If you want her, you'll have to play for her in the Niiwa like anybody else." He gestured to Kairo's inkless shoulder. "Leave us, liar, before I wake this whole building to find a rat in their midst."

Slowly, Kairo forced his legs to move. Around Verano he walked as calmly as he could act and went back up the stairs.

He cast a glance back at Aterah. She was staring up at Verano with eyes full of fear, and with a flicker, the white-colored flame extinguished.

18

EIDHIN

"You understand now that we of Aylavuera gain vuu through more profound means than the others." Sor'al's right hand hovered over his wooden piece. The House of Biology. *"There is a level of earning one's title. There is no such thing as the self-taught master. That is a game played by kingdoms like Sigu Nii, perhaps even Masikus."*

Sor'al didn't explain the rules, but after moving his piece closer to the center of the circle board, twice, Eidhin learned that the Aylan-board was a game of deception. You win by convincing your opponent, or opponents, of something utterly untrue. Sor'al was good at this game. He masked his convicnings in tidal waves of persuasive information that Eidhin knew nothing of. Any tad-bit of things within his statements—a number, a date, or a whole ideology that could be false—would result in gaining ground toward the center of the circle.

The board was made of an average-sized tree trunk, its bark lacquered slick along the edges. Ornate carvings ran deep beside the playable area, which had six starting places around the circular edge connected to six lines with five positions along each that all led to a center etching of a crown. Five thumb-sized figures stood on the starting positions, while the House of Biology stood four positions away from victory.

Eidhin still sat at the starting position. His eyes squinted, and his brain spun furiously through each concept that Sor'al dove through. The world around them gently throbbed in golden-blue colors.

Penoa El's hands lay folded against his chest.

Sor'al continued, *"It is no wonder, then, that powerful El, leagues smarter than even I, can manipulate the fundamental blocks of a creature's existentiality. And if they can do that, who's to say that perhaps a monkey could not be taught. If a monkey can be taught, then even it can demonstrate vuu."*

Eidhin shook his head. A physical assertion of falsehood that he regretted as soon as he began, the world and his body were too slow to keep up with his gesture. *No.* The thoughtful uttering shared between he and the El's consciousness vibrated with a tune of tangibility. *If a monkey could be taught, then we would see Sigu Nii with Illian vuu. If it were as simple as a teaching, there would be no such thing as Illian vuu because just anybody would have at least some. For that reason, I say vuu is not a nurture matter, as you've titled it.*

When swatting away the opponent's attack, you were granted the ability to name the falsehood for your own point. It increased the stakes of carelessly making something up that was untrue. But it was still a risk on Eidhin's half, because if he named the falsehood incorrectly, Sor'al would gain another space on the board.

Sor'al's lips curled into a smile as he moved his piece up. Slowed by the displacement of the perceivable.

You got me? Eidhin asked.

"Indeed. Though you played that space well. I found it advantageous to resort to techniques of deception that you have not yet conceived. Indeed, Illians do gain vuu through teachings, so it might suit you best to hang on every word mumbled by us in black-velvet robes."

You went past the lie, Eidhin answered. *Instead of masking a lie in truth, you put a truth within an obvious lie, therefore leading me to believe the entire concept was fallacy.*

The smile vanished from Sor'al's lips. *"It's your move."*

Eidhin's piece represented the school of Philosophy. He was beginning to decide the poorness of his choice. Though he knew the rough borders around the word, his lack of knowledge in the subject provided him with less-than-ideal ammunition to fire philosophical lies. He could hardly even think of any truths, and it was reflected by his lack of movement on the board.

To further the difficulty, the intimacy shared between them both provided uncertain grounds for thinking. Sor'al could feel his every thought. His every emotion. If Eidhin were to spin up something untrue, he would have to do it quickly, and with a degree of discretion. Though, Eidhin supposed, discretion and deception were not too far from each other.

I watched a man, Eidhin began, *standing on the stone steps to our church in Snowstock. He was clothed in rags. Dirt adorned his person like any of us others. A town of farm-folk we were. But he remained unwelcome inside. In fact, he was firmly shut out.*

Sor'al cut in. *"Stories don't count. You can't reiterate a personal story with false events and move your piece for it. Unless you played History."*

I'm getting there, Eidhin replied. *On the morning of that day, my father taught me of the usefulness of pruning brown leaves from an onion. We went around the whole patch doing this. Forty-seven of them. It was a matter of care, a tender maintenance, to cut decaying leaves from our future food. Because of this, I say that pruning is a good thing.*

There was silence for a moment. The discolored world throbbed rhythmically, as if in sync with the tunes of their hearts beating. Eidhin could feel Sor'al searching for the falsehood.

"I agree," Sor'al said at last. *"Everything you've stated is true."*

I agree as well.

"Then you take a pass?" Sor'al asked.

If that's what that means.

"*Indeed. My move.*" Sor'al's hand began to reach for the wooden piece of Biology. Less than a knuckle away, he hovered. "*Man was born of a monkey.*"

Eidhin's eyebrows raised. It was a large claim to make. He waited patiently for Sor'al to continue, but they hung in momentary silence. *Is that it?*

"*Indeed.*"

That's not fair. You've provided me with no reasoning, no convincing. I'm just to guess whether it's true or not?

"*Indeed.*" Sor'al seemed to be getting impatient, each affirmative coming more grumbly than the last.

Untrue. Eidhin decided with a mental shrug, careful not to let his body mimic his tone in case he were to accidentally commit to the gesture for longer than he'd wish.

"*It is true.*"

How can you say?

"*House Biology released the study a few generations ago. There are some who oppose the logic of the theory, but all in all, each of the six smartest in Zoë have agreed upon its soundness.*" Sor'al kept a straight face as he moved his piece closer to the center.

That was cheap. But if you say it is so . . .

Sor'al moved House Biology another piece forward.

What is that for?

"*Wording,*" said Sor'al. "*Though they agree man descended from monkey, it was not a sudden birth. It took an inconceivable amount of generations to take place.*"

That play sat ill with Eidhin. He allowed his lips to arch downward, his brows caving with the weight of injustice. *That is hardly fair.* But he understood. Sor'al interpreted his relenting as a swatting of sorts, which was incorrectly placed, giving Sor'al the additional space.

Sor'al did not respond. One space remained for his victory.

There was a man dressed in slacks and silver buttons, shining shoes placed against the edge of the cobblestone garden near a square in Gehni. He spoke to the passing crowds, but no one lingered. El Penoa called him a conspiracist and said he would not remain. Perhaps coin will not follow his words, but I say that for attempting to convince people of untrue things, he should be pruned. Chopped from us like an infected limb.

"Should be?" Sor'al repeated. "Should be, should be, should be." He threw the words around as if tasting them for logical discrepancy. "I agree. He should *be*." Careful to place emphasis on Eidhin's own wording, Sor'al's eyes squinted in preparation for his response.

I agree as well.

"Then you pass."

Indeed, said Eidhin.

"You've begun to play sloppily. Perhaps we grow tired of this game. I have achieved enough insight into your mind to assess your ways of thinking, if you wish to—"

One space left, interrupted Eidhin, and followed up with, *Finish.*

"My move." Sor'al hovered his hand over his piece, ready to move it to the crown center-space. "Vuu, in its essence, is human influence throughout Zoë. Whether it be Illian, Sigu Nii, or any other."

Your convincings are becoming cheaper and cheaper, protested Eidhin.

"Indeed, I wish to see how little I can tip my finger for you to bow."

Eidhin hummed, the sound low rumbling in his throat from time slowed. *I say you are correct. I've heard El Penoa mention something similar, though I confess, this claim seems of a different category than your others. I dare proclaim this is not from the House of Biology.* It was bold for Eidhin to retaliate. A simple agreement might have prevented Sor'al's victory. But if his counterclaim was proved false, it would be a free move.

"Indeed. It was of *Philosophy*." Sor'al moved his wooden figure backward one space. "I sense that you did not realize backward ground was particularly *possible. Failure to catch concepts aligned with a different house would still result in my gaining one space, it being deception of sorts. But because you called me on it, I lose one space. Your move."*

Eidhin paused for a breath. *If a man should be pruned for convincing with ill intentions, then I daresay that you and I should both be pruned this instant.*

Sor'al's eyes opened wide. *"My, that was a good play."* His eyes searched frantically for ways out, ways around Eidhin's claim, before retreating to inspecting semantics. *"My only route is to claim that I play this not with ill intentions."*

Eidhin refused. *Are you sure?* He could feel Sor'al's hesitation. Where his thoughts were previously quick, discrete, the logical corner was an echo for Sor'al's mental lingering.

"Indeed, it was a good play. If I were to recant your previous 'pruning is a good thing,' you would gain two spaces. If I continue to agree that I should be pruned—chopped from our society like a plagued soldier—you would legally have the right to do so."

Eidhin's eyes darkened. *I would?* Killing Sor'al was never part of his plan. He did not know it was even possible to legally murder.

Take your two spaces.

Eidhin found utter joy clicking his wooden figure forward, then up once more. Yet Sor'al was still two spaces ahead.

"W-well I—I—"

Are you stuttering? asked Eidhin. *That is surely an obstacle to be overcome.* That's what Sor'al had said, when he first heard Eidhin's stuttering. The attack spilled out from Eidhin's consciousness with an edge, but without intent.

A smile slithered across Sor'al's lips. *"I stuttered on purpose. Commentary against your opponent is forfeit. You resign."*

What? Eidhin began to stand up, but in the telepathic state, his whole body felt stuck in a kind of slow motion. *I didn't know.*

"I've given you advantages when you did not know. I will not revoke your disadvantages under the same argument." Sor'al knocked Eidhin's piece on its side. *"Shake with your left, touch my forehead with your right."*

Reluctantly, Eidhin did. The pulsating golds and blues drained from the world around them. Everything returned to its regular speed, and sights and sounds rushed at Eidhin like a crashing river—the crackling of the indoor fire, the puffing of the elder on his pipe, footsteps pattering across the ceiling overhead, and Penoa El's settling shoulders.

"What an ending," Penoa said, clearly impressed.

"Y-y-you c-c-ould-d—"

"Gracious me, quiet." El Penoa shuddered in annoyance. "I could not hear the conversation, it was in your head, but I saw how the pieces moved, and I can deduce that you relished going after Sor'al. A mistake only made by the emotionally dumb." He turned to Sor'al, who briskly pushed himself from between the table and chair. Penoa's voice was quiet, "He won two spaces in row off of you?"

"Indeed," huffed Sor'al El. "He played a Vylndaer Advance, on his own, unprovoked."

Eidhin did not know what that meant. But he saw the room shift for it. Each of the four velvet-robed El locked their eyes onto his, he could not peer around the room fast enough.

"I must bathe the match off," said Sor'al, brushing his robes with his chin raised. "He reduced me to play a spiteful Sehlyian Retreat. It smoothed over well enough, but still . . ." Sor'al turned for the staircase.

"Are we not to discuss his usefulness?" Penoa called after him. "You leave me on the brink of understanding, like a story cut too soon."

Sor'al stopped. "Best we wait until the children are in bed."

Eidhin shifted in discomfort. The robed teachers could not take their eyes off him.

"Indeed," huffed Penoa. "Let's introduce your flat mate." He laid a hand on Eidhin's shoulder and guided him up the stairs. They climbed the dark-lacquer switchback stairs and paused at each level. "These are our rooms." Penoa gestured down the second-floor hall. "You are not to be caught on this floor at any time, unless instructed to do so." Third floor. "These are the classrooms. You will find yourself in your designated seat each morning before the sun breaks the horizon." Fourth level. "The girls' hall." He looked Eidhin in the eyes. "You are not to be caught on this level either." Fifth level. "And this is your hall."

A dozen doors lined each side of the hallway. Some were open with soft candlelight straying into the hall. Others were closed, with darkness beneath the bottom of the door.

Penoa El turned and pointed at the upwards stairs, "The last stairway goes to the roof. There are student Aylan-boards up there and chairs for leisure. You may study up there, or peer out across Gehni's pleasing landscape. I'll show you to your room." With a guiding hand on Eidhin's shoulder, they walked four doors down and came to a lit room.

A boy sat in a frail wooden chair. He had bright blonde hair and blue eyes that lit up when he saw them enter. He laid his quill on a thick book. "El." His voice thick with Gehni's accent. "And a new flat mate." He glanced Eidhin up and down.

"Ecagaus here is one of our best," said Penoa. "His parents have been contributing salaries to our church here in Gehni for a generation. And when he came of age, it seemed only fitting that he join us in our rigor."

Ecagaus asked, "How did you do on your first Aylan-board?"

"I—I—I—"

"Oh," His eyes went wide. He glanced between Penoa and Eidhin.

"The boy's lips are lame. It will be something we attempt to work on." Penoa gave Eidhin a soft shove into the room. "Go on now, we will fit you for clothes, find books and the like in the morning."

19

NIIWA

Between the sun's first breaths and its peak in the sky, the lot of Yutarah woke slowly. Kairo and Arden wandered around and explored sections of vendors, ate lunch, and looked at funny Sigu Nii blades. The day proved particularly hot, though the air stayed much drier than the humid heat Kairo was used to. His throat constantly felt dry, and Yutarah had little beverage to offer other than wine or ale. The smoke from hundreds of campfires being lit throughout the day did little to help. By the hour after the sun's peak, the whole of Yutarah was covered in the same dense air that had polluted it the day before.

Fights constantly broke out between the Sigu Nii. It seemed that in every section of Yutarah they wandered, there were always Sigu Nii dueling to the death. Grashing, Arden called it. Kairo learned it was a manor of arguing, but to the death.

The duels would take place anywhere—near tents, in the middle of a path, sometimes the grash would spill violently across entire camps resulting in a number of collateral casualties. Kairo found that if there was *ever* a difference in tattoo ranking, the higher-level Sigu Nii won. They watched Sigu Nii grash over shinier swords, women, or even their own pride.

Sometimes, the Black Guard would get involved and grash. Kairo learned when this happened, it was because someone had broken one of Yutarah's very few laws. Then, the grash became a manor of policing.

Arden explained that it was a trial, if you beat the Black Guard in a fight to the death, then you've been found not guilty.

The Black Guard would incapacitate the accused, drag the criminal to a big wooden X, and slowly cut them in half top down.

Kairo gagged and turned away as split esophagus landed on either side.

In Renovia, if someone broke Graeynesh Law, they would be tried with words. Explain to the Chamberlains your circumstance.

It wasn't right, what happened to Rouen. It hurt Kairo's stomach to think about. And, counter-instinctively, it didn't help that the exile ended up being sort of correct. What with the raid immediately following and all.

Still, Kairo swore that Copt had been able to bring the war chief into his own demise—dragging him into the attacking snagaeri.

Once the sun began its daily retreat toward the horizon, there began an erratic shuffle toward a central point in Yutarah. The Niiwa arena. Kairo breathed deeply. *It's time.* Sigu Nii pushed past one another to get to the arena first. Vendors made their stands mobile and dragged them to the corners. Others wagged behind or stayed in their tents—Sigu Nii without ink or coin to be granted one of Yutarah's demanded Niiwa seating.

"Five copper pieces," a scrawny Sigu Nii at one of the gates muttered with half closed eyes. "Each." He added, glancing between Arden and Kairo and their inkless shoulders.

"Floor seats." Arden said.

"A silver piece, each." The usher moaned, exaggerating his exhaustion. Arden handed the guard half a golden disc. The guard stuttered, wide-eyed, and pocketed the coin. "R-right that way, El."

There were two wooden platforms nudged against the long side of the arena's oval, red and blue linens stretched across the top to provide shade. Most of the crowd would stand there to watch the coming fight.

Arden continued around the side and up toward the pit, which was a dugout oval several reaches lower and fifty steps in diameter at its long point. Wooden beams were built around the edge of the pit and occasionally down the sides, in order to maintain the integrity of its shape. There, between the pit and the stands, was a long wooden bench where Arden took his seat.

Kairo sat beside him, and beastly warriors followed shortly after. A Sigu Nii with a gorilla build and a level-three serpent sat two seats over, and a girl filled the seat between them after that. She had snagaeri scars running up her neck from under her tunic. Cheeks with a sand-like color pinched corners over her eyes; they had a soft vibrancy.

Kairo shook his head. The Sigu Nii were not soft. She was an animal, like the level-three snake staring at him from her left shoulder.

"I'm going to get a drink," said Arden.

"Again?" Kairo asked. The stoneman had been drinking all day. Kairo thought about asking him to not have any more. He grew frustratingly loud with each drink, not just in volume, but in presence. And he needed him to be regularly present—they were going to save Aterah this day. Right after the Niiwa.

Kairo glanced across the pit as Arden went to the closest corner of the oval, where the vendors were. The stands were crowded with waiting Sigu Nii. And a handful of Black Guard roamed the arena.

The arena grew louder as a thousand Sigu Nii hollered and shouted, laughed and talked all around. Kairo watched a group of them, near the vendors on the far corner, take turns pushing and old man. Kairo shuddered. The Sigu Nii praised the very things that NeoDerii exiled. They listened and respected their elders, gave them positions of importance.

Kairo had half a mind to walk around the arena edge and help him, but he waved the thought away. The old man had probably stood guard at one of the old prison cities and hunted brother Renovians down during the Egress. He was still just a barbarian.

Arden returned with two frothing mugs of ale. He sipped one on his way down, winced, and snarled. He set both mugs on the bench, uncarefully so that ale sloshed over, and bent over and scooped a handful of dirt. Air funneled out of his nose in repeated chuckles as Arden used Masikonian vuu to pour more of that clear liquid into each mug.

"Welcome to Yutarah's Niiwa!" An announcer yelled from the oval's curve. He shouted through a step-long cone with the small end by his mouth.

Kairo looked quizzically at Arden.

"It's called a megaphone. Makes the sound carry farther."

"Any and all failures to 'ccept the rules of the Niiwa will be punishable by grashing from the Warlord's Office. Round one, the Dagger." There was a tense pause from the announcer. It was like an invitation. Eighty-something Sigu Nii pushed their ways to the pit and leapt down. They unsheathed sword, hatchet, and dagger. "Begin!"

Sigu Nii began clashing metal on metal. Several of them around the pit were unlucky enough to have each Sigu Nii beside them turn their direction. Swords and knives pierced through chests of those caught in the middle.

Kairo's eyes widened in disbelief. He caught surprise from croaking out of his mouth. When he learned of the Niiwa game the previous night, he had thought it would be sparring matches. He leaned over to Arden and whispered, "They're hardly even men! They're all younger than I am." Most of them looked to be about Aterah's age—a generation old. But a handful of them could still be considered children—younger than two-thirds.

"Aye," Arden whispered back, his eyes fixed on the battle. "The Sigu Nii have until the generation after their birth to take the Niiwa. So, if you're born in Bora, you have until the end of Lotra before you count yourself inkless for the rest of your miserable life."

The words Bora and Lotra meant less than nothing to Kairo. He practically didn't even hear them, since they were drowned out by the sound of one child getting chopped to death and the crowd hollering with excitement. He tried to listen for a mother's wail or a father's roar, but he heard none.

Most of the contestants weren't skilled with the weapon they used. They just whacked. And the winners of the fights were just those who're whacked the least. Kairo watched many opt for swinging their sword faster than their immediate opponent, instead of just blocking. He leaned over to Arden. "Rules? What rules?"

"The first round of the Niiwa allows any kind of blade but no vuu. If you use vuu," Arden paused to belch, "you get disquantified. The rest of the rounds have rules too, but they're different—" Arden stopped at the screaming of a Sigu Nii whose legs were dismembered from his body.

The remaining contestants were covered in blood, head to toe. Intestines draped over the shoulder of one, eyeballs squished underfoot, and another used a severed finger to pick his own nose. It was Sigu Nii spilling Sigu Nii blood.

Kairo clenched his fist and beat it against the bench quietly beside him. He did not want Arden or the Sigu Nii woman to notice the turmoil within him. The tentative wandering through the jungle, the necessity of observant eyes and listening ears, all in fear of combat with these barbarians, and come to find out they fought themselves just as often.

The crowd was quiet and tense during the clashing of steel, then roaring and hollering as the individual battles around the pit ended in death. Finally, half remained, and the round ended.

A wooden ladder fell down the side of the pit as the announcer asked, "Will any of you stay for the second round?"

A large handful of them did. The rest climbed out.

Arden hummed.

"What?"

"Most'll die."

"Round two, the Flame," invited the announcer again.

"It's rare to see someone start from the Dagger and go through the entire Niiwa," Arden said. "It's foolish. You're tired, children. Take your tattoo and fight again next season."

Kairo glared at Arden. His commentary was not insightful, it was culturally cooperative.

Forty young corpses polluted the pit. Kairo quietly assumed the first Sigu Nii to descend would help remove them. But no one paid them any mind. The next twenty-something Sigu Nii making their way down stepped casually over, around, or on the majority of the previous contestants.

The new fighters looked to be about the same age as Kairo, some a tad older. They all had clean swords and blades strapped to their hips. Their leather and clothes were yet unstained by red.

"Begin!" The moment the announcer's call was heard throughout the arena, the Sigu Nii contestants' hands lit up in a glow. Three-step-long spikes of ice ripped out of the ground, small balls of fire exploded around the pit, and gusts of wind blew and redirected the fire. The whole arena turned into a frenzy of spells and vuu that Kairo could hardly keep up with.

"What are the rules for this round?"

"Elemental vuu only."

Almost half of the contestants found themselves dead in the first few moments of explosive action. Kairo watched the winners of the previous round. He winced when vuu blew their direction, scooted toward the edge of the bench when they locked into a duel, and felt his muscles relax and slump defiantly when he watched any of them die.

Kairo began one of these sit up apprehensions when he felt his neck stiffen. "Not aga-ohn." His speech cut short into a long groan as his jaw clamped shut. His leg throbbed in a motion that felt like it was getting slashed by the same sword again and again. A violent twitch in his stomach caused him to spill halfway down the bench. His feet were dangling over the pit. He didn't have enough hands to grab the parts of his body that were in spasms, and he had to use his only two to keep from falling into the battle.

Only the Sigu Nii girl beside him paid him any mind. "The infection," she said with aloof calamity. "How grotesque of them to use rusted blades against us."

The crowd cheered at some unseen victory down in the pit while Kairo growled and climbed his way back onto the bench. "They don't do it on purpose. . .?" It started a statement and ended a question.

Kairo did not know rust was a source of the infection to begin with. He wondered if the physicians knew this, and followed the thought to leadership, questioning whether their bronze metal swords were passed from soldier to soldier in order to weather them.

The girl only shrugged and turned her attention back in time to see the final contestant slain.

They were getting worse. A dreadful thought. Most watch Death approach by walk, Kairo felt him sprinting.

His right knee jittered up and down. He had seen the infection take dozens of his fellow soldiers. And by now, he wondered if he would survive the return journey with Aterah, back to NeoDerii.

Ten fighters remained when the announcer asked, "Will any stay for the next round?" One did and the rest climbed out.

"There were like forty when the round ended last time but ten this time." Kairo leaned closer to Arden and asked, still half out of breath from his spasms.

"Aye—well it's just half both times, boy," said Arden. "But the number of victors it takes for the round to end is different across each town, province, and season. It all comes down to the Warlord's Office. Warlord El Rai Ezs of the Ryalan Colonies is quick to fumble over demographics and what not. But the Pikemaster, Warlord over Ryvl, for example, just kind of. . ." Arden frowned and did a shooing motion with his hands. "Makes it up."

"Round three, the Skull."

Eight more Sigu Nii leapt down into the pit. They took their places around the edge of the arena. They were older than the previous contestants, and each of them bore the ink of flame. Swords and blades hung loosely at their hips, and they stood low in fighting stances. Of the eight, two were women, slender and sinewy, with their hair cut short or tied back out of the way.

"Begin!"

The contestants immediately dashed toward one another.

"Battle vuu only," Arden leaned over and whispered with a reeking breath. "Since I knew you were going to ask."

Two fell in the opening explosion of battle—a noxious green cloud so dense that Kairo had to squint to make them out. The two warriors neared one another, and while one was still pulling out his sword, the other punched with all his might. It must've been combined with vuu because his fist exploded straight through the other's face. Brains, blood, and skull fragments shot out of the mist and splattered the crowd.

The stands roared in excitement.

It took a lot for Kairo not to lean over and wretch. He'd lived in war his whole life, but he'd never seen such gruesomeness. He turned away as the surviving Sigu Nii fell to his knees coughing in the green gas.

"Ahht," Arden grumbled and grabbed Kairo's face. "You have ta watch, boy." His grimy hands thrust his nose back toward the pit. Kairo shouldered him off but watch he did.

The Sigu Nii dodged opposing attacks, they leapt and rolled, and they threw up their own vuu for counter-attacks. They were fighting for positions worthy of war-tribe leader.

Four contestants remained when the round ended. One stayed for the next round.

The sun fully descended. Great metal braziers around the pit were lit, flooding the arena with a molten-warm light.

"Round four, Blood."

Arden lurched up to get more ale, stumbling several times on his way.

Oh El, when will this be over? Kairo looked to the sky.

The woman to Kairo's right huffed, shuffled, and pushed herself to stand. He watched with horror as she braced her left hand along the wooden lip of the drop-off wall and jumped down. The bodies were piling high. He could hear each squish and squash of her walking along the corpse floor.

The five Sigu Nii in the pit were *monsters*. They moved in a constant fighting stance, and their eyes seemed both hungry and lifeless.

Arden returned with two mugs.

"What are the rules for this one?" Kairo asked. Exhaustion was his best disguise for the disgust he felt.

"None, no more." He belched.

"Begin!"

Offensive attacks didn't explode this time. Instead, blades of vuu filled each of their hands. One dragged a sword of ice out from his palm, another blew an explosion of fire that settled into the shape of an axe, another had bolts of lightning ripping down his arms, the woman that sat beside Kairo made great gusts of sand swarm around her hands, and the last had a green fire settle around his feet.

The crowd let out gasps and noises of impressed surprise.

"What a show!" the announcer called. "I haven't seen a colored flame in half a generation!"

All the Sigu Nii contestants uneasily eyed the man with green fire. The one with lightning pulsing down his arms was the first to act. He thrust his hands in the sand, and Kairo could see bolts of electric vuu rip through the ground.

The woman thrust her hands beneath her, and the shooting sand exploded her a dozen reaches into the air, avoiding the lightning. The man with the axe of fire measly jumped, but it was still there when his feet landed. He contorted a little before laughing belly first. "The sand and dust are bad for your vuu!"

Kairo marveled at the woman's acrobatics. He had not seen a Sigu Nii so agile.

"Why's it look like that?" He whispered to Arden and nodded at the discolored fire. The neon flames moved slowly, weaving and licking at the air.

"The green flame is El-tier vuu. It's the wil'est of the fires, it spreads and spreads, devouring anything it migh' call food. It's surprising b'cause Yutarah is ty'ically a heap of dung—oi why's there dirt in me ale?" Arden sat perched, curled over his clasped mug, inspecting it thoroughly with a roundabout sway.

Kairo thought about the previous night, when Verano Veligreen had sparked the tiny white flame that burned brighter and hotter than any normal candle flicker.

The man with green fire stirred. He whipped his arms out, and the fire rushed in the direction he thrusted. Everyone did their best to avoid it, the man with the fire axe smashed the ground before him, causing a small explosion of green and red flames. But the tiniest speck of green caught him, and in moments it was devouring him.

The snagaeri-scar woman blasted at the ground, jumping above the attack again.

The one with lightning swirling around his arms shot bolts of lightning at it, which only made the flames shoot up taller. He was a burnt crisp within the moment.

Kairo was growing frustrated. He wanted to scream, *just block!* All night he watched these beasts attack. Over and over, their blood spilled, and easily avoidable if—instead of trying to attack faster—they just blocked.

The man with the ice blade thrust his hands up, and ice walls three steps thick shot up in every direction. The green fire traveled about half-way up before the ice began to melt and the fire went out.

Yes! Kairo wanted to leap up and shout, like many others around the arena. Why had he been the first all night?

The green fire quickly died out everywhere except the small ring around its creator. The sandy reflected the night sky as the firelight glint-ed off thousands of tiny specs of glass. The woman landed back on the ground with a thud and crunch. She struck her hand out in a funnel mo-tion and sent a cloud of dust and glass at the man of green fire.

He leapt out of the way, but tiny shards imbedded into his torso.

Kairo sat and stared. His shoulders slouched back, and his arms slumped to either side. He knew that if he were to fight any of these beasts, he would be hopelessly outmatched. He wondered, for the sake of Graeynesh Law, how many Renovians it would take to take down *one* of these high-level Sigu Nii warriors.

Ten, he thought at first. No. He wondered if any number of Renovians could defeat one of these beasts.

The three remaining contestants—the green fire, the iceman, and the woman with sand—danced around each other, waiting for someone to make a move. Waiting for someone to make a mistake.

The iceman tilted his head and gestured toward the green fire. Gusts of wind blew from every which way. Sand and dust swirled around the green fire, and the flames whipped in the sudden gusts. The other made a face of realization and tried to beckon his own vuu to shoo away. But it was too late. Specks of the green flame carried with the swirling wind. The green fire turned orange, its typical color, as its source changed from vuu to the skin, clothes, and hair of its originator.

The crowd hollered and cheered, drowning out the noises of the Sigu Nii being burned alive. And then there were two.

"Alrigh'." Arden sighed and stood. "This is my las' one."

"Done already?" Kairo mocked. "We still have another round of this to go."

Arden frowned and looked around. "I doubt it."

A sword of ice ripped out of the Sigu Nii's hand and the woman caused a hardened rod of sand and glass to take shape in her hand. It was like a good old-fashioned sword fight.

"How does she control sand like that?" Kairo asked when Arden returned, mug in hand.

"What'dya mean, boy?"

"Instead of regular vuu, like fire, she uses—"

"Regular? The Sigu Nii can control almos' anything if it's in the motion of des'ruction. Some might like fire over ice, and practice with it accordingly, but still—there ain't no 'regular.'"

Clash. Clash. Vuu. Clash. The two of them thrusted and parried until they were both visibly weary. An occasional thrust of ice shards, or a sudden sand stalagmite ripping in his direction, but otherwise they sword fought until they could fight no more.

Who could outlast the other became the game. The two of them fought so long that the man could no longer lift his tree trunk arms to block her attacks. Finally, the woman raised her sandy-glass rod, and the man of ice had nothing left.

The crowd was in a frenzy. Kairo wondered if they ever grew tired of watching someone die.

"I am Furadii!" she shouted, her voice breaking from exhaustion. "Know my name and know that I am the gemstone of Yutarah!"

She would receive the level-four tattoo: four pieces of a serpent with a down-facing dagger beneath the first, a flame under the second, a human skull above the third, blood dripping from its neck, and *Yutarah* beneath it all.

The announcer cheered. "Furadii! Our Blood of the Niiwa!"

A member of the Black Guard came around by the dropping ladder, he clutched a small tan girl in one arm. She was young and had dark brown hair. A cloth gag was tied round her mouth, and her wrists were bound bloody behind her back. *Aterah.* Kairo leapt from his seat and stood there frozen.

"Are there no others?" The entire arena was almost silent. "Is there no one to fulfill the fifth round of the Niiwa? Come, any who bear the fourth tattoo, and battle for your prize."

"There ain' no blood-dy Bloods 'ere." Arden scoffed with a raspy voice.

They waited, and the crowd remained silent as everyone looked around.

"Then behold, Furadii. This witch has been promised to the Warlord of Ryala, El Rai Ezs. Your prize is to deliver it yourself."

Kairo began a laugh. The prize sounded like a chore. But his chuckle cut short as gasps echoed several times around the arena.

"Rewarded by a Warlord!"

Furadii climbed the ladder and snatched Aterah as soon as she was within arm's distance. She stroked Aterah's face with her hand, a wicked smile across her face. "More than a bit o' gold."

"Hey," a sharp voice came from Kairo's left. It was the arena entrance guard, the usher. He was standing over Arden with his palm outstretched, holding a small pile of dirt. "What is this?"

Oh no. Realization flooded Kairo. Arden's Masikonian vuu was draining. He hadn't thought anything of it before, since the stoneman could retain Kairo's Sigu Nii form even while sleeping. But it seemed the ale, however much of it Arden drank, affected his ability.

Kairo looked at the back of his hand. It was still a light yellow. That was good, at least.

"Oh lemme gethat for you." Arden reached out and pressed his hand on the usher's, using his vuu to turn it back into a golden disc. He looked up smiling.

Kairo had an awful feeling. An instinctual fear slithered up his spine.

The usher backed away, horrified. He dropped the coin like it belonged to the long list of poisonous jungle plants. It landed in the dirt with a thud. He searched around the arena with a sweeping gaze. It landed on a member of the Black Guard.

"We have to go." Kairo leapt to stand.

"Leave m' be. I'll-mma be up in jus' a momen'."

Forget him. Kairo had spent half the day watching what happens when the Black Guard were crossed.

The arena usher sprinted off in the Black Guard's direction.

Kairo took that as his moment to flee. Dirt kicked up behind each sure-footed step. His stolen boots dug into the ground with manufactured traction. Though they made his feet feel stuffy, he didn't mind their ability to get going.

He took off around the corner of the arena and hurled himself through the wall of vendors. Sigu Nii buyers and sellers hollered as he dove through the stands, and out the other side of the arena. He found himself just north of the main square, beside the tavern and looking at the black painted Warlord's Office.

The bone-thin, charred-leg seller from the previous day stood under a member of the Black Guard. He held up a pile of dirt.

A thin croak escaped Kairo. He had planned on running east, toward the tree line, but he would have to go south first and escape around the arena. He walked, trying his best to look inconspicuous.

The two of them looked up, suddenly searching for their suspect.

Just then, the tavern door slammed open. The glass all across the lower half of the building shuddered violently. The largest man in there, the barkeep, looked around, also holding up a pile of dirt. He made eye contact with Kairo. "You!" he shouted.

The Black Guard across the square sprung to motion.

Kairo spun around and took off northwards. He didn't know where he would go from there, but it didn't matter. On one particularly gritty stride, his left boot caught on the bottom of his right. He flung forward. His feet remained strained the whole way down, as if Kairo could muscle his way to the next step. He slammed into the dirt and slid into the previous Guard spilling out of the northern arena entrance, with a panting usher in tow. He leapt to his feet, but was stuck with the tavern on one side, and the arena on the other.

Kairo spun around again. He was surrounded. They closed in.

20

AYRAH

Castle Tamagai was in a flurry. Errta bounded through the halls in search of his wide leather boots. Ecanaes clutched an armful of scrolls, trying in vain to sort the information he had gathered on the Waterdome. The Tamagai were fighting this evening. Pratuel's strongest guild versus Waike's. It was the championship for the whole Gya province.

Amid all the dressing and preparing for their company's departure, Urota tugged on Ayrah and suggested they leave a little early.

Walking down the switchbacks from Mount Tamagai, she was still high enough to see above the distant walls of Pratuel's Niiwa arena in the north. Vuu flashed and extinguished on the sandy pit. She stopped.

A hand rested on her shoulder. "Come on now. It'll be worth it," Urota cooed.

"If you would just tell me where we're going."

Urota *tsk'd*. "You'll see."

The two of them continued on. It was midday, and summer was not quite at its end. Ayrah wiped her forehead from sweat another quarter's way down the mountain. She covered her eyes with her hands, squinting, and planned to ask Ecanaes why Pratuel's wooden structures glittered like gems.

The prey districts of Pratuel, where the commoners dressed in rough cloth and hid their lowly tattoos, was mostly empty. Ayrah guessed they were all at their coin-paying occupations. The few that peeked from wooden shuttered windows or meandered where drunkard's steps landed, bowed hastily from Urota's path. "El!" They called, groveling like rats.

"You guys must own most of this city." Ayrah's brows raised. The raggeds' eyes looked upon her the way she'd wanted to be looked at. Afraid.

"What do you mean?"

"Shops, taverns, brothels . . ."

"Oh, no, none at all." Urota waved a dismissive hand. "Respect for the Tamagai has been in Pratuel for clusters of generations. I don't know much about guild history. Malik might, he has a rabbit's ear for the pale things."

"Then . . ." Ayrah squinted. "How do you make coin?"

Urota laughed. "Money is for the poor. You'll learn that well enough after the king's Niiwa in Sehlya."

If I survive. Ayrah thought.

It's true, Ayrah recalled, that Herk and Boden never had to pay for ale unless it was at another guild-owned tavern. They had to pay coin for very little. Not fruit, vendor stands, or livestock. But they still needed money to stock their own bars and pay their own wenches.

No. There was a currency in Sigu Nii that was much, much older than coin: glory.

She ran a hand through her hair. It was softer than the day prior, but the front-left side of her head still had near-formed dreadlocks. A servant girl the previous night had offered to get them out with almond oil, but she liked the rugged feeling they gave.

"How do you like your clothes?" Urota asked.

Ayrah had chosen to wear some of Urota's spare clothes for the Gya championship that evening. Purple fabrics—lightweight, see through, and scratchy sounding when rubbed between forefinger and thumb—fell loose over her shoulders and down her rib cage. Over that she wore a leather vest tight against her breasts. Below that a red silk sash wound the fabric tight against her hips. Rubies bedazzled across her back in the symbol of Tamagai's insignia—a coiled serpent, eating its tail, with five daggers jabbed through its back meeting in the middle at a point.

"I feel like a Masikonian whore."

Urota forced a laugh. "Aye. Their eyes are tailored." Her clothes looked little more than shiny undergarments. Her sandals had a leather band around her big toe, and strings of the same leather wound from the back ankle of her sandal all the way up to her mid-calves like lace.

Ayrah had picked the most modest outfit she could find among Urota's closet. The girl's name meant "Dying Winter" in a lost Sigu Nii language, before Common Aylan took over Zoë. But she was hot, all the way down to her Tamagai insignia painted red across her arse.

As Urota led them south through the city, Pratuel's architecture changed. The sparkling wood and cobblestone, which Ayrah now guessed was something of a local resource, was still prevalent. Most of Pratuel's buildings had sharp corners and flat tiled roofs. They stacked on one another as the foothills of mount Tamagai spread through the city. Farther on, houses and shops were egg-shaped with roof peaks that resembled an onion or a lick of flame. Colors were deep-ocean blues and emerald greens.

The roads narrowed as well, and horse-drawn carriages had to squeeze through. "Where are we?" Ayrah asked. The commoners of this strange Pratuelian district wore clothes as ornate as their buildings. Golden rings on multi-colored hands. Velvet dresses, dyed in sporadic colors with gold and sapphire seams.

"Little Mas. It's a Masikonian ghetto, where foreigners come in search of their own coin." Urota did little to hide intrigue in her voice. "I come here for clothes and wines. And oh, the men here are wild."

Ayrah watched one of them, a Masikonian, whose hair went from a blindingly vibrant pink, and changed quite suddenly to a dark blue. "I guess I could use new clothes."

Urota hummed in thought. "Maybe after Sehlya. We don't quite have time for all of that today."

Ayrah sighed with relief.

Even here Urota was known by name. And the grand Tamagai insignia across Ayrah's back turned heads. Eyes lit up in delight. Lips curled into ovals. Suddenly, the foreigners swarmed them. "Autograph!" Parchment and quills were shoved into Urota's hands. "Good luck tonight, El."

Ayrah's blood boiled. Elbows nudged against her ribs. Her sandals were stepped on. She even watched a Masikonian hand, splotches of pale and tan, dart out and grab at her see-through fabric and dark-leather seams. "No, you don't." One moment she was covering her breasts, the next, the veins in her arms turned black.

The Masikonian crowd watched her change. Before Ayrah's black-ice-blade even fit in her palm, the foreigners backed off several steps, fear in their eyes, ready to sprint for their lives.

Urota laid a gentle hand on Ayrah's shoulder. "Thank you, all!" She waved. "But we must be going." Her hand gripped a wee tighter and guided Ayrah through the parting crowd. She led them into a dome-like building. A wooden sign hanging from an iron frame read: Mutations.

"Ayrah, they were exalting you. No need to get defensive."

"I just . . ." Ayrah's voice caught. Urota was right. Glory was all-sought. Why did her stomach turn so?

"No worries." Urota did something of a sigh. "Kizmaldi gets the same way when we pass through here. I think he prefers something a little more . . ." Her hand waved in circles as she thought. "Fear-like."

"Hello!" called a man rising from a stool.

The building's inside was lacquered hardwood floors, red painted baseboards and ceiling moldings. It was a calm solace from all the vibrance outside.

"Urota! It's good to see you again. And you've brought a friend. Oh, darling, how sweet. What's your name?"

Ayrah's eyes scanned this person. He was a man, but his voice fluctuated like that of a young girl. His pure-silk button shirt had the top four buttons undone, so that she could see his rippling pecs, moisturized, and shaved clean of hair. His hands never strayed far from his chest, even as he waved them while he talked.

"Ayrah V-v—" She stuttered. "Shadowa."

The Masikonian's brows scrunched, "I think I've seen your posters."

"This," said Urota, "is Ayrah Veligreen."

His hand, pure golden Sigu Nii skin tone, covered his gasping mouth. "So the girl is alive? Oh, don't look like that, darling. I'm nothing but a money-fueled mutator. I won't tell *any-one.*"

"A mutator?"

"She doesn't know?" He glanced at Urota.

Urota smiled and shrugged.

"Well! Let—me—just—" He rummaged through a paper pile on his granite countertop and handed her a thin paper pamphlet. "Here! Look through this."

Urota whined, "When are you going to just move in Castle Tamagai with us? Think of the honor! You would be the *exclusive* mutator for. . . Errta, Urota," She fluttered her eyelids. "Even Kizmaldi Tuio! Think of it!"

Ayrah flipped through, staring at collages of hand drawn pictures on each page. There were faces with thin golden wires embedded into cheeks. Hair with radiant colors, some pure, some assorted, some with strips of silver. Then there were breasts and butts, with clear implications of enlargement or shaping.

"You know me, darling." He replied, "I ain't exclusive to no one."

Ayrah felt her throat constrict. "Uhm . . ." She gulped. "You can put these on me?"

The Masikonian laughed, it was a high-pitched laugh like Ecanaes', but more squealy than nerdy. "I wouldn't say *on*. But yes, you get the picture."

Ayrah twirled her hair. The thin dreadlocks hanging from the front-left side of her head rolled between her fingers. It used to be auburn—heck, it used to be red! If you looked closely, you could see the previous color bounce off the black, in the right light. She wasn't sure why it was changing. Figured she was just growing out of it. Suits her right. It should just be black. "Do you have anything that would help in a Niiwa?" she asked.

"Straight to the power stuff, mmm?" He turned back to his counter and gave her the first pamphlet off the top.

This was more like it. Pictures of tiger claws, a cat's slitted pupils, bone-restructuring, fanged teeth, an entire page of assorted muscle refinement like calves and biceps, ear shaping and animal nose adaptations.

Ayrah turned the pamphlet toward him and pointed at the cat's eyes. "What would this do?"

"Oh, El Veligreen, you don't want those. That would be helpful for, say, a skull-ranked poacher down in Rya."

Ayrah's eyes raised. She'd never even been to the Rya province. This Masikonian must've been in Sigu Nii for some time.

"I'd love to suggest, darling, but you're not giving me much to work on. Let's start with this: How would you describe your style of fighting?"

Ayrah thought for a moment. "Agile." That was it. "Close-quarters."

The Masikonian grabbed a blank parchment and scribbled a list with his finger. "These?"

She looked at the list and read,

Full-body bone integrity enhancement
Full-body muscle refinement

Retina sharpening

Skin armor (category - animal)

"Is this dangerous?" She asked.

"Very." Answered the Masikonian. "In Aylavuera, they make you get a scholarly license to even practice on hair."

"Oh. So, you have one of those?"

"We're in Sigu Nii, darling."

"It's fine, Ayrah. I come here all the time. In Sehlya, you could face Ohaer. It's not just an advantage to have these, it's a disadvantage to not."

"Will it hurt?"

"A lot," said the Masikonian.

Ayrah thought. She sensed they were right. There seemed only one good choice. And she nodded.

"Follow me." He rounded the counter and parted a blue silk curtain in the back.

Urota followed.

Ayrah lingered half a moment and followed them. On the other side of the curtain, the walls were painted plain brown, and a single cot took the middle of the room.

"Lie there." The Masikonian sat on a wooden stool.

She sat on the metal edges of the brown hide skin cot and began to lie down.

"Ahht. Sorry, darling. Undress first."

"What?"

"Your clothes, take them off."

Ayrah clenched her teeth and told herself this man was more a girl than a man anyway. She undid her waist sash and vest and pulled her top from her shoulders. She untied her leather sandals and the red-ribbon-sash that wound around her calves, and let her trousers fall. Only her red underwear remained. "I'm leaving this on."

The Masikonian nodded. "It's fine."

Ayrah lay face up. The room felt drafty.

The Masikonian laid his hands on her right shin. She was sure she'd never felt hands as soft as his. Warmth began to radiate from them and crept into her bones. He stroked his hands between her knee and her ankle. Her right leg turned hot. Itchy. Her leg began to hurt, a soft aching pain, like the splintering of her shins when she was younger.

Crrrk! Ayrah's right leg cracked, loud enough for everyone in the room to hear. She bit down on her teeth. Hard. Dark-black-ice coated her arms from her fists to her elbows.

"Give her that piece over there!" he yelled at Urota. "Before we have to work on her teeth too."

Urota fit a thin strap of leather in Ayrah's mouth. *Get this thing out of my face!* was her first instinct. But bit it she did, as her leg cracked and throbbed with pain.

The Masikonian's pupils thinned like a cat's eyes as he leaned in. He scanned her leg. The man nodded and scooted his stool down to the end of the cot. With his soft warm hands he massaged her right foot. Warmth spread between her toes, the arch of her foot, dulling the pain completely from her shin. A soft "Oh," escaped her.

Crrrk! Her foot snapped. Two dozen bones cracked and shifted. Ayrah nearly felt her teeth touch between the strap of leather. Muscles and tendons all yanked and made way for her sudden out-of-place anatomy.

The Masikonian's eyes dilated and slitted back and forth as he examined her leg. Everything beneath her knee. He nodded and moved his stool around to her other side.

"Oh," Ayrah said again, but not out of pleasure. She had half-a-mind to tell him to piss off.

They went through the same two-round routine again. First her left shin, then her foot. He inspected them both with his magnifying eyes. He felt them with his baby-soft hands, which both massaged some of the pain away and surfaced the soreness of her re-formed lower legs.

Then he moved to her thighs. He did them the same way one at a time. Then her hips, which nearly caused Ayrah to swat him away with ice-gloved-fists when his hands wandered. The Masikonian reformed her ribcage, her chest, her shoulders, arms and elbows, hands, and neck. The most painful of them all surely being the last. She thought she would never get up from that cot. Any movement of her head felt like vipers' venom shooting down her spine.

"The bone integrity enhancement is complete," said the Masikonian. "Taking punches, sword-flats, blunt weapons, anything of that sort, darling, will be *grandly* less fatal."

Ayrah began to fit her elbows beneath her.

"Ahht." He grabbed her shoulder and eased her back down. "Now for muscle refinement, darling."

21

EIDHIN

Each of the twelve wooden desks had scratch marks from students fidgeting their nails into the wood or quills jamming through parchment paper. The lacquer on the seats was faded from use. Each desk appeared meticulously placed and distanced from one another. Three days had passed since Eidhin arrived at the School of Rai and played the Aylan-board against Sor'al.

Eidhin had been told his classmates were of similar orientations— new. But a quick glance around the room suggested otherwise. The other eleven all had thick scrolls, and they scribbled away furiously, as if El Sor'al's words were to be captured with continual urgency.

They were the crash and foam on a shipwreck of fading varnish. Their uniforms were long finely crafted robes of blue and white.

Eidhin's classmates would remain mostly the same throughout his graduation track, with some moving around as learning speeds developed gaps. New teachers would rotate through classrooms, delving the entire classroom into a single topic for one memorable, strenuous forecast after the other.

"Most of you will be on graduation tracks of two seasons," El Sor'al announced. "Some of you might find your way from here sooner, others later."

Heads shifted to the far-right side of the room. "Ecagaus," some of the students whispered in a good-for-you sort of tone.

"By a show of hands, how many of you have engaged with animals? Whether it be horses, dogs, farm animals, insects, etcetera. And I don't mean simply encountered but have actually spent time with, in one way or another."

Eidhin raised his hand and peered round the room. All but two hands were raised.

"Perhaps many of you have not had pets, like a dog, but it is the easiest example, so use your own apperception as necessary. Dogs are personable little creatures. Their emotions, though primitive, are malleable and observable. A single repeated event can shape its interaction with the world for the rest of its life. Forever. This is nurture.

"Humans are a gorgeously more complex species, yet the same principle applies. A single event can change the way you perceive the world. Forever. We will dive deep into how this happens, why this happens, and categorize influences great and small into possible outcomes.

"For your homework, each of you will receive a mouse from the tundra plains of D'shric-Ra'che. These little rodents are acclimated to our cooler weather, moderately stabilizing nature influences. A professor at House Biology's school in Vylandria has genetically modified an entire subspecies of these mice, with the help of Masikonian vuu, to reduce their lifespan to one day. These creatures are highly personable, with malleable and observable behaviors, like a dog. Each of you is responsible for being aware of how you treat it and how its behaviors reflect that treatment. We will convene back in this classroom at the appointed time, after the death of most of your mice, and discuss our observations. Any questions?"

A squeaky cart rolled into the classroom. Sor'al El flung a frayed tapestry from the top to reveal a cage full of near-infant white and grey mice.

"What are you going to name yours?" a student leaned in and asked Ecagaus.

"Oh!" A girl in the back squirmed and covered her face in her hands. Another student squeaked, pretending to be a mouse himself.

One by one, each student picked out their one-day-lifespan mouse and exited the classroom. Some of the students hardly adjusted their pace past the cage as they scooped up a mouse and continued on their way. Others gave each mouse an inspection and picked one that suited their fancy, whether by temperament or cuteness. Some held the mouse at arm's distance, flailing their tongues. Others touched noses or made a home in their white-robe pocket.

Eidhin paused by the cage of the six remaining mice. As per Sor'al El's instruction, Eidhin thought about his choice. Not which mouse he would pick. They were mice. That decision would hardly matter. But of how he would treat this mouse. The tenderness with which he would pick this little rodent from its brothers and sisters, and the attendance and nurturing way he would carry the creature around.

He decided, with a near spiteful recognition, that he would treat his mouse with more care than he felt he had ever been dealt. He would call his mouse Jillao, deriving from his oldest brother, who by now was most likely running the finer parts of their family farm.

Behind the worn steps of the staircase on the bottom floor was the cafeteria. A hundred cotton blends of white and blue all gathering around the dark, waxed wood of two dozen cafeteria tables. The setting sun rays fractured through the beveled glass windows.

Of a hundred students gathering, Eidhin could hear the squeaky squeal from his twelve classmates' mice.

Socially hindered as he was, he hated this game. Peering about the tables, analyzing who might talk to him and who might ridicule his lame tongue. Eidhin looked for his flat mate, Ecagaus. He spotted the student elbowing Seraii, one of the two girls who had not engaged with animals, which showed quite clearly as she handed Ecagaus her mouse hanging by its tail.

Eidhin joined them with a grimace, and hoped he was not denying Ecagaus the finer quest of romance.

"Eidhin!" Ecagaus greeted him with a jaw-clenched smile.

Servants clad in black gentlemen suits, with white aprons tied around their waists began setting plates and silverware. Their movements appeared automatic. Their eyes stuck to single points of interest. Rumor had it these were previous students who had graduated early. Too early.

"What's his deal?" Seraii asked, nodding at Eidhin, who was fixated on the servants.

He couldn't be blamed. The brown-leaf servants were leagues more interesting than getting cut-short three letters into a sentence. Well, one letter, repeated three times.

"His words don't work," Ecagaus answered, with a voice caught between solemn and tease. "Never mind him. Pretend like he's not even there. Continue about your namesake."

Seraii turned back to Ecagaus with her eyes lingering on Eidhin. "Uhm. Indeed. Uhm. Right. Anyway, great-grandmother Seraii came to Aylavuera in the Ar'lm cluster. She was fascinated with the architecture and our vuu, though I think she was more scared of dying than anything else. It was near the end of her big fighting career thing, and my mom says she wouldn't have made it much longer anyway. Supposedly, great-grandmother Seraii could have become some type of Lord Mayor, but it wasn't her fancy."

"That's intriguing," Ecagaus said in awe.

Indeed, Eidhin was paying attention too.

"So, do you have Sigu Nii vuu?" Ecagaus asked.

Seraii scrunched her nose and held her hands straining above the table. They wiggled a bit. "Nope." She giggled and let her hands down.

A servant wheeled a cart up to their table and passed plates down the rows. Eidhin eyed the servant, but the man's gaze was focused on the table. He looked like one of the horses that had absent-mindedly pulled the coach from Snowstock to Gehni.

"Maybe he's afraid he'll become one of them," Seraii whispered to Ecagaus.

Eidhin was sure that Ecagaus' chuckle was of the polite sort.

The dish was a salmon-steak, with a sauce of squeezed lemon and butter, three stalks of asparagus baked in spices, and a spoonful of salted peas. A more savory meal than Eidhin had ever eaten on the farm.

Eidhin pulled Jillao out from his robe pocket and set him on the table. The mouse was much the same size, though its whiskers were longer, its tail sturdier, and its fur coat had turned coarse. Jillao squeaked, itched its nose, and scurried toward the plate.

Seraii gurgled in disgust. And when her own mouse squeaked and attempted to eat from her plate, she swatted the thing away with a half-hearted backhand.

Her mouse squealed—a scream for its size. It turned to Jillao and Eidhin and crept cautiously across the table, pausing every few moments, wary of another backhand.

It crept up behind Jillao. Eidhin watched it, thinking how he did not care for this mouse. This mouse was not his. He had no emotional attachment to the thing. With his forefinger, he nudged the little critter away.

But it returned. The smells were too much to resist. As Eidhin thought about it, this was likely their first meal.

Seraii's little mouse crept behind Jillao and then leapt. Jillao squealed. They tumbled, their little claws digging into each other.

"Stop them!" Seraii clumsily rose, her hands waving in front of her face.

Eidhin's lips pressed flat. He wished Seraii would just take care of her own mouse. *Does she not understand the homework? Her little mouse is already becoming a nuisance because of her lack of nurture—her negative nurture.*

Eidhin reached into the mouse fight, plucked them apart, and set Jillao back into his robe.

Specks of mouse blood soaked through his white pocket.

Jillao acted differently after that. After dinner Eidhin took him to their room, bandaged him with thin cloth, and joined a gathering crowd on the rooftop. He could feel his mouse shivering at times, sometimes scurrying around the deep pocket.

The last pink-red rays of the departing sun illuminated Gehni's cobblestone streets and whitestone buildings. To the north, a blue expanse extended to the horizon. The Spar'adian Sea. Eidhin wasn't educated in geography, and until he saw the vast blueness, he had not even realized how close to the ocean he was.

Oil wick lanterns replaced the sun and hung from rafters of gazebos covered in ivy and jasmine. Ecagaus and another student sat on rain-stained wooden chairs beneath the gazebo, playing a crowd-intensive game of Aylan-board.

Ecagaus' mouse had drooping whiskers and a wrinkled tail that whipped around in confidence. It sat on Biology's space of the board, as if he were a player.

"Untrue," said the other player, aloud.

A guilty smile swept Ecagaus' face, followed by a shrug. "Your move."

Eidhin's eyes darted back and forth. They played audibly? He wondered whether it was a manner of people pleasing or a matter of lacking vuu.

Both players sat one space away from the center kingship spot. And the inter-class audience gradually crept tighter and closer to the board with each round.

Ecagaus played History, and said, "King Samuel Gehn's fifth generation great-grandfather won the crown from the Vylndaer bloodline off a
game."

His mouse pattered across the board and nibbled on Ecagaus' piece.
Eidhin studied the other student's face. He did not know the answer. His
eyebrows were crumpled and his nose scrunched, his shoulders rolled as
he turned to the varnished gazebo.

Say untrue. It was the safest answer. Figure Ecagaus was assuming his
final move to kingship. The claim held many possibilities for fallacy—the
chronology, the bloodline, and the game.

"Untrue." He leaned forward, waiting for the answer. "Well?"

Ecagaus plucked his piece from the mouse and moved it to the center.
The mouse squealed and tackled the wooden History figure.

Eidhin could feel Jillao shiver and scurry in discomfort. He assumed it
was provoked by the mouse's squeal. He took note of this while the others
praised Ecagaus for his victory.

Seraii's temperament had affected her mouse, which in turn influenced Jillao. Eidhin had assumed that he would be the one to influence
Jillao, but as the rooftop began to clear for the night, it seemed the biggest
event, and thus influence, in Jillao's short lifespan had come from this
unforeseen source.

Jillao died during the night. His white-fur coat had thinned to bare
skin from his hindlegs to his tail. His bandages were still wet when Eidhin
woke the next morning, and he blamed Seraii. Eidhin had planned to give
that mouse the best day possible, but by the end, he died shivering and
afraid.

"I hope after day-last, you can relate to the hardships of influence." El
Sor'al passed from one side of the classroom to the other, his hands folded
behind his back as he spoke. "You wish to be gentle, but roughness arises.
You wish to be careful but difficulties come. Each of these affected your

mouse in ways you had not anticipated. The vast variables in the world that have shaped each of you in turn shaped your mice. And the shaping of your peers shaped their mice. Which still, continues to pass along the authority to mold."

The words sank deep for Eidhin.

"The Illyadra have more than a rudimentary understanding of these things. The factors at play are wider than we could possibly cover in a single rainfall. I respect their grand authority and their supervision and intervention on our societal behalf in order to determine the best influences each of us are exposed to at specific moments of our lives. Most of you have not yet heard this information because it is a studious place like this where this knowledge is guarded. The six people of the Illyadran Council, the smartest in all of Zoë, direct our society with careful adjustments. As well they should."

Sor'al El paused. Every student was still.

"It is possible to be *so* intentional in how you affect each personal, moral, or ecological event you encounter. But the difficulty and brain space that is required goes well beyond any one of you. I urge you to consider an alternative. Release yourselves from influencing. Sacrifice what it means to radiate yourself onto others. Be still. Be quiet. And most of all, let your eyes begin to gloss over the unimportant."

22

RAVID

"Wait!" he hollered, holding his hands out in retreat. A single level-three was enough to frighten his whole Renovian squadron. Here, two sprung fire from their palms, facing his lonesome.

"It's your bloody coin." Spat the northern guard. "Warlord El Rai Ezs is finding it increasingly tiresome, having to rid his colonies of forgeries. Especially when it's *your* bloody coin! Prepare to grash." He lowered into a fighting stance.

"It wasn't me!" Kairo pleaded. They weren't listening. A ball of bright orange fire exploded toward him. Kairo's knees buckled and it whistled overhead, its smoking coattails lingered in the air.

"Ready the splitter," said the fighting guard to the one behind Kairo. "This one'll be easy."

He was talking about the big wooden X. Kairo rubbed the top of his head, desperately wanting it to remain in one piece. He felt a bubble pop under his hand. Then he saw another pop on his forearm. He hollered as pain enveloped him. His skull cracked and shifted. His eyes slanted back. And his skin boiled, top down, returning him to the Renovian ethnicity.

He had begun to run from this moment. But now, it probably saved him. The approaching Black Guard straightened, confused. "Hey! Wait, you're Renovian!"

"Aye," said the other. "He must 'ave a Masikonian El 'round here, somewhere."

"El is a title—" Began Kairo, but he was interrupted as ice sprung around his limbs, binding him stationary. The guard came up and drug him by the wrists toward the Warlord's Office. "It'll be the mines of Ravid for you."

Kairo squeezed his hands around the cold metal bars. He could make out slight, faded black stains of blood around the cell. Short wooden planks made up the wall behind him and to his left. Metal bars made up the walls in front of him and separated two other cells to his right.

This was Aterah's cell. That was Aterah's blood. He was one step behind her. And now she was behind hauled off to the Warlord.

Where was Arden? Why had the man-with-stone-tattoos not come and rescued him yet?

The ceiling thudded with footsteps, and dust sprinkled down from above. A figure appeared in the threshold.

There he was. Kairo put his face against the bars. "Over here—"

A soldier in full leather armor stepped cautiously down the stairs. A flame no larger than the lick of a candle popped up before his cell. Kairo flinched at the sudden vuu.

"Back." The soldier's voice was quiet.

Kairo didn't move.

Black-and-gold painted studs shone across his torso. "Back!" The guard grabbed hold of the cage with a rippling hand of neon blue electric vuu. The metal bars lit up and zapped, bright orange sparks exploded where Kairo's cheeks and hands had been.

Kairo hollered in pain as he flinched backward, hitting his head against the hard wooden floorboards. He wanted to lay there a moment and hold his face. But he pushed himself back to the far wall of the cell with urgent strokes. "Whe—" He heaved and coughed. "Where did you take her?"

"Renovian filth," the guard spat. He fiddled around his belt, found a key, and opened the cell door.

Kairo glanced at his hands. He had forgotten briefly which skin he currently adorned. Thinking back on it, he was sure that the Sigu Nii were going to kill him. It was only when Arden ceased vuu did they hesitate. Now he was a prisoner. He supposed it was better than dead, but if he didn't escape soon, the infection would have him anyways.

Hard, harsh hands grabbed him by the arms and lifted him to his feet. With Kairo's right arm under his grasp, the guard dragged him from the cage. They went up the stairs, through the Warlord's Office, and out into the dirt courtyard of Yutarah.

The sun was blinding, and he closed his eyes, stumbling along until he slowly got used to the brightness. Not even half the density of smoke polluted the skies this day, and the sun reflected harshly against the tan, sun-scorched dirt.

They made their way around the Niiwa arena and headed north through the busy Sigu Nii trails. Kairo peered through war-tribes and around corners of tents, expecting to see Arden waiting for him, but he was never there.

Sigu Nii tribes packed away their cream hide skin tents. Dozens of Sigu Nii wearing full knapsacks headed the same direction as Kairo and his captor.

Eventually, they reached the northern edge of Yutarah. Flattened, dead grass marked where previous war camps had been. Beyond Yutarah's edge, there was nothing but yellow grass and an occasional rolling hill. Kairo and the soldier stood at the end of a trail where horse-drawn wagons filled with barrels and crates pulled up to a wooden pavilion, and sweaty, inkless Sigu Nii tirelessly unloaded.

"Yutarah isn't the end to Sigu Nii, boy." Arden's voice echoed in Kairo's mind. It finally dawned on him. Yutarah was a mere outpost, with others like it, and a central hub of some sorts behind it. Horse-drawn wagons came from somewhere beyond, farmlands untouched by war, to feed their outpost. It was just like NeoDerii.

The Black Guard pulled Kairo past a large stable, with horses munching on hay. A dozen steps out from the stables, a line of people sat with their knees in the dirt and their hands bound before them. Dirt clung to them heavily, and their linens were tattered and patchy. Their skin was a dark sunset color. Kairo's eyes lit up. It felt like it had been ages since he had seen his own people.

"Here's another." the guard shoved Kairo down, and his knees scraped in the dirt. The line of bound Renovians all turned to look at him. Pity was in their eyes. Blood was on their arms, faces, and legs. They were skinny— starved, even. Kairo didn't recognize any of their faces. They were from different outposts than NeoDerii.

Each of them had been captured by a Sigu Nii tribe and dragged all the way out here. They still wore the old, weathered, tattered linens available to the rebellion. Kairo thought he must have looked funny, wearing Sigu Nii boots and leather and cottons.

"El." A level-two Sigu Nii handed something to the Black Guard, a glint of polished metal shining briefly between fingers. With that, the Black Guard turned and left.

"Horses are fed and the saddles are packed." Another Sigu Nii came up beside them. He was scrawnier than the first, a level-one tattoo across his shoulder. He drew two horses around the front of the line.

"Tie the prisoners, and we'll be on our way."

"El." The dagger-ranked soldier pulled out a long rope. He came around to Kairo and tied his wrists tightly against each other. He drew a longer rope around that knot and weaved it around each pair of bound hands in the line.

The level-two, flame-ranked Sigu Nii, mounted one of the horses as the other tied the rope to his own saddle and mounted. "Up!"

The Renovians hesitated, then scrambled to get to their feet, but the horse started, and the rope snapped taught.

Kairo stumbled, trying to make his feet move with the horse's gait and the line of fumbling Renovians.

Grass and slight rolling hills passed around them as they walked along one dirt rut of the wagon trail. He waited for Arden's mop of dreads to come peeking over something or another. And the rear view of Yutarah was eventually blocked by a grassy hill.

He realized, this would have been it. Aterah's pleading was for the present moment. Kairo and Arden could have taken Verano here.

They continued on as the sun dipped beneath the horizon, walking into the twilight. Kairo turned his eyes upward at the brightest of stars that appeared through the dimming sky. *Korta Ellanii. Help me. What am I to do?*

Kairo's throat choked in dry swallows, and his lips weren't far from bleeding.

A wave of unsettlement washed over the Renovian line as darkness enveloped the world. Kairo's eyes swept the horizon of rolling hills around him. It was bad enough that there were not any trees to block line of sight, but at night? The snagaeri would devour them.

The Sigu Nii must have seen the shivering prisoners, or they walked this route often enough to know what they were thinking, because the level-two growled, "Quit yur pissin'. The snagaeri only chase Renovians, right? Well, there aren't enough Renovians out here for them to spawn in the night. So quit yur pissin'."

The unsettlement lifting from the line of Renovians was a visible wave.

Another handful of moments later and the Sigu Nii yawned, "Alright." He slowed his horse to a stop. Kairo sighed in exhaustion, along with all the others. The two Sigu Nii hopped off their horses with a thud in the dirt.

The flame-ranked soldier handed the first in line a canteen of water. The Renovian drank heartily, the rest of them eyed him, groaning softly for just a sip. "That's enough." The soldier snatched the canteen and handed it to the next in line.

Kairo stepped out to peer down the Renovians. *Ten.* There would hardly be any left for him.

"That's enough." The soldier snatched the canteen and handed it to the next in line. Down it went, until the sweet water made it to the one before Kairo. He drank heartily. "That's enough." The soldier reached for the canteen, but the Renovian flinched backward and kept drinking. "That's enough!" Small thin lines of electric vuu sparked around his hand, and he jabbed the Renovian, who screamed in pain as his knees buckled and the hide skin canteen dropped to the ground.

Kairo leapt for it, watching the greedy ground soak up all his water. His hands wrapped around it, and he lifted it upright as fast as he could. But it was empty. He fit the nuzzle to his mouth, but only a few drops of water ran over his lips.

The Sigu Nii soldier huffed and took back the canteen. Kairo pleaded for another as he went back to his horse, but he fit the canteen in a satchel and turned to his fellow soldier. The other was laying two woolen blankets on the ground on either side of a small grass-fed fire.

The line around Kairo's wrists was painfully taught as the Renovian beside him remained kneeling on the ground. Kairo eyed him, disdain boiling within. After a moment, he joined the ground as well. Moaning with sore muscles as his rear found rest.

One Sigu Nii pulled a scaly serpent over the fire and watched as it cooked and filled the trail with its savory aroma. Surely, they could feel the eyes of a dozen captives on them and their meal.

A snake. Revolt compiled within him. What a morally foul creature to consume.

Once Kairo's mind lifted from his aches, his sore feet and legs, his groaning stomach, and his desperate thirst, sleep washed over him. His worldly conscious pains were only replaced by those unseen.

He dreamt of Verano and Aterah. He watched as Aterah's eyes slipped closed, the night surrounding her. Mumbles of speech slipped her lips, and her eyelids fluttered from whatever dream she was dreaming. Kairo tried to yell, but Aterah could not hear him. Verano eased himself over Aterah, placed his ear against her mouth and nodded in understanding. Verano reached around to a dead body beside them. Kairo hadn't seen it before. It was Adakon. Adakon lay dead beside them, his blood seeping into the grass they lay on. Verano dipped three fingers into the wound that had killed the famed general, and gently marked Aterah's face. He drew runes, words of Old Vulgarhe that Kairo couldn't understand. After a moment, Aterah's face was completely covered with the blood of their Renovian leader.

And then Kairo woke. The hunger and thirst of his physical body came rushing back.

With the demanding schedule of the sun at NeoDerii, and the sna- gaeri that came at twilight, Kairo used to feel that there was never enough time in a day. Each time he came close to accomplishing anything, *bam*, the day was over, and it was time for curfew.

On this trail in the middle of nowhere, it was the opposite. Each day had *so* many moments, all of them relentlessly filled with walking. On- ward they walked, northwest. The ankle-high yellow grass turned green, growing past Kairo's head. Boulders jutted from the ground and slowly began to litter the rolling hills around them.

Days passed by. It was difficult to keep track of how many, they all bled together. Nothing kept them apart, it was the same walking each day. They passed a small creek once, which was erotic for all the captives. They drank and drank, and they wallowed in the water to clean and cool themselves.

Kairo stopped the group on a couple of occasions, when his neck tensed up and his stomach spasmed. Each time he collapsed to the ground to grab his aching ligaments, and the wince staining his face let all the others know: he was going to die.

The level-two Sigu Nii cursed aloud. "He's infected! We can't sell the warden of Ravid a dying a prisoner!"

"He'd kill us." Agreed the level-one.

The first groaned, pondering further action, but made none apparent.

The Sigu Nii starved the lot of them. Each night Kairo watched them eat some other critter, a rodent, a reptile, salted pork. Not once did they offer a single bite to any of the prisoners. By the last day, it took everything in him to not fall over with each step.

Finally, they reached their looming destination. Massive stone walls rose on the side of a rolling hill. They were the tallest thing Kairo had ever seen, comparable to the height of Renovia's jungle canopy. Several hundred reaches high with thick cracks and black-green stains.

"What—What *is* that?" Kairo asked, unable to take his eyes off the walls. It seemed they stretched around a great circular distance.

Kairo was well acquainted with the back view of the Renovian before him. For days, oftentimes the only sight to look at was the bobbing head and peppering hair in front of him. So Kairo's eyes automatically darted forward when the Renovian turned. "You don't know this place?" He snarled. "This prison has kept our people for twenty-six generations." His head turned away. "I never thought I'd see Ravid again." His voice sounded as dry and weak as Kairo felt.

"Ravid," Kairo repeated. He had heard stories about it, one of the twelve prison cities. It was the third of the walled cities to be freed, to be broken by Adakon. It was where Commander Lezyne was born, if he remembered correctly. Here it was again, its walls towering over the grassy plains. And here he was with a handful of Renovians being dragged back into it in chains.

The grey stone seemed to grow darker as the sun lowered behind the walls, and the walls looked ever higher as the prisoners approached them. They came up to massive doors of solid black metal, fifteen reaches high and eight steps wide. Four Sigu Nii guards with wooden spears stood beside each other, facing the grassy hills.

"Eleven captures," said one of the men who had dragged them through the plains. The guards nodded and pulled levers on each side of the doors. Loud metal clanking boomed from between the stone walls. The great black doors slowly creaked open.

The group continued.

A nose-stuffing aroma blasted through the doors as they opened. Like rotten pork, churned dung, and roasting hair. Kairo gagged.

This was Ravid? The light tan dirt of the trail turned to light grey crumbling gravel. Bits of broken metal, wood, and dirt crunched under Kairo's stolen boots. Everywhere he turned, the walls towered over them. The sun was just departing beneath the far wall, which cast a great shadow over half of the city.

Ruins of stone buildings lay to either side of the gravel road. Only the outlines remained. A lone wall with a window, crumbling boulders that were once walls, and wooden framing peaking up beneath the wreckage. New, small shelters had been made out of the wreckage, flimsy sheets for walls and roofs. Metal grates and wire strewn between the buildings made pushed tight alleyways.

Trash and dung piled a story high along the gravel trail. A mountain of filth. Rats scurried about the pile. To either side of the trail were small gutters, trickling with black-green water.

Kairo couldn't believe this was where his people had come from. How long they had been held captive, and how there wasn't an Adakon to rise among them sooner.

The group passed beneath the shade as they approached the back wall where there was a hole in the ground, ten steps in diameter. It led down, under the wall of the city. Torches were stationed around, as well as wooden racks holding tools.

To the left of the hole stood a light-colored brick building. The only one that was fully intact anywhere in sight. Candle-lit windows shone out from the first and second floors.

A small group of Sigu Nii soldiers waited in a half circle between the building and the hole. They watched as Kairo's group of prisoners approached.

"Welcome back to Ravid. Make your way into the Stonehouse. Meals and rooms are prepared for both of you. I'll come by later to discuss price."

"El." The two Sigu Nii who had dragged Kairo through the plains nodded in appreciation and made off toward the brick building. One glanced back at Kairo uneasily, then the war-chief, and shrugged wearily. They disappeared into the Stonehouse.

Two Sigu Nii soldiers came around and pushed the line of prisoners parallel to the wall so that each of them faced the hole in the ground and three other Sigu Nii.

The one who had spoken wore a red button-up with patterns of black woven in and a long black leather jacket. Both were crafted to leave a hole above the left shoulder. His shoulder-length hair was black, cheekbones hard and high, and a mustache sprouted from his upper lip on either side of his nose. The other two wore studded leather, and bright shiny blades decorated their hips.

"You all must be hungry," Ravid's war-chief said.

None of them answered.

"Well?" He screamed. He thrust his hands forward and torso sized spikes of ice ripped out of the ground, each of them with a sharp point that stopped just before their necks.

Kairo flinched back, stumbling over his feet. He would have caught himself, but one of the other Renovians fell flat on the ground, pulling them all to the ground.

The war-chief laughed. "You all are going to be here for a very, *very* long time. One thing you best learn quick, is I'm as good as Warlord within these walls." He gestured to the towering imprisonment. "In here, I'm your Adakon." He twisted his body around, so that his left shoulder faced all of them. A clear four-piece serpent, with an inscription written beneath that read: *Vasara*.

The two Sigu Nii guards came around and cut their rope bindings.

"Every morning, guards will be stationed around the mine entrance. They'll hand you pickaxes as you enter and take them as you leave. With every stone's worth of hellinite that you find and deliver, you'll be given a food card. You can take that food card to the Stonehouse," He gestured to the only standing building in Ravid. "And they will give you food to eat and water to drink." He waved the group off and began turning toward the Stonehouse.

"Where are we supposed to go?" one of the Renovians called out to the war chief.

"Wherever you want."

Kairo looked around and massaged his wrists. They were raw and sticky. It felt weird to be a prisoner and allowed so much freedom. But it made sense. They were all starving.

Kairo walked back down the gravel trail along the gutter of sloshy green water. He was already beginning to get used to the smell of the place—an unnerving feeling.

Adakon began circling his mind. How he freed thousands of people from this place, and ten and two-half others like it. How did he do it?

How did he sneak in? How did he unite everyone? For twenty-six generations this was the wretched home for his people. Two had since passed. Few people were old enough to remember the troubles of this place.

Except for those now brought back. Here Kairo was, in the prison that no longer kept his people.

His mind turned to Aterah.

Two weeks had passed since the night of the raid. Two weeks of relentlessly chasing her through snagaeri-bound jungle, and Sigu Nii-taken lands. All to end up behind walls too high to climb, and too thick to break.

He felt stupid and helpless. He wished he could find a wall ready to collapse and lay beneath it.

How was she right now? It was hard to imagine. Soon Sigu Nii war leaders, *real* war leaders, would have their hands on her. As soon as they had an Oracle, they would know what has not yet come to pass. And once they did, Renovia and all the work Adakon had gone through would be wiped away.

Kairo's mind turned to Arden. He should have asked to stone man to stop drinking. Why had he been so irresponsible? Kairo kicked a rock down the street. Now he would die here.

Laughter pierced his thoughts. Kairo looked around. It sounded like a child. He didn't see anyone. It was getting dark, and he needed to find somewhere to sleep.

The laughter came again, high and soft. He walked around a heaping pile of trash. There sat a small boy, maybe a generation old, halfway atop the trash pile. Rats were scurrying all around him, nibbling at his fingers, and jumping across his lap. He giggled violently.

His hair was blindingly white, like Kairo had never seen before, though the short, curly locks were splashed with dirt.

"What are you doing?" Kairo asked.

The kid flinched, and he looked around in fear. Seeing only Kairo, he softened with relief. "Just playing." His voice was small and mumbled. He spoke gently but uncarefully. "Do you wanna play?"

A single chuckle of disbelief and uncertainty escaped Kairo. "Uhm . . . Sure."

The boy ruffled around the trash, moving so Kairo could have a place to sit.

Kairo eyed the place unsettled, he didn't want to go in there. There was dung, and hair, and piss, and dirty trash critters, but he had already agreed. Kairo tottered as he climbed the uneven ground and sat in the filth.

"So, what's your name?" the kid asked, his bright grey eyes shining wide in the dimming light.

"Kairo."

"Kairo . . . ?"

He didn't have a prison-city of origin. Neither did Aterah. Rouen had found them wandering through the jungles as small children. His gut felt hollow as he replied, "Just—just Kairo."

"That's okay. I don't have a last name either."

Little trash animals cautiously began sniffing at Kairo's side, and he instinctively drew his hand back. "What about you? What's your name?"

"Weksen." He smiled wide for a moment, but then his face fell. His lips pursed, and his brows scrunched in thought. "No, no, wait. We-Wes-Wesken. Wesken!" A violent giggle escaped him. "Dummy."

23

WESKEN

Sometime earlier.

The sun hung low over the Sea Masikonia. Wesken walked along a cliff that dropped hundreds of stretches into the ocean. His feet were getting sore, and his food had run out a few hours prior. He switched between enjoying the view of the long, jagged wall down and the ocean that stretched out beyond.

What's that up ahead? A voice asked in his head.

It looks like a ravine. The cliff angled inward to become a high, narrow abyss. Wesken walked to the edge and looked around. A small river cut through the bottom of the cliff, spilling its waters into the ocean. Thirty strides of empty space separated him from the other side. To his right, the ravine stretched beyond the hills.

Then he saw bit of material swaying in the wind, calling to his eyes from far away.

Is that a bridge?

Not just any bridge, a rope bridge! Wesken walked fast toward it. A thin layer of perspiration formed in the palm of his hands. The bridge extended all the way across the ravine and hung low in the middle. The rope was a dry green color, and wooden steps were missing or hanging. His heart palpated as he eased his foot onto the first rotting piece of wood.

The bridge swayed slightly with each step. He clung for life to the rope railing. Wesken tested his weight, easing himself carefully step by step.

Alright. This seems far enough. He turned to face the sea. The ravine walls on either side of him were above as he stood at the lowest hanging point. Dusty plant life clung to the cracks of the rocky tan walls. Wesken peered down over the rope rail, watching the river water race home. After a moment, he slid his knapsack from his shoulders and nudged it gently between two planks.

This is what, like a fatal height of like forty times over? Wesken asked giddily.

Do you want to die? another voice asked. It didn't sound like his own. It seemed feminine in pitch, but he couldn't place its owner.

Who are you? If you're concerned, then why aren't you here? His hands were good and sweaty, an unnerving feeling to think they might slip. He reached out and wrapped his fingers around the bottom rope that held the planks.

With only a moment's hesitation, Wesken flipped forward. He watched his knees fly in front of the horizon, his heart thundering. The rope bridge rocked hard from side to side as his body yanked it downward. His scabbard whapped against his thigh. His shoulders slumped up against his neck, and his feet dangled below him. He looked down. His mind felt like it raced an empty wagon. A sense of hyper alertness rushing through his veins.

How could anything be more neutrally exciting than this? Then he dropped his left hand, so that he dangled by his right. Wesken's pack shifted and eased its way between the planks. His eyes followed it the whole way down until it splashed in the river down below.

Whoops. Well, time to leave before that becomes foreshadowing. Wesken swung his left hand around and grabbed the rope above him. He muscled his way back up and walked the rest of the way across the bridge, less carefully this time.

I'm hungry, a voice nagged at him. He hated this one. It's always "*I'm hungry,*" or "*I'm tired,*" or "*I'm thirsty*" with him.

I know, me too. We should be up at a village after nightfall. The sun turned red as it began to blend with the sea.

How do you know? You lost your map in your stupidity.

I don't know. I just know we're supposed to head north, so north is where we'll go.

North where? Why are you even heading that way?

I don't know, okay? It's not like you're real anyways.

Well, that's not very nice.

Hush. Wesken shook his head. The cliff next to him began to lower as the ground he walked on took a slow descent. The land grew more luscious, grass began to sprout, and a wooded area came up on his right. He tried to remember people he knew, but no one came to mind. The only voices that started rising were his own.

You know, the only thing that would've made that ravine prettier, was if that red sun would've been there quicker.

And the only thing that would've made it more fun is if the rope would've snapped. Wesken laughed to himself. He couldn't help but enjoy the strangeness of the way he thought. Enjoying a pretty sunset but hoping for mortal danger at the same time.

As twilight turned to night, Wesken came upon a small moonlit cove. Fishing dinghies swayed gently in the water. A town rested at its crest, with a thin log fence wrapping around. He walked round the sandy shores, up to a gate in the fence that opened toward the sea. Two guards stood outside the entry. They held long spears, with rock-cut blades at the end.

"What's your business here, child?" One of them yelled at Wesken. They wore woolen clothing, covered with patched and unpatched holes. The other guard's brows lifted, as if he were awing at Wesken.

They're townsmen. Probably on some mandated shift to be here.

That means the town is poor.

Probably because they treat visitors like this. Wesken sniffed to clear his nose. "Just looking for a place to sleep and some bread to eat."

"We don't get too many newcomers 'round here," the first guard called back. His voice was harsh.

"You're right on the water, shouldn't this make a great port town?" Wesken's voice was soft. "You should be welcoming visitors!"

Just get the go ahead and mind your own business. No need to risk excitement where it's not necessary. There she was again. The voice of concern, though the word *excitement* was surely his own filtration.

Even though Wesken couldn't remember her, he knew that this voice, specifically, was the echo of someone he used to know.

"We used to be. . ." the second guard spoke up, his voice cracking from lack of use. He cleared his throat. "We used to be a good port city, but that was an age ago. The damn Sigu Nii burned us to the ground more than once in recent generations. They keep thinkin' we're hiding some of those filthy Renovians—"

"You're not Renovian are you?" The first guard interrupted, clearly worked up just by hearing the other.

"No, I'm coming from down south. Although, it seems like I might be headed that way." Wesken explained, and then pondered a little out loud. *I guess I am headed into war torn Renovia. That doesn't really make much sense, but it sounds like a good cure for boredom.*

"Into Renovia? You don't wanna be goin' that way. Nothin' but Sigu Nii killing, and Renovians gettin' killed up there. Best not to stick your neck in the middle of all that," the second guard warned. Wesken noticed he had gained his sympathy, or at least concern. The process seemed familiar, as if he had gained sympathy or concern many times before.

Why? Do I seem weak? Or is it just my age? He didn't care much for image preservation. He wondered if concern was something that could be routinely extracted.

"Well, what are you then, if not Renovian?" The first guard asked before Wesken could answer the previous question.

"Razite," Wesken lied. Truthfully, he didn't have any idea what his ethnicity was.

The first guard turned to the second. "You ever seen a Razite before?" The second shook his head. "Well, alright, I guess. Just don't cause any trouble!"

Wesken thanked him and started through the gate. The road was sloshy with mud. Horse tracks and footprints stirred the middle of the street. The houses around were all dark wood, with mixtures of planks and leaves for roofing. There weren't many people walking about, and those who were gave him no second glance. Shops and vendors and a small fish market were all closed for the night.

He continued through the town in search of an inn or tavern. He came to a handful of cobblestone steps, presumably reaching the more established part of town, where he found stone-trimmed buildings, wooden frames, and candlelit glass windows.

He found an old tavern.

"Ham pie, please. And a mug of your cheapest ale," Wesken asked the bartender as he sat at a table. The tavern was decently busy for the size of the town, although the sun hadn't been down long, so it was drinking time for the people there.

"Aren't you a little young for ale, son?" the server asked, making his voice audible past the bar. A few of the men sitting at the counter turned to look at Wesken. They were greasy and sweaty from tilling fields or fishing under the open sun all day. Large, burly Masikonian men.

"Depends on what makes a person old, if it's the calendar, then maybe. But if it's the things you've done and been done to in life, I'm well of age."

The men at the bar laughed but Wesken could tell it worked for the server. He made a strange face of surprise and didn't respond. Wesken waited there for a few moments and conversation spun in his head.

Do other people think in this way? someone asked.

Depends. Is this just a way of thinking? Or is this a threshold for intelligence in any way?

Maybe you just got wacked on the head as a baby. Wesken chuckled aloud and silenced as the server approached the table.

"This is the best ale in all the North. You seem like you could use it," the server said, setting a full foaming mug down.

"Oh, I can't . . ." Wesken reached for a pouch tied to his belt, realizing he didn't know how much money he even had.

"Don't worry, I'll charge you for the cheap stuff," he said as he turned back to the counter.

Wesken thanked the man.

He thinks you're weak.

How do you know he's not just being nice?

No one's nice.

"The same sauce for an old rock." It was an old raspy voice, but his tone was light and upbeat. Wesken looked up to see an old man. He had long, dirty white hair, bald on top, and a scraggly beard. The man leaned heavily on a dark bamboo staff with strange bright markings all around.

"Grandpa!" Wesken shot up from his seat and hugged the old man.

"Rocks and dirt be soft on the back?" He smiled with crooked teeth through his beard. He grasped Wesken's shoulders after the embrace. His eyes were bright, iridescently grey, gazing intently at Wesken.

"I'm good! I feel like I haven't seen you in forever. Have you been busy?" Wesken asked excitedly. He couldn't quite place how long it had been since he'd seen him.

"If Neo had any Nii!" the old man nodded. "Has the white river bent under the mountain?"

"I—"

"Quit speakin' in tongues. None of that foreign talk," the bartender interrupted, setting two mugs of foaming ale between them. "You're in Masikus, you speak Common Aylan."

Wesken hadn't even realized they were speaking a different language. He thought about pondering the event further, but it seemed a lot to think about amidst the current conversation, so he shrugged it off instead. "I'm headed north, like you said. It seems I'll be in war-torn Renovia soon." He said that last bit with a touch of playful poke, hoping to stir a positive or negative reaction from the old man.

Grandpa nodded with a distant look in his eye. "There. . . is. . . a. . . wooden prince—ahht! Young. . . man. . ." Speaking Common Aylan was obviously painful for him. Wesken understood. It was a simple language compared to Old Vulgarhe. "The Kraussing of Moments—mmm, it rests. . . upon him."

Wesken's eyes widened. "Wow, grandpa! That's a lot more information than you typically share about my destiny. Normally you're all," he did a playful impersonation of the old man, which was like rasping repeated nonsense. Grandpa normally spoke cryptic, even in his native tongue.

Grandpa croaked chuckles. "You'd. . . forget."

Wesken shrugged and nodded.

"Neo has him a Nii—gift! A gift."

"Grandpa!" Wesken exclaimed. Presents from this man were always the best.

"From my own—blah! Here. . . this." He handed his black bamboo staff around the table.

"What? No! You can't give me that. You've had this since like, before I was born!"

"Much me before the white—Mmm! Yes. . . Have."

"Wow." Wesken nearly felt guilty instead of appreciation for how great a gift. "Thank you, grandpa."

Grandpa didn't hear him. His eyes were defocused, like he was looking at something very far away. "Go time." He stood from the table and looked at Wesken.

Wesken got up and embraced him in a goodbye hug. "When will I see you again?"

"Don't forget."

"Forget what?"

Grandpa pointed at the staff.

"Ope. Yeah." He nodded.

Grandpa hobbled off and thunder shook the tavern.

Wesken sat back down, sipped at his ale, and stared at the walking stick. *How do you trust one of most important things this side of Yeshwin to the most forgetful person across Zoë?*

Daydreams took him for several moments, and when his attention neared reality next, it was because the burly Masikonian men from the bar were standing around his table.

"Oi," one snarled.

"We've decided that there's an export tax on our ale," said the other. "From our bar to foreign mouths."

"Well, that sounds pretty silly." Wesken sipped his ale. He eyed them. They were bored.

"Sing for us," said the first.

"I don't know how to sing."

"You're in Masikus, everyone can sing," said the second.

"I'm not Masikonian."

"Dance then. Put on a play," said the first.

Wesken darted between them both. They were really bored. They wanted to fight. And they would continue to poke until they got it.

That's what you get with a Sigu Nii Kortaes. Even the lowly, field tilling Masikonians like to get bloody.

He stood slowly and laid his hand on his scabbard. They towered over him.

"Oi, he's lookin' to fight!" laughed the first.

"Oh boy," groaned the bartender.

Wesken could feel his hands perspire. His heart was beating quickly but steadily. He knew he wasn't in the wrong. But if he were honest, he was a bit bored, too. "Maybe if you weren't so fat, you'd be the entertainer instead of the entertained."

Welp. Now you've done it.

The farther one reacted first. He probably wasn't about to attack quite yet, but his hand flinched toward his sword. The kind when you're about to do something, but still kind of contemplating it in your head.

Wesken didn't flinch, he hardly even told his arms to move, but they did. Before anyone else realized what happened, he was already back in his original position, his sword dripping with blood. A look of complete horror came over the second man as he watched his friend topple over backwards. He turned to Wesken and howled in fury as he drew a two-handed sword from his belt.

Too slow, Wesken thought, but he figured he'd wait for this one to attack first. Given the small amount of room from the bar to his left and the wooden tables to his right, the drunk fat man swung heavily from above his head—an easy read. Wesken stepped to the right and jabbed his rusty blade deep into the man's side. The man's sword hadn't even had the time to bounce off the ground before Wesken yanked his sword free.

Everyone jumped from their seats, yelling about their fallen town members.

This'll definitely be a good bit harder. Wesken stood for a short moment, assessing his surroundings. Questions by some unknown voice, different from the previous, shot through his mind.

How many are there?

Fifteen-ish.

Who will reach you first?

The bartender to my left.

How long do you have before the second person reaches you?

Not long enough.

What about the staff?

What staff? Oh yeah! Is that more than just a walking stick?

Good question. You wanna find out?

Yeah, okay. From the corner of his eyes, he could see the bartender jump over the counter, already preparing a swing. Wesken dodged to his right and threw his sword at the person who would reach him second. Without checking to see if his throw had rotated correctly into its target, he grabbed up the staff leaning against his table. He gave the staff a few swings around, just to get his hands comfortable before he had to block the bartender's blade.

Wow, this thing is noticeably faster than that old piece of rust. It felt light, but not so light as to sacrifice power. He thrust the old man's staff forward to meet the sword before it met his flesh. With a crack that sounded like thunder, the bartender's sword snapped into a dozen pieces.

The bartender winced, surprise filling his face before shards of his own sword pierced through him. Wesken felt just as surprised as he looked. He twirled the staff around. Taking note of the bright carvings. *I think I like this walking stick.*

Wesken spun in a circle, and with two hands he kept his weapon low to the ground. Two men knocked chairs and tables out of their way as they raised their swords on Wesken. He swept them off their feet, and the force of the ground meeting their backs briefly knocked the wind out of them. Without hesitation, a quick strike to each of their foreheads sent consciousnesses to dreamland.

Wesken paused, everyone gathered around him in a circle. His stance was clean, head low, and his senses were on high alert. He took in as much information as he could. The staff was firmly and evenly distributed between both of his hands.

This has to be the most I've ever taken on at one time, his brain yelled excitedly. *And they're still too slow.*

24

ATERAH

"Who was the boy?" He asked.

Aterah swayed with the horse. Her legs and loins were sore. Her left shoulder beat with a rustic ache along with the horse's gait. Verano's arms, dense and coarse to the touch, pressed against her own. He held the reins just before her, the front of his inner thighs rubbing against the back of hers. The yellow, sun-stained grass had long since turned tall, up to her waist even atop their steed.

"You knew him. How?" Verano weaved the horse around long, thin, scattered lines of Sigu Nii soldiers. They marched northwest, carrying knapsacks bursting with assorted dyed cloth and metal objects. Trash piled along the edges of the well-traveled road.

"Answer me!" The warmth from his arms vanished. Patches of frost formed on his skin. "He was talking to you in prison below the Warlord's Office. Any number of curious rats could have found themselves down there." He spoke loudly, clearly, and fluently in her ear. A crisp Sigu Nii accent most unlike the twang and slosh that came from the rest of them. "Then it turns out he was Renovian. How?"

Aterah watched it happen. Though, Kairo hadn't seen her, Furadii was dragging her through Yutarah toward her tent when the shouting began. And while Furadii and Aterah were watching her brother change skin tones, Verano came up behind and stabbed Furadii in the back. He slipped away with her in his clutches before anyone found out what had happened.

Some of Furadii's blood still clung to the back of her neck.

"He's my brother."

Verano paused. "He appeared to be Sigu Nii. How?"

"I don't know."

"I don't believe you." Razor sharp shards of ice ripped out of his skin. They pressed up against hers, with pressure close to puncture. "How?" he shouted.

The horse beneath them screeched, and Verano had to keep it from steering into soldiers below them.

"I don't know! There was a man with him. He was different. He had stone tattoos! That's all I know!"

"Stone tattoos?" He murmured. "Describe them."

"They were—were like boxes in shape, like a maze. They came out of his skin. I didn't get a good look. I've never even met him." Aterah whimpered. "I've only seen him in my dreams."

Verano kept silent for a moment, then speaking to himself, "Masikonian. No doubt. But Alkalii? What is he doing here?" His voice turned close to a grumble. "This is treason!"

Nothing he said meant anything to Aterah. *Masikonian? Alkalii?* She might not have even known what treason was if it weren't for NeoDerii's library.

Verano *tsk'd* his lips, "Well, your brother is dead now anyways."

He's not. Aterah kept quiet. *I've seen where he's going, and it's not to Yeshwin.* Her eyes turned hesitantly up to the grey slab against a rolling hill on the horizon. Ravid. Though she knew Kairo had not yet even departed from her very same cell in Yutarah.

Aterah shook her head of the thought. *He'll come for me.* Yet she hadn't seen it in her dreams. She only knew her brother's character. "Where are we going?"

"To Vasara."

The city of old. Her eyes widened. "Why?" She wondered what had become of it.

"Because it's the closest Tuidiia. They're too expensive to put in the likes of Yutarah."

That meant nothing to her. She turned to the marching soldiers beside them. "What about them?"

"Vasara, too. They will trade in whatever muck they've taken from you for coin. Trinkets, ears, scalps, eyes, toes, whatever." Verano sighed, almost longingly. "Then they will make their way home."

I thought they never quit. Aterah pondered this for a moment. "But there are so many of them."

"The season is over. The winter garrison will take their place."

"Garrison? I thought these were all independent tribes."

Verano's knees shifted as they rubbed against her own. "They huddle together on their own. But their interest in Renovia is fed to them."

"By who?"

"The Warlord."

"And what makes you special? What makes you different from *them*?"

A single chuckle escaped him.

"Well?" She asked.

"I'm stronger." He shrugged. "A *lot* stronger."

Aterah *hmph'd*. "Is that all you care about? Being strong—"

"Of course not," he growled. "Keep your Renovian lectures from my ears before you soil them. Everything about you reeks of meekness and weakness."

She remained quiet. *Graeynesh Law IV: A king will come from the line of Graeynesh and restore Renovia to glory.*

Queen Epheriia. Aterah let the name roll through her mind, careful to pronounce each syllable. *The Oracle before me.* Aterah wished she could talk to her. A deep longing turned something in her chest. *The things you saw before you passed. The wisdom that you possessed.* Aterah could feel Verano lead the horse off the dirt trail. *Help me.*

"We will stop here for the night." Verano dismounted, wrapped his hard, calloused hands around Aterah's waist, and heaved her from the horse.

She looked around as Verano unstrapped the saddle and packs from the horse. They were adjacent to the dirt trail, in a patch of flattened tallgrass that had been previously slept on. Ten steps in a loose circular fashion, with head height reeds of grass around.

Aterah couldn't quite place it, but atop the horse, being able to see as far as the horizon in every direction felt wrong. She felt safe in the little compartment of grass.

The exhausted horse neighed as it knelt to the ground. It ate the grass beside it and Verano poured a water canteen into a small bowl. He tossed the packs on the far end of their circle, then offered her bread and water.

"Try and get some sleep. We will not stay long."

Aterah slept almost immediately. The world fell away, the snoring horse, Verano Veligreen, the dry air of the grassy plains.

A new world took its place. Aterah stood without shoes. She could feel coarse, shelly sand squeeze between her toes. The air felt heavy like the Renovian jungle, but with something else that clung to her hair and itched at her bare scalp. Roaring water crashed behind her, *The Maua?* she wondered. *No, it's too rhythmic. The Maua is steady. Crash, peace . . . crash, peace . . . crash, peace.* Aterah shuffled her feet, she ached to turn around, but her dream kept her facing forward. The ground took shape before her, as if her dream was slowly building itself, each piece materializing as she focused on it. A palace rose out of the fog, surrounded by courtyard-sized sections of dew-laden grass. The whole building was stone, like from the old days. There were giant windows in its face, with a thin, colored sheet of invisible material keeping the inside and outside apart. Glass. She'd read about it. These people had access to things she'd only read about.

Aterah felt her feet move toward the grass, some of the sand still clinging to her soles. *Let me turn! I don't want to go in there!*

The palace drew near. Sunrooms and towers, pavilions and courtyards between them. A small, plainly painted door called to her. Aterah's hand fit around the brass handle and listened as the door popped open. Cold air spilled out of the palace, ruffling her hair. She tried to resist, she tried to turn and run the other direction. But quietly the door closed behind her. Her new surrounding was dimly lit. Chills ran down her arms.

A familiar scent found her nose as her eyes adjusted to the dark. Ink and parchment, paper and leather. With another soft smokey scent mixed in. Slowly, long tall shelves took shape around her. Each of them filled with hundreds of books and scrolls. A single candle flickered a dozen steps away. It rested on a three-prong iron stand and illuminated a single folded leg.

He's here. Aterah shivered.

He was sitting deep in a leather chair and smoking a long wooden pipe. His crossed legs were covered by a silk robe of black, clinging so that the long skinny shape of the leg could be seen. Leather strapped sandals covered the foot at the end.

The figure leaned forward into the light. His head was shaved bald, circle rims covered his sharp blue eyes, and his skin was ghostly white. "I can see you, witch." His voice ripped through the darkness.

Aterah gasped. Her heart pounded. She tried to turn and run, but her legs continued toward the figure.

His hands pushed off the arm rests so that he stood a whole reach over her. His eyes searched her face, a feeling that caused a twinge in Aterah's gut. "I have waited awhile for this moment. Though, I wonder, did you even know it would come?" He smiled. Bright white teeth shone clear through the shadows. "I have met you several times. Though, you don't even know who I am."

Aterah's breath escaped her, slow and uneven. "How—how can you see me?" She looked around. "Aren't I in the future?"

He huffed through his nose. "And soon, I will be too." He reached out a hand, long pale fingers that wrapped around like claws. They settled before her forehead, just around the crest. But she couldn't feel his hand. Not so much as the warmth of his body. "I can't wait to dissect you."

She sat up with a start, panting shaky breaths. She was covered in a thin film of dew. *Or is this sweat?* she wondered, rubbing the wet from her arms. Aterah looked around, the foreplays of twilight were scratching at the sky.

Verano shifted, he turned to look at her, still lying in the flat tallgrass. He sighed, "What did you see?"

Aterah glanced at him, her dreams of the night flooding her mind. "I saw him. The Warlord." She spoke unevenly. "He could see me."

Verano picked himself up and stretched his arms. "Aye."

"But how? I dream of things not yet come to pass."

"He's probably in your head. You can do a number of things from in there." Verano spat, seemingly out of disgust. "Whoever heard of a foreigner becoming a Warlord of Sigu Nii?" He turned to the horse, who was already awake and munching loudly on the edges of their camp. The saddle and his knapsack bags clinked and ruffled as Verano strapped them around the horse. "Let's go."

From pre-dawn through the morning until the skies gradually descended into twilight, Aterah rode quietly in front of Verano. The grey slab on the horizon grew nearer, the high walls of a prison city.

She tried to keep herself from looking upon it. Ravid. She had seen it in her dreams, it's inside, and Kairo's slaving work to be done. Though at the moment he was still only on his way. And on foot. To see Ravid still standing, and once again collecting Renovian prisoners, made her shiver. It was like a backhand to their most legendary leader, Adakon.

They passed it without stopping.

For days, they continued through the grassy plains between Yutarah and Vasara. The grass rose and fell with the hills, and occasional grey boulders would jut out of the ground. Each time they passed a creek, Verano would lead the horse to drink.

Aterah didn't see any Sigu Nii tribes or soldiers after Ravid. She asked Verano why. "Those that we passed, those who couldn't afford a horse, left the night of the Niiwa. We're in the front of the line now."

On the evening of the fourth night, they stopped a few dozen steps off the sand trail, and the night grew cold. "We should have brought your tent," Aterah scolded.

"Hush," Verano snapped through jittering teeth. His arms flexed, a molten glow lighting through his veins, and fire steamed and withered the wet grass around them. "Come here." He held his arm out.

"No." Aterah shook her head. Vivid ghost pressure caused her ache, accompanied by images of her first night.

"*Here!*" Verano snapped, his teeth grit together in a snarl. He snatched her arm and dragged her closer.

"*No!*" she shouted, her legs flailing, she tried to tear her arms from his grip. But as she drew near to him, he wrapped both his arms around her.

He was warm. And the night was cold. *His grip is too tough to break.* She thought wearily, ceasing her resistance.

On the evening of the fifth night, they began to come across Sigu Nii soldiers once again, this time heading in the opposite direction. "The winter garrison?" Aterah asked. Her eyes swept across huddled lines of them. But their eyes lingered. They stared at her. Some looked angry, others confused at her presence. "She's on a horse!" one shouted.

"Aye," Verano answered, unconcerned.

The rolling hills began to stretch out. The jutted boulders and head-height grass fell away. Creeks and small rivers became more frequent, along with short, knotty trees with twisted branches. Bright yellow flowers clustered along wide hillsides, and dark red flowers grew in vines around the knotted trees.

As the skies darkened, a long wooden fence ran along the dirt trail. Farmlands stretched out toward the horizons. Verano had to steer their horse off the trail on a few occasions as large horse-drawn wagons passed beside them, filled to the brim with barrels, sacks, and shiny metal blades.

They passed three other horseback Sigu Nii soldiers with various lower ranking tattoos. The three led a herd of cattle so big it could feed all of NeoDerii for multiple dry-seasons.

And finally, in the distance between clusters of trees and a lake to the east, a village appeared.

Gravel crunched as the horse walked. Singing and shouting carried downwind. "This is Vasara?" Aterah asked. *It doesn't look at all like the stories I've read about our capital.*

Verano chuckled. "No. No, Vasara has a number of towns surrounding it, and villages surrounding those. This is one of those villages." He waved his hand north. "We will be there near this time tomorrow."

The twisted, flower-covered trees fell behind them, and they passed under a wooden arch made of two tall fence posts connected by a curved piece on top.

The road cut straight through the middle of the small village. Large wooden buildings clustered around the edges of the road. Behind them stood wooden farmhouses with half-beam framing and grass roofing.

At a glance, Aterah could see two types of Sigu Nii passing each way. Half of them were dirty, with soil and manure clinging to their clothes and skin. They seemed to come from the fields and the lake in the east. The other half wore studded leather armor with swords hanging on their belts, thickly padded boots, and serpent tattoos. They walked in herds, passing between a stable to the right of the middle trail, and two other large buildings.

Shouting and singing, laughing and banging came from the latter three buildings. Aterah watched as two armored Sigu Nii soldiers groveled and wailed on each other.

"He-e-ey!" a guttural slithery voice erupted from below her. A hard and calloused hand wrapped around her ankle. She yelped in surprise and turned to see a Sigu Nii soldier smiling at her. He tugged on her ankle with strength enough to pull her off the horse. "Whatchya got there?" He laughed.

"*Off!*" Verano bellowed and shoved a fistful of ice needles across the soldier's face.

The soldier howled in pain, his hands clutching the blood flowing down his cheeks. He fell to his knees, and a moment after that, he fell quietly to his back.

An idea struck Aterah. Like the flat of a blade hitting her in the gut, the idea made her short of breath.

Verano steered their horse into the stable. He heaved Aterah from its back and began relieving the steed of its saddle and baggage.

Her eyes swept the streets. Her pulse picked up in pace. She hugged the back of her arms tight. Yes, she would try it.

Verano led them toward one of the buildings that the Sigu Nii herded around, passing soldiers and farmers alike.

Breathing deeply from her gut, she said loudly, "So where *is* this Warlord? How much farther do we have to go?"

It seemed to work. One or two of the street noises halted. Aterah could feel a soldier's eyes turn toward her.

Verano stopped in his tracks and turned slowly to meet her in the eye. He squinted. "He's in Ryala."

"And *you're* going to lead me there? All by yourself? You understand I'm an Oracle. I literally see the future."

Several more of the street noises ceased. A dozen heads turned toward them. "Renovian witch." Whispers. Gravel and boot scraped against one another. Soldiers slowly drew near.

"They will die," Verano said, searching Aterah's face.

She glanced at them with a worried expression that said, *Help me!* One of them got a good look at Verano's left shoulder.

"He got no Niiwa!" the soldier shouted.

Verano flexed and lowered into a fighting stance. Black ice ripped out of his skin.

Aterah began to back away, nothing sudden. She felt her feet collide with something, she looked down. Large boots stood around her own. Hard calloused hands clasped her shoulders. Her arms flailed, she tried to swat the soldier behind her away.

"You gonna deliver this here girl, all by your onsie? I think you need some help," roared the Sigu Nii behind her. Approving growls followed.

"You won't win," replied Verano casually.

A sword of black ice flew past her with lightning speed. It tore through the soldier, sloshing audibly. His blood spilled down Aterah's left side. It was warm. A croak escaped her as she backed away. She glanced at Verano, he wore a face as if to say, *I will find you.*

Aterah turned from the Sigu Nii soldiers piling around Verano and moved her legs as fast as they would go. Down the gravel street, between houses. She passed soldiers and farmers staring at her in disbelief. She paused on the outskirts of the village, a lake stretched out to her left. Fishing dinghies waded out in the water.

She took off again in a sprint, completely unsure how long Verano would be occupied. *Hide in the farmlands.* She hurled herself over a wooden fence into a field of tightly packed crops and began to slow, the stalks swayed visibly around her. She came across a narrow gap between rows. *A water ditch?*

She crouched and paused to slow her breath, then slowly raised her head. *There.* Verano had already finished, his cloth clothes covered in blood. He hadn't seen her, but he was searching.

Careful not to touch any of the reeds around her, she continued. A farmhouse stood at the far end of the ditch. She crouched and went that way.

I killed them. Aterah felt her throat close up. She didn't want to cry. *No.* She refused. But she felt the guilt of those soldiers' lives lost. Yes, they were the enemy, but this wasn't territory marked for war. This was their home.

"Hey." someone whispered.

Aterah's heart dropped. She stood frozen in fear.

"Hey!" The whisper came again, this time more aggressive.

It sounds like the voice of a child. She turned, searching the rows. There, stepping toward the ditch. A Sigu Nii child with a sewn doll in hand stood staring at her. His head was shaved, and his clothes were dirty from playing in the field. It was strange, seeing a barbarian child standing there, looking so dormant. *Not sure that I've ever seen one of their young.*

The boy glanced around. He could sense that something was off. That Aterah was hiding for some reason. "Follow me." He ran up the ditch toward the house.

Aterah hesitated for just a moment, then chased after the boy. The narrow trail weaved and cut, the dirt dipping unevenly from running water. *Remember, this boy is less than human.* She came to a halt by the edge of the wheat. *But he looks so . . . innocent.*

"Come." The boy gestured and ran into the house.

She took a step out from the farmland and bolted after him.

The house was two stories, its structure rickety, torn holes, splintering planks. Nothing compared to the golden carpentry of NeoDerii.

Aterah prayed to the Korta Nii that when she turned, her eyes would not meet Verano's. She closed the door, but it wouldn't shut. Its hinges were uneven with the threshold.

"Renovian!" a deep, sloshed and twangish Sigu Nii accent bellowed behind her. The man stood in a candle-lit hallway, confusion clear across his face.

She turned, bringing her finger to her lips, her heart pounding. "Shhh," She pleaded. "Please."

The man's unshaven face softened.

"Mak'er tea, Papa!" the boy yelled from somewhere behind.

He waved a hand to come near. "Tea?" he asked. His brown tunic stretched around his bulging belly. His trousers were coarse, tough for field working.

Aterah nodded and walked cautiously toward him. She peered at the walls, worn daggers and swords hung as decoration. The hallway opened to a small eating area, a four-step-wide circular table in the middle, with the child sitting in one of three chairs. A faded tribal insignia hung over the table. The man turned right into a narrow kitchen with dark metal plates hanging over a metal basket of wood. He snapped his fingers to make a flurry of sparks over the log. "Jus' be a momen'," he said, putting a closed-pot on top, and gestured toward one of the chairs.

Aterah pulled it out and collapsed into it. "You don't seem like a barbarian."

"Wha'?"

"Nothing, never mind." She sighed and leaned her elbows on the table.

"What're you doin' out this far?" he asked, pulling up a chair across from her.

She paused. "I—uhm. I escaped from Yutarah." A lie. *I'm telling a lie?* It didn't sit right, and she had a gut-churning feeling that caused her heart ache. *A lie.*

"And you came 'ere?" The man glanced around and pointed east. "Renovia that way."

"I never got to meet a Renovian before," the child said. He wouldn't stop staring at her. "You do 'ook a li'le frail."

A knock came from the door. Loud. Aggressive. Aterah's heart slithered up her throat. Her joints felt frozen.

The man's brows came in. "Who's chasing?" He asked, getting up from his seat.

Aterah shook her head. She didn't know what to say. *Nobody?* She pondered. *An inkless monster?* She forced herself to move, just out of view of the door, and pressed her back up against the kitchen wall as the man started down the hallway. The door creaked open before the man would have reached it.

"Who're you?" the man bellowed.

A tense silence.

"Verano Veligreen, eldest son to Warlord Nahkon Veligreen."

No! She looked around. *Where to go, where to go, where to go, where to—* The pot whistled. Aterah jumped, her heart wrenching in her chest. *Why is it doing that?*

"Who are you making tea for?" Verano asked.

"My boy—"

The hallway filled with a choked gurgling, blood and organs spilled across the wooden floorboards. Followed by a loud *thud* of the seasoned soldier toppling to the ground. The child started screaming.

Aterah's back slid down the wall behind her. She sat, hugging her arms. "No," she cried. Her voice drowned out by the harmonious wailing of the boy and the pot.

"There you are, witch." Verano peered down at her.

The child started punching Verano's legs.

"Off." Verano sighed, before punching a wave of ice needles across the boy's face.

25

AYRAH

The day grew late as Ayrah limped with an arm over Urota's shoulder. Her whole body ached. She had lain on the Masikonian's cot for hours—full-body bone integrity enhancement, muscle refinement, skin armor, and the sharpening of her eyes.

"It will pass quickly, I promise," Urota assured. "You'll feel like a reborn warrior before we even make it to Waike's arena."

Ayrah didn't respond. Each step sent boiling surges down her spine. She eased her eyes open, dried mucus and tears cracked from her parting lids, and the world was a blindingly bright and blurry place. Ayrah didn't know where they were. She didn't know who was around them. She felt wholly and humiliatingly vulnerable.

Being aided by an El-tier warrior hardly helped. Commoner gasps echoed all around them.

"We're going to walk up some steps now, aye?"

Ayrah tipped her head. She forced her eyes half-open, in hopes to ease them into being useful. But the brightness of the whitestone steps they climbed were like razors being jabbed through her newly mutated retinas. She peered upwards and saw a blackstone triangle stretching high into the sky. If Lyta Tuio's sigil painted in gold across the high-middle section of the tower weren't so recognizable, she wasn't sure she'd have been able to see it.

The Warlord's Office of Pratuel. Even through Ayrah's near-unusable eyes, she could feel its grandness—as opposed to Simula's squared-off clay building, whose only distinguishing feature was some black paint.

She wiped her eyes and felt the itching crust flake off across her arm. Her skin was rough and leathery. She pinched it. Nothing. She kept pinching as hard as she could. She could feel it, like the numbness of a hand that's been slept on. But no matter how hard her forefinger and thumb strained, it didn't sting. She hoped she looked much the same, at least.

"El," said Urota.

Ayrah heard someone *hmph*. "So that's where you two ran off." It was Malik's voice. He sounded unenthused. "I'll take her from here. Hurry on to the Waterdome Arena."

Ayrah could feel Urota nod and ease her arm off her shoulder. A moment passed by where she swayed alone, her hands raised hoping to grab Malik, her head raised, hoping to spot him. "Malik?" Her voice sounded how she felt. Small and cracking. *Where did he go?*

An elbow gently nudged her lower shoulder. "Let's go."

Ayrah clung to him. She could feel each time Malik stepped with his left leg, his body would shake and shift weight, demanding his right leg to race back beneath him.

"El Malik," said a man in full black-and-gold armor. He and another guarded a pair of double glass doors and collected two silver coins from a lengthy line of commoners.

Muffled thunder erupted from inside the building.

"Wait," said the Black Guard, and stepped in front of them. He squinted and looked closely at Ayrah. "This is the Shadowa girl from Simula!" His eyes widened, and green fiery vuu sprang in each hand.

Dread surged through Ayrah's stomach. Her hand slipped from Malik's arms, frost coated them, and her head tipped up at an uncomfortable angle so as to see her accuser through the slit between her eyelids.

"She's with me," Malik replied rather impatiently.

Several more Black Guard filed out of the building and descended into low, firm stances, ready for battle. Yelps came from the line of commoners as they backed into one another, pulling away from this potentially fatal encounter. "But El," The original complained, "This one killed five Black Guard out in Simula. And a retiring officer of your generation!"

"Lord Mayor Gabya, aye." Malik nodded. "He was a prick. I know who she is. Stand down, she's with me."

Ayrah watched uncertainty pass over their faces. Knees eased up, shoulders settled, and faces scowled.

The bouncing echoes of thunder seeped outside, coming from deep inside the Warlord's Office.

"She's number eleven on Gya's most—"

"I *know*," the seasoned Tamagai guildhead growled. "She is not just some whore, this is Ayrah Veligreen."

"Oh." Their eyes widened, as horrifically surprised as if they had mistaken Kizmaldi Tuio for any city rummager. Gasps came from the nearest commoners, but unlike those for Urota, these weren't filled with excitement, rather a *oh-my-bloody-El* sort of gasp.

The whitestone steps leading up to the Warlord's Office filled with whispers as news spread down the line. "Nakhon's daughter." And, "I thought she were dead." And, "Aye, she's wanted in Gya now too."

Ayrah whipped around, her black ice blade raised in her heavy arms. "What?" she screamed at the line of people. She decided she would kill them. Kill them all. A hundred of these flame-ranked, muck for-blood peasants were not worth her power.

News would spread that Ayrah Veligreen had resurfaced. The new Warlord Pikemaster's bounty hunters would begin narrowing in on her, and she would have to run again.

The sound of muffled thunder disturbed the silence.

"Come." Malik grabbed her shoulders and steered her into the War-lord's Office.

"How did you disarm the Black Guard?" Ayrah protested, peering at the soldiers, who lingered by the door. "They're the Warlord's extension. If Lyta Tuio says I'm wanted—"

"Aye, aye, aye," Malik shushed her. He tapped his left shoulder. "They've only got the fourth tattoo. I'm a victor. I am El, even to them."

They wanted to arrest her, but with Malik stepping between them, he was essentially demanding that the Black Guard publicly grash him. A thing he knew they would not do hastily. Malik was in charge of one of the strongest guilds across the kingdom. Even *if* they won the grash, they would be hated for it.

Ayrah peered around the interior of the Warlord's Office. Her eyes and limbs and skin felt leagues better, like after cracking a stiff neck.

The glistening tile floor mirrored a spectacular painting on the ceiling of Warlord Tuio. Long golden locks curled around frigid red eyes, down her thin, snarling face, and looped against Vulgarhe engraved armor.

Hellinite trimmed each corner of the room, like supporting pillars, which made the whole place feel like a demonstration of black and gold.

Hallways led from this room to others, Ayrah could just peek the fall-ing outside light in an adjacent room, and a commoner loading a wagon with crates.

Thunder cracked inside, Ayrah jumped, startled by the deafening noise.

The line of commoners continued inside the room behind a black vel-vet rope on the far-right side. They shuffled along at a snail's pace, holding their shoes (boots, sandals, the like), and eyed Malik and Ayrah as they strolled by. Across from them were triangular indentations in the walls, just big enough to fit a large person. Signs above the twelve indentations included all six of the provincial capitals, like Waike, Ryala, and Gryyn, a few larger cities around Gya, and of course, the Sigu Nii capital: Sehlya.

This was the Tuidiia. Ayrah had heard of its majesty as they began popping up around the kingdom during the past few seasons. But never had she seen one from inside.

A member of the Black Guard policed the commoners, asking them questions like "Where to," and "what for," and "for how long?"

Ayrah and Malik arrived parallel to the front of the peasant line and the Black Guard left the next-in-line in the middle of his own question. "Evening, El. Go right ahead." He gestured to the indentation behind him, under the sign that read, *Waike*. His eyes flickered across Ayrah's.

Malik nudged her. She started forward, toward the wall of indentations. She began unlacing her boots along the way.

"Ahht—uhm, you don't need to do that, El. I'll do it for you." The Black Guard forced an awkward laugh and chased after her.

"Oh," she said. She stepped onto the black metal plate. It was riddled with Old Vulgarhe inscriptions that she didn't understand. The Black Guard bent down and touched it with his finger—just the tiniest of human interactions to begin.

Imagine that. Ayrah frowned. *A piece of metal having vuu.*

Dusty black sparks crawled across the pad, they darted all around her, and with a deafening crack of thunder, as dark lightning struck through her, she was gone. There was nothing. For the briefest of moments, Ayrah did not exist. And then she was back in the Warlord's Office. She looked around, confused, but the painting on the ceiling was of someone else. And the Black Guard were different.

She had teleported.

Ayrah was impressed. As Warlord of Gya, Lyta Tuio led the networks of command that ran each office across the region. She was already in charge of so much. With the Tuidiia, Lyta Tuio had found immortality through integrality. Surely, she thought, the Tuidiia would go down in the pale-historian's writings as an eternal mark on Zoë, during the Kortaes of Sigu Nii.

Black lightning, and the accompanying ear puncturing thunder cracked consistently around the room. Dozens were exiting other divots in the wall, adjacent to hers.

Halfway toward the office doors, Ayrah saw a room adjacent where the hellinite plates were several people large. Sigu Nii peasants loaded them up with barrels and sacks of grain.

Ayrah's eyes widened. It was a whole other teleportation room. One for cargo.

Boats, roads, wagons—whatever. Ayrah couldn't imagine a network of transportation more powerful than this one. Even if somehow, say, Masikus figured out how to mutate wings onto people for a long enough time for them to *fly*, it would not leave such an affect.

Imagine if the filthy bark-eaters across the eastern sea *did* start to punch above their weight. All of Sigu Nii could realistically arrive within a season.

She turned back and waited for Malik. But when black lightning finished flashing above the plate, Kizmaldi Tuio strolled out.

The heir of Gya. His full suit of armor glinted with red, with delicate gold leafing, and with engravings of Old Vulgarhe. The dead language covered entire portions of his armor. The Tuio insignia shone bright and clear on his right peck, a hand with lightning ripping through the palm. His pitch-black hair was oiled slick-tight against his head.

The boy heir had many Masikonian mutations. His knuckles were large and sharpened, as well as his elbows and shoulders. His skin seemed rough, leathery, almost gritty like sand. And the boy's pupils were a tad narrow, almost vertical ovals.

"Kizmaldi," she said, surprised. "I thought Malik was behind me."

He scoffed, as if he had expected her to call him *El*. "Yeah, well, everyone worth a gold coin is trying to get here right now, so he might be a moment."

It was true. A vast variety of people with flame ranks, skull ranks, and places of Niiwa like Pratuel or any number of cities around Gya kept coming and coming.

Many of them halted, their boots screeching on the white tile as their eyes caught sight of the famous boy. "El!" some said. "The Warlord's son," others whispered. Each of them who drew near found that Kizmaldi was not the approachable sort. He sent them scurrying away with a glare in his eyes or flash of vuu on his hands.

"Will your mother be here tonight?" Ayrah asked, loosely following Kizmaldi toward the full glass doors. It was nearing dark, and clouds overhead threatened rain.

The boy shrugged. "At the end when we're winning perhaps. She and I were meeting with Coryndal Nia Makri; we're beginning to build these things in the Masikonian city-states now."

"Coryndal?"

Kizmaldi waved his hand, "The Masikonian equivalent of a Warlord."

"You seem pretty confident in our victory."

"You're using 'ours' now?" He laughed. "Undoubtedly, we'll win. You know, I could've joined any guild across the kingdom. I could have chosen the Kaeselwa victor from the last championship. I could have chosen *the most* El-ranked guild, and they would have had little choice but to kick out their weakest player to make room. But there's no glory in that. I chose a decent guild, and I plan to be the reason that it's the best. All this Kaeselwa nonsense, it's just training for my days to come as Warlord." He took one stair down the whitestone steps, turned, and stuck his chin high. "Don't get in my way." He turned to the city.

Ayrah watched him go, thinking about how young the boy was. Still, it felt like he was older in all the ways that counted.

"So, this is Waike." Ayrah sighed, folding her arms across her chest. That small action still brought her soreness from the mutator. But at least she could see, now.

Waike was mostly level, with buildings stacking several stories high. From the steps of the Warlord's Office, she could see the Niiwa arena to the north.

A ring of vendors with wooden stands and multicolor linens stretched over surrounded the office in a circle. Beyond them were thirty-step-wide cobblestone streets in each cardinal direction, fronted by blocks of low-Niiwa housing. Wood and tin shacks stacked vertically, whose stability relied on the shacks stacked on either side. Thin alleys ran between some of these structures that were so densely packed that lanterns lit the way.

From the top of the whitestone, Ayrah watched people with carved pipes, long and straight, inhaling and collapsing from seizures and pelvic thrusts. She knew that guilds offered indeclinable protections to shops and houses alike. They fought in the allies, dealt assorted drugs, and moved black-market blades and armor.

Sigu Nii was run by guilds. They were clans. Gangs. Even the Warlord's Office, the giant black and gold pyramid behind her, was a guild of sorts. The Black Guard enforced Tuio's glory across the entire province.

Then you have the Kaeselwa guilds. The Tamagai. Waterdome. Korlaii. There were hundreds across the six provinces. Teams of professional fighters, young—in their prime even, dueling for names of international recognition.

And still you had these, the guilds of the underground, like Herk and Boden. They owned the taverns, brothels, inns, the restaurants. They owned the common man's day to day. They enforced their glory through the grash, a duel between warriors, recognition was the currency, and ownership of property came with.

"Were you afraid you might get lost?" Malik strolled past her, down the whitestone.

"I was remembering," she chased after him.

"Yes?"

"Just the time I spent as Shadowa. It's still strange being introduced as Ayrah Veligreen."

"Seems you'd better get used to it, or you might not be called that much longer."

Vendors hawked their trinkets and foods to them. The older of them felt compelled to tell Malik that they were of his age and remembered his defeating assorted guilds in his younger days. Malik shunned them away with a purple-fire ignition in his outstretched palm. It was a threat to most and a life-long scar for the few who drew too close.

Ayrah tired of Malik's self-aggrandizing. "I would've fought the Black Guard, back in Pratuel."

"Then you would've died. There were at least a dozen of them around the building."

"I can take them. I defeated five in Simula and Lord Mayor Gabya at once."

Malik scoffed. "What does this city make you think?"

"It seems larger than Pratuel, but dirtier."

"Aye. Waike has an average Niiwa rank of two-point-nine. Pratuel's is three-point-four."

"What does that have to do with anything?"

"It means not all Niiwa are equal. It means taking it here would be easier than taking it in Pratuel. It means that when you fight in Sehlya, with an average rank of four-point-five, you won't be able to think, 'I can take them,' and leave it at that."

Ayrah remained silent.

"I'm strong, Veligreen. Very strong. Two generations ago, I blew my opponents out of the sand. A true Pratuelian victor. But I'm no Warlord. See, the Kaeselwa doesn't just recruit victors, there are plenty of those. The Kaeselwa is made up of the youngest, fittest, most prestigious Niiwa victories across all of Sigu Nii." Malik poked Ayrah's shoulder with some force, "You got good blood. And I admit, if you deem yourself worth the glory, your presence on this team would be El."

Ayrah frowned. She *did* like glory. No more grashing for scraps of food. No more sleeping with both eyes open on a bed of straw if she was lucky. Perhaps the threat of death was worth the chance at exaltation.

The arena was the size of four city blocks. Its walls slanted outward, with hellinite structural beams every thirty steps around the external oval. The stone slabs were gargantuan. *How could anyone or thing carry slabs so large up here?* she wondered. They must have been twenty steps from corner to corner, weighing way past unliftable.

The indoor crowd roared. Explosions went off. Masikonian-mutated voices boomed, "The Waterdome versus the Tamagai!"

On the main walkway leading up to tan-grey stone steps and a half-circle corridor for an entrance into the arena, vendors sold their goods. And all around them a dense crowd of Sigu Nii peasants pushed, shoved one another to get a seat.

Gusts of wind swirled around Malik's hands, picking up dust and trash from the cobble stretch. He thrust his hands before him, and wind blasted through the crowd. The commoners yelped and stumbled as Malik parted his hands, splitting the crowd in half. They strolled right through the middle.

Ayrah fixed on Malik's uneven steps. His knee-length olive-cloak glided along corridors with paintings of historic Waterdome fighters. One had bolts of lightning coiling around a chiseled shirtless torso. Another shoved blades through blurred enemies, with spattering blood.

"It's funny that you of generation Yaerta call this the Waterdome Arena," said Malik as he began down a stairwell. "The guild had only just climbed Waike's hierarchy when I was fighting. When Waterdome took over as Waike's El guild, it sent heads turning. They rose to power overnight, and next thing all of us Tamagai knew, we were scraping off shin blades for Warlord Tuio to deem us Gya's champion. The Waterdome has been here a generation, and already we forget their predecessors."

They climbed down a flight of stairs and turned onto another hallway curving around under the arena. The shouting and stomping of thousands reverberated through the ceiling. To Ayrah's right, they passed sectioned off, ground-floor viewing compartments. Ten-reaches-high boxes for officers and lord mayors of Gya's outlying regions. Beyond them lay the sandy pit and Masikonian dancers putting on a choreographed prefight show.

"Lyta Tuio. She was Warlord back then?" Ayrah asked.

"Aye."

"How? I pictured her young. Fierce and agile. Enough to deter someone grashing for her title."

"Aye. All of those things. The woman has been Warlord since I've been alive. She's Ohaer. She and others like her have powers still unknown to the rest of us."

"People like my father?"

"Aye." Malik stopped as they neared a compartment with Tagon, Ecanaes, Ryan and three Masikonian whores portioned between them.

The shadowa-skinned Razite wore a white, hellinite decorated shirt that parted down the middle, with one side drawn over the other, and tied at the waist with a linen belt.

The pale-skinned Illian, with his golden locks curling sweaty against the copper of his spectacles, wore a dark blue suit. He wore a shawl on top, with an ornate sigil hat clasped the shawl together.

Each of the three Masikonian whores took on the fashionable Sigu Nii skin tones. A light golden-yellow. The color of a Sigu Nii who might train in an enclosed arena, like this one, rather than baking under open sun. Snakeskin, pelts of fur, and fish scales grew from their skin, covering their privates as if each were convinced the word "clothes" had a malleable definition.

They stood near the middle of the oval, prime positioning to watch each player and each event unfold. Ayrah could see thirty steps across the width of the pit to the middle viewing compartment on the opposite side. It was twice the size of their own. Black-and-white clad servants scrubbed the walls, the fruit bowls, and the single golden chair with black velvet cushions.

The last of the pre-fight Masikonian dancers exited. Thousands held their breaths as the Tamagai and Waterdome took fighting stances on opposing ends of the pit.

"Begin!" screamed a Sigu Nii voice, mutated with Masikonian vuu to boom through the stadium.

The Tamagai began with defense heavy positioning, Tayo and Saechii stood closer to the half-line. Urota, in her shining silver undergarments, held her foot over the unwritten mid-line, with hands straining upwards for thick neon ice barriers to erupt from the ground in front of each of their players. It was a contingency shield, for ducking and finding cover.

Ayrah found herself impressed that Urota could put up defenses, whatsoever. Sigu Nii vuu only worked in order to destroy—not protect. She must be doing some emotional acrobatics to convince herself that these ice-walls were intended to destroy incoming vuu.

"Ecanaes, what's the reading?" Malik asked as he scanned the players.

Ecanaes shook his head. "I spent a whole season studying the Waterdome. I watched them fight each aspiring guild in Waike, and I individualized profiles, but I highly doubt a single of ours read them."

Malik hummed in distaste. "Tagon?"

Ayrah watched the Razite close his eyes and lift his hands, palms forward, toward the sand. Then gradually his hands wandered across each of the ten players. "Zhe depths of our vuu is grander than theirs. Mostly," He added after a moment, "Because of zhe boy."

Errta and Kizmaldi stood toward the back of their side, evenly distributed halfway. White fire exploded into a circle around Kizmaldi's feet. Ayrah winced and shielded her newly sharpened retinas. The boy heir punched, spun, and kicked a storm of fireballs. Each blasted forth, leaving a trail of light like a comet, and cracking with thunderous force.

The veins in Errta's skin illuminated a dark molten red. The braziers of fire, piles of wax-soaked coal stationed around the arena wall, raised their flames in response to Errta's flexing his biceps inward.

It reminded Ayrah of their fight only three nights earlier—how this same flex ignited bonfires in a perfect circle around them.

Errta tore his hands inward, and they throbbed with rhythmic light as vuu channeled through his straining palms. The braziers all around the arena crashed forth, flying in droves toward the opposite end of the pit. Fire and coal clashed against the Waterdome players in a storm of sparks and hot metal.

That was the whole arena's source of light. Not only did Errta lightly injure an opponent or two, but he also made it much harder for anyone to see the Tamagai. Kizmaldi's blinding white-fire made them like silhouettes.

"I tried to warn them about this," Ecanaes said in his crisp Illian accent.

"Aye." Malik nodded.

Ayrah wasn't sure what he meant. The infliction would leave life-long scars and white fire had them dancing and crashing into one another.

It was five on five, on enemy territory, unforgettable by rumbling sound of the stadium wincing at each smack and hit. Peasant fans punched their hands in the air and commanded their team to exercise competency.

They did. One moment the Waterdome players were vainly swatting away enemy attacks, the next they were funneling hands together, channeling vuu into a single cast of dark-blue, vibrating energy. They released a ball of destructive force that shot forward. Urota reached out, and a spear of ice shot out of the ground, to intercede the ball. But on contact the ball flattened and streamlined into a slow-spinning continuum that ripped into the arena walls, the crowds, and through Tayo.

The small nosebleed section filled with fatal screams, but they were quickly overtaken by rest of the stadium's cheering.

Everything above Tayo's waist disappeared without a trace. His legs stood in place for a moment, hidden behind Urota's cracked ice barrier, the ends of his were knees charred and steaming, and they fell to either side.

"*No!*" Malik bellowed.

A subtle snickering reached Ayrah's ears. Ecanaes faced the ground, his head shook lightly.

"You're laughing?"

"In Aylavuera, I'm actually, what you might say, *strong.*" Ecanaes pushed his glasses farther up his nose. "And yet all this vuu, all this knowledge, all of this intent to come and see the El of my generation's Kortaes, and I can't get a single Sigu Nii to *listen.*" He gestured to the pit with shrugged shoulders. "What is my purpose in this place? This was the very thing that I warned about in great detail. *Specific* detail. The timing, the placement, the cooperation. All of Waterdome's vuu would have been rendered useless had Kizmaldi or Errta just *listened.*"

"You talk too long." Ayrah's eyes turned back to the fight. "Too many words to say too little. Doesn't your vuu involve holding my attention? Make your points smaller." Ayrah waved a hand to dismiss the conversation. Ecanaes' gaze ingrained into her, but she didn't care. She wanted to watch her team fight, a whole man down.

The pit now turned into several man-on-man battles. Fighters were littered across both ends, no one kept to the responsibility of the middle line.

Kizmaldi fought two Waterdome players at once. He wrapped his hands gloved in white flame around necks, leaving scorched and melting tissue with one hand and squeezing a head clear apart from its body with his other.

"Now *that* is strength. To be taught by a Warlord." Ayrah mumbled to herself.

"Taught?" Ecanaes' voice came clear, his voice pitched high with excitement. "Sigu Nii don't gain vuu by being taught."

Oh El. Here we go. Ayrah hung her head in visible exhaustion. Errta had warned her about this.

"You are about to take king's Niiwa, are you not?" Ecanaes said with displeasure. "Maybe you would be interested in understanding how you might best grow your vuu."

"Alright. On with it." She kept her eyes down.

"Sigu Nii vuu is genet—" Ecanaes paused as the crowd screamed with delight. "Hereditary. Unlike Illian vuu, which has a much higher percentage of nurture influence. And yet, your father had little time to train you before he grashed king—"

Ayrah waved her hand. "The point? Before I grow too old to reach Ohaer."

Ecanaes huffed and spoke quickly. "A very loose 10 percent of Sigu Nii *skill* comes from training. And that 10 percent is only useful for understanding one's capabilities and limitations. The other ninety comes from your parents, parents' parents, etcetera." Ecanaes shrugged. "That is the reason you find Errta enthralling. It's a subconscious instinct to reproduce that power."

He wasn't making any sense. "Would you speak Common Aylan?"

Something broke in gaze. His smile slipped. His tone had the slightest edge. "It is called the Common Tongue. For everyone. It's like you're calling it 'Kaeselwa Jargon,' or 'Niiwa Mouth,' or 'Kick the Ball Talk.'"

Ayrah had to keep herself from laughing.

"You should know, by the way, that an Illian giving you information—*real*, solid information—is a grand honor in my culture."

"Thank you," Ayrah mumbled. "But I'm not sure what good it does me."

"El, Veligreen." It was an unfamiliar voice. Ayrah's skin crawled hearing her House name, especially from an unknown source. *Bounty hunters*, she thought. A small ice blade filled her left palm, and she turned slowly. A Black Guard stood patiently behind the threshold of their private viewing compartment. His eyes were locked on hers. "The Warlord El Tuio requests your presence." His eyes shifted past her own as he raised a hand to gesture across the pit.

Ayrah turned and saw the Warlord Lyta Tuio sitting in her double-sized box, atop her gold-and-black chair. Her hair was golden and fell in loose curls around her shoulders—an odd sight to see the thin, grainy hair of an Illian atop the calloused, yellow tan of Sigu Nii.

She felt her throat constrict and squeaked, "What does she want?"

The Black Guard shrugged.

Ayrah's eyes darted back and forth. From Malik to the pit to the several steps of space on either side of the Black Guard. She could make it, she decided. She could take this guard, kill him if necessary, and be up the stairwell before anyone knew what was happening.

Explosions on the pit shook the arena, and Ayrah from her mind.

"I could come," Malik offered. But there was disdain in his voice. It was no peace offering. It was a suggestion of meekness.

Ayrah knew this was the moment. Either she met Warlord Tuio, the all-powerful leader of the Gya province, who decreed Shadowa number eleven on the most wanted list or run forever.

She knew her brother had failed this test. And most likely, he was subject to running for the rest of his life. It was a lifestyle that Ayrah found to be beneath her.

"Just me." Ayrah approached the Guard hesitantly. He turned and gestured for her to walk the curving hallway first.

Around the pit they walked. Passing other guilds from Waike and from cities all around, fighters who quite literally had killed in attempts to be where the Tamagai stood.

They passed Black Guard officers, in charge of all inner-city policing. They passed lord mayors and blood-powerful nobles in charge of every other city aspect from travel to construction to the networks that supplied produce, wood, and metals. Any and all of these people, who might have attempted to have Ayrah call them *El*, would just as quickly have sacrificed their first born than come face to face on Lyta Tuio's request.

"So, the great bloodline of Veligreen has returned," said Warlord Tuio, facing the pit. Air funneled through her nose as Errta repeatedly smashed a Waterdome face with ablaze knuckles.

Ayrah approached. A white glass bowl of fruit sat on a decorative table beside the throne. She could only see the Warlord's hair over the golden back, and her right hand wandering through the bowl. Ayrah looked down at herself, suddenly worried about the openness of her borrowed garments from Urota.

"El," acknowledged Ayrah, the word caught in her parched throat like a salted cracker. She had only *ever* relented the title of respect on a few occasions, in her life, and even they were when she was a child.

"Bow," said Tuio. Her hand waved impatiently.

Ayrah stared at the ground. It was a clean ground. She had watched servants sweep and scrub furiously in anticipation of the Warlord's arrival. The contemplation of sacrificed glory, the means of exchanging exaltation from one to another pierced her gut. "No." Her voice was low. "Your title of El is good enough."

"Oh?"

Thunder cracked through the arena. Crowds fell silent as black lightning webbed and sizzled around the Warlord's chair. Center-pit explosions halted as heads turned to the deafening sound of Tuio teleporting behind Ayrah. "El Shadowa has not met someone worth bowing to."

A hand landed on the back of Ayrah's neck as quickly as the dark lightning vanished. The hand was neither hot nor cold, no blades, bristles, or poisons tracing through her fingers.

"Bow!"

Ayrah felt her knees buckle. Her hands hit the floor.

El Tuio guided her head down with a soft hand until her nose was pushed against the tile.

"You've been chasing the dead, I hear."

Ayrah watched her feet, dressed in glittering flats, pass with soft steps back to her chair. The Warlord whistled, and action gradually resumed on the pit, crowds regained their attention for Gya's championship.

Ayrah stretched her hands in and out, her wrists cold against the stone. She had bowed for the first time. A currency worth more than any coin. When it seemed safe, she straightened her back, still kneeling. "Aye." Her voice was cold, bitter.

"Ridiculous," said Tuio, "The errand killed your brother."

Ayrah swayed. "Verano is dead?" Besides command and authority, there was a manner of safety in having the blood of a Warlord reside in her veins. Sure, their specific circumstance had Pikemaster bounty hunters chasing after them for nearly half of a generation. But being as powerful as they were, danger was not a major concern.

Verano was dead? By whose hand?

Lyta Tuio turned and peeked back at Ayrah around the gold encrusted backing. "So, you've sought refuge among the Tamagai." She laughed small, breath heavy, nearly snorting. "As if Malik would hesitate on my request to be done with you. Tell me, Shadowa—Ayrah, daughter of Veli-green Castle—are you as foolish as the rest of your bloodline?"

Ayrah's teeth were clenched. "No, El."

Warlord Tuio turned back to the arena. She watched as her only son pumped his chest high with biceps straining on either side, a victorious gesture, and white fire beamed from him to chase the last standing member of the Waterdome guild, blasting him off his feet, melting parts of his chest, and crushing him against a pillar of the drop-off wall.

"Good," said Tuio. "Then I look forward to watching you attempt the Niiwa in Sehlya tomorrow evening."

26

EIDHIN

Eidhin waited with one hand in the other, trying to count the rows of wooden pews that faced him. *Three, four, five—* A moth distracted him as it spun furiously around the hellinite chandeliers, white candle wax threatening to drip off. Then El Penoa straightened each of their robes, flitting his hand like a duster across shoulder and stomach. *Six, seven. . . seven. . . e-e-e-*

Eidhin was smart. He knew that. Perhaps his lips could not keep up with his brain, or perhaps his brain was too fast for his lips. Either way, counting really was a tedious task. Best leave it to the El, right? Surely, they had already taken account of Gehni's population size, density, and drawn conclusions on how many pews would best fit their congregation.

He turned to the others. Ecagaus stood straight postured, like a line drawn from his upper-back to his legs. But his eyes, they looked so empty. Eidhin might have assumed any amount of daydream passed behind them, with his pupils ingrained on the blue-stained-glass, but he looked like a blank-eyed-horse.

Seraii's remaining feistiness may have carried on internally, but like the others, she stood tight-lipped, stiff backed, and with nearly locked knees. Another student was the last of their. . . four. Eidhin had not spent much time with him, but his narrow mind made him an early champion on rooftop Aylan-board games, though once his ways of thinking were determined by other students, he lost increasingly.

They held their breaths when the first of their new El breached the church doors. His head was clean shaven. His pale face was absent of any whiskers. The only accessory visible on his person was his gold-rimmed spectacles.

"El, welcome." Penoa closed the distance between them, meeting the newcomer half-way from the stage. "Come." He motioned for the other student.

Who is this man, whom even Penoa calls El? Awed a captivated Eidhin.

The bald man studied the graduating student up and down, fixing his glasses along the way. "Indeed. And what level of discretion must I use when speaking around him?" His accent was new. It was suave and flowed off one syllable to the next.

"Well, none at all, El." Penoa stifled a smug smile. His Gehni accent sounded especially crisp, but his rhetoric seemed to bend to this newcomer. "I assure you, the caliber of scribes produced from our Freedom Encryption program are far from the humble quality of your previous endeavors. Perhaps you purchased a great number from the Dajo family, but their scribes are easily persuaded by any passerby."

It was strange watching them interact. Previously, Penoa El was the grandest, smartest man Eidhin had ever encountered. But watching the two speak, observing their postures and tones, Penoa seemed like a brown onion leaf beside the bald man.

"I might suggest bringing him around for maintenance, but being a scholar in King Gehn's own regiment, I'm sure you're capable of such an accessible assessment."

"Indeed," said the El with little contemplation. He flipped open the button of his leather satchel and handed Penoa a rolled-up parchment.

Penoa unfurled the top and mumbled aloud, "Generation De'lm Bora. Accounts of misconceptions. Yes." He looked up. "This will do splendidly. I am of Bora, if you did not know, so—"

"I can see." He glanced toward the door. "We are done?"

"Indeed, indeed."

Eidhin was thrilled awaiting his new El. Of what stature would they be? He hoped their sole vocation would be to discover unknown principles. Papers on papers, scroll after scroll for him to copy and edit and study himself.

"Prepare yourselves," mumbled El Penoa after the others left. "The coming customer is a left-handed Masikonian trader. He uses his vuu in unorthodox ways. Do not let your faces show disgust." He warned.

When the church doors opened next, the unruly beast that entered was like something straight from a Sigu Nii fever dream. Rough, grainy hair of black and grey, silver-tipped like frost, covered his wolf-like paws. His deeply bent ankles shook as he clawed down the aisle. What great big teeth hung from his closed, slobbery, black-gummed mouth. And the beast wore no clothes, his canine part swung with each gained ground toward the Penoa El.

"Ah," said Penoa. "The Silver-Fur of the Opulent Roads."

What daunting creature was yanked from the depths of mythical underworlds, to derive such a stutter-provoking name? He imagined briefly how many seasons it might take to say his name aloud. Eidhin prayed to Hwaerta that this El was not his.

"Oi, am I in the right place?" The beast's voice swayed violently, between the grouch-ish growl of his clear wolfish anatomy and the high pitch hueing of stranded confusion. Like a musician playing the highest and deepest chords without any build between the two.

Saying that Eidhin knew vuu could do such things to a man, would be like saying Eidhin knew the capital of Sigu Nii was the city Sehlya. It was not an intimate relationship—this knowing. Stories of Masikonians mutating themselves to take whatever shapes they pleased certainly drifted this far north, but Eidhin never would have guessed he'd actually encounter one.

It made him feel uneasy and embarrassed. The Silver-Fur of the Opulent Roads was rather hard to look at, and Eidhin found his gaze returning to the hellinite chandelier.

"Indeed. Come Ecagaus."

Eidhin expected Ecagaus to chase reluctantly. Perhaps even shoot a glance back at him and Seraii. But the graduating student walked briskly and steadily to stop patiently near Penoa's side.

"Well," began the Silver-Fur beast, "This vacation of mine has been . . . informative." He said it as if exhausted. "Several of the Isle Lords said I just had to stop here and pick up the most obedient slave I could imagine. Here I am. So I ask, do their downstairs work?"

"Wh—that—yes. Yes, you may do as you please. I apologize deeply for my momentary loss of composure, but we do not typically receive a request so abrasive."

"And I can pay in gold?"

Penoa scoffed. "As if your gold had any value."

"I can turn this whole church gold."

"No."

Eidhin was astonished with El Penoa's decision. Even just a single gold coin would have been life changing on the farm. To turn the whole church gold? That would be a lot of money. Was Ecagaus' assistance with study worth that much?

"Fine, like I have any use for this." The beast reached his human-like hands, covered in fur and tipped with black-painted claws, into folds in his fur and pulled out a scroll.

Penoa mumbled aloud, "Historical Accounts of the Masikonian Kortaes. Origin—ooh," Penoa tipped his head, "An original copy. This will do."

Ecagaus gave one final glance back at the rest of them as he and the beast exited the building. His face and eyes were mostly blank, perhaps the tiniest hint of wistful horror.

And then it was only Eidhin and Seraii, anxiously awaiting their El. They had been told several days prior that they had studied adequately and were being passed on as scribes, apprentices, students of El greater than those they had been hitherto learning under.

They were told the El taking them under was greater than any other and he would acquire them both.

And when the doors opened, a stout, sweaty, chubby man waddled in wearing a gentleman's suit that clung to his rolls. His hair was brushed over a sun-spotting bald head, and red-hair chops sprouted on either side of his chin.

"Tuladrna," Penoa said with an escaping breath.

"Indeed." The man bowed what little degree his belly allowed. "The El Illyadra Kalyn Vylndaer is predisposed to beckonings by the king. Would it be, I humbly hope that I might be suitable in his stead."

Penoa waved an impatient hand. "Yes, yes. Alright, okay." The affirmations spilled from his lips. "I've told El Vylndaer an encounter longer than a greeting would be sufficient for any of ours. What have you brought me instead?"

"A complete map of Zoë, and her greater regions."

The church doors opened, and two casually dressed men carried in a large scroll. So large that when Penoa began to unfurl it, he instructed Eidhin and Seraii to move the pews out of the way.

And it was beautiful. To have been taught geography is a valuable thing. To receive a mastered, detailed illustration of the known world? It was El.

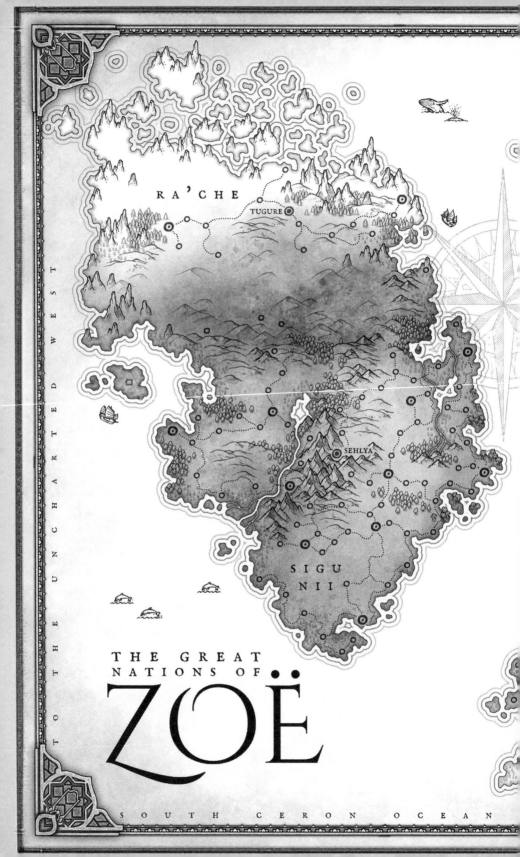

RA'CHE

TUGURE

SEHLYA

SIGU
NII

THE GREAT
NATIONS OF
ZOË

TO THE UNCHARTED WEST

SOUTH CERON OCEAN

27

MINES

The subtle sound of high-pitched laughing stirred Kairo from his dreams. His eyes opened slowly to the thin sheets of metal around him, tacked to thin wooden boards to form crude walls and a roof. He had taken shelter in one of Ravid's various shacks.

Kairo had almost forgotten the white-haired kid. But there he sat with arms wrapped around his knees staring blankly at a corner. Had he laughed? Kairo pushed himself up and rubbed his eyes.

Kairo was thinking of something to say, like hi or good morning, when his stomach grumbled and broke the silence. Wesken turned slowly, his eyes hesitating to unfix themselves from the corner.

"Oh no." Wesken's brows caved.

"What?" Kairo asked, worry filling him.

"You're hungry. That means we have to *work*."

Kairo scoffed. He pushed himself into a crouched stand and held his hand against the low flimsy metal ceiling.

"See look. We're already going now." Wesken's voice was small and mumbly, as if his tongue hadn't learned to properly enunciate.

"You can stay here." Even as Kairo said it, Wesken scrambled to stand. The kid crouched under the low ceiling, though he was short enough to stand upright. His clothes were strange, foreign somehow. An assortment of deep blues were long faded from his thin dirty tunic.

"How long have we been here?" Wesken asked. They walked down an alley, opening onto the broken streets of Ravid.

"What? I just arrived last night. I was about to ask how long *you've* been here."

"Oh. You were? That's funny. I'm sort of psychic, so I probably heard the question before."

Kairo stopped and faced Wesken. "You're an Oracle too?"

"Ora-what?" Wesken laughed a small, high pitch, rapid sort of laugh. "No, no. I'm psychic."

"What is psychic?"

"It means I can see the future."

"So, you're an Oracle. You have dreams of the events to come."

"Dreams? I hope not! My dreams are *crazy*. No. Nothing like that. I just think about what might happen, and then it happens."

Kairo let a sigh escape him as he kept walking. Something about his emphasis on crazy rung true.

The high grey walls around Ravid hid the sun, casting a long shadow over most of the city. Though from his time spent in the rebellion, meticulously planning on the rise and fall of the sun, Kairo could tell it was a little over an hour into daylight. By the feel of the morning, the moisture, the way the light looked and felt, he knew the time.

Something ached within him, a pinching, churning feeling in the top of his gut as he watched several other Renovians rise from piles of trash and crumbling stone. They filed in before him and behind, all shuffling toward the north wall. All of them were covered in dirt, some had long cuts on their forearms or dried splatters of blood somewhere on their bodies.

The sound of a foot scraping on the street and pebbles kicking up past Kairo made him turn. Wesken had stumbled. The white-haired kid looked up and pursed his lips. "I tripped." He said.

"On what?" Kairo gestured to the mostly even ground.

"My attention."

"That doesn't even make sense." Kairo turned back as they approached the slowing crowd of Renovians by the hole. Two dozen, Kairo counted. Hardly a step between each of them. What is it with Renovians and standing so close? He itched in the crowd, unable to move freely. The smell of rotting flesh came from the prisoners beside him, in front of him, and behind. Here they were again. Slaves to vipers.

Kairo found himself in the front of the group. The ground in front of his feet declined steadily until there was no light to be seen. Sigu Nii soldiers stood in a circle around the hole, talking wearily amongst themselves in the morning hour.

A tall Sigu Nii with a two-piece serpent coiling around his shoulder lifted a pickaxe for Kairo. The tool had a wood handle, smooth and grimy where the hands would grip.

Kairo mumbled a word of appreciation out of instinct and began the walk down. The tunnel weaved and curved round and round, the light above fading away. The sound of Kairo's steps echoed off the hard rock walls, along with that of a dozen other prisoners. As the light disappeared, he used his free hand to feel the way.

"Do you want to hear a joke?" Wesken's light-hearted voice couldn't have been more out of place.

"Sure."

"Okay. Uhm. How many Renovians does it take to kill a Sigu Nii?"

"Well that would depend on—"

"None! The Sigu Nii will do it themselves!"

Kairo let a bit of air funnel out of his nose. Warm light began to glow around the corner of the dark stone walls, along with the sound of metal colliding on stone.

"I guess you might not find that one funny. Uhm," Wesken hummed in thought. "Okay. Why is Masikus called the country of the colorless coin?"

"I've never heard—"

"Because dyes cost coin!"

"That doesn't even make sense."

The tunnel opened to a vast cavern that was sixty staggered steps across, between boulders, with various tunnel entrances, and an assortment of rock spikes with drips of water between them. It was warm and humid in the cavern, a feeling that reminded Kairo of the jungle. Along the walls, several torches dimly lit the room.

Renovian prisoners parted from each other in every direction. Some smashed their picks against the walls in the cavern they stood, others continued down more tunnels.

"What are we supposed to do?" Kairo asked, looking around the cavern.

"We have to find hellinite. It's a hard, dark metal that Sigu Nii mix with a bit of iron and copper, and they use it for just about everything."

Mix? Kairo's face hued quizzically at Wesken. Metal doesn't mix—it's metal. "Okay. . ... How do you know when we see it?"

Wesken scrunched his brows together in thought before giving a weak shrug. "Follow me. I know a good spot." The kid began down an adjacent tunnel on their right.

"Wait!" Kairo called and ran after him. He found it difficult to run with his heavy pick rubbing against his right shoulder. The kid was fast. Kairo worried that he was faster even than himself. With heavy breaths, and bright lights flashing across his vision, he decided food was an urgent necessity. "So . . . this is it?" Kairo asked. The kid had stopped nowhere of note. It seemed to be in the middle of a random tunnel, up against a random flat of wall clear of vertical pick marks.

Wesken nodded, and without any hesitation, turned to the wall and began heaving a pickaxe much too large for him. The tunnel rang with the sound of metal and rock clashing, and small bits of stone broke and fell against the ground. The tunnel was dark, but a small bit of light made its way through.

Kairo frowned, heaved a deep breath, and swung his axe against the wall. The handle vibrated violently. A handful of broken stones fell. After swinging a sword countless times he thought his hand would be used to the impact, but at least his hilt was wrapped with leather.

"So how . . . did you . . . end up . . . here, anyway?" Kairo asked between swings.

A moment passed. Wesken didn't answer.

"Wesken?"

"What?" The kid turned, leaning on his pick.

"How did you end up here?"

Wesken stared at him in the dim light. Kairo watched little thoughts running behind his light grey eyes. "I'm . . . not sure."

Kairo let a single, confused chuckle escape him. "What do you mean? How do you not know?"

"I don't really, uhm—*quiet!* I don't really remember things like that."

"Things like what?"

Wesken turned back to the wall and shifted the wood handle in his hands. "Like *how* things happen."

Kairo hesitated. "Explain."

Wesken laughed. Another high-pitched, rapid sort of laugh. "Every day I forget what happened the previous day. And sometimes even more often than that." He spoke soft and quickly. "I think—I think I remember *why* things happen a bit better. Like information. Not events."

"Oh. That's why you asked me how long we had been here."

"Sure." Wesken laughed and shook his head.

"Well, I'll tell you what. Let's get back to this hellinite stuff, so we can eat. I think I'm about to starve to death."

"Starve to death." Wesken laughed. "As if I could starve."

Kairo scrunched his brows. "Have you never gone hungry?"

"Probably. But no chance something as silly as starvation—"

"It's not funny," Kairo snapped. "I've seen people starve. Your body eats itself until there's hardly even skin left to eat. I'd rather die by fire than starve."

"Why don't they just eat food?"

Kairo softened his voice. "Sometimes they don't have any food to eat." He wondered how Wesken was so young. When he was Wesken's age, he had already fought a Sigu Nii to the death.

"Just eat the little friendlies. The furry ones. They climb around the trash."

Kairo blinked, and started under his breath, "I didn't even think—" His voice came close to a growl. "Why didn't we eat one last night?"

Wesken shrugged. "I probably wasn't hungry."

The morning was still fresh as Wesken climbed through a decaying pile of trash. "Here little friendly!" He called in an exaggerated high tone, and then grumbled in an exaggerated low, "Mr. guy wants some yummies!"

Kairo watched, amused. He watched the half-step long critters, with rubbery hair and leathery tails scurry about the trash and peek their heads out at the call of Wesken's voice.

Wesken pursed his lips and made silly noises as the critters chased him down the trash. He ran down a narrow alley with a drove of critters in tow.

Kairo chased after him. He rounded a corner into the thin box-framed shack where they had slept. The shed couldn't have been larger than seven steps and five reaches. In one corner black soot marks rose against the tin where a fire had been, a small pile of ash underneath, along with several twigs up against the wall.

Wesken sat cross-legged in the middle of the shed, a pile of trash rodents screeching and chasing each other in a circle around him. "Okay, who's the yummiest? Tell me. Tell me which of you is the yummiest." One jumped up and squirmed in Wesken's lap. The kid smiled and patted the rodent, then clenched its neck and twisted.

A small snap, and the rat fell limp. The other critters screeched in fear and piled over one another as they fled the room.

Kairo's eyebrows rose, and his lips parted to say something, but nothing came out. He sat where he had slept the previous night and watched as the kid took one of the twigs, gently nuzzled it into the critter's tiny mouth, and drove the stick all the way through its body.

Wesken piled the remaining sticks together in a triangle tent fashion, with the rodent's stick poking diagonally above it. He stopped and stared for a moment. "Light," he said. The pile of sticks didn't. He sighed aloud, grabbed two of the sticks from the tent, and began rubbing them together furiously.

Kairo heard a noise gargle out of his own throat.

Wesken twisted around. "What?"

"I've changed my mind." He said. "These rodents are filthy. I would rather just mine for their hellinite."

Wesken shook his head. "We can cook the dirt off—"

"Not on the inside. Filth is just as much a moral trait as it is a physical one. Like the barbarians. Their stinky must is a sign that they need a bath *and* some prayer."

"Oh." Wesken's brows arched in curiosity for a moment before descending back over his eyes in a squinty apprehension. His chin slowly descended. His neck lowered toward his torso, and he gave one singular audible sniff. He frowned and shrugged. "I'm not too stinky. But I don't want to be stinky on the inside! Not even lightly! Fix it!"

Kairo chuckled. "What? How would I do that?"

"Just use your vuu."

Kairo's lips curled up over his teeth. "I don't have any." He said it with pride. "There's nothing *stinkier*." Arden had begun to convince him otherwise. Slowly. But after the Niiwa, and his imprisonment in Ravid, his worldview did an inadvertent assertion of the fact.

Wesken frowned. "Me neither. Actually, I don't even know what I am, much less what vuu I would have." He shrugged and giggled. "*Rai* is, I don't remember anything, anywhere, or anyone I've ever met before yesterday."

"Can I tell you something?" Kairo asked.

Wesken didn't respond but waited silently.

"I'm going to die." Kairo sighed. "I know that sounds crazy—"

"It doesn't sound crazy. You know what *does* sound—wait, no. Stop! Sorry, keep going."

Kairo let a single chuckle escape him. "My leg was slashed, and it got infected. If I had to guess, I only have a handful more days to live."

Wesken made a slow swatting motion. "Nah. You're not gonna die."

"What? How do you know that?"

"The same way I know you're going to escape from here. You've got a cloud of destiny around you that won't leave you alone. You've got places to be, friends to save, enemies to kill. You won't be here long."

"You're a strange kid, Wesken."

28

EIDHIN

Gehni Isle, City of Gehni, Gehni's Harbor. It was a bleak day. The water was dark, nearly black under the dense overcast.

Tuladrna led Eidhin and Seraii past an ocean-front market, around floating boardwalks, through a jungle of ropes and poles and fish smells. He caused the day's lack of shine, saying, "We have a five-day sail ahead of us," he waddled his way to a sloop and crossed a working line of sun-parched, wind-burnt, shark scarred, and snarly skinned men to step aboard. The runes *De.Ae.Ar.* were burned into each crate and barrel in a pile being loaded from the dock to the boat.

At the start of the current forecast, Eidhin had the impression that he would meet his El on this day. Now he had to endure Seraii, whose complex resembled a cherry tree on some days and a Sigu Nii with a splinter on others. "This is our vessel?" Her voice was like a cat's hiss. "One might think the Illyadra of Philosophy could afford more than a dingy."

Eidhin winced, ready for Tuladrna to whip a scold across his new scribe. But he wasn't the one who turned.

"Dain't you talk twice, lil' girl." Several surrounded her. The sea dog who spoke had a tobacco roll stuck between his lips, muffling his ocean-soggy accent. They picked up Seraii, to her yelling and kicking, and tossed her aboard.

Each of them had their own cabin below deck, a first for Eidhin. That night, long after they watched Gehni's Harbor roll away, he lay awake. Alone. The bow of the ship faced the waves, so the rocking went from his feet to his head. Each time he closed his eyes, vision swept his mind: drowning. Flailing in the black waters of night. He couldn't breathe, and his fingers were scraping against drenched cloth. The blue Church of Rai sigil passed his sight. Was it a pile of robes waterboarding him? Eidhin opened his eyes, sighed a shaky breath, and laid awake.

"W-w-w-"

Tuladrna's fingernails scratched against the boat's side rail, he shivered as he swept his book out of the way. "Not while I'm reading." His blubbery face and orange chops shook when he spoke. "I can tolerate your stutter when prepared, but dear Hwaerta boy, not while I'm reading."

Eidhin slumped and waited to see if El Tuladrna would offer his attention, but the book took him back. It was good to know: Do not disturb him while he's reading.

Each time Eidhin spotted land on the horizon he rushed to the deck, his head and shoulders leaning over the side rail as he peered beyond the blue. But Aylavuera was crowded with islands. Small ones, big ones, sometimes they had to maneuver the boat between reefs and sharp black rocks jutting from the ocean.

On the third day at sea, Eidhin felt so bored of daydreams that he prompted himself to talk to the captain. A large man whose burly hands were found clasped around the wheel more frequently than not. His whole presence radiated Sigu Nii, but his skin, however sun tanned as it were, was fair-colored.

"Wh-wh-e-re a-a-are w-w-we g-g-goin-ng?" Eidhin asked.

The captain's eyes passed over Eidhin, up and down. The corners of his lips curled over. "You don't know what you are, do ya?"

"A st-st-t-tud-d-den-nt-t."

"Argh!" The captain winced. "North, 'round the city of Spar'ad. Then 'bout ten to twenty degrees east, toward the port town of Talynguard." He spoke quickly and began to inspect the integrity of the wheel.

"Dirt in me britches!" yelled one of the sea dogs on the evening of the fifth day. It was the first time Eidhin watched an island pass the nose of the boat. Tuladrna and Seraii made their way to the bow and leaned against the railing.

They watched Talynguard approach, a shanty wooden sea town taking up the only visible beach on the small island, which was mostly cliff touching water. On the highest point was a castle of whitestone with towers overlooking the ocean.

"Vylndaer manor."

"What is he like?" Seraii asked.

"A genius, by any measure." Tuladrna's voice was wistful. "But Vylandria has demanded more of his time than anticipated. He won't arrive until tomorrow evening."

It was a bleak day.

The men with calloused blubber for skin yelled and hollered, ropes flung this way and that. The boat secured, they slid a plank out from the deck. The three disembarked, and the sea dogs unloaded most of the crates they had brought aboard.

The boots of the three clacked down the long dock. Waves jostled between boats and dock pylons, and mountainous cliffs loomed to either side as they approached the beach.

The wood from the boardwalk melted with dirty sand as they passed the first set of buildings. Eidhin avoided dark rocks jutting from the path and murky brown puddles alike. Many of the shack-like shops were closed, and long-dried twine nets hung everywhere.

The *De.Ae.Ar.* sigil was ingrained all over Talynguard. A dozen laid on the mud-stuck planks from the shack beside Eidhin. Some of them were full, each rune visible, others were sawed to fit corners, or broken into bits so that just a burnt line of *De* could be seen.

It seemed the shipping company and its corresponding crates, delivered more than just supplies and resources, but building materials. Eidhin's lip curled up. These people were poorer even than himself.

"What happened to this place?" Seraii asked, a horror muffled in her voice.

"Sorry?" Tuladrna asked.

"I just—I imagined Illyadra Vylndaer's living to be spectacular. A grand city with markets, schools and lecture halls for travelers all around to come and sip from the El's cup of knowing."

"The El Kalyn is quick to a solitary setting. A preference you had best understand. Though he does teach classes in Vylandria once a season. The capital is only a day's sail away, in good weather." Tuladrna sighed and gave a quick glance around. "As for Talynguard, they receive the first fruits of El Vylndaer's social philosophizing. A testing ground for how people could be."

"Whatever is being tested doesn't seem to be working," said Seraii.

Tuladrna huffed. "They are between experiments. Kalyn starves them of attendance to reset them."

Eidhin awed at that. He had commented on Seraii's lack of nurturing her mouse as being unintentional negative influence. But here, the Illyadra ignored his people on purpose. To reset them. He ignored them long enough that his previous influences would go away, so he could test new influences.

The shanty town climbed the face of the mountain. The path became broad stairs of wooden frames holding compacted sand. Water trickled down a ditch beside them.

Tuladrna paused frequently for breaths.

Eventually the buildings were replaced by farmlands. Eidhin peered down the valley and saw that rolling hill upon rolling hill was covered in terraces of tall green crops ready for harvest. They came to two tillers in a field. "A bit o' truth, El?" They asked, hands stuck out and tongues passing over sun-dried lips.

Tuladrna ignored them. He forced each shaking leg to the next stair.

"A s'ribble o' words?" they pleaded.

The worker's skin was even darker than the captain's. But they looked frail, their skin brittle and already bleeding. When you're working on the farm, you're always breaking skin from something. Sometimes it's not until dinner that you notice, when Mum would holler for staining the tablecloth.

Eidhin lingered, empathetic. He came from a place much like theirs. A bit of attendance is what an onion needs. "Y-y-you n-n-need t-to—"

Their lips unraveled. The corners pinched up near their nostrils, and laughter spilled from their cheeks. They laughed and laughed, they slapped their knees, dust billowing from their trousers. "Slave boy," one of them squealed.

Eidhin's face burned. He could feel his heart slam against his chest. He watched them for half a moment, his mind racing through all that he could say. Like the Aylan-board. If he could just let them into his mind, they would understand. He was hardly conscious of his hand reaching for their foreheads.

"Eidhin!" Tuladrna's voice cracked like a whip. "Come here, *now*."

Like a gutter unclogged, every boiling emotion drained from him. His face cooled, and his lips felt chapped. And why were those two farmers laughing again? Tuladrna was calling him. He raced up the sandy stairs. "S-s-sorry, E-e-el."

The man sighed, his belly rolls spilling back over his buckle.

The path to Vylndaer Manor turned to white brick with golden grout. Eidhin nearly dropped to his knees, he fought the urge to dig his finger-nails and scrape out the gold grout. And it shone. In the orange light of the falling sun, each white brick had a radiant halo.

A cliff wall to their right shortened with each stair gained. Above it sat what Eidhin assumed to be a wing of the manor, a humongous dome building, whitestone, with all sorts of metal tubes and glass.

They now stood atop a blackrock cliff that guarded the south and west sides of the manor, with sparkling ocean stretching across the horizon.

"It's beautiful," said Seraii, but when Eidhin turned to agree, he saw that she faced the manor. A palace of a building whose roof was dominat-ed by two triangular gables, shingled with slate, and tinted glass windows looking out from each. Between the gables was a flat area with gazebos and trees and a greenhouse. A circular tower rose behind the dome building.

Nearly everything was made of whitestone. But there was a strange blue gem that trailed through the walls like veins. The gem was deep, splotchy, with a soft light emanating from it on and off, slowly, hardly noticeable.

The dark double doors, seamed with ornately forged hellinite, opened at their approach by two suit-clad servants. Their postures were stiff and their faces blank.

Eidhin and Seraii shared a glance and wearily followed a waddling Tuladrna. Everything was ornate, grand, and expensive. Across the rug, floorboard, and tile, Eidhin kept his steps light, afraid that sand clung to notches in his boots and might come off on anything. They walked from a tearoom to a room with a fire pit and a lingering tobacco smell, from a dining hall with crystal chandeliers to a kitchen with a Masikonian hard at work.

Tuladrna went through a door that led back outside. They followed a dirt path around hedges and lawns, statues with water sprinkling into bowls, and came upon another wing of the manor. The walls were painted a creamy-yellow, cracking, and with shutter windows.

Tuladrna opened a wooden door. Inside was musky, like a closet full of shoes and no ventilation. Bunk beds lined the cracking stone and plaster walls. Eidhin began to count them, but Seraii interrupted in her pitched voice, "Why are you showing us the servant quarters?"

"Oh, of course." Tuladrna shook his head. "I forget that you arrive under the pretense-fixation that the El Vylndaer is your solitary instructor. Let the notion fall from your mind, children. Many serve the Vylndaer family, hoping to squeeze table scraps. I am no different, though my competence has earned me a bedroom in the manor and responsibilities that have consequence."

Seraii strode to one of the beds and swept a finger across dusty sheets. Her mouth trembled. "We're just slaves, aren't we?" Her eyes looked wet and she bobbed up and down as if her knees were aching.

Tuladrna sighed heavily. "Listen little—"

"No!" Seraii shook her head and clasped her ears. Her eyes shut tight, and she sank to the ground. "I don't want to hear anymore!" she cried.

"I swear, you can never find good help these days." Tuladrna waddled to her, bent over, and ripped her hands away. "Information is warring within you, girl. Let me settle the disagreement."

"No!" Seraii screamed. Her voice wavered from strain but she kept screaming as if another heard word from Tuladrna would kill her.

Tuladrna's arms shook. He cursed, and he slammed the crevice of his palm across her forehead. The screaming ceased. There was silence for a moment.

Eidhin's hands dripped with sweat. There was very little air flow in the quarters, and he was practically rubbing them raw. He had never seen so much emotion shown, ever.

The girl complained about the state of the boat. She quivered at the state of Talynguard. Now, she revolted against the quarters of the Vylndaer

Manor. When El Penoa traveled to her region, and preached advocation for discontentment, he must've been singing with Rai. *An intellectual harmony to persuade her very core,* Eidhin frowned.

Tuladrna's hand lifted from Seraii's forehead. She gasped for breath, the bunk bed screeched as she strained back, her feet slid out against the cement floor. She rocked gently, her eyes fixed on the door, though there was a glaze on them that suggested she stared past it.

"There are clothes laid out on your beds." Tuladrna pointed wearily down the aisle of bunks. Beads of sweat lined his scraggly orange hair. "Come to the kitchen as soon as you're changed. The Vylndaer Lady and offspring need serving."

"Elbows high, like this," Tuladrna raised Eidhin's right elbow.

The black clad gentleman's suit, omitting a jacket, felt taught around his body. The flexibility that Tuladrna required for something as simple as pouring liquid into a cup felt unnecessary. Though, Eidhin admitted, the bottle of wine caressed in his hands was probably worth more than his father's farm.

"Indeed, that will have to do." Tuladrna gave him a nudge through the double-swinging kitchen doors.

The dining table was long enough to fit all of Snowstock, but each ornate, gold-and-blue chair sat empty save four at the end of the hall. It was a walk, and Eidhin couldn't help but let his eyes slide across the decorated walls. There were portraits of old men under a gleaming gold crown, webbed by the same blue gem that he had seen outside.

He realized, this family used to be a royal dynasty in Ages past.

The Lady Vylndaer sat nearest to Eidhin. Her golden hair shone in the chandelier candlelight, and her clothes were frilly and puffy and lacy.

The Lady's three children sat around her: a girl near Eidhin's age; a girl in her mid-pubescent age, who wore gold-rimmed spectacles and strips of real silver in her hair; and a young man with short black hair, in a puffy white button-down shirt and a black-and-gold-trimmed coat on the back of his chair.

Eidhin tried to steady himself. His hands were shaking. *Elbows high.* They were near the end of their meal. He approached the Lady's glass and made a gesture to ask if she would like more. He prayed to Hwaerta that she understood and wouldn't have to use his stuttering voice.

"They look ridiculous. If your eyesight were improved any more, you would be able to see through walls." The Lady nodded vaguely for Eidhin to pour.

Steady, pour. Steady.

"They're called spectacles, Mum, and they don't have any concave. They're the latest fashion trend in Vylandria. You wouldn't understand."

That's a full glass. Did I pour too much? Everyone else is too young, right?

"Hush now. The golden glasses, the silver hair, the slick clothes, haven't we taught you to rise from such peasantries? You should be setting trends, not following them."

"Hold. You there, servant," the young man spoke. His voice was strange. "Come 'round and fill my glass. My family's comfortability with dull insights has me thirsty."

Eidhin began around the table. The Lady Vylndaer caught him by the arm. Eidhin winced in fear. But her attention was not on him.

"Kal, you know how your father feels about alcohol."

Kal. He was like Eidhin. The last generation in a cluster, receiving a shortened version of his father's name.

The young man sighed, "You drink, Mother. And when did feelings get Father anywhere?"

"Well, I don't have a kingdom to maintain, or even a portion of it. My wits were enough to land me you mother, but now they do me little use." The Lady's grip tightened around Eidhin's forearm with each sentence passed. "If you presume to take Kalyn's place eventually, you'll need to retain all that you were given at birth. Please, Son, unless you want to end up a servant for some other Illyadra, don't take the drink."

Kal glared at his mother, "If my cleverness is in question, damageable however much by one glass, then note that my attention is not. I find it difficult to muster care for this eroding kingdom you say I'm to inherit. Perhaps if my amusement was moldable, say by drink, then maybe I would find myself ingesting more of Father's countless books and lessons."

Eidhin felt his eyes gloss over. *If only. . .* A momentary absence in his train of thought. It was brief, and when he came to, he noticed that whatever El Kal had been saying, it worked on his mother. The Lady released her grip on Eidhin's arm.

He continued around the end of the table, and just as he raised the glass bottle, an explosion in the adjacent room shook the manor. Like the cracking of thunder. The crystal chandelier jingled dangerously.

Kal slid a hand on top of Eidhin's and guided the bottle of wine beneath the table, hidden from view.

The dining hall doors threw open, slamming against the walls. The figure's head was downturned, his long black hair soaking and dripping water across the tile. His calf-length black overcoat swayed behind him, glowing with blue gem buttons. His head whipped up. Wet hair clung to the sides of his face. "*Tuladrna!*" he shouted.

The Illyadra Kalyn Vylndaer looked young. Much younger than Eidhin might have guessed. The color of his eyes were black, with a ring of solid blue bordering his pupils.

Tuladrna's racing down the hall was a sight. His orange combover threatened to unslick from the top of his head as his waddle resembled a keeling ship. "El." He bent his back as perpendicular to his legs as his belly allowed.

"Send for the ship. I've returned without them." The Illyadra's tone contained the utmost urgency.

"At once, El. But why have you—"

Kalyn threw up his palm for silence. "Someone has convinced me of something untrue. I can feel it. It squirms around my brain. Feeding. I will be in my study until I find it. No one enter. No one send for me. Void all upcoming responsibilities, lest I infect one of you. And Tuladrna,"

"El?"

"It's time I employed a Razite."

29

WESKEN

Wesken sat in the middle of the shack, staring at a corner with wispy black soot marks. *I'm bored.* Nagged the bored voice. He was similar to the survival focused, *"I'm hungry"* voice, except the only conversation he was capable of spinning revolved around. . . *I'm bored.*

Yeah. Agreed Wesken. *What do you want to—*

Ooh. Let's get in a fight.

That sounds pretty fun. Who should we fight? Wesken glanced at the Renovian sleeping by the tin wall of his shack. The bones of his elbows were pointy, the skin around them clinging to what little meat they had. His face was sullen, his cheeks like dark pockets. His brown hair was oily with dirt clinging to knotted locks. *He's too skinny.*

Fight me!

Okay. The shack faded away as Wesken imagined fighting his self. He giggled audibly.

The sound of dirt and cloth ruffling against one another tore Wesken's mind back to the shack. His eyes itched to turn behind him but unfixing his gaze from the pile of ash was difficult. A strain to readjust the dimension of his attention.

"Eghem." The Renovian coughed as he pushed himself into a sitting position.

Wesken locked eyes with him, which provoked a long moment where the air drew heavy and the hair on the back of his neck stood on end. A sensation like slabs of marble falling in his stomach made him feel queasy. He wanted to break the silence, but the first thing he wanted to say caused a double-back on the beginning of the whole uncomfortable moment—he forgot the dude's name.

"Are you ready, Wesken?" asked the Renovian. "We have a long day ahead of us. And I'm quite certain that if we don't find hellinite down in the caves today, then I'll not have enough energy left to pick up a pickaxe, in which case I will starve to death."

Forgetting the name forgetting thing, Wesken swatted through the air and giggled, "Starve to death."

The Renovian shot him a glare that would have sparked fatal manifestations of Vuulguard in the world around them, had the guy any vuu.

Oh no! Cried the voice that Wesken had nicknamed Greg, when Kairo began to stand. *Now we have to work!*

Yeah. Agreed Wesken. *I'd rather stay here, and time travel the time away.*

We could daydream, like—uhm, what if all the clouds in the world suddenly turned solid and dropped out of the sky?

Wesken giggled at the funny sight in his mind, which caused the Renovian to glance sideways at him, which in turn silenced the afore-mentioned giggling. Despite the knots of dread that stirred within him, Wesken stood slouched in the tin shack, ready to follow the Renovian into the mines.

Along the way, he daydreamed an Illian getting plucked out of Aylavuera and dropped into the middle of a Niiwa, where the man had to fight for his life with nothing but his words. The scene depicted in Wesken's mind was so engaging, vivid, and entertaining, that when the gravel street inclined slightly, Wesken stumbled.

The Renovian scoffed. "You literally did that. . . never mind."

"My attention," Wesken answered.

"Amazing." He shook his head.

The two of them joined a clustering crowd of prisoners walking at a crawl's pace toward Sigu Nii guards at the mine entrance. Wesken watched his prison mate. He itched in the crowd. His face contorted into such pain, it looked as if a tsunami were crashing down upon him while he stopped to tie his shoelace. It was fear-stained like moments before torture.

Is he scared of being slow?

I'll bet it's his upbringing. You can always blame a man's tasteless features on his upbringing.

Truth be told, he understood, Wesken hated the slow trudge also. But it didn't torture him enough to poke cries from his soul. *Look,* laughed a voice. *It affects him so visibly!* Wesken's attention returned to his eyes from the realm of contemplation. Kairo was more than showing discomfort—he was rolling on the ground in absolute agony.

I'm not sure this is due to the crowd. He replied.

Kairo's face widened with a fishhook pinch at the corners. His chin thrust at the crowd. Wesken thought he was showing off his teeth, but they weren't well kept.

Kairo's back began to arch in such a degree that the trash rats might've used it like a bridge to cross the green-gutter streams. His hands darted out, each finger stiff, like a zombie bursting from a grave, and grabbed portions of his body like they were running away.

"Uhm, do you want help?" Wesken offered Kairo his hands. Not to help him to stand, rather, they were turned up in pleas of retreat. He jiggled them as if to say, *Take my hands and delegate them to be most useful in this time.*

Kairo only continued to roll.

By now, the Renovian crowd had backed away. Whispers and murmurs took them. A singular choice word repeated from every direction, "*Infection!*"

Sigu Nii shoved through the crowd and spilled into the inner circle of the spectacle. The soldiers' faces each turned from accumulated annoyance to disastrous surprise. "Get the warden," growled one.

"Ohh," Moaned another, "El is going to be *pissed.*"

"This one hasn't even gotten a food card." Yet another Sigu Nii guard hummed with fearful anticipation. "Not one." He turned back through the Renovian crowd and sprinted off toward the Stonehouse.

Kairo's back returned to the ground in a sudden kerplop. He began bending and unbending his leg at the knee, while resting its weight on the ground.

"Aye," Growled the first guard again, "Everyone back to work." It wasn't so much a command, since the prisoners of Ravid were free to work whenever they wanted. Or, more accurately, their labor was forced by more nuanced elements than a whip and chain.

The crowd dispersed.

Kairo was attempting to sit up when the warden arrived. An oily haired man that dressed in updated Masikonian fashion—for not-Masikonians, of course, since the powerful ones just sprouted animal parts for clothes.

He had the tattoo markings of Blood rank. And a mustache ended point-thin on either side of his nose. "What's going on?" He asked. His voice was not particularly deep or scratchy, but he growled because a grumpy tone of voice was practically a staple of the Sigu Nii accent.

"This one appears to have tetanus, El," replied the guard.

The warden cursed. "Do you have any cuts, filth? Show me."

Kairo nodded. His brow glittered with sweat in the morning hour. He avoided eye contact with the warden, and his hands shook as he peeled back his trouser pant leg. Though, Wesken figured, the fear-like symptoms could be due to the previous episode, rather than the fact that a man with the prerogative to kill Renovians with a swoop of his finger curled over to inspect his thigh.

The revealed gash evoked a genuine gag from Wesken. "That's disgusting." He said with a hand over his mouth.

One of the guards laughed in agreement.

It was black, blue, red, and white. Infection may not be technically visible, but oh boy, did this gash look infected. A small portion of the scab ripped during the unveiling process, and white-yellow puss oozed down the sides of Kairo's leg.

The warden cursed again, more violently this time. "They sold me a dead worker!" He shuddered with anger.

Wesken imagined miniature men in wet-retardant loincloths diving from the bouncing points of the warden's mustache.

Kairo winced in beat with the warden's pacing and cursing. Wesken was unsure if he was scared that the Blood ranked Sigu Nii would turn and punish Kairo for nearing death, or if Renovian culture was so prude that bad words kindled visible anguish.

"What the bloody El am I going to do?" The warden asked.

"Kill him." Shrugged one of the guards.

A blankness descended another of the guards' eyes, briefly, and there was the tiniest difference of crispness in his accent. "Pass it on," he said.

"Pass it on?" asked the warden.

"Aye. Pass it on. There's a cargo wagon headed to Vasara this evening."

"Pass it on. . ." Repeated the warden. The statement ended with a peculiar voice. He was definitely one to include a throaty nasal pitch towards the punchline of a good joke. "I'll sell him to Lord Mayor Ryaff!"

"Uhm, El?" Inquired the first guard. "Are you going to kill the slave traders that sold him?"

"Aye." Nodded the warden casually.

"Then won't Ryaff kill you?"

The warden hummed in thought while pinch rolling the ends of his mustache.

"Just lie." Huffed Wesken. "Tell him you didn't know."

"Wesken!" Kairo scolded.

"That's perfect!" yelled the warden. "We have to get him there quick; he would die on the walk."

30

AYRAH

"I still can't figure out what Lyta Tuio wanted," Ayrah muttered, peering at her rubbery, mutated hands in the morning hour.

They were still in Waike.

Sure, many of the commoners were furious with the Tamagai for defeating their home team, even killing a man, but last night had still been a party. And Waike, the capital city of the Gya province, parties hard.

There were honorable deaths in Sigu Nii, and dishonorable deaths. Dying in the Niiwa, for example, is a rather mediocre death. There are thousands of those a season. Dying in the Kaeselwa, however, was quite honorable. Tayo would be remembered dearly. . . at least until the current members of the Tamagai still lived. It wasn't *that* honorable a death. It wasn't so honorable that a statue would be erected in a town square, ever. At least it wasn't a grash, though. Of all the ways to die, that one was the worst. That was a mockery, no matter how strong you or your opponent may be.

Like the death of Ayrah's father. Even though he was a Warlord—even though he was grashed by whom Ayrah assumed to be the only being on the face of Zoë that would win, King Ash, it was a death that would be remembered by the world, for several generations. It was humiliating.

Tamagai-employed servants gathered swords, socks, Urota's favorite pillow, loose underpants, and the rest, and hauled it to a wagon outside. Their rented, inner-city manor was trashed. Bottles of bourbon lay upside down on couch cushions. Tapestries that looked generations old now had corners burnt off, and charr and ash several reaches toward its middle, where Ayrah and Errta had drunkenly swatted it the night before. Vases lay smashed on the cold tile. And the five of them that remained, slowly picking themselves up and making their way out the door, ignored it all.

Ecanaes shrugged. "To let you know that she knew who you were."

Errta hurtled the soft linen-covered couch and stuck his head between them. "You said she forced a bow. That's what she wanted." He waved his hands over his head, "*I'm a Warlord. I have people bow to me, low and high.*"

Ayrah giggled and pushed Errta's face away. It felt good. Laughing. For a sweet, brief moment, she had entirely forgotten about the king's Niiwa that evening. The Niiwa of Sehlya.

Until Ecanaes brought it back. "So, it's entirely up to you, El Veligreen. I understand the instinctual realm of Sigu Nii is something left desired among us other-colored peoples. But, having—"

Errta snored.

"*Having* studied combat analytics, I might be a useful tool to have at your disposal."

"What, like, you would be in the pit with me?" Ayrah asked, stifling an incredulous laugh.

"Don't be ridiculous. I would engage my thoughts with yours."

"That sounds distracting."

"I would remain utterly quiet when need be. Speaking only when of the utmost importance. From the stands, the elevated point of view, an Illian's insightful perspective could be El."

Ayrah hesitated. She recalled Ecanaes' pouting from the previous night. How he tried to warn the Tamagai of a Tayo-evaporating play by the Waterdome. "Okay. Aye. But if I tell you to get out of my head, I need you out."

His pale cheeks glistened. "Yes, of course. Splendid indeed."

Errta, Ecanaes, Ayrah, Urota, and Tagon passed their luggage-burdened wheezing servants straining to lift Urota's chest up onto the wagon.

Waike was festooned in decorations. Banners hung from every corner celebrating Warlord Tuio and the end of the age. Even the highly-ranked of Waike, with their horses or carriages, were covered with golds and reds and faces painted resembling their ancestors.

"It's going to be a party tonight!" Urota danced with her hips.

"Aye, even harder than last night." Errta smiled knowingly.

Summer, winter, fall, and spring—those seasons marked the turn of the weather across Zoë. The Oscillation however, marked the end of a season in the afterlife. It didn't follow strict increments of momentary measurement, not at least in the way that harvest-based seasons did. And this season was the end of a very, very long age. It was going to be a party, alright.

Ayrah just hoped she'd be alive for it.

The name of tomorrow's age was yet unknown, still unnamed by the Dii'raxis. But Sigu Nii had been Kortaes for so long now, it seemed that they were spreading *another* marking influence: transportation. Teleportation. Perhaps they would not only be the last Kortaes of the previous age, but also the first Kortaes of the next one. Truly, glory to Sigu Nii.

Tagon pulled a crystal from his pocket and dangled it by chain over his offhand. His eyes followed the swing, reading it, understanding it.

Ayrah's father had said something about Razite's timekeeping vuu when she was a child. Something or another about how seasons in the afterlife affects vuu, which does something to like, the weight drawing on the pendulum? Ayrah frowned, unsure.

Imagine if the long-lost healers, the Renovians, before they turned all savage-like, found out that Ra'che picked up their calendar? Ayrah chuckled. They'd probably be furious, maybe even damning the pendulum itself.

Urota told the Black Guard soldiers at Waike's Warlord Office that their servants were coming a few moments behind, hauling all their luggage, and not to make them wait in the daunting peasant lines or make them pay the fee. The Black Guard nodded. This was the treatment Ayrah received with Herk and Boden. Though the guild from Simula was a tiny, infant organization compared to the Tamagai, they were still El-tier in the small town. Even though Ayrah didn't have a Niiwa tattoo—yet—she was known as one of their members.

Black thunder struck through the Tuidiia as each of the Tamagai members teleported to the Sigu Nii capital.

Sehlya had no office. Instead, Warlord Tuio's growing international network of Vulgarhe teleportation pads was styled in the likes of a large garden square. Her black-and-gold insignia, the hand with the lightning striking through, was an inlaid brick mosaic between the plates. Great northern pines lined the square as a windbreak.

They passed over a thin ring of hellinite, separating the courtyard from the rest of Sehlya. Ayrah couldn't hear the ear-piercing thunder on the other side. She stopped and looked around. "How does that happen?"

Ecanaes smiled, always excited to explain something. "The Old Vulgarhe," He nodded at the strip of hellinite that they passed over, it had inscriptions on it. "It uses Masikonian vuu to distort the air density above it."

Ayrah hmphed. *The more you know.*

Sehlya, located on the northeast crescent end of the Ryvl mountain range, was drastically colder than Waike. Ayrah shivered. She hated being cold unless it was by her own vuu. In a sudden attempt to destroy it, she channeled warm vuu into her palms, puffed a breath of fire, and stroked the back of her arms.

Sky-reaching towers, made from ice as black as Ayrah's sword, blocked sight of the horizon. They radiated chill generations old. She realized, as her eyes traced up balconies and clear-ice windows, that the tops of the towers were all connected to something else—a dark, oval cloudlike something.

"What is that?" She asked, her sharpened retinas slowly telling her brain that the cloud was a solid structure.

"Sehlya's Niiwa arena," said Urota.

"It can't be . . ." Ayrah said breathlessly.

Sehlya and her towers were illuminated by red-and-gold paper lanterns. Each passerby wore the painted face of another, someone important or powerful in their bloodline. People sang, they danced in the streets, and cast vuu into the skies as the Tamagai passed through them. Errta snatched a mug full of ale out of someone else's hands and drank.

The crowds dressed in silk and hellinite armor alike. On display were Niiwa tattoos that moved and radiated unorthodox hues, or shone like gold, or swayed like shadows behind a fire. It was the staple of a Sehlyian victory. Instead of the city name being an inscription beneath the serpent, it was the only Niiwa tattoo in the world that had style.

"It's good to be home," said Urota.

Ayrah turned to her. "You lived here?"

"Aye."

"But your tattoo says Pratuel."

"Aye." She shrugged. "I wanted to be a victor more than I wanted Sehlya's branding."

Ayrah swallowed. Even Urota had not dared to take this Niiwa. Come to think of it, not even Kizmaldi Tuio had fought here.

"At least you only have to win the fourth round." She shrugged, probably seeing the look on Ayrah's face.

Of course it would only be the fourth, thought Ayrah reproachfully. The fifth round was practically a farse in every city besides this one. Each round had its own set of rules on what style of Sigu Nii vuu was allowed. But the fourth took out those rules, you could fight with Sigu Nii vuu however you wished. The fifth? Other kinds of vuu were allowed. It was a battle between the Ohaer.

There're so few Ohaer, that it was only here, in Sehlya, that the fifth round was authentically utilized.

Errta laughed. "Don't be too scared. But you won't be facing any Renovians today."

Horns sounded behind them. They were loud but harmoniously gentle on the ears. Their tunes echoed off the black ice towers all around them. Ayrah turned and saw a host of Masikonians marching down the black-stone street. "Make way for King Drastos!" they yelled, as inviting as it was demanding.

The Tamagai moved off the street and watched as four giant men, whose skin looked like rock, carried a float. Their synchronized steps were slow and mechanical.

The float was made from gold and platinum and silver, with glittering rainbows of gems. Dancers and singers leapt, transformed into birds in a blink of the eye, and landed on human feet once again. They spun and kicked, singing with ear-melting melody.

Atop the first float stood the most gorgeous people Ayrah had ever laid eyes on. With blue and white fur adorning the queen's privates like clothes, and hair like a river of silver. Her face looked young, with edges still soft. "She can't be older than a generation," whispered Ayrah. She was basically a child.

Ecanaes snorted. "Like Lyta Tuio couldn't be any older than two? They're all Ohaer. They all have the same power. Masikus just prefers 'cute.'"

Even King Drastos, with a carved, sharp, warrior's jaw, looked really rather cute. Not handsome. A little sexy. But mostly cute. Ayrah dared say, with her sharpened retinas, it looked like whiskers grew from his cheeks.

And his nose looked a bit cat-like. His pectorals and abdominals were rigid, but as Ayrah's sharpened retinas studied his skin, it was the tiniest bit. . . furry.

The chosen mutations of Masikonian royalty.

Ayrah's lips curled up in disgust. She didn't care for this cute. She didn't care for it at all. Attractive was powerful, not. . . not *this*.

A crown of near-white metal sat on his head, his thick brown locks curled around the heavy, spiked ring. It hurt her eyes to stare at. The way the black-ice towers sat backdropped behind it, or the way Masikonian dancers blurred when they passed near it, made Ayrah think it was less than just white. Like, this crown had no color at all.

Ayrah couldn't take her eyes off of it. The crown. A coarse, mouth-watering, stomach-throbbing, hunger kept her attention planted on the colorless crown on his head. It was the Masikonian Archeodon. And Ayrah wanted it.

"Why are they here?" she asked, using disgust as a disguise for desire. But she knew. They were here for the Niiwa. To watch her fight.

"Make way for Prince Agora!" Their heralds sang the incoming of a second float adorned in similar majesty to the first.

Prince Agora waved his hands at the Tamagai and the Sehlyian commoners alike, as if his stupid mutated eyes could not tell the difference. "Watch for me tonight! I will be among you in the arena!" His utterly cheery voice sent chills down Ayrah's spine.

"What the bloody El did he just say?" she asked. "He's fighting?"

Urota shrugged. "It would not be uncommon."

Errta laid a hand on Ayrah, "Best hope, for your sake, that he has not won the dagger yet. If you can catch him before vuu is allowed, he should be less of a worry than the rest."

"Or hope that he already has won the fourth round and has come to win the fifth and final round."

"You all continue to miscalculate what determines the vastness of vuu," Ecanaes said.

Errta snored.

"Let me talk, El." Ecanaes snapped. "The girl is scared because of bloodline. But heritage does not define strength for the Masikonian ethnicity."

"I'm not scared," seethed Ayrah.

"Yada yada, dah dah." Errta held up his hand like a mocking puppet. "Fight me." He stuck his nose against Ecanaes'.

"Let 'im speak." Tagon spoke for the first time since they were in Sehlya. He did not look at Errta.

Errta glared at Tagon but said nothing more.

"Being daughter of a Warlord is what makes you strong. Being the son of the Masikonian king means his direct parents have *the most* vuu in their entire kingdom. But bloodline does not articulate where Masikonian vuu comes from, like for Sigu Nii.

"We call the factor, back home, 'talent.'" Ecanaes paused as he thought about how to word the next part. "Talent is like. . . well, it's sort of just random." He shrugged and giggled his geeky little laugh. "You inherit a tiny bit of vuu genetically, from you parents. You learn a little bit of vuu, and practice as you get older. But really, it's all kind of just. . . *random* over there."

Errta growled, "So I was right. 'Best hope he hasn't taken the dagger yet.'"

Ecanaes nodded slowly. "Yes, but there are many subtleties you misunderstand."

Errta paused. He turned to Ayrah, and in a casually grim tone he asked, "You want me to kill him?"

Urota chuckled and shook her head. "It's about time we head toward the arena," she explained that each of the six Warlords owned a tower in Sehlya, each made of black ice. They were like inns for visitors and merchants, or officers on official business. The lobby was bright, each wall made of ice dyed into a mural. Hellinite beams supported the ceiling.

Ayrah followed the four other Tamagai members. They squeezed inside a small icy box whose walls were like thin, polished sheets. A servant of the tower was with them, and when he strained his arms upwards, the whole box lurched toward the sky.

Ayrah grabbed onto Errta for stability.

He chuckled. "Are you nervous?"

She shook her head. A lie. It was the end of an Age. The whole world celebrated tonight. And Sigu Nii was Kortaes. The most powerful country in the world. That made Sehlya the partiest of all party places, with the king's Niiwa being its most prestigious, rigorous, and fatal.

"There is a strange mixture in the Niiwa," said Ecanaes. "Between contestants targeting those with the weakest vuu for the quickest, easiest kills. And targeting those with the strongest vuu for the most glory. You should decide when one is better—and when the opposite might be true."

By the time he finished speaking, the ice box halted and opened to a torch-lit blackstone hall. They were all quiet. They came to a fork in the hallway, and Errta said, "The blood of Rahktavah be with you."

Ecanaes touched his two inner fingers to Ayrah's forehead. A small horn, like a trumpet, sounded in her head. *I'll be your educated eyes.*

Ayrah scanned for opponents she recognized and slid her foot through the knuckle-thick layer of sparkling, black volcanic sand. There was Ty Ryaff, the second son of the Lord Mayor of Vasara. Ayrah smirked. It was ambitious of him to be here. The Niiwa of Ryala would have been challenging enough.

Delrah Zerii, the third daughter of Zya's Warlord, twirled twin silver axes, glittering with rubies. Delrah bounced the handles off her inner elbows, caught them in the opposite hands, twirled the blades around her wrists, and caught the handles again. Another Warlord offspring. Ayrah would need to keep her in periphery.

Of bloody course. Thought Ayrah, whose eyes landed on a smug, smiling Prince Agora. Ayrah squinted, scanning his shirtless torso for mutations. Maybe he was a furry, like his dad. She chuckled at the thought. Instead, she found that his skin was shiny grey, in thin and frequent splotches, like a leopard. His skin was metal.

She cursed. What a fine mutation. She glanced down at her own palms, they resembled more a hippo's arse than actual armor.

Ayrah's eyes swept around the oval. Nearly a hundred contestants prepared on the pit, stretching their arms, offering praise to their ancestors, or shouting their dominance. Some wore thick hide skins, with ram horns protruding from mutated shoulders. Others wore thongs and strapless bras, glittering with gems and metals. The vast majority were Sigu Nii. But there were a handful of other colors. Black, white, and the flair of Masikonian mutated skin. Ethnicity didn't matter much, not this round. Vuu was off limits. Sizing up the opponent was the only measure of power.

Ayrah was the oldest person there. She frowned, hoping it was not too dishonorable. A Sigu Nii has until the generation after their birth to take the first round. This was the last Niiwa she would have been able to take, ever. And it showed. There were children present.

Though, Prince Agora looked like he could be turning two generations old soon, as well.

Some of the other colored people looked smug, hopeful. Perhaps they thought playing a Sigu Nii game before the Sigu Nii were allowed to use vuu was a smart or entertaining move. Ayrah smiled and drew the hellinite blade from her waist. She was an El with swordplay. A monster up close.

Ayrah stood at the corner of the designated oval, and even turning behind her, the nosebleed section was very far away. She briefly remembered Errta's instruction, that dominating as large an area as you could was El for a Sigu Nii. But turning back the other direction, to face across the pit, she could scarcely imagine shooting a single, streamlined bit of vuu far enough to reach the other wall. The arena was huge.

There were two sets of rows between the edge of the pit and the far wall of the arena, one on top the other. Their only break was in the middle, the flat of the oval, where large blackstone viewing compartments were built into the wall that the second-story balcony was built on. She could see royalty with her sharpened retinas. There was the Masikonian family, there were other Warlords, there were Coryndal and Wardens and Illyadra, there was Lyta Tuio. There was a break in the vast ring of boxes, in the middle of the oval to Ayrah's left. A throne. It was as tall as the second-story, and as wide as the flat section of the oval.

Lightning, black and dusty, cracked and danced across the chair. It was him. The King. He was magnificently huge. His head was the size of several people whole, his body larger than the courtyard of Castle Tamagai. His skin was grey and rough, it was cracked like a dried-up lake. Black horns protruded from his shoulders like sun spotted freckles. His red eyes fixated on the pit, and his mouth hung open in delight under a hellinite crown. Black shadowa mist decorated the crown like jewels. White fire outlined the crown's edges and took the shape of a singular Old Vulgarhe rune, right in the middle. Twisting black horns kept his crown in place on his bald, grey, cracking-skinned head.

"Round one, the Dagger." The king paused. "BEGIN!" His voice was a grash between mountains. It thundered across the pit, stirring the black sand. Ayrah wondered if even the commoners down in Sehlya could hear him—the god-king Ash. Rahktavah.

Her limbs jolted into movement.

"Back up," warned Ecanaes from the stands.

Ayrah leapt backwards as a saber and a double-edged sword clashed against one another from both sides. One was held by a child.

How different he is from me, she thought.

She swung her hellinite blade in a simple backhand motion and amputated the boy's knee. The child wailed and flailed in the sand.

The other, on her left, was older, near Ayrah's age. She snarled, and her teeth snapped in sync with the darting of her saber.

Ayrah dodged left, right, and swatted incoming attacks. The first round was the easiest. But it was even. She wasn't the daughter of a Warlord, here. She was just a girl with a sword fighting another girl with a sword. They were both nobodies, simply hopeful that they could make it through the first round, so they could show their power to the world in the second and third and fourth.

Ayrah spun and feigned a swing toward saber girl's forehead. As the saber was coming up to block, Ayrah pulled her swing to the side and sliced the flesh off the girl's forearm. She screamed, and Ayrah decapitated her head.

While Ayrah ceased the first child's screaming, Ecanaes insightfully picked apart the remaining groups, then concluded, *"The number of contestants is soon nearing the final amount. You must reach Prince Agora now, while he only has a sword to fight with. If he reaches the next round, and is allowed to use vuu, there will be no stopping him. Tagon informs me that his vuu vastly outweighs your own."*

Ayrah snarled at that last bit. The Prince already had a handful of contestants crowding around him, with similar goals of slaying him quickly. But he defended himself well. He swatted away incoming blades with Masikonian mutated speed and agility. Ayrah didn't know what ligaments he had changed that allowed him to swing so fast, and by the looks of her own body, neither did her mutator. His splotchy metal skin fended off penetrating blades as well, which was almost half as often.

The pit was a thunderstorm of clashing sparks and spewing blood—a cage for the glory slaves. Nearly a hundred fighters—a number that was quickly falling, turned into groups of three, five, even ten. And she had become one of them.

Ayrah growled, teeth grit. She needed to save strength for the coming rounds. But there was little chance, even in the afterlife, she would be caught hiding in a corner. She began a trot toward him.

There was a battle of three to her left, and a battle of seven—no, now six, to her right. She jogged between them.

"Ayrah, behind you."

"Veligreen." It was a girl's voice.

Ayrah stopped in the middle of the pit and turned. "Zerii." Blood and organs in her wake, Delrah Zerii, the daughter of Zya, marched toward Ayrah.

A stomping drumroll spread through the arena. The people in the stands did not yet know who Ayrah was. To them, Delrah Zerii had closed in on prey.

Delrah's thick brown, single braid swayed behind her. She wore zigzags of red paint across each cheek and adorned the thick cloaks of poached lion from the savannas of Zya.

"We need to take out Agora first." Ayrah urged.

"Coward." Delrah replied.

Ayrah tsk'd her lips. That had done it. She descended into a fighting stance. *How many has she slain?* Ayrah asked in her mind as she unsheathed her hellinite sword.

"Enough for adrenaline to fill her veins, but not enough to be weary," said Ecanaes.

Delrah Zerii kept her dark brown eyes locked on Ayrah. She raised her two silver axes and deliberately cut each arm. "Don't mind me. Just planting bombs around the arena for the next round."

"Tsa." A snicker escaped Ayrah. "You won't make it to the next round!" She made an upper cut with her blade.

Delrah caught the swing in the crux of her axe's blade and handle. Ayrah tried to pull it free, but Delrah pounded the hellinite sword down

ILLYADRA

with the blunt edge of her free axe. The ring of the metals colliding lingered in the air.

The sword ripped downward and buried into the blackstone. Ayrah pulled and yanked, but it was stuck in the stone. Delrah gloated and raised both axes at Ayrah.

There's no way anyone could hit that hard. No way.

"Indeed," agreed Ecanaes. *"And the king will feel it."*

Ayrah whispered, "You used vuu."

Delrah scoffed, "Pfft."

"You used vuu!" Ayrah screamed and kicked Delrah away.

The arena descended into chaos. They shouted and screamed.

The ground shook as the king rose to stand. He spoke, "You challenge the king to a grash?"

"No!" Delrah pleaded. "No!" She fell to her knees and bowed her face into the sand. "It was an accident! A stretch of the arm!"

He approached. The entire arena quaked. "Stand to fight." Ayrah backed away, afraid that the localized weight of the king would tear a hole through the arena.

When she had backed out of the foreground, she turned, dropped to her knees and vomited. She hesitantly peeked over her shoulder. Delrah had still not risen from the ground, and King Ash's hand descended on her.

Ayrah's thighs twitched. Her ankles fidgeted. A fleeting burn within her to save Delrah. Was it a second opportunity? Perhaps one to make up for the last?

What could she do, though? It was the king. The only king Sigu Nii could even remember. If she dragged Delrah out of the way, either Ash would realign on Delrah or include her in the taking.

The King's palm encompassed Delrah with grey, cracking knuckles.

Ayrah's leg unfolded, her boot slid flat through the sand. *Save her. Save her. Save her.* Her heart thundered against her temples, it womped the sides of her eyes, making her vision grainy.

A pillar of fire and smoke exploded from within the king's hand. When the king pulled away, Delrah was a charred silhouette, and whimpering. She was still alive. Hardly.

Ash gestured his hand the smallest degree, and columns of black sand erupted out of the ground, crisscrossed, dragging Delrah's limbs taught. She was in the middle of a giant black X.

Ash took the crown from his head and yanked it into a sword. He struck Zerii's remains, splitting her in half from head to bottom.

Ayrah cried. She couldn't believe it, real tears rolled down her cheeks. She breathed, shaky, heavy, and stuffed her throat with salvia. And when she thought of how horrific a place for these to boil up, with ten thousand eyes on her, a sob forced its way out.

It was a near perfect image of Nahkon Veligreen's death. The very thing that had kept Ayrah from taking the Niiwa all these seasons. Here it was before her, happening again.

Ash returned to his throne and the fight resumed. How was Ayrah supposed to pick herself up after that?

The question didn't last long. Action coursed through her veins. She looked at her hands. They glowed black. The shadow wanted to be released. But she couldn't let it, not yet.

The king's Niiwa concluded with a quarter of the contestants remaining. One round down, three to go. And they would only get harder.

31

ATERAH

A chilling night of restless sleep. Tossing and turning. An incessant itch where her hair had been torn from her scalp, one that seared to scratch. A stab shot through her left shoulder with each turn, where her own people had put an arrow.

There were several bedrooms in the second story of the farmhouse. Each with an accommodable bed. But after her attempt the previous night, Verano would not let her out of his sight. Together they slept, bunched up on a small bed with reeds of straw poking into their skin.

"Quit it," he would growl throughout the night, each time Aterah turned to her side or raised a hand to scratch her scalp.

The child's wailing filled her mind. It was the sort of scream that any Renovian might utter, given the circumstance. She began to wonder, *are the Sigu Nii more like us than we thought?*

Verano lacked moral civility, though. The vuu that coursed through his veins and the remarkable absence of hesitation was more than cause for concern. It was damning. *So, wondered Aterah, is it only their strong? Is it vuu that makes a man less? Are the lowly of their conglomerate the most human?*

The next morning couldn't come soon enough. Verano raided the farmer's kitchen, piling the table high with bounty. Breads and cheeses and corn. He ate by the handful. But the smell of the farmer and his boy wafting through the house made Aterah queasy. It stung her eyes, like the heat of a fire. It sat heavier and ran thick down her throat. But as they crossed the threshold of the farmhouse and Aterah drew in the fresh breeze, she revolted at its similar taste. She wondered if there were more bodies, or if those inside stained even out here, or if it was her heart that carried the stench with her.

They came upon the village stable to find their horse missing. Verano cursed and cursed, slamming his fists against the pavilion posts. He scanned the street for anyone suspicious. His eyes eventually met the un-moved bodies scattered among the far side of the road.

Verano snatched up a saddle and reigns that were not his and strapped them to a horse adjacent.

"What are you doing?" Aterah asked.

"Some dastardly coward stole from me. If someone comes to claim this one before we depart, I'll be glad to pay."

"With the metal?"

"By killing them."

"Oh."

Verano aided Aterah's climb upon the steed before he leapt up behind her. He guided the horse backwards, out from the wooden rail of the pa-vilion, and snapped the reins once they faced the north road.

The northbound road began to stretch, and hours passed.

Aterah imagined Vasara, the capital of Renovia's Kortaes. *A different time in our history. When ours was the influence that wrapped the world.* She had seen her already. Her houses and structures, her courts and the Graey Castle. Many times she had visited this kingdom hub back in her corner of NeoDerii's library. *I wonder how long it's been since a native Renovian has been there in person.*

Villages occasionally appeared on either side of the road. An assort-ment of war-tribe banners hanging over each of them. They began to encounter growing numbers of Sigu Nii soldiers, farmers, and cargo wagon drivers passing between towns and villages, going to and from Vasara.

And finally, on the northern horizon, Vasara rose. There was a statue of some guy casting vuu in the middle of the city. A big one. *I don't remember ever reading about him.* She asked Verano, "Who is that?"

"Ryaff." He huffed. "The Warlord assigns his best subordinates as Officers and Lord Mayors over larger cities. I watched my dad hand pick several for the greater towns around Ryvl. And Ryaff is Lord Mayor over Vasara. Means he's basically in charge of the entire war against you. He splits the whole lower class of the Ryalan Colonies between Yutarah, Brair, and Tseren."

The taste of dust collected in Aterah's mouth. Airborne dirt from the hundreds making along the wide road. Her excitement turned sour. *What have these barbarians made of my home?*

Graeynesh Law II: Renovia will fall from Kortaes and enter a time of exile.

Verano slowed the horse's gait amid the people as they marched toward a flimsy archway. Most of the people around them were leaving the city. Her eyes looked from one soldier to another as they passed by. Their knapsacks covered their backs and reached above their heads, with assorted cloth and skins sticking out.

The horse strode under the arch and the watchful gaze of the Black Guard. Their gold-leafed chests shone with the swirling eye of Warlord Rai Ezs. On the inside of Vasara, the dirt road turned muddy and filled with the sound of boots and horseshoes smacking in and out. Shacks piled up along the road on either side, three stories high. Self-built homes of metal, wood scraps, sticks, and cloth. *How do they not collapse in on each other?* She watched Sigu Nii go in and out of the shacks, dressed in rags pinned together at each shoulder.

Vasara reeked. Aterah wrinkled her nose and stuffed a sneeze. Flies and gnats flew across her face every few moments. *This?* Aterah felt a sense of loss come over her. A painful wrench in her gut, and a heat that came about her ears and nose. *This!* Her fists clenched around the horse's hair. *This is what they've made with it?* She gritted her teeth.

"War Guild Taii! Tryouts for War Guild Taii!" a man shouted from the side of the street.

"Twen'y-seven members, and count!" other soldiers from different clans shouted similarly.

Verano nudged her arm. "Keep your eyes to yourself."

She faced forward, trying not to peer at all the cruelty. *"They've ended entire societies before,"* the man with stone tattoos had said in her dream. That was back when she had hope that Kairo would save her before they reached the edge of the jungle.

"Five copper for an ear!" a man shouted.

"Eleven for a pair!" someone down the road yelled.

They've made my city a hub for their war. Aterah felt her throat close. *Korta Nii, how can you stand for this?*

"Two silver for an eye!" a violent feminine yell came from the other side of the road.

Verano chuckled. "Eyes are the best. They decay in a matter of days." The eyeballs hung by their own optical cords. "Even if you ran from the Delkop, they would be dried and shriveled by the time you got here." He paused a moment. "Means you have to bring their hosts alive."

Aterah tried not to look at them, but she wanted to note how they dressed. They were dirty. All of them. But it seemed half of them were dirty with blood, while the other half were dirty with dung.

Verano turned down a street left of the north road, and the sound of the crowd and soldiers' calls faded behind them.

"Are we staying here?" she asked hazily.

He snapped the reins. "No." The horse took off in a gallop. Up a shifty gravel hill the shacks gave way to solid houses and buildings of wood and stone. War-tribe banners hung over each of them. They reached a crest, and Vasara stretched out before them. Aterah could tell there was more that lay behind nearby hills. She peered east, hoping she might be able to see a grand mark of history.

A stone arena lay to the north. *Are these blood sport houses in every one of their cities?* she wondered. Her eyes moved past it. *There.* On a hill just beyond the eastern edge, with corridors and stone roadways radiating into the city, the Graey Castle. Towers stretched dozens of reaches, grand halls with shining silver roofs, and she knew there would be courtyards and trees hidden from view.

Wooden scaffolding covered these things like a brown smudge across Aterah's vision. She frowned. Far away laborers heaved stone up by the brick.

The hill descended, and the houses blocked her view of the castle. She remained staring in its direction, dreaming of its interiors.

Verano led the horse onward. Several moments passed before they turned onto a cobblestone road, and noises of a crowd returned with more Sigu Nii screeching for coin or trade.

Before them rose an eerie black triangle, many stories high. Each brick appeared to be trimmed with gold. The swirling eye of Warlord Rai Ezs shone across its face. The setting sun cast a broad triangular shadow on the street.

Sigu Nii flooded back and forth from this building. Most of them were clean, no dirt, dung, or stench. Some carried shiny black blades and some no blades at all.

The entrance was a doorless opening decorated in carved designs.

"I thought you said we had to go to Ryala?"

"Aye." He led the horse up to the steps of the building, dismounted, and brought Aterah down. A young man with a red vest approached. Verano gave him a coin, and the young man gave Verano a red wooden token with a number on it, then led the horse away.

Aterah felt the sore in her back and loins from days of riding. Verano guided her up the steps and through the entrance. The crowd of Sigu Nii clustered into a long line, each of them nudging and pushing each other in wait.

Verano passed them. A Black Guard held out a hand before him and checked his lower left shoulder. "Back." He pointed toward the line. "Or six silver."

A moment of silence passed. Aterah stared at Verano. She could feel heat rising within him. An unsettling thought, *I've been with him long enough to know when he's mad.*

"I have a delivery for the El Rai," Verano said in his clear accent, firmness in his voice as he nodded at her.

The Black Guard glanced between them. "You're it?"

She squirmed under the guard's gaze.

"Aye."

The guard frowned but let them through.

Metal and leather boots from various roaming guards and soldiers clacked against the unpolished stone. The voices of the crowd echoed off the high circular ceiling, painted in the likes of a demon she had never seen: dark cracking skin, horns erupting out of a shaved head, and eyes with wisps of red mist.

Three black metal plates lined the wall around the dome, with signs above them that read the names of cities, one was Ryala. The metal plates indented into the walls had inscriptions on them, runes of Old Vulgarhe.

Aterah watched in awe as people from the line stepped onto the metal plates, and after a moment black lightning cracked and thunder echoed throughout the building. The people rippled and disappeared.

"What is this?" she whispered.

"The Tuidiia," Verano said it in a grumble, not with pride. He gestured toward the plate that read Ryala.

Aterah looked at him. Nervousness gripped her, and she clenched her fists as she took the first step. A tingling shot through her body. The plate faded under black electricity. Black lightning and thunder. Half a moment passed where there was nothing. And then she was back in the building. But Verano wasn't there. And the guards were different.

"Renovian?" One of them yelled.

Dread shot through Aterah. Her legs twitched, and she wanted to bolt. Her hands were shaking, and her whole body descended into jitters.

A tall man dressed in black-and-gold-trimmed mail snatched her elbow. His grip hurt as he dragged her off the metal plate.

"Who do you belong to?" the guard asked.

Aterah looked at him, at a loss for words. In her mind she went back to NeoDerii, where she was at home, secure, and everything was simple and made sense. The intricate language they had created, the calls and chirping of birds. Graeynesh Law and how dearly they held to its teaching. Home.

They could teleport at will. They could move any amount of people, foods, weapons, whatever distance they pleased. The barbarians could teleport.

"She's mine!" came Verano's voice.

"Just keeping her from slithering off." The Black Guard paused as he glanced toward Verano's Niiwa. "You're it?" He huffed and shook his head. "Warlord El Rai Ezs is waiting for you. There's a carriage outside that will take you to his manor."

The exit to Ryala's Tuidiia was carved stone like a delicate design of an eye. Several limestone steps laid out beneath them, a cobblestone road, and a red painted carriage with gold and blue stone decorating its exterior.

She could see all Ryala, and a vast neon blue beyond. Like a giant hand pressed up against the world, the mountain beneath them spread in five spinal fingers through Ryala.

Aterah looked to the sun. It was higher in the sky than it was in Vasara, another couple hours before sunset.

"Come on." Verano placed a hand on her back, guiding her toward the cart.

A man with pale white skin jumped down from the driver's seat. His clothes were strange—a black jacket with shining buttons and a white long-sleeve shirt beneath. His trousers looked poorly crafted, frail, like they would tear just at the sight of a hanging branch. His shoes were shiny, and Aterah moved her head to see if she could see her reflection in them. She watched his eyes, how they naturally glided to Verano's lower left shoulder. The man frowned and opened the carriage door.

"How long?" Verano asked.

The whiteman pointed down the mountain's forefinger. It was too far to see, but it seemed his point ended just along the white, sandy shoreline.

Verano slid into the carriage and glanced at Aterah as she sat the on the narrow, cushioned seat and the oddly dressed man closed the door.

Gold rimmed each of the inside corners. Thin lace curtains hung over two glass windows on either side. Wooden trays jutted out from the side walls in front of them, with bottles of dark liquid inside.

She could feel each brick of cobblestone they rode over and tried to pull back the curtain, but it was wrapped around a silver pole on both ends of the glass. She glanced at Verano. His knee bounced up and down rapidly. *He's nervous as well.* She wondered why. *What could he possibly be nervous about?*

"So, your father . . ." Aterah started.

Verano's gaze whipped in her direction.

"He's strong right? He's a Warlord?"

"Was." He turned away. He tried to pull back the curtain but met the same resistance. His arms lit up with a faint black glow, darkness in his veins. He ripped the curtain from his window and turned to her. "Here." He huffed, stretched over her, and ripped her curtain down.

"What happened?"

"He died."

"Oh." She paused. "How? I thought Warlords were strong—"

"Grashed." Verano's voice was steady. "By the king."

Aterah searched for the tiniest speck of difference, but he hid it.

"And he lost?"

Verano nodded.

"Why?"

"The crown." He said it obviously.

She shook her head. "What crown?"

He squinted at her. "The king has the Sigu Nii Archeodon—it's what makes him king."

"And that's a crown?"

"Sometimes." Verano nodded. "Other times it's a sword, fending off the ambitious."

"Like, if your dad won?"

"Aye. He would've become king."

"Oh." Aterah turned from him. "What a way to determine authority." She looked at her palms. "Seems primitive."

Verano stared at her. "I'd kill you right now, you know that?" She could feel his eyes ingrained on her side. "If it didn't mean my own death, I would do it. And you'd have as much chance as a beetle trying to stop me. *That* is primitive."

Silence surrounded them for a moment. She listened to the bumps and grinds of the carriage wheels.

He responded again. "The fact that you can fight Ash for a chance at the crown is honorable." He nodded. "Unlike Aylavuera where the commoners are too dumb to know what kind of world they live in, let alone face their king in a debate or whatever. Though, I'll admit: No one has beaten Ash in a grash. Ever. Not in the Kortaes-and-a-half-time that he's been king."

There was silence again.

"Why are you doing this?"

He remained quiet.

"What will this man do for you?"

"You would not understand."

Aterah looked at his shoulder, the one facing her. "Your father's death, is that why you don't have the tattoo?"

Verano glanced at her and pulled his cloth sleeve down.

Aterah let silence own the carriage. She turned back to the window. Glass. Using her forefinger, and her long, dirty, unclipped nails, she tapped on it. It sounded. . . *tattery*. She braced her knees and legs forward as the cart gradually descended the mountain. Time passed as she prepared her mind for the Warlord.

The carriage shifted and bumped until the light started dimming. She rubbed her shoulders. Images of the past fortnight crossed her mind. *Such a journey*. She was exhausted and ready to meet this Warlord and be done with it all.

The carriage made a right turn. Fields of well-trimmed grass passed on her left, populated by whitestone statues of winged beasts, crowned kings, and fancily dressed men with scrolls in their hands.

The coach turned a wide left before stopping beside a pond surrounded by whitestone, with structures rising out of the middle and spewing water in the air. Aterah gasped. *How does that happen? It must be some trick of vuu.*

Verano's door opened. The pale, oddly dressed man stood holding it, every joint in his body locked in a straight position. Verano pushed himself out, Aterah behind him.

A palace stretched before her, fronted by a wide porch with wooden rocking chairs. Pillars thicker than Aterah and Verano combined held up a white overhang. Above that rose a wall of blue window.

Verano's boots clacked against the stone steps. She followed a step behind. The high double doors were dark with intricate engravings. They clicked and swung open with a blast of cold air.

"Good evening," a crisp, elegant, high-pitched voice came out. A short man popped out from behind the door. Pale in face, dressed in the same strange clothes as the coach driver, with wispy black hair drawn over an otherwise bald head.

"What is it with all the bloody white people?" Verano yelled. "Is the Warlord bringing all of Aylavuera to aid him?"

The hardwood floor seemed hollow underneath, so that each time someone moved, the floor creaked under their feet. Hallways extended in either direction, and in front of them rose a wide blue carpeted staircase that narrowed slightly with each step and had waxed wooden handrails on each side leading up to a vast second floor. Ocean blue light shone down the stairs. A little way from the double doors, hanging from the ceiling was a candlelit crystal chandelier. It looked so fragile that Aterah itched standing beneath it.

She rubbed the back of her arms. "How is it so cold?" Even during the dry season, NeoDerii never got so cold.

"Aye." Verano nodded.

The little man waved a hand and led them toward the hall behind the staircase. "The El appreciates the coolness of his home kingdom, says the air is too moist here in Ryala." The pale little man paused. "I would not know, El . . ."

"Verano."

They passed tapestries, paintings of landscapes, and portraits of long-past kings and queens.

"Not very defensible. The Warlord must be challenged to grash often. Any Sigu Nii worth a serpent would think 'if an Illian is Warlord, then I could be too.'"

"Ah, the El Rai's manor." The man turned, his black jacket swirling as he made eye contact. "He told me you Sigu Nii have a liking for castles. Something-or-other about the bioregionalistic architecture of your culture."

Verano blinked. His mouth opened, but nothing came out.

"Perhaps the El needs nutrition? Surly, he must be after such a long and tiresome journey. The El Rai employs one of the most *prestigious* chefs in all city-states of Masikus."

Verano turned and looked around. "Is he not here? Where is he? I thought I was delivering this"—he gestured to Aterah—"to El Rai himself."

"Yes, yes. He will arrive shortly. A brief meeting with the champion fighting guild of Ryala, preparing them for their first match in the Kaeselwa, and he would be on his way." The little man balled his fists and shook his hands. "I hear we are to go against the champions of the Gya Province first. So exciting!"

Verano sighed. "Food is fine."

"Oh, splendid." He turned and led them down a hallway to their right.

Aterah paused beside one of the hallway's paintings. She reached up and touched the thick, fading and cracking paint. A family portrait. Their attire was rich with jewelry, and elegantly woven clothing. A wooden crown adorned the top of the man's head. *Whoever heard of a wooden crown?* she wondered. In stories, crowns were always overzealous with gems and glory. But the only shine that this frail looking thing had, were little twisted veins of silver. Aterah recognized the symbol that the silver faded into. The Silver Tree of Renovia.

Her mouth dropped open. *A painting of a Renovian king? Why would the Warlord have this?*

"Witch!" Verano yelled down the hall.

Aterah flinched and hurried in his direction.

He stood on the threshold of another room and gestured. "Come."

She glanced back at the painting. She turned the corner and entered a long dining hall. Three clusters of candlelight were holstered to the ceiling with a majestic array of see-through stones. The table was wooden. She let her fingers glide across its smooth, waxed surface. Many golden chairs surrounded it.

"I would just fetch the chef. It should not take him longer than a few moments to prepare." The short man ran off.

Verano yanked a chair from the table. He tossed himself in and threw his feet up on the wood. "Manor." He scoffed. "Forget his bia-region-ism. This is but dirt to the *fortress* I grew up in." Verano pinched a bit of dust from the arm rest and sprinkled it over the floor.

Aterah walked around the table, letting her fingers run over the backs of the chairs. She felt the dense, cold, shiny metal, before letting herself collapse into one across from Verano.

He stuck his chin out and glared at her for a moment, before turning his attention to nothing in particular.

A few moments passed, and the little pale man returned with a tall man in tow. His arms were larger than Verano's, his muscle carved like a statue with opaque, shining green scales. He wore a thin blue tunic with three horizontal lines of wispy white dye and long, dreadlocked hair with strips of real silver. He disappeared through a swiveling door on the far side of the room.

"Can I watch?" Aterah asked.

Verano and the pale man both looked at her. The pale one turned to Verano, and Verano shrugged. "Not my problem anymore."

"She wishes to see Masikonian vuu in action?" The pale one chuckled. "I think it's fine."

The kitchen was a world in itself. A wooden island in the middle, shining pots and pans hanging above. Several stove fire ovens lined the far wall. She walked to the other side of the island, there was a metal pot large enough for her to climb inside. It was full of ground slop. She could loosely make out bits of meat, vegetables, breads, and liquids. She touched it. *Yep. That's some slop.*

"Oi!" a guttural growl.

She flinched.

"Getchur bugger 'ands outta there!" The cook snatched her by the wrist. His hands were soft, unlike his voice and appearance.

"Sorry, I—What is this for?" She tried to back away.

"Cooking." He eyed her with bright grey eyes. "You're the witch, huh?" He sniffed.

"Can I watch?"

He hesitated. "Aye." He grabbed a pot from the metal overhang and brought it down to the wooden island. Then, before Aterah's very eyes, his cupped hand melded together. The skin between his fingers melted in an instant and scooped slop from the pot beneath them. He pressed his free hand against the slop. Then he slowly tipped his squeezed hands over the pot, and a dark liquid came pouring out. He repeated the process several times, creating different liquids, with different colors and consistencies, mixing each one into the pot.

"Aterah?" The pale little man peeked through the door.

She looked up at him.

"He's here."

32

ROADS

They didn't give him a spoon, but Kairo didn't care. He dug each finger joint, down to his knuckle, into the white and brown sludge. His fingernails scraped against the smooth bottom of the wooden bowl, while picking up plenty of gruel along the way. He pinched, squeezed, and pulled as far under his fingernail as his teeth could reach.

It tasted dung-ish. Kairo had overturned rotting logs in the jungle and eaten many of the critters found there on desperate occasions. And they tasted better than the sludge by far.

Rice was the only recognizable ingredient in the dish. And not just due to cultural or geographical differences. But because every other source of nourishment appeared to have been chewed and spat back out by at least five others.

Kairo's fingers audibly plopped out of his mouth as he sucked the sludge off along the way. How many days had he gone without food again? Nearly a week, he guessed.

Wesken whimpered. He sat with his back to the road, leaning on the latch that the driver had undone to let them aboard.

Kairo sat across, his back leaning against the same plank of wood that the driver leaned on. Occasionally his head would brush against the man's back, or vice versa, which prompted a huff and a shift from either of them.

The driver was a level-one Sigu Nii. He hadn't the skill or talent to kill Kairo with vuu alone. He probably didn't even possess the power to seriously injure. But he did have vuu. He was capable of little things to help in a fight. Like electrifying a sword or forming ice under an otherwise sure-footed step.

Graeynesh Law didn't say anything about a level-one. Kairo was free to engage alone. But his thigh throbbed. And the spasms were becoming far more frequent and painful.

Kairo eyed the child. His tunic hid the definition of his muscles. Kairo wondered if the boy had ever killed anyone before. Doubtful. The playful tones, the unaware eyes, the far from ready posture—Wesken was innocent.

And they didn't have a weapon.

He could turn quietly, wrap the inside of his elbow around the man's neck, and squeeze. But the Sigu Nii could ignite fire from his skin or something.

Kairo slouched back, deciding that, for the moment, escape was off the table.

Kairo shoveled another handful of gruel into his mouth. He grabbed all the portions sticking to his fingers with his lips.

"Please. *Please*, stop eating so loudly." Wesken's face held untamed, child-like disgust.

Kairo had never heard such a request before. Everyone at NeoDerii ate like this. Were there so many different ways of consuming a meal? He supposed a little less suck as his fingers left his mouth wouldn't kill him. Though, he was darn hungry enough to be convinced otherwise.

Sigu Nii guards had piled a number of crates, sacks, and barrels on the cart around them. They jiggled and shuttered as the horse drawn wagon drug across the uneven sandy terrain. They gave him this bowl of sludge as they left Ravid without a word. Kairo wondered if it was to keep him alive on the journey, or to make him appear livelier before this new Lord Mayor Ryaff.

Wesken scooched and wiggled, making the sacks comfortably fit the outline of his body, all the while commenting on being here with Kairo, "I can't believe I get to come too. I guess I just get to do what I want."

But Kairo knew it would've been far too obvious for the warden to pass on just one captive—the dying one. And Wesken was simply unlucky enough to be in proximity at the time.

Kairo finished scraping the final wet lines left around the bowl and tossed it over the side.

Trash and human waste were removed from NeoDerii carefully, so as not to let the Sigu Nii know there was an outpost full of Renovians present. Even a fire would not do, since it would give off a banner of smelling smoke similar to that of Yutarah. But out here? It wouldn't matter. Kairo could already see plenty of trash and ash firepits nestled against the road.

"So. You have no idea where you're from?" Kairo asked.

"Nope." Wesken let the word slide from his tongue.

"And you're telling me that if you passed, say for example, your father, you wouldn't even recognize him?"

Wesken shifted his shoulders. "Uhm," He paused a notable while. His eyes looked like they peered past Kairo, over his left shoulder. Then his eyes glided back to Kairo's, and he continued as if unaware there had been the pause. "Maybe! But I'm pretty sure I was spawned."

"What?"

"You know, like hatched or whatever. Let's just say I came from Yeshwin and fell from the sky."

Kairo sat up, intrigued. "Yeshwin? You know the city of El?" It was the final resting place for fallen Renovians and it was where the Korta Ellanii looked over the world. It was the fifth entry in Graeynesh Law: *At the end of the generation, Yeshwin and Vasara will collide.* Few Chamberlains claimed to understand what that meant, since far longer than a single generation had passed since its foretelling, and Vasara was now all but foreign to them.

"Sure." Wesken shrugged. "Like I said, I've been."

Kairo frowned.

"Do you believe in the gods?"

"I believe in the Korta Ellanii—"

"Korteous," Wesken interrupted with the point of his finger. "You call him the King of Life."

Kairo had never heard this—not another name for El, nor what his common name meant. He wondered if Aterah would know about this, since she was so well read. "Are there others?"

"Sure." Wesken nodded. "But I guess it depends on which you can call a 'god.' Cause like, Yeshwin's got plants and animals, right? So they're el, with a little *e*. But they're not *gods*."

Kairo blinked repeatedly. "Uhm—"

"If you had an extra eyeball and could put it anywhere on your body, where would you put it?"

"What a strange question."

"Where?"

"The back of my head. That way I can—"

"That's what everyone says."

"Alright. Then where would you put it?"

"The tip of my finger. Cause then I could peek around corners, under doorways, or even behind me." Wesken demonstrated the maneuverability by wiggling his finger in all the directions.

Kairo let a single chuckle escape him. "Clever." Though, he had a difficult time picturing having another eyeball at all. So much of his navigating the world around him revolved around his sight. The world would look so different with just one more.

"Your turn! Ask me, ask me!"

"Alright . . ." Kairo paused as he thought. "How did you end up like this? Your memory and all."

"That's like, the exact type of thing that I wouldn't remember," stated Wesken bluntly.

"Right." Kairo tried to think of a new question. Information—not events. The child seemed to have very foreign understandings of how the world worked. Maybe some of them would be useful. He felt like several questions had arisen in him before, questions he would've died to have answered, what were they? Oh! "How is King Ash still alive? He was the Sigu Nii king when Renovia fell, right? It's been twenty-eight generations; how could he possibly still be alive? Vuu, right? It's just gotta be vuu somehow."

Wesken widened his eyes and brought up his hands, closed, and opened them in a popping motion as he said, "Time travel!"

Kairo sighed. He really thought he would obtain some insight from the boy.

The driver continued a few hours into the night. He pulled off the road and stopped by a small creek. After the horses were fed and watered, the driver had Kairo and Wesken sleep with their hands tied to the wagon.

It wasn't a very restful night, and the journey resumed at first light.

The boulder-speckled hills gave way to meadows, bright yellow flowers covering the horizon, with single lonely trees then and again.

The driver spoke up around mid-afternoon. "We're getting close."

Long wooden fences acted like borders on either side of the road. They passed animals that Kairo had never seen before, and plants that would produce some unknown food.

"Their farms go on forever," Kairo said. "I thought they were just tribes that hunted and gathered for food. Maybe even barbaric enough to eat us."

He turned to Wesken, looked him in the eyes, and with a sad smile said, "Turns out, barbarian is just a mask they wear."

The road came to a village with a wide lake glistening in the east and fishing boats across the water. They passed under a wooden archway and the smell of baking bread wafted downwind. It was a plain smell, absent of spices, cheeses, or any other flavors. But it was bread, and it caused Wesken's stomach to growl audibly.

"We'll stop here for food and continue on for Vasara."

Vasara. Kairo's heart crawled up his throat. That's where this Lord Mayor Ryaff was? Vasara? Hope flickered across his eyes. That's where Aterah was headed. Would she still be there? Could he rescue her before this infection finished him off?

"Ooh," Wesken brought his arms up against his shoulders and stretched loudly. Then he began to sing and dance, quietly, as if to himself. "The hungry voice is hungry, the hungry voice is hungry, the hungry voice is hungry."

The wagon stopped beside a pavilion stable. Kairo sat up and took in his surroundings. The village was cut in half by the road. On this side, Sigu Nii workers hammered a vuu-looking illuminated sword, fumbled with leather, or brought in fresh fish from the lake. On the other side, Kairo's attention paused on several bodies. Their limbs were crumpled into fatal positions and blood stained the gravel in a wide pool beneath them.

"What happened there?" Kairo wondered aloud.

The driver came around and unlatched the back of the wagon. He glanced over the bodies and shrugged. "This way." He guided them across the street, hand on his hilt all the while.

They entered an open-air tavern. It had three walls and was open facing the street. In truth, Kairo didn't know what to call the place, but the tavern in Yutarah held the closest resemblance. There were the tables with benches. But no giant barrels. And no upstairs with rooms.

The driver muttered a strange name to the woman behind the counter, and then said, "Three of them."

The woman inspected his Niiwa tattoo. "That'll be nine copper."

"I'm on official business between the warden of Ravid and the Lord Mayor Ryaff."

She shrugged. "Then you'll've been paid for the trip."

"It should bring you glory to serve me."

"What's your name?"

"Ryudon of the—"

"Aye, no, I've never heard of you. Nine copper."

The driver, Ryudon, scoffed and tossed the coins onto the counter. He began to turn and guide them toward a table, but Kairo spoke up. "Why're they there?" He pointed to the bodies outside.

The woman shook her head with unease. "An inkless beast passed through. He looked like he was running the slave-trade route, like any other. But it turns out he was delivering the thing to El Rai. Anyways, he had no ink, but he possessed the power of shadowa."

Kairo croaked with urgency. "How long ago?"

The woman shrugged. "A couple days." She rolled her eyes. "And now *I'm* gonna have to move the bodies, before the stench scares people away from my shop."

She was here. Kairo stared at the bodies in the road again, just to make certainly clear that none of them were Aterah. She had just been here.

The three of them sat at the table. Wind caught on one of the side walls, giving the shop a nice breeze, containing only the slightest aroma of human rot.

Kairo felt his jaw begin to lock up. He remembered being a child in NeoDerii, when he was still young and had fun climbing trees—rather than the practiced, survival necessary motion they became with age—there had been one time when he fell a decent distance. He didn't break any bones. But the moment his hands slipped, the gut churning feeling of knowing a fall was coming, resembled the current feeling of a spasm coming on. It was about to hurt. A lot.

Kairo spilled off the bench, grabbing his thigh, his stomach, and his neck. It was like a foot cramp, a calf cramp, and a tongue cramp all learned how to communicate and attack with decision. His lower back stretched off the ground. He began slamming it up and down, unintentionally.

And he couldn't breathe. The whole while, air was locked out of reach. Each moment that passed during the spasm brought him closer to death. He had watched several of his fellow soldiers suffocate during a moment just like this one.

The spasms passed and he gasped desperately for air.

Vasara. Kairo prayed to the Korta Ellanii that Aterah would still be there when he arrived, and that he would be given the strength to escape whatever walls he was put in. He prayed that, in this next couple of days, he would be limping home with Aterah in hand.

The shop woman brought out three steaming wooden bowls and set them on the table. Kairo peered inside. There was fish in there. That he recognized. Some green stuff. That could always be trusted—he joked. And hundreds of tiny snake-like things.

Wesken used two sticks to pinch the snake things into his mouth. He did so with an urgent vibrancy. He hummed tunelessly while he chewed.

"What a morally fowl—" Began Kairo.

"Oh, just eat the stuff," moaned Wesken with a mouthful. He swatted through the air. "It's fine."

Kairo frowned at his bowl.

"You really should eat up, filth," said Ryudon. "Once you get to Castle Graey, the Masikonians will be turning dirt into something edible for all you slaves. They're not the expensive ones, they can only maintain its shape for so long. Means your body will be sucking out the nutrients, sucking, sucking, sucking, bam! All the sudden your intestines are filled with bloody dirt. Emphasis on the bloody. Trust me."

The three of them returned to the wagon after the meal and resumed the journey north.

They rode through the day and into the night. The cart had several round wooden stakes, one on each corner. Netting weaved between the poles, keeping crates from bouncing away.

Unable to sleep, Kairo laid with his back pressed against the net and his left leg propped on a sack of grain. A synthetic hammock. His face hung up, watching the stars spread across the heavens. That was one thing he could never do back in the jungle. NeoDerii had curfew before sunfall. And out on missions, the only stars he ever saw were little glimpses between the canopy high above.

Wesken was curled up on several sacks of grain. His eyes were open, though he lay unmoved.

"Wesken."

Nothing.

Kairo wondered what was going on up there, in that head of his.

Kairo closed his eyes. He wanted to dream the sort of dream where you're not wholly asleep and powerless over the dream. The sort of dream where you thought about what you liked and did what you liked. The sort of dream that Aterah had, and Wesken. But when he closed his eyes there was nothing. Just the darkness of his empty eyelids.

33

EIDHIN

I don't understand, said Eidhin, sounding out the syllables in his head for Tuladrna to hear. He swept the kitchen floor, picking up dust and dirt and potato peels. *I'm sure there's a number of things that I'm convinced of that are untrue. I can't be right about everything, I'm only human.* He squeezed the thistles of the broomstick in the small corridor between the cutting board island and the pale-orange tile.

"Well that's the difference 'tween you and him," Tuladrna sat on a kitchen counter, a near-empty bottle of wine sat beside him and he scraped expensive fruits from a bowl to his mouth like they would go bad at any moment. "A sour notion, a bitter persuasion, a handful of dirt—ridden with worms, worth of an encouragement, on a man of Illyadra Kalyn's stature?" Tuladrna offered a lazy chuckle, "And I thought, 'blessed me, for I have a job with consequence.' No. See, there is a gulf between you and me. And between me and the El Kalyn Vylndaer?" Tuladrna plopped a grape in his mouth. "That would take coordinated flagships to cross."

What sort of consequences, El?

"For Kalyn?" Tuladrna hummed while he chewed. "Well, he's an Illyadra. Means he's in charge of all philosophical thought in Aylavuera. Probably, you could make an argument for the world. So if he were to calculate. . . say, uhm, what a good way to be was, and it turns out that way isn't all that good, well now he's taught and convinced half of Zoë's curious what to do-n't. And do-n't they would. Savvy?"

I think so—uhm, indeed. He corrected himself, remembering his manners. *What about the Razite, who is that?*

"Mhm." Tuladrna hummed and held up a finger but didn't chew any faster. "El Kalyn is Ohaer. Means all the other types of vuu are available to him. But Razite vuu is tricky. It's not based on genetics, or learning, or even talent for that matter. It's based on emotion. Makes it especially difficult for an Illian.

"The aristocracy of Ra'che, Wardens I think they're called, sell the employment of poorer Razite at ridiculous prices to people like Kalyn because, get this, Razite can *see* vuu. Even the invisible types, like Illian. That's a really valuable power, and the Wardens know it.

"Some say," Tuladrna glanced at both of the kitchen doors, "Some say the Wardens are the leading members of a secret world government. A cabal. The Dii'raxis. They've already taken over the calendar. Not that Renovia is still around to put up a fight, being jailed up in those big prison cities and all." He shrugged and chuckled. "But it's all rumor. Hard to believe, what with Ra'che being the most desolate chunks of wasteland on the face of Zoë."

Eidhin nodded but it was difficult to follow along. There was a fog in his mind. A sort of distantness. *So, El is buying a slave?*

"Well," Tuladrna frowned and waved a dismissive hand. "No, no. They're paid a fair share. And Ra'che is so torturous a landscape to live in, they love being taken away, really."

Eidhin hummed in thought, then monologued, *I'm done with my chores for today.*

"Indeed. Do as you please." Tuladrna slouched further against the clay-brick wall and turned away.

Forest surrounded the grounds. Broken branches, twigs, and fallen leaves covered the soil. Nature's waste. Eidhin picked up a decent looking stick, nearly twice the length of his forearm. He gave it swing and twirl, then sheathed it in his belt.

He found a tree with a thick trunk and branches hanging low, as if their arms were too heavy to hold themselves up. He climbed up and notched his feet, then tore out his sword and held it up before him. *Argh! Pirates on the portside!*

"What are you doing?" It was a young girl's voice.

Eidhin's heart plummeted through his stomach. He hid his wooden sword behind his back. Aesa Vylndaer stared up at him from the ground. The El's youngest daughter.

Eidhin shrugged, praying to El Hwaerta that he would not be forced to speak.

She giggled. "Talk."

"I-I w-was p-p-playing p-p-pirate-s." He closed his eyes over some of the more difficult letters. His chin swung up and down, as if trying to strong-arm the syllables.

"I want to play," said Aesa, already swinging herself aboard. She climbed nimbly and without thinking, as if she had been up here before.

Of course she has, stupid! It's practically her *tree.* Eidhin scooched himself back, letting her stand comfortably. She had to be within a few seasons of his own age.

"You think loudly," she said, peering about his face with wondering eyes.

"I-Is that-t b-b-bad?"

"Baah, baah." Aesa giggled out sheep noises.

Eidhin's face reddened.

"Here." She held her palm up toward his face and paused.

It was like when Penoa could communicate with his mind back in Snowstock's inn. Or when he and Sor'al poked each other's foreheads and rid themselves of communication. Even Tuladrna had come into contact with Eidhin's thoughts.

He nodded and she let her palm wrap around his forehead. He expected trumpets to blast and the world to look gold and blue, but these didn't happen. Eidhin wondered if Aesa's vuu was stronger, if she was sneakier, or if she accessed less of his mind than the other times. He wasn't sure.

"Look out!" She pointed past his chest.

He looked over, and behold, a misty galleon swayed in the air, just out of reach. It was small, made to look far away. It flew the Tyrodeon flag, a bandit insignia of a rogue Sigu Nii armada that gave the northwestern isles trade difficulties. "W-what?"

"You can just talk in your head. I can hear you, it's easier that way."

Like this?

Aesa nodded.

How are you doing that? Eidhin pointed at the ship.

Aesa laughed. "You can't? It's just an illusion. Illian vuu. Like the way I can talk with you head-to-head. Father says I'll be doing more than silly party tricks when I'm older. I tell him, 'Okay.'" She rolled her eyes. "As if I'll ever stop playing pretend."

Aesa and Eidhin stayed up in the tree for hours. They fought pirate ship after pirate ship. They dined with a misty King Samuel Gehn, and he personally thanked them for their bravery. They traveled to meet tribes on remote islands of Aylavuera, whose social pillars and technological advancements were still stuck in the third Kortaes.

Eidhin thought he was imaginative, and his daydreams were entertaining. But Aesa? Her daydreams were real. They had life. Characters with names, islands with cultures, frames of time based on real history that he had never learned. Her daydreams, playful as they were, were informed.

Commotion came from the south wing of the Vylndaer Manor, as the day was nearing its end.

I need to get ready for dinner, he told her.

She sighed and stared at the manor with a longing in her eyes. "Me too."

"Well haven't you enjoyed the most splendid of times?" Seraii's voice shook. She had dust streaks across her face.

"I-I-I—"

"I-I-I!" She mocked. She closed her eyes and let out a slow breath.

Tuladrna opened the servant quarters' door. "Eidhin, Seraii. Come with me."

"We haven't changed for dinner yet."

"Forget about that tonight. The El Kalyn wishes to speak with you."

They both froze. Their eyes locked on Tuladrna. "What did we do?" Seraii asked.

This is what she wanted, thought Eidhin. But he understood. He felt the same. As if he were walking toward the gallows. Eidhin and Seraii shared a glance and followed Tuladrna toward the manor.

Tuladrna turned left at the gravel intersection just before the north wing entrance. It seemed the main manor was not where they were going.

They walked along the edge of the building. The path turned to a narrow trail in the grass. To their right was the ocean cliff and the gold-and-white staircase to the manor. They came to the dome they had passed on the way up from Talynguard. The dome was made of rounded whitestone bricks, with a blue gem that wove through the stone. Bronze gears stuck out from the building, moving and chugging. Brass tubes covered portions like armor, steam and smoke spilling from some of the seams.

"What is this place?" asked Seraii.

"El Kalyn's study. You are never to enter here unsummoned."

Tuladrna tentatively opened the door. A gust escaped the building, cool and dark.

It took their eyes a moment to adjust to the dim light. Eidhin sniffed, a distinct smell of blood and pine wafted through the building—plus another steamy, unidentifiable aroma that stung at his nose. The floor was cement, inlaid with circles of brass and strange runes. If he were as tall as a man grown, he could have reached up and touched the low ceiling.

"I've done it," came a hoarse voice around a corner. Before them was a hall of floor-to-ceiling bookshelves, with papers and books flung around the floor. Narrow doors lay on either side of the bookcases.

At the end of the bookcase hall, El Kalyn wandered into view. His black locks surrounded his face, and he stared at the sword he held. It glinted from an out-of-sight candle. A milky white hilt, with a blue gem for the pommel, and strange runes burned into the metal. "A blade that will not dull."

Tuladrna shuffled between all the books, cautious of what he stepped on. "Splendid, El Vylndaer." He spoke with relief. "You can begin a fruitful trade alliance with Sigu Nii."

El Kalyn snapped in his direction. Eidhin and Seraii both flinched, having followed Tuladrna into the main room. "I will not." He laughed. "You have a poor imagination, young Tuladrna. I have discovered a new vuu. A vuu that doesn't require human muscle. A vuu accessible only to the Ohaer. This isn't just a good sword, dear Tuladrna. This is a prototype for the biggest advancement of our age." Kalyn licked his lips and shook his head, "No. No-no. This sword will end the Age of Under. Come the end of next generation Yaerta, *I* will begin a new age. An age of Old Vulgarhe. The Age of Vylgarhe."

The four stood in a weighty silence.

Kalyn's eyes snapped to Eidhin and Seraii. "You two! You have not been vetted. You might be spies. You might be spies." He snatched Eidhin's upper arm and thrust him into a chair. "Sit." He shot a look at Seraii, and she raced to the rickety wooden chair sat beside Eidhin.

Written words and applicable attempts seemed to cut the room in half. On Eidhin's left, the main room was walled off from the previous by more bookcases—floor to ceiling, wall to wall. On his right, a long, lacquered desk was built into the curved wall of the dome. Hundreds of little trinkets sat on the desk, with smoke whispering from runes of Old Vulgarhe burned into the sides. There was a pen, a book, a chestplate, an apple, papers upon papers flung across the floor, each smoking but not catching fire.

"I checked them in Gehni."

"Do not say his name," hissed the Illyadra. He stooped down in front of Seraii so that his eyes were level with hers. His black coat hung around either side of his knees. He held his hand out, palm forward, halfway to Seraii.

Terror flashed across her face. She wriggled her head away, but it continued to draw forward, as if propelled by some unseen force. Her forehead landed in the crevice of his palm.

Eidhin gripped his hands and chewed the inside of his cheek. His heart thudded in his chest.

She squirmed, her face contorting and straining under his grip.

"Educated by . . . parents and family members. Who were educated by . . . parents and family members. An average sensory processor for your region. And . . . an adequately small amount of vuu."

El Kalyn lifted his hand away, and she gasped for breath. Tears formed at the corners of her eyes as she leaned back into her chair.

The El turned to Eidhin. His long black hair hung heavily around his sharp face. His eyes, a solid ring of blue amidst a black sea. He held out his palm.

"Come," a voice whispered in his mind. Eidhin winced and found he was unable to resist. He leaned his forehead into Kalyn's palm.

A hard wind whistled in his ears. It fluttered his wispy, blonde hair and snapped Kalyn's jacket back and forth. Kalyn's face became grainy until his nose fell off and shattered across the ground, rupturing into a thousand salt grains. The wind tore off his arm, it splashed against the bookcase like a thrown snowball. Eidhin peered down, feeling an ache in legs. And they too melted like heaps of sugar. A sandy mist tormented the study, blowing and breaking everything in sight, until there was nothing. A void.

Eidhin hung loose in the empty darkness.

"Who is Eidhinro?" A whisper echoed through the black.

Eidhin peered down at his hands, they were covered with wrinkles. *He was—Grandad?* His voice was not his own, but the old rocking-chair bound man who wheezed when he talked. Ground took form beneath him. Soft dirt. Rows of it as far as the eye could see. Onions formed in his palms.

"The first of Generation Bora acquired himself a plot of land. You're a farmer." The whisper sounded amused, pat-on-the-back like. *"And what guidance has sought you?"*

In the distance, out of the tilled mounds, rose a stone building with stained glass and the blue Church of Rai sigil across the front doors.

The whisperer laughed. *"So, none at all."*

The hand pulled away from Eidhin's beaded forehead. Reality came back to him. He gasped for air.

El Kalyn looked at an arm-folded Tuladrna. "This one is like you." He pointed at Eidhin.

Tuladrna's arms fell from his pudgy chest. "What?" He sounded offended. "This one here?"

"Exceptional intuitive processor. Nearly zero education—no vuu." Kalyn nodded. "He's perfect. Have him begin scribing immediately."

The room fell silent.

"The other is good just as she is."

"This one here?" Just to make sure, Tuladrna walked over and stuck a finger in Eidhin's face.

"Immediately."

"Indeed, indeed." Tuladrna raised his hands in surrender. "Let's go, then." He huffed and pulled Eidhin and Seraii out of their seats.

When they reached the door to the study, he paused to let Seraii through, and shut the door.

He turned to Eidhin. "Seems you'll be allowed in here after all." He strode to the door on the left of the bookcase hall. Moaning. Sighing, pained and soft, spilled from the eerie underground staircase.

Tuladrna lit a match and held it to an oil wick lantern. Its light danced across the walls. Eidhin assumed they used to be whitestone. But now they had become brown and black with soot and sludge that leaked through the grout.

There was an interesting smell about the air. Eidhin sniffed for investigation, but the sudden blast through his nostrils had him forcing down a wretch. It was like pressing his nose against a corpse's arse.

The moaning grew louder as they reached the bottom of the curving staircase. They stood in a short hall of iron cages. Three young, naked men stood shivering in separate cells. They were bone thin and had hollow sockets instead of eyes. None of them had any arms, and when they moaned again, Eidhin saw a scarred nub where a tongue should be. Their heads turned, Eidhin wondered if they sensed his and Tuladrna's presence. But with what? Their ears were a pile of melted skin, Eidhin couldn't see any hole.

"W-w-w—" He probably would've been stuttering, even if he didn't have a stutter.

"Other Illyadra—take Grandon Delshau for example," Tuladrna's voice was casual. He continued down the hall, with a terrified Eidhin in tow, explaining in detail. "He has such extraordinary observational vuu that he can infiltrate the minds of his subordinates and operate their bodies totally simultaneous to his own. Live their lives for them, without much sacrifice."

It sounded like El Hwaerta, the god of truth. He had a quadratic attention—or the ability to focus on four people praying simultaneously.

"Then you have Kalyn Vylndaer, whose intuitive processer is much stronger than his observational. He infiltrates these savants here, unsociable little weasels with minds as great as any, and thinks with the speed and depth of four."

Eidhin was horrified. He shivered down the aisle, keeping as close to the middle, away from the cages, as he could. What did their minds look like? He wondered. Could they see what Kalyn saw? Did they think what Kalyn thought?

They arrived at a door at the end of the hall. Tuladrna opened it, revealing a closet-sized room housing a simple chair and a small, unvarnished wooden desk under stacks of scrolls and papers. From a drawer he pulled out ink and quill and set it neatly on top of the mound of papers.

He pointed at everything atop the desk. "You're to copy these papers . . . onto these papers." He pointed to a fresh stack of clean paper under the desk.

Eidhin held his breath.

"You are not to repeat any learnings you might encounter here—including the location of your scribing. Else you'll end up one of those three. Do you understand?"

He nodded like his life depended on it.

"Enjoy." With that, Tuladrna left.

Eidhin's throat constricted. He wanted to cry. He wanted his mother and father and the farm.

The sounds of the savants moaning in the cages were louder than his sniffles.

Eidhin wondered how long it would take just to organize the papers. And copying them? more than one sitting, that was certain. He shuddered at the thought of having to pass the savants again and again.

Then he thought, *At least I finally get to scribe for one of the greats. To copy and copy and learn as I go.*

But as he began to copy the first few runes of Common, something was off. He could read the letters, all of which he knew well. And he could discern the words. But he could not understand any of them. Was it in a different language? No. It was his native language. Why could he not process the meanings? The findings of an Illyadra sat before him, and he could not understand his words.

34

VASARA

The lantern-bearer climbed over the eastern horizon, Kairo turned his hungry, tired eyes to the north. A sight more spectacular than he had anticipated. Vasara. There were three perfectly parallel points with which she stood against the sky: a black and gold triangle thing, a statue, and a castle. Beneath them—grandiose weavings of gargantuan human construction, and beneath them—a vast city spread out over many rolling hills.

Kairo lifted himself with his elbows, peering over the wooden cart panel that separated the driver from the cargo.

Each bolder-sized brick in the pyramid, black with a solid gold outline, caught morning sun, creating hundreds of rectangular halos. In the middle of the triangular face was an eye, its pupil swirling the black and gold into a point. It was the insignia of Warlord El Rai Ezs.

"Lord Mayor Ryaff," huffed the driver.

Kairo wondered if he was addressing the statue. It looked new. The black metal that the Sigu Nii use so frequently was polished and without rust. He stood in a wide fighting stance, Kairo wondered how many dozens of buildings stood between his feet. And his hands were funneling to a point, facing east—where Renovia was, with bolts of electricity running down his arms. Ryaff's left shoulder faced away, but Kairo didn't doubt there would be a level-five tattoo visible for great distances north of the city.

A small mountain rested at Vasara's northeastern edge, with Castle Graey spilling down its side. It was the oldest thing Kairo had ever laid his eyes on. Well, besides the dirt and rocks and trees, of course. It was older, he figured, than even the river pass over the Maua. It was apparent that the hillside cluster of a fortress used to have wood decorating many of its parts, but even many of the stone structures were in pieces. Despite all this, scaffolding covered its entire eastern face. Kairo was still far away, but it looked like people were actively working on it.

The cart jerked and slowed suddenly. They rolled past soldiers, farmers, and Sigu Nii of all sorts.

Vasara. This was once the capital of the world. But that was a very long time ago. Kairo shifted in uneasy apprehension. What will the barbarians have done to his city?

Wesken rolled and twisted, sat up, and looked around.

"Well, good morning." Kairo gave a weak laugh. The boy did not know what boredom he had left Kairo to for most of the night.

"I wasn't asleep." Wesken rubbed at his eyes. "Oh! You mean because I was—right." The child laughed his rapid, high pitch little laugh.

A stench infiltrated Kairo's nostrils. Violent and aggressive. Kairo sat up suddenly, his hands clasping his nose as if a bee had flown straight in. It was worse than Yutarah. Worse than Ravid. Like genitals washed in dung. Perhaps that wasn't what caused the smell, but once Kairo thought of its similarity, he couldn't banish the comparison from his mind. It took great restraint to keep from hurling over the side of the cart.

As Vasara grew nearer the cart slowed more and more. Kairo could distinguish loose clusters of war tribes. Banners attached to the backs of men, insignias painted on leather armor, war chiefs on horseback marching with a steady gait, regardless of who was in front of them.

"What are we doing here again?" Wesken asked as he shifted around the grain sackcloth.

"Aterah. She'll be here," said Kairo confidentially with blocked nasal passages.

"You're being sold as slaves to help restore the Castle Graey for Lord Mayor Ryaff," barked the driver.

Wesken pinched his nose. "It smells like poopy."

A flimsy metal archway hovered over the road. Everyone coming and going passed beneath it.

Past the arch, on either side of the muddy dirt road, thin metal sheet shacks stacked three stories high. They abutted the road as closely as they could and leaned like an arching canopy. Dozens of strings extended between the upper floors with clothes and fly-ridden hide skins hanging to dry.

The Sigu Nii built themselves a Ravid.

The wagon hit a bump and rocked. The jitter sent a sear through Kairo's leg that made his teeth gnash. He glanced behind them to see what they ran over. A corpse. Horse trodden, carriage sawn, rodent nibbled, fly infested, with organs and intestines spilling halfway across the road.

Kairo felt the blood drain from his face. And the smell of the rotting body added a punch to the gut. He clutched the cart's poles and wretched over the side. He laid there a moment, not daring to look at anymore of Vasara.

Why was he so shaken? He had seen worse things on the warfront, where he had literally grown up. His hand had taken many lives. Why did Vasara shake him so? Perhaps it was the way the Sigu Nii seemed wholly unmoved. Their way of living, though reluctantly more advanced, was just—so—barbaric.

Wesken had no such reaction. He wore a blank face—no pity, no disgust, not a trace of empathy behind his eyes. "When do we hunt for the girl?" he asked, exaggerating a hungry croaking voice.

"My . . ." Kairo smacked his lips and took a moment to spit through the net of the cart, "Sister."

"Right, sister. When do we hunt?"

"I guess I'd say we are. Now. Look for her."

"Ooh, I hope we get in a fight."

"Please El, no."

"Ears! Four copper apiece!" a woman called. She was tucked under a red fraying cloth stand. Kairo saw no ears hanging from her tent. But then Sigu Nii warriors approached and handed *her* ears. From the slight caramel shade, he knew the ears were Renovian. Soldiers lifted entire strings of them from their necks as the woman handed them shiny bronze-colored metals.

The swaying canopy of tin and cloth shacks gradually gave way to cobblestone streets and wooden buildings with stone slate roofs. War-tribe banners hung from these too.

This wasn't at all how he imagined their home territory to appear.

Yutarah had been horrifying to walk through, because often even when the Renovians outnumber the Sigu Nii, their wicked vuu hands them victory in battle. And Kairo was well outnumbered in Yutarah. But that's loosely how he presumed their living. A bunch of tents.

Kairo marveled at Vasara's use of wood, like NeoDerii, and stone structures, like the old river pass.

As they continued, Kairo's mind ran on about Sigu Nii culture. He had learned so much more about the beasts than anyone he ever knew in NeoDerii. More than Copt and Norly, more than Captain Rouen. More than the team of Leadership, probably even Commander Lezyne. Even the generals and the elders had never seen Yutarah or what had become of Ravid, and especially not Vasara. Kairo wondered, what did Adakon know? What had he seen in the time spent between the Egress of each prison-city? Had he adorned a hooded cloak and wandered these streets? Or did he pass through uninhabited areas around Renovia's stolen lands?

Foremost on Kairo's mind was that the Sigu Nii were not as entirely barbaric as he had thought. Morally, yes. But structurally? Their carpentry, their Lockes and Wheelhouses, their barracks and their sense of Graeynesh Law VI: adhere to the process of rank, was better. Was it all due to their vuu?

And the Niiwa. What a despicable, brutal blood sport. Why does competency in battle determine so much? It seemed that their capability of vuu really did distinguish a decent work of carpentry from a poor one.

Kairo raised his hands to press against either side of his head. He felt nauseated. *Korta Ellanii, what do you call these people? Do you call them yours? Or do you despise their way of living? Help me view them as you do.*

"You sure are thinkin'," Wesken said in an exaggerated twangish, Sigu Nii farmer-like voice and giggled.

"Yeah." Kairo sighed and lowered his hands.

They came up a small hill, and most of the city stretched before them. He was breathless as he swept his gaze across it all. Towering shack houses were prevalent along the outskirts, but the structures grew sturdier and more elaborate with each step toward the center of the city. A grand stone arena stood a way's north of the great black and gold pyramid.

The cart turned northeast, towards Castle Graey.

A stone archway separated the strip of shacks where Vasara ended and the hill of Castle Graey began. Carved womanly figures stretched out of the pillars, as if they were trying to climb out of their stone encampment. They were cracked and crumbling but remained distinct in shape—the el of realms unseen.

Six shirtless slaves passed in front of the cart; a trunk laid between each three. Kairo's eyes lit up as he recognized ethnicity. Renovians! They trudged around the bottom of the castle's hill. The sun waged against vuu-scars, which perforated more of their skin than not.

He began to call out to them. "H-he—" The first letters spilled into a stutter as he realized they didn't have any ears. All of them had been cut off, leaving a lump of scar tissue around a hole. And upon closer, heart wrenching inspection—two out of the three on this side of the log didn't have eyes either. Lids flapped like loose bags over the empty sockets.

Kairo's stomach rumbled in threatening revolt. "Not again." He moaned. But he managed to keep it down.

The wagon turned sideways from the hill that Castle Graey ascended and turned toward a collection of buildings beneath it. Between them was a dirt courtyard as big as the West Deck. Groups of Renovians were separated by task. Some were shoveling a grey slop onto itself. Others were gathering up wooden poles and twine to make scaffolding. And others still were hauling things this way and that. Among each of these groups, Kairo saw a Renovian or two who still retained their preceptors.

Thin white dust clouds navigated the trail. Kairo wasn't sure what it was, but many of the Renovians were covered with it. The white powder clung to their sweat.

It was a new Ravid for him, thought Kairo.

"Aye. 'Ere we are," said the driver.

The buildings were made out of wood and stone but they looked thrown together. Kairo understood—sometimes temporary shelters are necessary. But low effort construction in the jungle was just twine and sticks with leaves tossed on top.

The driver made around and unlatched the back. Wesken jumped out and Kairo scooched, being sure not to irritate his throbbing thigh.

A soldier in polished black and gold armor greeted them with folded arms. He looked each member of the approaching party up and down.

"Ravid passes on these most excellent workers, El." The driver bowed.

"Aye. We'll take 'em."

"Y-You don't even want to inspect them first?"

"Nah," said the Black Guard. "Orders from higher up. These two've been expected." The Black Guard motioned to a Renovian waiting silently behind him.

He came forward and escorted Kairo and Wesken to a pavilion, looking grim all the while. "Strip." He said.

"Dibs on being the one who gets to keep his eyes." Wesken giggled while taking off his tunic.

"W-Wait," said Kairo. He didn't recognize this fellow soldier, so he was probably from a different outpost. But they almost certainly followed Graeynesh Law religiously and punished disobedience with exile. *Strip*. It was commanded of Rouen.

"Strip!" His fist came up and connected with Kairo's left cheek.

Kairo stumbled back. His hands flailed in front of him for balance and protection. Something hard flew against his foot while he was shoved into it. His shoulder hit the pavilion's smooth stone floor. He moaned in growing soreness.

Wesken lowered into a fighting stance. A delight descended his face. The child's abdomen flexed in unison with his tensing biceps.

"Wait!" Kairo didn't want Wesken to get hurt. "Alright!" It came out a wail of hopelessness. A half-sob puffed out after it, divided by the fear that a snagaeri or a war tribe might hear him. Then he sniggered breath-heavy and sobbed again.

The Renovian lowered atop him, straddling Kairo's chest with each knee. He held a spoon.

35

AYRAH

Ayrah kneeled and dusted the black sand from her boots as the next wave of forty-some opponents took their stands around the arena. A large handful of them were remnants from the previous round, like Ty Ryaff, several others who had caught her eyes, and Prince bloody Agora.

The rest were newcomers, people who had won the first round in a past season. She studied them with mutated eyes. They were all older. Men and women who had lived long enough to gather callous and scar. They all wore clothes comfortable for agility rather than tough metals to resist blades. And they all carried the tail of the serpent on their left shoulders.

Ayrah took some solace that she did not know any of their names.

Ecanaes snickered at that, like a siren wailing through her observation. *"It would be El to know, Ayrah. Might I inform you?"*

Hush. She thought.

Masikonian contestants were sparse. And the few who were present looked over at the king's son with sudden regret. One had arms that transitioned into greasy, metallic points for hands. Another took the shape of a bird-like thing.

The dark-skinned Razites were few, as well. Only a couple around the pit. And unless they were Ohaer, they would be of little note. The pale-skinned Illians were completely absent.

"*Ayrah*," urged Ecanaes. "*One of the Razite is Ohaer.*"

She rose to a fighting stance and swept her gaze across each of the shadowa-colored people, searching for the one standing above the rest.

Ayrah scanned him with her sharpened retinas. His nose ended wide. Age had streaked white into his otherwise thick, curly hair. White dust was sprinkled over his face, a thin film of powder-like war paint, stopping just above his mouth, then one large dot on his chin.

"*He's El Baaor, Warden of Dun'tugda-Ra'che.*"

Ayrah assured herself that despite his superior accumulation of vuu, the second round of the Niiwa was of elemental vuu—and despite his power, maybe he had not practiced as much as she with a black-ice sword. She swallowed hard.

Ecanaes described the heritage of each Sigu Nii her eyes passed over, in the speedy mental relaying that he controlled. The pit was filled with daughters of lord mayors and sons of officers.

Ayrah assumed that her winning of the last round would make her a higher valued target to eliminate quickly. But as she looked into the eyes around the pit, they did not appear to care. She reminded herself that she was the daughter of a Warlord, but it rang hollow between her ears. There was a prince and a foreign Warlord equivalent standing before her.

"Round two, the Flame." King Ash's voice shook the arena. "BEGIN!" The black sand danced with the thunder of his call.

A skin-stinging cool coursed through Ayrah's left arm. Little icicles ripped from her elbow to her knuckles, and she pulled a black sword from her palm.

Vuu exploded across the pit. Colored fires sprang to life, blue, green, and purple. They cast assorted rainbows across the arena. A black fire settled around Baaor.

"*The fighter to your left is hesitant, his eyes linger on you; be careful of his observation. The fighter to your right looks to his right; he is not an immediate threat.*" Ecanaes' rapid insights filled Ayrah's mind as she looked the opposite directions. There was no comprehension time. When Ecanaes communicated, it was like food that had already been digested.

She feigned to the right while thrusting her left hand in the direction of her attentive opponent. Black-ice vuu sprang from the tips of her fingers and coated the sparkling volcanic sand all the way up to his shins. Momentarily taken care of, Ayrah spun and hurled her blade at the contestant who had turned away from her. The black tip carved a half-circled gash across his upper back and sank lopsided into his lower spine. He screamed and collapsed to his knees then to his face.

"*Good kill, Ayrah. The other breaks free from his bonds.*"

She spun around as her captured opponent kicked the ice free. Misty frost sprinkled from his shins. He brought his hands back, and the volcanic black sand around him followed his motion. He hurled his hands forth, and the sand erupted toward her at skin misting speeds.

Ayrah threw her arms up to materialize a black ice wall in front of her, and the sand pelted against it. She threw all her weight into a kick and sent the wall crashing toward her opponent.

He leapt away then charged his vuu, lighting up the veins in his arms and his face in a bright glow. When he released it, a flurry of small flaming orbs chased after Ayrah. She ducked the first several. But Ecanaes informed, "*They turn back for you!*" So she raced towards the man himself and instinctively slid through the sand. The orbs flew over her head and pummeled his chest. She drew a black-ice-sword from her palm and snuffed his final breaths.

"*Twenty remain,*" said Ecanaes. "*Most crowd around the prince and the Warden. The match will conclude after four more are slain.*"

Ayrah turned to the Ohaer Warden of Ra'che. Five contestants surrounded him, all with drool hanging from their chins at the thought of gloriously slaying someone of more vuu than they.

Another seven contestants fought Prince Agora, as well as each other, simultaneously. The remaining five consisted of duels, most still in their starting positions.

Ayrah had half a mind to explode a white gust on each duel, but Ecanaes urged, *"Ayrah, there is a reason large vuu is not predominant. White fire is tiring to cast.*

"And additionally, it is doubly important that you go and slay either Prince Agora, or the Warden, this round. Both would be desired."

Ayrah began toward them, snarling. She enjoyed the elemental vuu of the second round, and she was not too proficient the with battle-styled vuu of the third.

"And if you let them arrive to the fourth round with you," Ecanaes commented on her thoughts, *"Where Sigu Nii vuu has no more limitations, you'll be done for. They are stronger than you. Kill them!"*

The duels around the pit were ending as Ayrah arrived on the Warden. Ecanaes counted down how many more people needed to die before this round ended. *"Four. . . three. . . two. . ."*

Sweat streaks made rivulets through the white dust on the Warden's face. Slabs of ice coated the backs of his arms. He swung them around, blocking firebolts here, a spear of ice there. A stalagmite of black volcanic sand materialized in his thrusting hand, piercing one of the contestants fighting him.

". . .one."

Ayrah roared. She charged a ball of fire and threw it his direction. She chased after it, sending gusts of flame behind every step, propelling her forth at wicked speed.

His eyes met hers; he let out an exhausted snarl. Baaor raised his arm to block the cast, but Ayrah was already upon him and punched a razor-sharp ice-covered knuckle into his gut. He screamed. Blood gushed from his stomach onto her. A thin razor of black-ice formed on the side of her palm, he fell to his knees, she sliced his neck.

"Silence!" bellowed King Ash across the pit. The round was finished.

The other contestants that were fighting Baaor looked at Ayrah. There was a mixture of emotion in their eyes. *Who the bloody El are you?* And, *how dare you take my kill!* And even still, *Thank Rahktavah we don't have to fight him next round.*

Ayrah glanced over at Prince Agora's collection of fighters. They were all weary, but alive.

The stadium was a constant wave of cheerful screaming, though the harsh Sigu Nii accent made it sound like they were at war.

"Who will stay for the next round?" asked the king.

Ten fighters exited the pit. Five of them stayed. Prince Agora was one of them.

Ayrah didn't want to admit it, but she was sweating.

The crowd stirred in a brief intermission.

Round three, The Skull, saw fifteen new contestants, each of them well known. There were several sons and daughters to Warlords and only one other-colored person: a Masikonian.

He had tattoos of stone, maze like, coming out of his skin. Ecanaes informed that these were traditional markings of the Alkalii, the Masikonian's hand-selected military. The Alkalii were nearly all men, powerful, and unfit for regular society. They weren't funny. They had no desire to be pretty. They didn't care to amass coin or sing for the peasant masses. They were soldiers through and through.

The round played out differently from the previous two. Battle casts, the allowed style of Sigu Nii vuu, was rather niche and allowed one to punch with much more force than biological muscles would allow. And poison was cast everywhere—on the tips of blades, in puddles on the ground, and in wafting mists.

Contestants were no longer cautious about their reservoirs of vuu. Power was of the utmost importance for victory, and that meant spatially large casts.

Ayrah ducked and weaved, closing in on prey that she and Ecanaes deemed the weakest. Most of the contestants held their ground, content to defend their positions. But Ayrah was a close-quarters fighter.

A vuu-powered kick to the chest sent her flying across the arena. Her ribs would have shattered if it hadn't been for her mutated bones. Yet she struggled to her feet, gasping for air.

The round ended as Ayrah channeled fireless explosions into the Masikonian's obliques, sending him headlong into the pit's drop-off wall beside him. Ayrah heard bones crunch on impact. Prince Agora illuded her again. Was he avoiding her?

Weary, she took her stance for the fourth round, Blood. This was the final round for her.

There were no limitations; all Sigu Nii vuu was allowed. Contestants of this round would channel uses of vuu that have been perfected for generations. Like herself, a shadowmancer.

There was the Golden Spear, the Pikemaster's eldest daughter. She made snarly faces directly at Ayrah, and called across the pit, "My daddy put your daddy's head on display, right outside castle *Veligreen*. And it's still bloody there." She laughed.

Ayrah's teeth were probably near shattering against one another. Anxious sweat bore into her forehead.

There was an Illyadra, whom Ecanaes fawned over. Ayrah demanded his sworn loyalty to her, then and there, that he wouldn't suddenly have a change of heart over his allegiances.

With the recent downfall of the Church of Rai, this Illyadra is of a new thought-school called 'Lm-Waerta. It means, 'Cluster of the Dead' in Old Vulgarhe.

Ayrah had heard that Rya's Warlord was growing too old to rule. It wouldn't be long before someone grashed for his title. His eldest son, Hacht was present for the fourth round of the Niiwa, and she could see in his eyes that he would kill his father.

It was another source of Ayrah's humiliation. That neither her, Verano, nor their father, Nahkon, would have the honor of an in-house grash. She would've passed it to her brother. Becoming a Warlord was not her interest. But still, the shame weighed. Watching Hacht stirred her insides.

Ayrah could feel Ecanaes shuddering at the thought of killing his own father. Ayrah smirked. How else were you supposed to keep your enemies from gaining the title? How else would you ensure your children picked up where you left off? You grash for it.

King Drastos' son, Prince Agora, wore a smug face over in his corner of the pit. He was a beautiful young man, probably a similar age to Ayrah.

"Make no mistake Veligreen, even though he's your age, he is very Ohaer."

His rippling pectorals and quadriceps seemed more for aesthetics than actual function. They shone with glittering splotches of metal mutations, armor for skin. He wore no shirt and no pants. His parts were covered by a thick coat of lion's fur, grown straight from his skin. His eyes scanned the stadium, he wore the dumbest smirk Ayrah had ever seen.

"BEGIN!"

Frost traced down from Ayrah's elbows. She pulled a black-ice-sword from her palm.

Bright lights flashed across the pit. Dozens of parallel lines formed around the Golden Spear. Ayrah didn't know what they were until they began flying her way—spears, dripping with molten metal.

Ayrah held her hands up, an icicle wall erupted out of the ground, and the spears smashed against it, spraying white-hot liquid.

"You've been deemed the weakest," warned Ecanaes.

It was true, Ayrah noticed. All eyes were on her.

"*There are five contestants. Only two will succeed.*"

Hacht was to her left, the Golden Spear to her right. The Illyadra and Prince Agora were on the far side of the arena, across the middle of the pit.

"*They're charging vuu,*" said Ecanaes.

All of them amassed an attack and began to aim at her.

Ayrah dropped to one knee and pulled the wraths within her. She had wanted to save this for later. Especially since she grew so weary after using it. But she needed to establish ferocity. She needed the other contestants to second guess their choice of fighting her first. The black shadowa mist erupted out of her. But instead of sending it in a ground chasing cloak, she willed the mist to make walls around her. She silently cheered. She had never demonstrated such control over it before.

Light evaporated as the mist closed around the last airhole. Darkness enveloped her. It was silent of the most deafening kind. She could feel the slightest tremor in the sand. If it weren't for Ecanaes, she wouldn't have any idea what went on outside.

"*Stay, Ayrah. . . stay. Your shadowa consumes the likes of Sigu Nii vuu of which I've never seen: Hacht stands in the middle of the pit, and shards of lightning are stretching even into the stands!*"

Ayrah's eyes widened. She could scarcely imagine getting vuu across the length of the oval in one precise cast, let alone covering the entire arena. Every moment that the mist maintained intangibility, she wearied. And she was quickly growing exhausted.

I'm going to punch through the mist and send it in a single stroke at him. Can you feel the direction I'm facing? Ayrah asked.

There was some hesitation. "*Yes. Turn fifteen degrees east—*"

Ayrah was good with directions. But not that good. *I swear, white boy, if you don't start making sense. . .* Ayrah relayed the rest of the threat in a mental picture.

"*Yes, yes!*" Ecanaes wobbled, "*Indeed, turn to your right—too much! A little left. . . ahm, eh, this could be good.*"

His lack of certainty wasn't inspiring. Ayrah punched the mist with her cross hand, and it shot out in a single, streamline stroke. All of the mist around her chased after the momentum. Like throwing a rock with a cloak draped over.

It beamed through Hacht. It nearly shot through Agora as well, but he puffed an instinctive breath of white fire.

Hacht turned to her, a fist-wide hole through his chest. Ayrah briefly saw a startled Agora through it, before blood and organs spilled in its wake.

Ayrah paraded herself, stretching her arms high above her, orchestrating the stadium cheers like music, while silently noting Prince Agora's knowledge of Sigu Nii vuu, and his practiced instinct to act upon it in an instant.

The Golden Spear and the Illyadra were locked into a duel, and Ayrah told Ecanaes to ask Tagon to compare her and Agora's vuu again.

"*Tagon says it's difficult to distinguish Sigu Nii vuu from the man's entire storeroom. He has more than the rest of you combined. But how much of that weight is in Sigu Nii, alone? He isn't sure.*

"*I say, since his parents are so powerful, it is safe to assume that he inherited enough, he is probably capable of winning even the next round. A true El of Sigu Nii.*"

Ayrah darted past Hacht's limp corpse, brought another black-ice sword from her palm, and hurled it at the Illyadra. Even while he fought the Golden Spear, he whipped around and caught her sword by its hilt. Ayrah smiled and willed it to explode. Black ice shards obliterated the lower half of his arm. He screamed, and the Pikemaster's daughter flung a molten spear into his face.

"*One more remains on the pit than is necessary.*"

The three of them eyed each other. The Golden Spear. Ayrah. Prince Agora. They began the encloser—the slow circular stepping, drawing nearer to one another, waiting, watching for mistakes. Watching for weakness.

Ayrah and the spear made eye contact. Ayrah wanted nothing more than to tear off her fingers, break her teeth, or suck the juice out of her eyeballs. But Prince Agora was more powerful than them both. And at a glance, they seemed to agree on that. They both turned toward him.

Chaotic chanting and cheering filled the stadium. Whether they were Sigu Nii and rooting for them, or Masikonian and rooting for their Prince, they were loud.

The Golden Spear opened her palms toward the prince, and hundreds of bolts of white fire blasted forth at wicked speed. They deflected into the sand around him or against the arena wall and exploded into bright orange flames.

Ayrah ran at him.

Ecanaes pleaded, "*You are more vulnerable next to him. Agora will target you rather than the Spear. And the Spear will be happy to aim at you both from afar.*"

But Ayrah was a close-quarters fighter. It was where she felt most comfortable. And most dangerous.

She whipped a sword from her palm and slashed it against his rippled and metal abdomen. Her sword broke into a dozen shards. It didn't even leave a mark. The Prince smiled with bright white teeth. "So ugly." he said. The veins across his nearly naked body illuminated a glowing blood-red. He clasped her by the shoulders.

Ayrah tried to shake him off, but his muscles were much stronger. Razor-sharp shards of ice jutted from her skin, pierced his hands, but he held tight. His veins grew brighter, his smile crept wider.

Ayrah yelled. Her chest squeezed. The veins running down her arms turned black. And before Prince Agora could unleash his charge of vuu, the black shadowa projected from her mouth to his face.

Agora yelled, and white fire blasted from his mouth.

White and black warred.

Mists of her shadowa slipped through his fire and streaks of flesh disappeared around his right ear.

Puffs of his fire blew past her shadowa and seared her left eye. She winced and shut it tight to fight the pain.

They continued yelling their vuu, face to face, knuckles apart, praying that the other would let up first. Ayrah was running out of breath. But so was he.

And finally, as their voices began to croak, Ayrah's final breath of shadowa met no resistance. Agora's head disappeared from his neck, with a seamless cut. Her black mist rolled into itself and turned to small tangible marble. Prince Agora's headless body toppled backwards.

"Oh my. You did it."

Ayrah collapsed to both knees, breathing hard. She squeezed the sand between her fingers.

The crowd roared. She had slain a prince.

"Silence!" yelled the king.

Ayrah looked to the Golden Spear, her eye still held shut, she approached slowly. Ayrah wished it had been her. The Pikemaster's daughter. The look on her face was somewhat. . . shocked.

The air cracked between them. Black sparks darted. Lightning erupted, thunder blasted, and King Drastos stood tall, looking down on Ayrah. His mouth hung open. The tips of his canine teeth were little and sharp. They looked cute. A tear was forming over the crest of his soft, fuzzy-skinned eyelids. His gaze, which was sort of glossed over, darted from Ayrah to his son's headless corpse behind her. "You. . ."

Dread. A ball felt as if it were crawling up Ayrah's throat. It hurt. Her foot stretched out through the sand—an instinctual preparation, should she need to stand and fight within the coming moments. Would he challenge her to grash? She tried swallowed the ball down. It stabbed her throat. She didn't have any strength left. Nothing. Black vignettes played at the edges of her periphery. She was passing out.

Drastos knelt, his knee pushed into the volcanic sand, he laid a hand on her shoulder. "You won." Tears mounted his eyelids and sogged the golden fur beneath. He twitched. His chin came up. Calloused pride flooded back in. "A prize then." His voice was harsh. "What do you want different about you? Name it. Anything."

Ayrah tried to swallow the ball down again. Her head bobbed as she strained to stay conscious. She tried to think. Change something about her? What? She wasn't sure she wanted to look any different.

"I will mutate whatever you ask of me, and the affect will be permanent." He explained as a way to encourage Ayrah to answer.

"My hair." It was all she could think of. "It used to be red."

"And it will be again." He removed his hand from her shoulder, Archeodon crown from atop his head, and reached it to her hair. Along the way, the colorless, but not-quite-white, and not-quite-invisible crown transformed into a sword. For a very brief moment, the fear that they were about to grash returned to Ayrah. But the flat of the blade landed gingerly on the crown of her head. "Now everyone will remember you. You're the Prince Killer." With a crack of black, sandy lightning, he was gone.

Ayrah pushed herself to stand. She looked at her front-left locks, they were still dreaded, but they were vibrantly red now, instead of black with a reddish hue.

"What are your names?" King Ash asked. "And do you fight in the next round?"

"The Golden Spear of Ryvl declares no, El."

Ayrah peered at the king's giant red eyes, like she were only a grain, and felt like he already knew the answer. "Ayrah Veligreen declares no, El." For a brief half-moment, she thought he would, reach out, and grash her just for being her father's daughter. But he didn't acknowledge her last name at all.

The crowds, on the other hand, roared.

"Come, receive your marking." His voice was monstrous.

They approached the throne. He leaned over, his size was suffocating, and he touched Ayrah on the lower left shoulder. When it lifted, a beautiful Niiwa tattoo remained in its place, styled in the likeness of her shadowa. Four pieces of a serpent. There were no inscriptions, and no inner symbols—everyone would recognize the sleek, dancing vuu, styled from the Sigu Nii capital, Sehlya.

High ranking peasants stole glances at her from all around their section of the stadium. They whispered, "Veligreen."

She sat next to Errta. She was struggling to stay awake for the fifth and final round. He put an arm around her. She felt safe. It was a safe place to sleep, nestled under his meaty, hairy arm.

Ayrah missed round five. But when Tagon spoke of it later, the round where Ohaer was allowed, he said that he could hardly watch. It was like looking at a light too bright. And during the Oscillation, of all times. The standard measurement of many moments passing from now to the next. Vuu raged. It was a battle between gods.

36

CASTLE

Kairo fumbled around in the dark. He was crying. In fact, he was pretty sure that he was wailing. No need to be worried about the Sigu Nii finding you out, now.

His hands were trembling. He reached up with tentative care, to feel his searing eye sockets, and found the hot stick of blood streaming where tears should be. He screamed.

Someone approached. Their footsteps were nearly silent. Definitely not Wesken.

"Time for the ears." He said. It was the Renovian. His knees came down on either side, the full of his weight landing on Kairo's chest.

Kairo choked on a sob and wheezed. The top of his ear pinched between finger and thumb and stretched away from his head. He winced, teeth grit. A cold metal touched the crevice of his ear and began sawing furiously.

Kairo screamed again. His knees jerked up in protest. His arms writhed by his side, under the Renovian's knees. But he kept his head still. No sense in making that mistake.

The Renovian ripped his ear off the rest of the way.

Blood soaked his hair, it gurgled in the remaining hole, it pooled between his head and the dirt.

Then the blade began on the other ear. "The Lord Mayor Ryaff," said the Renovian, "Recuperates some of the overhead by selling your parts to the Warlord's Office."

Kairo didn't understand. Half because the sound of his voice traveled through Kairo's wailing, and into holes filled with blood. And half because the words he was using didn't make any sense.

Who was this man? He spoke like them. Acted like them. Tortured like them. Perhaps even loved like them. He must not be Renovian then, Kairo reasoned, but some wicked beast turned to look the ethnicity of his people by Masikonian vuu. The same way Kairo had for the Sigu Nii. In a way, this man was the opposite of Kairo.

He lifted from Kairo's chest. "I said strip." He ripped Kairo's boots off, one foot at a time, and tore his shirt apart. Both were Sigu Nii anyways, stolen from the gathering.

Kairo's sobbing was like rapid intakes of air, his upper lip flapping in the draw. Blood dripped lightly into his mouth.

"You," said the torturer. "Are to relay instructions quickly and efficiently. Or we'll find someone else to do the hearing and the seeing."

"Sure," said Wesken casually.

"Interior renovations. Get to work," said the torturer.

"Interior Renovians. Get to work—wait! That didn't count. Reno-reno-vations," Wesken declared the last couple syllables triumphantly.

A moment passed. Kairo was certain the torturer had left. Was he expected to get up? Floppy feet approached rapidly, and a foot connected with his stomach.

"*Hegheww*," Kairo wheezed.

"Ope." Wesken's voice was muffled, perhaps a hand drawn over his mouth. "Ohmygosh, I'm so sorry!"

"Why," a cough, "Would you do that?"

"I really thought you would've gotten some superhuman hearing, and like, stopped my kick."

"*What?*" Kairo rolled over to his hands and knees. He coughed. A bit of blood came out. He could hear it splatter against the stone. His left thigh seared, as well. Which was strange, because it wasn't involved in the previous event at all. He prayed silently to the Korta Ellanii that a spasm was not coming on. He decided to hold his breath, just in case it would be his last for some time.

"Wow, you are *struggling.*" Why was the child's voice always so amused? It wasn't maleficent. Rather. . . innocent.

The lockjaw threat passed. Kairo let all his breath go at once.

"Here. The guy gave me this. Let me do it." Wesken approached. He unfoiled something clothe-sounding and started wrapping it around Kairo's head.

A yelp escaped Kairo as the bandage drew tight. He could hear it. Sure. But the sudden pain and the effort his throat made didn't match what he heard. His cry was muffled.

Wesken did well to leave his nose and mouth free for air. He helped Kairo to stand.

They stumbled forward. Kairo scrapped the bottom of his foot across the stone with each step, as if he'd lose track of where the floor was. They moved along slowly. Step by step, until the warmth of the sun landed on Kairo's open back. It was breezeless, wherever they were.

Kairo held onto Wesken like a raft. An itch bore into him, dreading each coming step, shuffling along at a pace beaten by a caterpillar. "I hate moving slow." He said.

Wesken didn't respond. Was he daydreaming at a time like this?

The sun-warmth disappeared. Kairo tilted his head, trying to listen. He couldn't hear anything. A panic arose in his chest. Rational thought departed from him. It was as if, because he couldn't move—he couldn't think. And terror took its place.

He imagined beasts lurking around him, from every direction. Each sneaking in at a pace that he couldn't detect. Kairo sniffed in a vain attempt to observe them with his only available preceptor. Then laughed. He chuckled aloud. No need to resort to what-if's, he shrugged, it was fact. The wicked barbarians were all around him. *Where*, you might ask. What would that matter? There. He nodded in a make-believe direction. And there. He gestured someplace else.

"Here we are," said Wesken.

Sound. He had heard the child speak. It was real. Kairo felt like he was losing his mind. "Uhm. Here where?" He asked. Certainly, of all possible directions, *"here"* was most objective. Kairo quickly imagined then, when he soon died, that Yeshwin might be a palace of forever *hereness*.

"Hey, yeah," said another man. Kairo's ears were too bandaged, too full of blood, and too cut off to deduce ethnic accent. But even if it were of Renovian descent, he doubted that would make leaps or bounds in the field of trust at the moment. "We're good here actually. Go on further up the castle, there's a group working on the tile. I'm sure they could use you."

Wesken started forward again. Kairo chased after him at what he imagined to be a quarter-step an hour pace. He followed in the direction he thought he was being led and was promptly redirected with a push in his arm. Kairo, full of it, threw his hands around, saying, "I can't do it! Just go on without me."

"Well, no you have to, though," said Wesken. "Cause I called dibs on not getting my eyes *schlooped* out, but uhm, they would if you just stopped there like that."

Kairo hadn't any idea what these *dibs* were, but he understood the rest of the words. He frowned and kept forward.

Kairo's outpost-bound occupations were scout and carpenter. And besides being labelled a swordsman, his primary position within his squadron (under Rouen) had been scout as well. He kept watch through the jungle—constantly aware of the north side of their company.

Now, Kairo had no idea where north even was. He had nothing with which he could use to perceive information. He could still smell, sure, but it was a tool more useful for deciding when food was too rotten to eat than any type of navigation.

He was lost. And he couldn't right tell how far they'd gotten, but half the day seemed to pass before he felt the panic begin again. "Wesken." He said. "Talk to me. Please."

"Sure." The boy nodded. "Uhm. . . ooh! If you had an extra eyeball and—"

"Not that one." Kairo's stomach threatened a revolt, reminded suddenly of the pain boring into his skull from so many directions.

The child knew that his memory was lame, so he didn't press for more information. "Uhm—"

Thunder echoed through the castle. For a sweet, sane moment Kairo was aware of where the walls were, the pillars and the ceiling, even a group of toiling Renovians up ahead because each had made a distinct shaking or yelping loud enough for Kairo to hear. A thin sheet of dust fell down from above.

"Is it raining?" Kairo asked. Maybe a light shower approached.

"No," said Wesken. The child's voice was newly serious. His arm broke away from Kairo's grasp, leaving him immediately and desperately alone. Even if the child were a step away, he was not within Kairo's ability to see, and therefore—*alone.*

"Wesken?" he asked, fully aware of the tremor in his voice.

A raspy, tappy, knock approached. Kairo then discerned a pair of sluggish steps in company. Who was this old, limping person? Had he teleported? It wasn't Arden. No. But someone with as much power came this way. Kairo gulped. He felt himself shrink. Graeynesh Law would probably instruct him to run, but. . . .

"Grandpa!" yelled Wesken, promptly startling Kairo.

"Wait, *grandpa*?" asked Kairo.

37

ATERAH

Aterah entered the dining hall and gripped the back of a golden chair. Boots knocked, and armor clinked like a herd of animals pounding through the hallways. Verano pulled his feet from atop the wooden table. A dozen Black Guard entered the room and filed in around her and Verano.

Then *he* entered. His sandals tapped softly down the hall. His black velvet robe swayed gently. He paused in the doorway, approachable blue eyes landed on hers. Rigid face, high cheekbones, thin lips, and a pointed chin. His hair was blonde, shaved close to his head, and golden rims over the bridge of his nose held round slivers of glass. He smiled with bright white teeth. "Hello there." The Warlord's voice was soft, gentle even.

Aterah shivered. She rubbed the backs of her arms. "H-h—" She meant to respond but couldn't find her voice. Everyone's eyes were on her. Even the Black Guard seemed to be surveying her presence.

"What a journey the two of you must have had! Filled with at least some excitement, I hope?" The Warlord stood behind the head of the table. He turned his gaze to Verano.

Verano glanced at Aterah. "Once or twice." His voice was loud, clear, he took care to pronounce his words.

The short, balding, strangely dressed pale man ran and pulled out the chair that the Warlord stood behind. The Warlord held his robe as he graciously lowered himself in.

"Doesn't seem like much to me," one the Black Guard grumbled. He hawked phlegm in his throat, glanced around, and swallowed it.

"Make off." The Warlord waved a hand.

He huffed and turned. His metal boots clacked on the stone dining floor then down the hardwood hallway. The rest of them followed him. All of them shuffling and clinking against one another. Some of them stole one last look at Aterah.

"Excuse my Officer of Ryala. He forgets his manners." The Warlord Rai chuckled. "I hope you are hungry." He looked up at the door on the far side of the room. "We can discuss your reward over dinner."

"Aye." Verano shrugged.

"But . . . If you would not mind, I find myself immersed in curiosity for your heritage. Is it true that you are the Warlord Veligreen's son?" Warlord Rai propped his elbows on the carved arm rests.

Verano shifted uncomfortably. He glanced around and nodded. "Aye."

The Warlord slapped the table. "Well!"

Verano winced.

"I find myself in the presence of nobility! What an exquisite guest I have in my halls. Please, if you would not mind, where have you been all this time? I was friends with your father, you know?"

Friends? Aterah glanced between them.

The Warlord turned to her. "Do not worry, my dear." His eyes were sad and blue, searching deep into hers, as if he had heard her thoughts. "I don't mean to ignore you, but courtesies and curiosities instruct that I should converse with dear Verano Veligreen first."

Aterah nodded.

"After the grash, I . . . my sister and I fled the province. The Pikemaster sought to end us in case we tried to take back our place in the Ryvl Provincial government." Verano placed his hands on the table and looked down while he spoke. "The two of us made it as far as Gya Province before I'd had enough running. I left her and came here to join the warfront. A waste of my talents, no doubt. But I did what I had to survive."

"Here?" The Warlord asked, intrigued. "You have been here, in my province, this entire time? Oh, El Vuulguard." He brought a hand to his forehead. "You should have come to me. I would always welcome someone of your blood. What resolve you must have." His lips never parted far from each other, and his eyes never moved one direction or the other, though his voice took on emotional hues with each word and point that he made. "You heard about the Oracle job I sent out through Vasara, and you took it. And that has brought you here, for me. How fascinating."

"Yutarah," Verano corrected. "I picked up the job in Yutarah."

"Of course." The Warlord's laugh was soft, controlled even. "I've created a never-ending network of *pass it on.*

"I will say, though." He continued. "When I first received news of bronze within Renovia—swords, nails, the like—I celebrated their long overdue re-entry into the civilized world." The Warlord shook his head and *tsk*'d his lips. "Their single-handed departure from neolithic barbarism. I'm sure you can imagine what a jab in my heart it was when we learned of your father's treason."

The door to the kitchen opened, and half a dozen Sigu Nii, short, and scrawny, entered carrying silver platters. The tall Masikonian chef stood in the doorway, proudly surveying the table. The servants set the platters down between the three of them, as gently as a Sigu Nii could, and lifted the lids. Steam spilled from the seams, a sweet and savory aroma took the room.

Aterah's mouth salivated at the roasted chicken, peas and carrots, mashed potatoes, fish, and salad. She couldn't believe all these things, or *any* of these things had once been a handful of slop. The Masikonian was powerful.

Servants set white plates, bowls, and silver utensils in front of each of them, as well as tall crystal glasses filled with a red sour-smelling-liquid. The Sigu Nii servants cut the chicken and fish, with spices and sweet sauces on the side, and dished them out to the Warlord Rai, then Verano, and then Aterah.

Her hand shook as she picked up the fish and sank her teeth into it. She dipped the spiced chicken into her potatoes. *Oh. Have I never had food before?* Her eyes rolled as she lost herself.

Verano stayed staring at his meal. He glanced briefly toward the kitchen door. "This isn't going to turn back into a sword, or ground up glass, or electric eels while I'm eating it, right?"

"If it did," Replied the Warlord. "The eels would be dead, at least." He laughed politely. "No, it will do no such thing. A Sigu Nii keeps his Masikonian chef loyal with threats and violence, an Illian—by persuading his beliefs that he wouldn't *want* to."

"And how do you keep him in check?"

"I'm Ohaer, dear boy."

Verano's jaw clenched, and he began eating.

"An Illian, a Sigu Nii, and a Renovian sharing a meal together. That sounds like the beginnings of a bad joke." The Warlord glanced around the table.

Neither responded.

Aterah noticed that the Warlord used silver utensils to bring small portions of food to his mouth. Aterah glanced at him, then Verano (who was doing no such thing), shrugged, and took another sloppy, greasy bite of her fish.

"So, your reward then." The Warlord Rai wiped his mouth with a linen and turned to Verano. "Name your prize, whatever you would like." He paused for a moment and glanced to the ceiling in thought. "Niiwa." He nodded. "You would have me give you a Niiwa. One that would certainly suit your talents, and the vuu that accompanies your blood." He smiled gently and shifted his weight to one elbow.

Verano halted, his hand were dripping with chicken grease. "You can do that?"

"Of course." The Warlord's brows scrunched together as he gave a soft chuckle. "I can do whatever I want."

Verano looked down. His eyes met his food. "I . . . I think . . ." He returned his gaze to the Warlord. "I would become your sword."

Rai Ezs *hmph*'d. "Interesting. You, a Sigu Nii, would serve under an Illian?"

Verano glanced from side to side. "Aye. A Niiwa would bring me immediate glory. The things you would have me do might reward me with as much, and more in time."

Aterah's brows rose.

The Warlord hummed in thought. "The son of a Warlord in my possession. And the first Oracle of the Age." He smiled to himself. "You have yourself a deal, Veligreen."

"One condition." Verano raised a hand over the table.

The Warlord raised his brows.

"Spare me your tricks. I come to you of my own accord, my own mind. I wish to keep it that way."

The Warlord's face went blank. Any sign of emotion disappeared. "Done." Even his voice sounded different. "You can rest for the day. I will have much for you to start with tomorrow." The excitement, awe, and fascination in his words vanished—replaced with a monotone beat. The Warlord's pale servant pulled his chair from the table. He stood and turned to Aterah. "Come with me." He spun toward the door without a glance back.

I don't want to go. Without instructing her limbs to do so, she pushed herself to her feet. *I don't want to go.* She turned to Verano, who sat still at the wooden table, his eyebrows twitching in wonder. She followed Rai Ezs out to the hollow, squeaky floors of the hallway.

Through my eyes, he is about to learn everything there is to learn in the rebellion. No. Worse. He will learn things not yet come to pass.

She followed him five steps behind. His gait was long paced, in no hurry to go anywhere. His velvet robe swayed with each step; his sandals padded softly against the dark waxed wood. She followed him to the front of the manor. He turned right, toward the west. They passed through a large living area with leather couches and waxed tables and a fireplace.

"I will dissect you fully, to be sure," he said.

Aterah shivered. It was still so dreadfully cold. A glass wall stretched before them. On the other side, fifty steps of cut grass, whitestone statues, and candles on poles illuminated the grounds in a wide circle. Stars glistened across the night sky.

"But first, appropriation of the future should be in order." The Warlord gestured to a deep leather chair beside the glass. Studded armrests on each side kept the hide skin in place.

With her hands around her elbows, Aterah lowered herself. She looked up at him. He stood over her, with absent blue eyes. No emotion, no twitch or glance to show where his mind ran.

"Rest yourself." His voice took a gentle tone.

Like a wave crashing over her, Aterah felt her pulse slow, her arms fell to the cool leather chair, and she leaned back. "What are you going to do to me?" Her voice was small.

"Firstly, I must insist that you call me El." The Warlord leaned over so that he was at eye level with her.

"Graeynesh Law I: El is a Vulgarhe title reserved for the Korta Ellanii, Kortaes of realms seen and unseen, whom all living things flow—"

"Quiet." The Warlord's voice ripped through her voice and mind, trapping her tongue in the back of her throat. "I know Graeynesh Law more intimately than yourself. On one half, a wasted rambling from a woman thought to be wise. On the other, a methodical set of regulations for a people-group stained by oppression." He leaned in close. "We agree on one thing, I might assume. Oppression taints. And in a world where freedom is a trickle-down luxury, you are but a *slave*. Even before you were mine, your political circumstances have distorted your culture, and therefore your value-hierarchy, and therefore your definition of 'El.'"

The Warlord glanced to the ceiling as he laughed. "'Kortaes,' she says. A mere title. Do you even understand the ripples of influence that come with the word?" Slowly he reached up a hand, fingers out, palm forward. "Show me what happens next."

Aterah tried to lean back, but something held her in place. She tried to twist her head away, but it was locked. She couldn't move, couldn't speak, couldn't think. His long, pale, claw-like hand wrapped around her forehead.

The world shook, like an earthquake jarring her brain. Everything in her vision faded, like a pile of salt blown by a steady wind. The last thing she saw was the Warlord's bright smile disintegrate into darkness. Aterah felt the chair beneath her fall away, her arms and legs grew senseless, her thoughts turned to distant mumbles. A dream-like state. A raw, mere Aterah, hung loosely in a void.

"Oracle." A whisper drafted through the dark. *"Show me your power."* The words felt tangible, as if Aterah could reach out and grab them, had she any hands. They floated around her, grazing her body-less conscience.

The void turned, and a blinding green light surrounded Aterah. She tried to cover her eyes, but her body was still not with her. Gradually the light faded, and she found herself in a dim bedroom. Paper hung like rotting peels from the walls. A master bedframe lay in splinters. And there were people.

Kairo. Aterah's mumbled thoughts echoed. She watched her brother in this room, he was angry. He threw fists against another. The man with stone tattoos. Clutched in his hand, a wooden crown. Dark green mist fell from the crown and dissipated before it reached the ground.

"That will do." The whisper came out from under Aterah. The words grabbed hold and lifted her up. Faster, faster. She flew straight through the ceiling. Darkness. Void on the other side. She looked up. A deep leather chair fell toward her at racing speeds. Glass walls, a pale Warlord, and a bony, dirty Aterah slammed against her.

The clammy pale palm lifted from her forehead. She inhaled aggressively. Her hands clutched the studded armrests on either side.

"The lost Archeodon," the Warlord whispered under his breath. His face remained unyieldingly blank. "And a member of the Masikonian military. *Fascinating.* Tell me, Oracle. How far ahead do you typically see?"

Aterah shook her head, her breath still uneven. Her mind felt different. As if there were a bug squirming in her brain. "A few days, El."

The Warlord turned his gaze to the glass. He looked out over the grassy grounds and the stars beyond. "We will need to speed that up." He paused for a moment, his eyes shifted rapidly, seemingly searching for something. "The Masikonian . . . I cannot find. Though your *brother* can be passed on to Vasara, at once." He turned back to Aterah. She shivered under his rigid blue eyes.

"My, my. What an interesting story we have. Do I tell his Elness? The lost Renovian Archeodon!" He forced a laugh. "Of all these clusters of generations, *lifetimes*, the crown decides to return while I am here. Maybe he'll name me King of the Renovians." He forced another laugh.

Aterah didn't respond. She breathed deep, slowing her pulse. Her eyes closed, to rest a moment, but the radiating presence of the Warlord kept them from staying closed for very long.

"Verano!" El Rai Ezs yelled. His voice was not deep or powerful. But it seemed to echo in Aterah's mind. "Seems I would use you sooner than previously anticipated."

38

EIDHIN

Half a generation later.

Eidhin set his frayed feather-quill on the desk with a sigh. The shaft was dull and beginning to crack and the downy afterfeather was slicked from old sweat. Plenty of spares lay in the drawers beside him, but he preferred to get his full use with the current. He massaged his eyelids. All sense of time down in the closet-of-a-study seemed to vanish as he scribbled and scribbled away at El Kalyn's endless writings.

It wasn't good, what happened to El Tuladrna. Overly round as he may be, and a tad stern on the servants, his illness didn't sit well with Eidhin. Looming mortality seemed to hang heavy in the Vylndaer Manor.

Servant to one of the smartest, most powerful men in Zoë, and no amount of herbs or special insights would cure Tuladrna's wretched cough. The servants and El of Vylndaer watched him pass.

I should get these copies up to El Kalyn. I could use a walk before I start on the new set. He grabbed a heavy stack of parchments. Six different copies of one very long study. Try as Eidhin might, he had yet to ingest a single word of all his writings. He recognized and faithfully reproduced every letter, every word. But he could not absorb or retain the meaning of any of them, even the ones written by his own hand.

"Grraaahn!" The naked men groaned at him as he passed. Eidhin didn't think they could actually tell he was there, what with their arms chopped off, their eyes gouged out, their ears melted over, and their tongues cut out. They lived in an empty world, cognitively connected to El Kalyn.

Eidhin ascended the stairs and exited the computing room—that's what Kalyn called it—and paused outside the bookcase hall. *El Kalyn. Six fresh copies for "The Rai of Masikus" study.* Eidhin waited. He hoped it was near the dead of night, which would explain his utter exhaustion. The only reason he even knew the title of the research in his hands was because Kalyn had permitted him so, in order to differentiate between copies.

Moments passed with no response. *El? Are you asleep?* Something rustled on the other side of the bookcase, along with the quiet, unmistakable cursing of the El Kalyn Vylndaer.

Eidhin walked in. El hunched over his curving-wall-desk. Eidhin swore El never slept.

Ikondu, the Razite child, sat bored on the desk on the other half of the room, his legs kicked back and forth beneath him. He wore plain, undyed linens, tattered from poor stitching and many winters of use. His skin looked much the same. Dark and heavily scarred.

Aesa Vylndaer stood on Kalyn's other side.

Eidhin paused. It had been a season since he last saw her. What a sight she was. Her hair was still wispy, as if permanently blown by the salty ocean air. Her eyes had grown lighter, though the hints of brown still remained. Her lips were full, and her cheekbones round.

El Kalyn gestured to a place on the floor, and Eidhin set the parchments down. "Eidhin. Good." He gestured for Eidhin to enter the room. Aesa's big eyes watched him as he moved. "My little girl is growing up." He looked at her. "She's getting ready to take the Aylan at the Library of Vylandria.

"Every Aylan, before the games, King Gehn summons the council of Illyadra together. In the past, Tuladrna has been my personal servant.

Nothing too difficult a task. But with his passing, it seems I'd use you. Tell me, Eidhin, how does going to the capital sound?"

"Oh, please do come, Eidhin. It's been far too long since we've talked!" Aesa had dark bags under eyes, as if she hadn't slept decently in days. But she smiled all the same.

"W-W—" *What about Ikondu?*

Ikondu couldn't hear him. But he stared at some invisible space between them. Eidhin wondered if he was seeing the vuu that it took to relay thoughts, nonverbally.

Kalyn hardly looked a day over two generations old with his black and blue ringed eyes pinching at the corners. "He'll come as well."

Eidhin nodded. *I'll come as you wish, El.*

"Indeed. Sleep well and prepare your things. We depart in the morning. Pack whatever you need, we'll be there until the Oscillation."

Ikondu's ears pricked up at the mention of the calendar.

Eidhin waded through snow back to the servant's quarters in the dark. Kalyn's study was secluded, even from his own manor, let alone the world. *Vylandria.* He nodded, wondering what his parents would think. He doubted they had ever left Gehni's Isle.

"Up! Up, up, up!" Seraii's shrieking pierced Eidhin's dreams. She shook him till he woke. "We have a big morning. A big meal for the El, and a big departure. El Kalyn will be gone for half a season!"

Eidhin moaned and propped himself up on his elbows. Her messy hair contained growing specks of grey, her teeth were yellowing, and bags had formed under her eyes.

"I-I-I—" *am going with them.* But she couldn't hear his thoughts.

"I-I—*need* to get out of bed? Yes. You do." Seraii ripped off Eidhin's wool blankets as she left.

Sluggishly, he got out of bed and changed into his slacks and jacket. He pulled out his bag from under the bunk and started packing for the rest of the generation.

"And where do you think you're going?" She stood with her hands on her hips. Her mouth opened again to yell something. But then she realized. "You're going with El? You're going to the capital?"

Still groggy, Eidhin looked at her and nodded.

"Hmph! Well. That's no-thing. I'm sure a dozen others are also accompanying the crew to El's Vylandria manor."

Eidhin shrugged. Too tired to disagree, even with physical indication. Once his bag was packed, he lifted the strap over his shoulder and left the room. He trudged to the front lobby, where a pile of luggage was accumulating.

Breakfast for Kalyn, the Lady, and Aesa came and went. Eidhin ate flavored oats and bacon in the kitchen, waiting for their departure. When it came time, he and five other black-dressed servants began at the pile of luggage. Being his first time outside of the manor grounds in six winter seasons, Eidhin was quick to follow behind the others. They went ahead of El and his daughter and trekked down the long hill into Talynguard.

Eidhin stared at the frosted mounds, where crops would go in the spring, vividly remembering the last time he had passed them, led up the mountain by a wheezing Tuladrna. Eidhin glanced at the farmhouse at the bottom of the valley. *Peasants.* He smiled and held his chin up.

The morning was still early, and fishermen were pushing dinghies into the water and preparing bait and line. Children of a vast age assortment followed after a young woman. They carried books in their hands.

Though Eidhin did not witness the building's construction, he remembered Kalyn's initial experiment here in Talynguard. A testing ground of public information—free schooling. Eidhin had doubts about the concept, like what incentive the young woman had for teaching. But Kalyn said it would take them a generation to observe sufficient differences in the people's way of life.

Somehow El could afford that long. Somehow, El showed no apprehension for his heirs receiving the fruits of his research.

Then again, El did not seem a day older since Eidhin first arrived on the island.

They walked down the long dock to a moored schooner that took up the port. It boasted three masts of furled sails, and its crew was preparing for departure.

Waves rolled under the dock and crashed against the snowy shoreline and the cliffs to either side.

Eidhin followed the other servants aboard the ship, then below deck, where they stored their personal luggage among the hammocks of the crew. Several of the servants took the Vylndaer's bags to the aft cabin.

After that, he waited. He watched idly as sea dogs climbed rope nets and rustled about in the crow's nest. For a moment, he wished Aesa and he were still kids, playing pirates in the old tree.

The El appeared, and the commoners praised him as he passed. Aesa followed beside him, her gait matched his long, certain strides.

"Ikondu," the Illyadra's tone was rushed, but not urgent. He sounded busy. "What's the weather in Vuulguard—or the weight of vuu around us—or the moment in the afterlife—or however it is that you manage to tell time—what is it, child?"

The small, generation old, dark child pulled from his tattered trouser pockets a white wool string, cleaner than anything he was wearing, with an expensive looking purple crystal tied at the bottom. He dangled it over his other hand, while chasing after the Illyadra, and said, "It ez a calm forecazt, El. There ez little friction around us."

Aesa nodded in understanding.

And El Kalyn muttered, "Good."

The moment the Illyadra climbed aboard, the captain shouted, "Ready the sails! Release the lines!"

Dock hands released the mooring lines, sails unfurled, and the ship eased forward. Eidhin and Aesa shared a glance, but El directed her to their quarters.

Talynguard gradually disappeared beyond the horizon until there was nothing around them but blue stretching out in every direction. The sun climbed its way up the sky, mostly behind a ceiling of undulating clouds.

"Hey," a girlish voice called behind him. He picked his chin from the stern rail. Aesa, dressed in a long silk-spun gown of reddish gold with white frills, smiled at him.

Hey. He said, clear and crisp in his mind. Eidhin raised a brow, wondering if she could still hear his thoughts.

"*Of course I can, dummy.*" She giggled as she came and rested her palms on the railing beside him.

Eidhin watched her gaze across the vastness of the sea and its rising and falling swells. He tried to think of something to say, but he felt empty. It had been so long since they had last talked that their momentary pause weighed heavy.

A mischievous glint came across her eyes. She raised her right hand slightly, so that the tips of her fingers hung over the water. Out of the spraying mist, where the keel and draft mingled with the swells, a magnificent ship appeared. A galleon with massive sails, rows and rows of cannons, and men dressed in cliché pirates' wear crawled all around. "Pirates to port?" Aesa said and smiled.

Arrgh matee, Eidhin responded light-heartedly, but not enthusiastically. After a moment, the pirate ship slowly disappeared into misty water.

So, you're taking the Aylan soon?

Aesa let her head droop, so that she peered down where the ship and ocean met. "Indeed."

It's like the Aylan board game, right?

"Indeed. Just another manner in which a bunch of smarties can attack each other."

You don't seem very excited. I thought the Aylan was a big deal. Eidhin turned toward her.

"It is." She offered a chuckle. "The aim is to defend a point so well that your vuu drives the opponent to suicide."

He tried to imagine it. *You're nervous?*

Her eyes kept steady on the water. "No, I'm the daughter of an Il-lyadra. I've been raised for this my entire life. My brother and sister succeeded with ease, and so should I."

Then what is it? Why do you look the way you do?

She shrugged. "Well." A sigh escaped her. "It just seems cruel. First the suicide bit. And then everything that comes after. The Aylan is our vault. It's the proponent of our knowledge-based currency. It's like the Niiwa for the Sigu Nii, or the Algris for Masikus, except instead of coin traversing foreign waters, it's our language. Do you get it? I'm winning the Aylan just to rule over people. The whole system I'm to inherit seems narcissistic. A system in direct opposition to the values that we teach people like *you*, to keep you from stepping out of the lines *we've* drawn."

Eidhin blinked a few times. *I . . . don't think I'm getting the picture. You're upset about becoming smart?*

Her brows came together for a moment. "Not just smart, Eidhin. I'll become one of the smartest. My only competition, after I win the Aylan, will be my brother, sister, and the children of the other five Illyadra. King Gehn has no children yet, so . . . about fifteenish people of Generation Lotra will all be fighting over the six positions of Illyadra—and the crown. That's nothing compared to the *millions* inhabiting Aylavuera. And get this—even if I do fail to earn the title of Illyadra, I can still wed to one of them, or become lady over an isle or something."

Eidhin shook his head. This was all too much for him, but he strained to keep up. *Wait, wait. But if there are fifteenish of you, won't at least one of them be in the Aylan? Challenging another Illyadran offspring would be . . .*

"No. *Anyone* can compete in the Aylan. But all the Illyadra get together in a big meeting and plan which of their kids are to take the game and when. That way, none of them have to face each other. So they—we—al-ways win against the less-smart commoners."

Like me.

"*Yes.*" She paused.

He could feel her indignation.

"Eidhin, they're not just the smartest because they research. They're the smartest because they hoard every study ever done by anyone of note, for the past *ever*. The classes they teach in Vylandria? Watered down, deceptively diluted concepts, given only in order to maintain the vuu-bound-leashes we hold over people throughout the country." Aesa's tone was heated. She was almost yelling, and practically panting. "You say, Il-lian vuu is the greatest in the world, because anyone can learn. I say, Illian vuu is the cruelest, because personal libraries have remained in the same families for generations."

"It ez exploding from her," a very foreign accent squeaked behind them. "She will burst his encryption."

"Aesa!" A voice thundered across the deck. They turned to see El Ka-lyn and Ikondu standing just outside the aft cabin. His ankle-length coat flapped in the wind. "Come here."

Aesa turned to Eidhin. *"Do you get it?"*

He paused for a moment, trying to process all she had said. But some-thing wasn't clicking. He knew his mind was sharp. He was smart, not dumb. Yet while she spoke, his ears seemed to gloss over her spoken words the way his eyes glossed over the words of El Kalyn that he copied. It was as if she were trying to till flagstones. Eidhin grimaced, shook his head, and looked at her sadly.

Aesa sighed. *"That's what I thought."* She returned a sad look, then turned and walked to her frowning father. The three of them disappeared into the stern, and Eidhin was left staring at the Illian seas.

The day ran its course, and he watched the sunset with the other suit-clad servants, then made his way with them down to the hammocks. He slept, or just lay there, all night and most of the next day.

By late afternoon the second day, Vylandria came into view. Mountains rose as a backdrop to the grandest collection of buildings Eidhin ever laid eyes on. Tiled roofs on beautiful stone buildings, majestic domes trimmed with yellow sandstone and Kalyn's blue gems, and bridges that connected hill summits and towers.

The ship began a turn, wide and sweeping toward a beachside manor a decent stretch outside of Vylandria, far enough to avoid the commotion but a quick carriage ride into the city.

With the captain's shout, a heavy chained anchor dropped into the ocean beside a long floating dock. It stretched all the way to the entrance of Kalyn's capital manor. The servants grabbed their luggage as well as El's. And they walked down the dock as it bobbed up and down under their heavy steps.

The manor was no palace, but still a dozen times larger than Eidhin's farmhouse on Gehni Isle. He followed the servants to their wing of the house, where they quickly made themselves at home in a set of bunk-beds. Four servants were already there and greeted them as they entered. It seemed they were the ones who kept the house clean and in repair while El was away.

EIDHIN

Eidhin returned to the common area. Servants were bustling in all directions, preparing Kalyn's departure for someplace else. The Illyadran Council, Eidhin remembered.

Ikondu sat on the armrest of a soft linen couch, holding a pendulum swinging over his free hand. "It ez time."

Kalyn was passing by at that moment, eating something quickly. "What did I ever do without you?"

Ikondu smiled.

"Let's go. The carriage is waiting." El gestured to Eidhin and Ikondu.

Aesa fumed across the room, toward the glass doors to the seaside. "You're going to bring *him* and not me?" She shouted.

"It's forbidden, Aesa. You know that. He's too dumb to understand," Kalyn pointed at Eidhin. "And he protects me from being persuaded to hand over your inheritance." He pointed at Ikondu.

39

ARCHEODON

Hands slapped on backs—Kairo imagined a warm embrace.

"Misted canals appear only at noonday." He wheezed. Dust surrounded his nonsensical sentence with an age grander than the Chamberlains.

"Banana reign," Wesken agreed in his typical mumbly voice.

"What?" asked Kairo.

The old fellow hummed a ponderous tune and laid a hand on Kairo. "Let the Wooden Prince search the thoughts of the Unseen." The words rasping out of the old man's mouth shifted and clicked, suddenly forming nearly distinguishable sentences.

"Who-who are you?" There was a sense of cosmic understanding whistling about the old man—er, Wesken's grandpa.

"El Neo Nii."

"Blas—" Kairo began a protest. None are called El but the Korta Ellanii. The self-titling of the Sigu Nii was such that an example of their wickedness. But Kairo stopped short, and he wasn't sure why.

"Search his father's bedchambers," said the old man. "There, he'll find the Prince's coronation: a relic of Kortaes' past."

He was speaking Old Vulgarhe, Kairo realized. A lot of it. And where Kairo previously lacked the ability to detect intelligible thought, he now was only confused at the point trying to be made. Somehow, this old man had given him the ability to hear. But he needed the ability to understand. All this cramped into a single, dull, "What?" on Kairo's behalf.

Kairo heard the faint sound of the old man smacking his lips.

"Forealsies," mocked Wesken. He attempted to translate the old man for Kairo, reiterating the point in a fresh, differently understanded way. But he ended up just repeating what his grandpa said first, word for word.

Kairo laughed. A real audible laugh. Each chuckle was a beat of ripping pain, throbbing in both eyes and ears. But he continued laughing. Its external pain was matched with an intense joyous relief, beat by beat. Finally, distinguishing that the two crazies were speaking of a location, Kairo gestured in a wherever direction and said, "Lead the way."

The old man offered a hesitant hum. "A moment finds itself clinging to the present. I've to go see it along." He croaked. "But first, a gift."

"What? This?" Wesken's surprise was speckled with both guilt and longing. "I can't take this!"

Kairo wondered what it was. Unable to see it or hear it, he was left guessing.

"Mhm. Don't forget, now." Their talking ended in another hug, and the old fellow shuffled away.

"I wonder if the moment he spoke of was this one," Pondered Wesken. "Or if there's actually some spoonful of time somewhere that needs be hurried onwards." He started forward, leading Kairo by the arm, and a raspy, tappy, knocking came from his other side.

A walking stick. Kairo frowned. The old man couldn't have left something more helpful?

Thunder shook the castle once again.

So, the old man had teleported. Who was this grandpa of Wesken, that his power might match Arden's? And, if he were so wise, as to even speaking in Old Vulgarhe, why had he given the child the walking stick, rather than the literal cripple? Kairo's frown deepened. He wanted it. The relief it would give his thigh—oh—so—great.

It was amidst this thinking that they arrived upon stairs. *Stairs.* Kairo's frown opened. He stepped up with his left leg first. "Ahh-rgh." He moaned. Definitely a mistake.

"Argh, matey," Wesken replied in a strange voice.

Kairo opted instead for stepping up with his right leg, doing a sort of hop, and dragging his left leg up after him. Which all would have been awful if he could see the stairs. But he couldn't. So, it was nearly impossible. Wesken gasped and darted out to keep Kairo from falling back down.

He leaned himself and began climbing up with his hands.

Why did Castle Graey have to be built on a hill? Who does that?

"Only one more," cheered Wesken.

He would hit the kid. He would. One more, he said. It had only been a handful in total, not a whole flight, like the rooms built over Yutarah's tavern. But still. Climbing up the sky-bound jungle trees was more difficult with all four, fully functional limbs, than up these stairs with three.

Halfway through the final upward motion, a muscle spasm enveloped him. There was no warning. His jaw did not tighten beforehand, though it certainly was now.

It was a full body spasm. He rolled to his side, but the old stone steps crumbled in his grip, and he started sliding. His hands flailed out in roundabout motions. Kairo wanted to scream, but it was like a full-grown boa constrictor had wrapped around his throat. And he hadn't drawn a preemptive breath. Choking noises gurgled from his mouth.

This was it. His butt crashed and sent his torso headlong into a tumble. He was in perfect trajectory to connect with the corner of the stairs. Not that he could see them. But he could tell.

Then, something unwieldy happened. Wesken beat him there. From standing in front of him, to help guide him, to chasing Kairo's falling body down the stairs, Wesken caught him before he landed. Kairo awed. The speed was inhuman. Or his blind perception of where Wesken had been, was wrong. He wasn't sure.

The spasm didn't let up though, even as Wesken laid him gently lopsided, upside down on the stairs. He could feel the child strain, as if trying to drag him upright. Or to a more comfortable position to agonize in, at least. But the kid hadn't the strength.

Oh, this one hurt. Kairo's wincing pulled muscles in his face, scrunching over his still bloody eye sockets. His back arched up through the air, and his head wasn't enough to keep his whole-body stationary. He continued down the stairs. It was a slower, more controlled fall this time, but each old, crumpled corner of stair left streaks in Kairo's open back.

A loud cracking sound reached Kairo's blood filled ear holes. Had he broken the stone steps with his calves?

"Ope," said Wesken in an uncharacteristically grim voice.

Then the pain flooded in. He hadn't even hit the bottom with that much force. But his leg muscles were cramping, constricting even, with such force, that his right leg snapped. Kairo's wailing came first through his choked throat, and then through his locked-together teeth, so that he sounded more like a dying animal than someone capable of speaking intelligible words.

His chest roared. He needed to breath. He laid in a pile of pain at the bottom of the stairs, right-leg broken, about to suffocate to death.

And then, as sudden as it came, the spasm lifted.

Kairo wheezed, drawing in air with a fatal desperation. Then he wailed. Loudly.

He knew people, back in NeoDerii who had broken bones, but there were not many. Most of them didn't fight anymore. And not for lack of youth. No. A soldier that couldn't move at full speed, what with his hands, his feet, or his head, was a soldier that put the rest of his squadron at risk. Broken-boned soldiers were retired. They worked the kitchen or kept watch on the Locke.

"Help me up," Kairo growled. Something gnashed in his mind. He was not broken.

"Uhm." Wesken hesitated audibly.

Find his father's bedchambers. It was charged to him by the old man. And even though he hadn't any idea what that meant, he felt an unquench-able drive to do so. He plopped an arm up on the first stair, drug himself up, and threw his other arm up the next. An indisputable something was charging him irresistibly onward.

"Ahm." Wesken dangled his hands over Kairo and wiggled them with audible discomfort. He didn't know how to help.

"Just lift me up a little. Even a stone's worth," said Kairo between clenched teeth, dragging himself up another stair.

They mounted the final stair. Sweat boiled in his plump, bandaged head. His forearms were covered in scrapes and scratches.

He wished he could stand. He wished—wow, he wished he could go back to limping with Wesken in his clutches. He'd even take the day he woke up in NeoDerii, all bandaged and sweating on the Wheelhouse floor, over this.

Outside was near. Kairo could feel the breeze trickling in and the temperature fluctuate. And he could taste it. Freshness. The snap of cold altitude fluttered in. Kairo thanked the Korta Ellanii that Castle Graey was far enough away from Vasara's previous rotting-genital smell.

Wesken helped him continue to crawl along. They passed over rubble and debris. Kairo winced as rocks rolled under his stomach, scratching his skin most of the way down. They reached it, outside. Though the floor was still stone.

"Oh wow," Wesken awed. "You should see this place."

Kairo felt his lips curl up, but he waited for the child to describe it. He didn't.

"The things I would do, to watch the fight that took place here. . ..
A battle between *gods*—and I don't toss that word around all willy nilly."

Kairo frowned. "C'mon. Help me forward."

Wesken resumed lifting Kairo slightly by the waist, and they continued to cross what Kairo figured was a courtyard. The stone floor had many
cracks, each one scraping down Kairo's abdomen. He stifled a scream as a
rather large one caught on his broken leg.

Across the courtyard, into another wing of Castle Graey, riddled with
things that Kairo had to sweep out of the way with his hands, so they
didn't stick into him as he crawled along. It was painfully, penetratingly
clear that the renovations hadn't begun this high in the castle yet.

They turned a room.

"This should be it," said Wesken. "It feels very bedchamber-y."

There was a feeling in this room. A nostalgia, almost. But that wouldn't
make sense. No, the feeling was more physical. It vibrated; it churned in
waves. Something was in here, giving off this feeling of immense power.
Kairo crawled toward it. The vibration grew overwhelming in viscosity.
Kairo reached his hand out, sure that he was about to plug its source.

"Don't touch it, boy. Lest you surely die." It was grouchy, low, and
wavery. Like the voice of someone who had just woken from a long
slumber.

Kairo's heart plummeted through his chest. Some Sigu Nii had finally
found them. Then he recognized the voice, "Arden." His brief fear was replaced by anger. He pushed himself higher up on his elbows, facing where
he thought the stoneman was, "Where have you been? I kept thinking you
would save me! You left me to rot!"

"Quiet, boy." He stepped forward, kicked a large stone across the
room, and stumbled into a kneel.

"What are you doing? What is it with you and the ale?" Kairo's voice
trembled with rage; each and every one of his wounds were throbbing.

Both of his empty eye sockets, his cut off ears, the infected gash on his left thigh that was slowly killing him, and his broken right calf bone.

"The Archeodon." There was a drunk glint in his voice. Arden said it through a smile.

Then he realized, Arden was reaching for the thing. The source of the power. "Oh no you don't!" Kairo yelled, and grabbed the nearest piece of debris, a chunk of brick, and chucked it at where he thought Arden was.

"Argh!" Arden hollered. The rock must've connected with his face, every other part was protected by his stone tattoos.

Wesken giggled faintly someplace off in the corner.

"Relax, boy!" Arden yelled. "This is in 'ur interest, as well."

Kairo highly doubted that. He searched around for another rock with his hands. The old man had charged him with the coronation, of what he was increasingly suspecting: the King to Come. Arden seizing this relic, of all people, was revolting.

But there was nothing else he could do. He was, in fact, a broken soldier. His readying shot turned limp, falling slowly to rest against the stone. A less crippled Kairo could not stand against this man.

Kairo listened as Arden fumbled around and grabbed hold of something light and wooden. Vicious power blasted through the room—no, Kairo was certain, even if he were back in NeoDerii, he would feel this moment. It sounded like a sky-bound tree had been snapped totally in half, or several cracks of lightning were striking around him simultaneously.

Kairo could only describe the power blasting forth like this: it was as if he were dropped into the Maua river, at its fastest, rockiest river rapid, with stones on all his limbs so that he couldn't move with the river. But it exploded around him with lethal force.

Something stabbed his eyes. He wondered if it were Arden or Wesken, but a reactive swat through the air told him there was nothing there.

The feeling came again in his ears. Then both his legs. They seared, more than they had just a moment before.

Kairo blinked, and instead of it feeling like two flapping hemp bags in the wind, he felt them round the smooth marbles of his own eyes. He blinked again. And tore his sweaty, bloody, plump ball of bandage off his head. He looked around.

A vibrant green mist swarmed the room, opaque so that he could see Wesken wide eyed in the corner, and Arden standing tall with a wooden crown in his hand. Kairo blinked again. He was in total disbelief. He looked at his leg. There was no gash. And his other? No break. He wiggled it around in awe-worthy health.

The mist subsided. A spoonful of anger returned to Kairo. "Is this what you wanted, all along? Did you use me to find this? Did you ever intend to save Aterah?"

Arden growled. "Relax, *boy.*" He put the most patronizing, you-know-nothing emphasis Kairo thought available to him. "Do you not feel different?"

He did. He was fully healthy. Kairo could feel, deep within him and his leg, the infection totally gone from him.

"Well drink up! You've been granted access to Vuulguard's most sought-after treasure." Arden's lips curled up, revealing his stained yellow teeth. "Vuu."

"What?" The question ripped out of Kairo in untamable disgust. He was not capable of vuu. He was not wicked enough. He pushed himself to stand and wobbled a moment.

"It's your race, boy. You and all like you are tied to this thing." Arden snuggled the crown atop his dreadlocks. Its edges were lined with silver, which swirled inward with ornate patterns to form the Silver Tree of Renovia on its face. "You just needed someone to wear it."

"Awh. I wish *I* had vuu!" Wesken pouted.

"Who the bloody piss just said that?" Arden spun around. Fire enveloped his hands in the instant, casting a warm light through the torn-apart bedchamber.

The two of them made eye-contact. Arden seemed off, taken aback.

"What the bug are you?"

"I'm a Wesken!"

"Easy, Arden. He's just a kid," Kairo mumbled absentmindedly. He was positive that the old man had charged *him* with the coronation. Arden? The King to Come? He couldn't be. "He came with me from Ravid, helped me all this way up here."

Arden turned back to Kairo. "You weren't—no one was supposed to come with you from Ravid!" Something in his eyes was off, something close to fear.

"What?" Kairo moved to stand between them. "What do you mean, 'supposed to?'"

"Big boy got the powa," said Wesken.

"I ah—I'm an Oracle, too." Arden replied quickly and effortlessly. Almost like swatting the loaded statement away. His eyes drifted from the child's bright white hair to the black walking stick. Arden's mouth hung open. "Where did you get that?" He scanned the stick and took a drunken stumble backward.

"Arden, you're beginning to freak me out."

Arden stepped forward. Hunger was in his eyes.

"It was a gift from his grandpa."

A single panicked chuckle escaped him. "Gift?" He laughed. "*Grandpa?*" Without warning, Arden's hand darted out. Kairo couldn't be sure, but he thought he saw ripples of dusty black lightning course through the air.

Wesken moved just the tiniest degree out of Arden's reach. Enough that readjusting trajectory on Arden's behalf cost a fleck of thought and muscle impulse, but with that, Wesken was already nearing Kairo's opposite side.

"Hee-he-hee!" Wesken giggled. "Can't catch me!"

Arden rocked on his feet, seemingly pondering what to do.

"Arden!" Kairo yelled. "What? What is it?"

"It belongs to El Neo Nii." Arden's voice was grim, but his eyes suggested desire. "Not a thing you just *find*, boy."

"Grandpa!" exclaimed Wesken.

Arden looked him up and down. He squinted. "Nah. No way. That old bug? Having *kids?* Nah." He frowned and shook his head repeatedly. "I don't even know how that'd work, his being El an' all."

"He's not a ghost, silly," said Wesken. "No more than a snagaeri is."

Arden's frown deepened.

"What?" asked Kairo. None of the words, or their stringing together, made any sense to him. Did blood still fill his ear holes?

Both of them looked at Kairo with impatience.

"So . . . I have vuu now?" He didn't quite believe it. Although, upon recall, that is what Arden suggested when it was just the two of them marching through the Renovian jungle, nearing the Mauan valley between the Delkop range. The crown. *What did Arden call it? Arch-odon?*

"*Ark-A-O-don.*" Arden spat. "If you don't start thinking quieter, I swear, I'll rip that unused brain right out of your skull. You'll have every Illian worth a tattoo swarming the place."

"Oh boy," Wesken giggled, his voice high in jesting hue, "He's thinkin'!"

Arden shot the child a glance. Then took back to Kairo. "Aye. It's been more 'an a few generations since anyone had Renovian vuu. A sword might be the extension of your arm, but vuu is the extension of the soul. Bes' you learn how to use it on the walk. The witch been in Ryala since the turn of the weather." He surveyed the space around them with drunken urgency. "And it's not a calm day in hell today, neither."

They walked back to the courtyard. Wesken had described it quite well—the wing of castle they had traveled through held a giant hole running horizontally through its center. Kairo could see hallways, a portion of a grand stair and balcony, bedrooms, and the like. He could scarcely imagine what would do such a thing.

The courtyard suggested a monster had done it. There were several ginormous footsteps in the stone, leaving a web of cracks arching out in every direction. Kairo winced, remembering his crawling blindly over them.

Was this the power of King Ash? He looked around him. This was the final battle. Their dethroning. The coronation of their exile.

Arden stood still in the shadows of the afternoon sun as he solemnly fidgeted the crown atop his dreadlocks. The muscles between his stone tattoos were tense.

"What?" Kairo asked, catching up beside him. Then his eyes found the blemish on the far side of the courtyard. "Verano," Kairo croaked, feeling a ghostly ache in his thigh, like shards of bronze ripping through.

The young man stood with his arms loose by his side. His feet were planted in the great footprint. His spiky black hair fluttered gently in the crosswind. His clothes appeared nicer than they had in the prison cells under the Warlord's Office of Yutarah.

Kairo took a step past Arden and asked with guttural command. "Where is my sister?"

"Who?" Verano cocked his head.

"Oooh," Wesken cooed, his voice rising with excitement. "I know where this is going!" The child tapped his walking-stick against the stone.

"My sister!" Kairo yelled, his fists arching behind him. "The Oracle."

"Oh." Verano shrugged. "Well, that's of little importance now. She is not with me." He pointed at the wooden crown on Arden's head. "And I have come for *that*."

"We're not gonna give it to him, right?" Wesken asked, his face in a wide-eyed smile. "Oh, but he wants it. Oooh. That only leaves one—"

Kairo stepped forward, but hard calloused hands grasped his chest.

"Best leave this one to me, boy." Arden peered down at him, amused. He began toward the middle of the courtyard, stepping casually, stretching his arms.

"The Masikonian, then." Verano nodded and stepped forward to meet him.

"Wait, wait, wait," Wesken whined. "*I wanted* . . ."

Verano stopped ten steps out from Arden and bent his knees, his hands held out before him. A fighting stance.

Arden swayed, nearly stumbling so that he had to catch his weight with a shift of his foot.

Verano rose slightly, his arms fell. "Are you drunk?" He sounded insulted.

Arden chuckled. "Aye."

Verano *tsk*'d his lips. His biceps flexed and his forearms shot down. Bright white fire, hot enough for Kairo to shield his face from so far away, exploded in a circle around Verano's feet.

Kairo shuddered. This was the flame Verano used to light the cells in Yutarah. It was only a lick, then. And he remembered how afraid he was of that bright little flame. Here Verano had a bonfire of the stuff, all at his command.

Arden hardly reacted. A mere nod.

Verano huffed, as if he expected the man to be more impressed. With a kick and a punch, he sent two sizzling white fireballs hurling toward his opponent.

Arden caught them. They vibrated in his hands, white smoke steaming from between his fingers for half a moment, before they turned to stone. Starting from the fire nearest to his hands, and encaptivating the whole of the flame, they dropped to the ground with thuds.

Something close to wonder flashed across Verano's face, vanishing as quick as it came.

"'Ave you fought many Masikonians?" Arden asked.

Verano didn't answer. Instead, he punched the air rapidly, sending a flurry of white fire across the courtyard. Kairo and Wesken dove for cover.

Arden grabbed the wooden crown from his head and whipped it down with a flick of his arm. The whole thing, and all the intricate silver within, snapped straight into what appeared to be a sparring sword. A wooden plaything, with the Silver Tree shining greatly in the flat of the blade. The cross guard like roots, the pommel a soft green gem. Arden struck the sword through each of the white fires racing toward him, and they dissipated with a green mist softly tracing through the air.

Verano shifted uncomfortably. "Only one man in all of Zoë has seen Renovian vuu—King Ash. Parting you from that crown would be enough glory for a lifetime. I'm going to make my name known off of you." The man closed his eyes and brought his hands swirling together at a point. The ground rumbled around him, and a storm of darkness erupted from the cracks of stone. Near-tangible, malleable darkness. It shot from the cracks and surrounded Verano in a ball, before swirling in on itself to fit in his hands in the shape of a blade. Like a blade of night.

The sight sent chills down Kairo's spine. This was the blade that took his fellow-brother during the raid of NeoDerii. This was the blade that led to Norly's death, and nearly his own.

"Shadowa," Wesken said in amazement.

Verano launched into a sprint. Fire exploded behind him, propelling him off the ground through the air, his night blade held out before him.

Arden was calm. He held the sword vertically.

They smashed into one another. Verano swept the wooden sword away with his own. The two strange blades colliding in a flurry of black and green sparks. Arden's left elbow came exploding upward, and the stone tattoos smacked Verano clear across his inner cheekbone.

Verano hollered in pain as he stumbled backward, his night blade hung loose by his side as he clutched his face.

The last time Kairo had seen this blade of night, it had swept through Norly's bronze sword, and his neck, without resistance. As if those two things were not even there. Kairo wondered what it was about the wooden Archeodon that could fight the darkness' intangibility.

Arden stomped forward, his right foot making a new smaller set of cracked stone. He clawed his free hand through the air, and a storm of sparks chased his fingers. A swirling whirlwind of bright orange fire moved toward Verano.

"You're *Ohaer?*" Verano's eyes matched his voice's mixture of awe and fear. A hint of nasally hue suggested that blood filled his nose. Kneeling, he clashed his hands up together, and a thick wall of ice formed around him.

Ripples of black lightning flashed. Thunder cracked—loud and echoing throughout the courtyard—and Arden disappeared. The next instant he stood behind Verano and his wall. "Aye." He sent a punch through the solid ice, and it cracked and melted to nothing.

Verano stood to flee from between Arden and the whirling fire-wind. But Arden snatched him by the elbows and stared down with upward curling lips.

Verano hollered in pain before they were both engulfed in fire. And then they were gone, hidden from Kairo's view. Only the swirling orange flames remained.

A wooden sword swept through the middle, and the tornado dissipated. Verano was gone. Parts of Arden's tattoos were glowing from the heat.

"What—what happened?" Kairo asked. "Is he dead?"

"Let the boy live." Arden shrugged. "Not without leaving my mark though. He'll be feeling this battle in the next phase of the moon."

40

AYRAH

The Warlord's Office sat on a mountain top, with five ridges of foothills that melted into Ryala. A vast blue expanse stretched across the horizon, complete with fishing dinghies, mercenary armadas, and cargo ships to and from the greater regions around the colony.

It was a tropical Sigu Nii playground with fruits hanging from trees in the patches of vegetation adjacent to the Tuidiia. Colonized, any remnants of architecture from the Renovians who once lived here had long perished.

This day felt fresh. Ayrah slowly inhaled the winds that carried smells of salt and street food. It was a new day. And a brand-new cluster: Wy'lm, beginning again at Generation Bora. It was a whole new age—still yet unnamed.

The Shadowa tattoo on her left shoulder shifted constantly. It never settled. It stirred a great sense of accomplishment within her. She had done it. She had taken the Niiwa of Sehlya and come out alive.

The Tamagai had a couple days in Ryala before their first national Kaeselwa. A time for rest, vacation, and light training for the event. Each town with a name across Sigu Nii had battled their little league guilds—most of them resembling the inadequacy of the guild from Simula—then the victors would battle the victors of the other cities, until finally, each province had picked one team to represent it. The Tamagai were to fight Korlaii, the victor guild from the colonies of Ryala, at the end of the forecast.

Ayrah was now a respected member of the Tamagai. She had found a route of living worthy of her bloodline. She had teleported first and smiled at Errta as he joined her on the office steps. Urota came next. Then Ecanaes and Tagon, and behind them a whole host of their lesser servants to make their vacation manor homely.

"To the beach?" suggested Errta, he bounced up and down like an excitable dog.

"Lovely," said Urota. "We can get food on the way."

A stagecoach pulled up and stopped abruptly before them. The passenger door opened, and a suit-clad whiteman peered at them from inside. "Tamagai," he said, his voice high pitched and gentle. "The Warlord El Rai Ezs requests your presence."

Errta's face fell, his voice caught in "Ahk," and "Ugh."

Ecanaes glistened, his hand frayed across his chest. "He wants to speak with us?" His disbelief of a totally different orientation than Errta's.

Urota sighed and told the servants to continue to their vacation home. They all clambored in.

"We should be careful of what we say," urged Urota as the stagecoach jostled along.

"Nonsense," said Ecanaes. "El Rai is a gentleman of class and intellect. And a Warlord, lest you forget."

"An Illian Warlord," growled Errta.

Ayrah scrunched her nose at the sight of his castle. It was prissy. Weak. How would he defend against attackers with so many frail windows? And what function did the marble statues serve on his personal lawn? At least the doors were solid, barred aesthetically with hellinite. They opened as the Tamagai approached.

Chill funneled out in a breeze, parted by his Elness, the Warlord. He stood on the threshold, his robes a silk and cotton blend of black and blue. His face was rigid—cold blue eyes, high cheekbones, thin lips, and a not-so-recently shaved head of golden fuzz. "Welcome." His voice was soft like a whisper but jaded with precise pronunciation. He turned and gestured them to follow.

The Tamagai entered haphazardly, boots knocked against the floor-boards, sharp breaths from the sudden cold, and a near huddle beneath the dangling crystal chandelier.

"What is it you want?" asked Ayrah.

The Warlord maintained his flat expression, "It is typical for me to greet visitors of note entering my province." He motioned to a hallway sat beside the middle-of-the-room staircase. "Might I interest you in something to eat?"

"Food." Errta hummed and nodded.

"Excellent."

They clambered down the hallway, uncarefully brushing past paint-ings and swinging them off center. They passed a common room with a chimney fireplace and leather couches. A small Renovian girl was curled up beneath a book.

Strange. She was a far way from the jungle. And didn't look too. . . slave-like.

A right turn down a hallway, and into a long dining hall with golden chairs and red velvet upholstery. Silver platters were already laid out, as well as plates and utensils and full wine glasses.

"What is it you want?" Ayrah repeated after a long moment. She had not yet touched her food.

Errta snarled with fish smacking between his teeth, and still shoveled more.

"The Prince Killer." The Warlord sighed; his head tilted down. "I must congratulate you on your Sehlyian tattoo. Most skillful." He nodded.

"It seems you Veligreen children have decided to pop back into the lime-light at the same time." He chuckled politely.

"Verano? He's alive?" Ayrah stood up and gripped the table.

"Oh, very much so. He is under my administration at this very moment. 'I would become your sword,' he said, or something another. He is not here now, unfortunately. I have him off accomplishing some remedial task of mine."

Verano was alive. Her eyebrows twitched as she recalled the last time she had seen him. He abandoned her. Because low life was simply too low for his blood.

Tuio lied. But why? For what reason?

"I find myself indubitably curious." The Warlord put his hands together apologetically. "Does it trouble you to be so near the central ground of your father's demise?"

Ayrah looked at him. She knew he could see her absence of this knowledge pass her face.

"It is true. Your father and I worked together for many seasons. I sanctioned his weapons factories to be built near the edge of the city. It was just heart wrenching what he was up to." He shrugged.

"And now that it comes to mind"—the Warlord held out a finger—"I do have some use for you. There is an Ohaer Masikonian militant running around my province, causing me all sorts of headaches. He's proved to be quite powerful. Since you Tamagai have shown yourselves capable of capturing even a Warlord, I must plead that you help me with this matter."

"Yes," said Ecanaes with a sharp voice. "Anything you need, El."

Errta rolled his eyes and let his arms slump against the table. "So much for our vacation."

"What information have you gathered?" Ecanaes asked.

"A good, studious man you are." Bright white teeth peeked between his smiling lips. "He was spotted in Vasara this morning. If I assume correctly, he is headed this way sometime tomorrow. He wears the stone tattoos of the Alkalii. I must request, deal with him by any means necessary, and retrieve any artifacts he might have about his person. It is most important. And take care not to touch his things, whatever they might be. Who knows what diseases he has encountered near Vasara's slums. But I'm sure a measly handkerchief between finger and thumb and say, his sword, would suffice."

El Rai's carriages brought them and their servants back to their rented manor near the Tuidiia. Errta grumbled the whole way. "I was going to splash in the waves. Can't even try Ryala's sweet wine now."

Ayrah patted his hand, her mind elsewhere.

Their vacation manor rested on the east face of the mountain so that it overlooked the ends of Ryala where slums met road. The two-story house, topped with a red clay tile roof and graced with black iron balconies stood out as a contrasting symbol of wealth. Servants bustled inside and out, caretaking the grounds, and dusting each glass and vase left for eye pleasing fragility.

Ayrah and Errta had picked its location.

Now that she was officially Tamagai, Errta could explain why they were charged to arrest Nahkon Veligreen, without the king's Illian spell getting in the way. And before getting into the details of the execution, Errta told her, "You know we're in the same city as your father's factories. Go. Search them."

Ayrah dressed herself in black leather trousers that stretched tight around her legs and a black shirt that laced down her arms.

"Don't be long," said Errta, as she passed their common room. "We leave for the Masikonian at first light."

"First light it is." She didn't care. She had her own mission to pursue first.

A pink-orange halo spread across the mountain ridge as the sun dipped farther down the other side. Ayrah had a familiar urge to take alleyways but told herself, "I'm Ayrah Veligreen. Daughter of a Warlord. Member of the Tamagai, one of the most powerful Kaeselwa guilds in all of Sigu Nii. The Prince Killer. Ayrah Veligreen does as she pleases, the only ones above me now are Warlords and kings."

Eyes of commoners widened as she passed, their eyes drawn to the black, misting tattoo on her left shoulder.

The mountain road leveled, and tin shacks arose around her. Wire strings stretched between them, with tunics and trousers hanging to dry. Trash piled on the sides of the dirt road. And peasants fled from her path. In their midst, her father's factories were built in sporadic, assimilated fashions.

Blackstone chimneys rose silently from a dark, broken carcass of a building. Glass covered great walls, irrevocably soot stained, barred in a grid, with many shiny bits crunching beneath Ayrah's approaching boots.

Ayrah came to a rusty metal side door. She stretched her arm and blew the door down. It flew and scraped against the concrete. Yelps echoed from inside, followed by whispers. Ayrah stepped in and looked around. There were a hundred cotton blankets, folded up as pads to sleep on, and just as many ragged, inkless peasants watching her enter. Each young face was wrinkled as if a plague had swept them. Wooden pipes were held in their hands, smoke still puffing lightly from the bowls.

"Get out," said Ayrah. In truth, she did not care that they were here, but she didn't like their staring. "Get out!" she screamed, white fire exploded from her mouth, illuminating each horrified face in a blinding, unflattering light.

A hundred pairs of bare feet brushed the concrete as the addicts struggled to their feet and ran for the doors around the factory.

When they were gone, she turned to the vast network of conveyor belts, furnaces, and the dusty pits marked for raw hellinite ores. What was once a loud and busy place now lingered in a ghostly silence.

Ayrah walked around. She inspected each component to the sword making process, desperate for something to catch her eye. Something so unbelonging that it would cause the replacing of a Warlord. Nothing seemed amiss.

She passed offices with parchments flung around the floor. She peeked into dusty meal rooms and a bathroom with sewage connections. Nothing looked out of place.

She searched for a long while, each room and area of the factory less promising than the last, until finally, she found herself in an office larger than the rest. In it sat a leather chair, a dark waxed desk, and a calendar with incremental dates set to twelve Oscillations prior—all of it covered in dust. Was this her father's place of authority when he visited? Or was it the office of another person delegated to command his work?

Ayrah inspected some of the scattered parchment. They had her father's signature. She looked harder, parchment after parchment, hoping for some clue of what had happened. Nothing.

In the far corner of the office, a brass pipe jutted from the wall. Vulgarhe inscriptions encircled it. She nearly wished she had brought Ecanaes to decrypt the old language. She pulled, twisted, and tugged on the pipe, hoping it was some type of lever, but it had been fixed into the stone wall.

Ayrah's desperate hope was becoming a nuisance to her.

Power went out from her. She felt it. A slight draining of her vuu. She turned back to the pipe, and Vulgarhe letters fizzled with light then darkened.

She fixed her eyes upon them this time and drew near. Her shadowa tattoo lifted from her arm, it made like a funnel toward the pipe, but it could not reach. A smile came across her face, and she gave assent to the torment growing in her gut. It grew to be like a swirling storm. She let a fire consume her mind. And the shadow erupted from her. The black, intangible mist exploded from her palms and blew from her mouth.

Together it funneled like a whirlwind into the pipe. The Vulgarhe letters grew white, and the ground beneath her feet jolted.

Slowly, the walls around the room began retreating upwards. The ground declined diagonally, the desk rumbled, the papers scattered, and she braced herself with a wide stance. Her heart pounded, and her pulse throbbed against her temples.

When the floor screeched to a halt in its descent, Ayrah found herself in a narrow hallway. Wooden crates lined the walls, filling sectioned-off alcoves. She cast a flame in the palm of her hand for light and tore open the first box she came to. It was filled with swords. That didn't make sense. Her brows scrunched together. Why would they be hidden? This was a sword factory.

Ayrah picked one up, inspecting the strange brass blades. Why would these swords be made of a brittle, inferior material? Did her father sell these to Vasara, in hopes to hinder their peasants? She turned the sword in the light, emblazoned in the flat of the blade was a large tree with many branches and many roots. Whose insignia was this? She had not seen it on any Kaeselwa guild or Warlord administration. It did not match any city's crest that she knew of.

She dropped the sword back into the crate, and its metal clanged against the others. She tore open another. It was filled with the same bronze swords. She opened another and found the same. She made her way down the hallway, searching each crate, and all were the same. Who were these swords supposed to go to? Why were they hidden? Why did they get her father killed?

After closing the room with the same vuu, Ayrah trekked back up the mountain road, tired from the pouring out of her shadowa. Her pace slowed. She was in no rush to get back to the Tamagai. She reflected on the past quarter-season and how her whole intention of joining the Tamagai had led to that moment in the factory. Ayrah took the Niiwa of Sehlya to learn of her father's treason. It all felt hopeless now. Useless. A total waste of her regaining recognition and stepping back into the world of glory-driven death matches. An urge took her, she wanted to run. To do away with all that she had done to arrive at such an unavailing moment.

She trudged back to the manor.

"Learn anything?" asked Ecanaes.

Maybe he would know about the strange insignia, but Ayrah had been exhausted of hope that day. "No." She went straight to the bedroom the servants had prepared for her.

Ayrah's gaze absently scanned the teleportation pad that came from Vasara. Errta was on her right, and the other members to his right. She didn't want to be there. She didn't feel like fighting some Masikonian, regardless of how strong he might be. She had fought enough in Sehlya to last her quite some time.

"He would just change his appearance, right?" asked Urota.

"We will recognize him by his stone tattoos," said Ecanaes. "From what I hear, those things are permanent. They will remain long after his body has rotted away."

"Now remember," Errta's tone was grim. Ayrah had to remember that he was the only one among them that had actually fought someone Ohaer before—her father. "If black lightning starts crawling through the air, either we all have to grab him, so that he a, doesn't have enough vuu to drag us all anywhere or b, we all get dragged. If only one of us is in the spot to grab hold of him, while he begins to teleport away, let go! Last thing you want is to find yourself alone with a hostile Ohaer."

The Black Guard took on their normal responsibilities in the Warlord's Office, gatekeeping and instructing nameless nobodies to their destinations. But their eyes kept watch on the Tamagai. They were on guard for whatever battle would take place.

Thunder repeatedly cracked and fizzled with the black sparks around the metal pads. Ayrah figured by the time they were done, her hearing would need a touch up from a mutator.

Ayrah told Errta what she found last night. The bronze swords. She told him about the tree. "So, what is it? Why was he executed?"

Errta smiled, there was calamity in his eyes. "They're the swords that the bark-eaters use."

"The Renovians?"

"Aye."

"Oh." That made even less sense. Nobody helped the Renovians. It wasn't just a law. It was bloody senseless. They didn't have vuu. They were basically just animals. Why, why in all of Zoë and the afterlife, would a Warlord help them?

They stood and watched people teleporting for half the day before they saw him. He was tall, taking up the full height of the indented plate. His tattoos were indeed stone, carved like a maze. His eyes were bright purple, and a somber recognition took them as they locked with Ayrah's.

41

ATERAH

Aterah's eyes opened, and a spine-shivering tension crawled up her chest. Her hands furled around smooth purple-silk sheets.

"Splendid morning, isn't it?" El Rai Ezs's cold voice ripped through her waking. He sat in a wooden bedside chair; he curled over her. "What have the gods shown you?" He jerked his hand forward.

She flinched away. "Wait." Her mind raced. The past several days began with this same morning ritual. She had seen shipwrecks in an industrialized port district of Ryala, and a small dark-skinned child arrive through the Tuidiia. But this time she had seen Kairo. "I didn't dream. You woke me too early."

"Nonsense." He forced his clammy pale palm over her forehead, and the two of them relived her dream together.

Aterah drew her arms and legs in, curling up beneath the sheets. Her eyes rested on the wall opposite the Warlord, a splendidly vacant space. The tension in her chest drained. Everything drained.

El Rai tsked his lips. "A waste of a night. I've seen this already."

"I dream of—" Her voice cracked. A sensation descended upon her. A sound like mountains breaking apart reached her, from far, far off.

"Thing's not yet come. Yes, yes. But see, I can think with my own brain on how things will play out. This night was elementary." The Warlord made no notions as to having heard the sound or sensed the odd feeling, he even turned to leave.

Her stomach dropped. She lurched upright. It was familiar, but she trembled. Her vision faded to black, and a voice erupted from her mouth, as if in a multitude of voices,

"You will call Him the Restorer,
But He will be your injustice:
Your glory comes like ridicule,
Even a mouse takes your knowledge,
And your riches are like burdens.
A Kraussing of Many Moments.
He has been your great destroyer."

Her vision returned to her. Her head throbbed.

The Warlord stood halfway toward the door, wide-eyed. He surveyed her composure. "That was. . . *interesting*." He offered a fake giggle, then continued in a voice as if to himself, "I'll bet the militant has just come into contact with the Archeodon." He continued toward the door, and called back to her with a distant voice, "Breakfast will be ready shortly, get dressed for the occasion."

Aterah continued to lay, unmoved. Tears mounted the crest of her eyelids; she blinked them away. *What was that?* She hadn't any idea what it all meant, and many of the words were slipping away already. She understood the gist, though: It was about the King to Come.

Apparently, breakfast was an occasion calling for splendor. The Warlord had left a dress laying by the foot of her four-poster bed. It was a vibrant, shiny red in most places, but such a soft material that it appeared black in others. Even after putting it on, Aterah felt like she had to constantly hold it up. It clung loosely to the middle of her bicep area with thin crisscrossed ropes that were decorated with jewelry like golden beads or hanging gemstones.

There was also an ornate golden collar, half the size of her neck. It wasn't solid, it moved snake-like in tiny chain links, and there were portions where her neck that showed through, and others bedazzled by deep red gems.

Platters of shining silver were carried into the dining hall by several low-ranked Sigu Nii servants. Aterah waited with a grumbling stomach, still clutching her dress up as the servants revealed omelets, bacon, biscuits, poached eggs, and a tray of honey and jams.

Warlord El sat at the head of the table. He picked up his silver knife, and instead of taking it to the food, he drew it over the back of his forearm. A thin line of blood dribbled out. He brought his other hand over the cut. It shook. His fingers strained. It only lasted a moment before he huffed and wiped his arm. He wrinkled his nose in thought.

The two of them sat alone at the table, eating in silence for several long moments.

"El," said his pale-skinned servant. Short and dressed in a black costume tailored to his roundness. "Today's events."

"Proceed."

"Lord Mayor Ryaff of Vasara requests a meeting regarding Castle Graey's structural integrity—something or another about the gaping hole through its upper wing. Then, the Kaeselwa guild Korlaii requests further insight on the Tamagai's weak points. Also, a black-parchment letter has arrived from Ra'che. Another letter from the Illyadra of 'Lm-Waerta has arrived. And Verano Veligreen approaches the manor—I've been informed that he is . . . in a bit of a mood after his loss in Vasara." The servant waited patiently for the Warlord to respond.

"Mmm." Warlord El Rai Ezs dabbed his mouth with a linen. "Yes. Lower the buying price for severed Renovian organs by two copper pieces and raise the buying price for the enslaved delivered to Ravid and Zetola by a silver piece."

The stout servant scratched etchings with a quill on parchment. "Done."

"Prepare the two letters in my study. And bring my pipe at once."

The servant bowed deeply and backed out of the dining hall.

The big picture, thought Aterah. *That's what Adakon said I would be good at.* Before she was taken from NeoDerii, she had spent hours contemplating what it would be like to be aware of the rebellion's many moving parts. Moving them around, placing each according to their strengths and weaknesses, and using her visions to react to the not-yet-outcomes. It seemed that here she was, fulfilling that vocation. But for the wrong side. The side of the snakes.

Hurry, Kairo, she pleaded.

The front manor doors slammed apart. Even from so far away, Aterah could feel the walls shake as the carved wooden doors nearly shattered against them. Verano had returned, and from the sound of his stomping and groaning entry, he was not in a good mood.

Aterah gulped and looked to El Rai Ezs. The Warlord sat patiently; his hands folded.

Before Verano found his way into the dining hall, the stout servant brought in a golden tray with a purple velvet pouch tied at the top with golden strings, and a long wooden pipe. El Rai untied the pouch, dipped two fingers in, lifted out stringy brown bits, and pressed them into the bowl of his pipe.

Verano stumbled into the room and bumped his shoulder into the doorpost. He turned, giving the wooden-frame a snarl, and bashed it with his shoulder as if to punish the wood for being in his way. A gash of seared flesh covered his lower left cheekbone, and he clutched his left arm.

He looked up blankly and moaned, "He bloody cheated." His voice shook, his lips pressed flat between words. It seemed painful to talk. "I failed you." His shoulders settled limp.

"Might you be a fellow, and light this for me?" The Warlord nodded at the bowl of his pipe.

"Uhm, aye." Verano walked over, reached his hand, and a small lick of flame transferred from his finger to the bowl.

El Rai Ezs sucked in deeply. His eyelids shut tight as his head rolled back. His breath held a moment, until a sigh released creamy-white-smoke from his mouth and nostrils.

Aterah wrinkled her nose. It smelled funny.

Verano punched the table, and she jumped at the burst of anger.

"Do not punish my table." Another deep intake of smoke. "It was quite my fault, really." His voice was like one with phlegm in the back of his throat, and his words spilled out with coats of smoke coiling around each syllable. "Knowledge is most literally my department, and I commanded your mission with insufficient information. For that, you fought against an Ohaer Masikonian. It's lucky he let you live."

"I would be victor if I just—"

"He let you live, child." The Warlord waved him off. "If someone Ohaer wanted you dead, you would most definitely be dead." With his brow scrunched together in thought, he leaned his head back. "It is interesting, though." He paused and inhaled. "The Masikonian militant is not registered on any census. None of the proper Sigu Nii have heard of him. None of my friends in the city-states have heard of him, it's not like there's anyone in the jungle worth asking, not even—and this is quite startling—any of the Illians, whose sole duty it is to keep track of the powerful in this world, have heard of him." The Warlord frowned. "And now he possesses the Archeodon. Most frustrating."

"What are we going to do?" Verano asked.

El Rai Ezs leaned in and looked Verano in the eyes. "I've taken care of it. All and all, it is fortunate for us that he seeks to come this way." His gaze turned and met Aterah's.

"Who did you send, instead of me?" Verano tried to not sound insulted.

"The Tamagai." El Rai searched his face. "They're in town for the Kae-selwa, and they've proven themselves against an Ohaer, in times past, yes?"

"Yes—aye." Verano's voice was hoarse. "They helped in the arrest—"

"Of your father, indeed."

"May I be excused?" Aterah asked, no longer wishing to be a part of the discussion regarding her brother and his new mentor's capture. It felt like an age had passed since Aterah felt that she was allowed a restful moment alone.

The Warlord nodded.

Aterah wandered the manor and its many halls and rooms. There was a destination she sought loosely, and she enjoyed the historical paintings and tinted glass along the way. One painting, interpreted by its plaque caption, was "King Ivan's Final Stand." The Graey Castle stood on its hill, with decorated Sigu Nii warriors spilling through the courtyards.

Eventually she found herself on the lower level of the west wing. The room was dim, illuminated by a single candle on a three-wire-pronged-nightstand. The aroma of parchment and leather bindings sent Aterah back to the library in NeoDerii, and she hoped the smell would linger past the point of accustomation. She passed shelves stocked with books and scrolls, each compartment labelled with absolute care—author, date, and title of the work.

Captivated, she pulled several titles and brought them to a deep leath-er chair beside the nightstand. She noticed stain rings around a singular spot and two letters tucked behind the candle.

Aterah opened the first book, titled *A Tale of Many Masks*. The begin-ning pages described it as a piece of fiction, though she didn't know what that was. The author was a Masikonian entertainer, allowed to stay among the Alkalii for inspiration, which he described to be like sleeping in a room full of not-so-secret military police.

Aterah decided she would enjoy the piece. A tale that was not true. A story written for entertainment and thought provocation. She set the book down, page marked, to bring to her room and read as she fell asleep.

Aterah held up the other two works, letting the candlelight fall across their titles as she decided which to open. *The Aliyah Demise* by Hera'd Xen and *El Rai Ezs*. She picked the latter.

All the pages were handwritten. The work took the format of a journal. The entries were deep and long, several pages each.

El Rai Ezs, "The Truth of God." Aterah translated the Vulgarhe inscriptions into the common tongue. The corners of the parchment pages were stained red with blood.

She began reading: "El is Old Vulgarhe. The ancient hieroglyphic has been found on every continent, predating any tribal language yet discovered. It is local to everywhere. But it means something different to everyone."

Aterah paused, remembering Epheriia's third entry in Graeynesh Law. This was exactly what she had prophesied! The disarrayed uses of El. She continued. "It's no doubt that the different Archeodon across each kingdom have provided the grounds for the forming of this word. The crowns have chosen systems of value for us. They have a man imagine his best self and his worst. A dumb man in Aylavuera cannot be El, for El in Aylavuera holds the very definition of being knowledgeable. A weak man in Sigu Nii—"

"What are you doing?"

Aterah flinched up, the book fell across her lap. On contact of their eyes the room grew blurry, and grotesque scenes of Kairo being ripped limb from limb flooded her mind. Uncontrollable dread shot through her stomach. No other moment in the world existed as El Rai Ezs ate Kairo's brain whole. Blood splattered and stuck to her face, seeped into her mouth.

"Answer me." His voice ripped through the illusion.

Aterah shivered. Her hands wrapped around the backs of her arms. Tears streamed down her cheeks. And nothing had even happened. But the Warlord's eyes moved across hers with passion. Kairo stood up, skull ripped apart and brain removed, and came after Aterah with a mindlessly chomping mouth.

"I meant no harm." Aterah held her hands up in surrender. "I just like to read."

"You like to read." The Warlord laughed. "Who teaches a bark-eating soldier how to read? Poorest population control I've ever heard of."

Kairo fell over. Dead. And his body dissipated in a fading sickly-yellow mist.

"Do you feel any different?" he asked. "Tell me!"

"No! No. I just—I saw the tale of masks, and then I saw your name, and I wanted to be alone."

"I can understand that." He snatched the study away from Aterah. "But you're never to enter this room again. Ever." The Warlord sighed. "If you want to read, you're to ask me for something." He handed her the Masikonian tale and laid a hand on her shoulder. Black lightning exploded through her. She screamed, but she was still alive, standing beneath the manor's main stairway.

42

EIDHIN

The stagecoach pulled to a smooth stop before the king's palace. The carvings in the whitestone pillars loosely resembled an ornate seashell design.

Despite the majesty of the palace, the ivy and ivory mingling with one another along the walls, the glowing blue gem that trimmed the corridors, Eidhin knew they walked through a side entrance. Perhaps a calculated avoidance of philosophical nonsense uttered by any commoner in contact with Kalyn. *Like, really,* thought Eidhin, *one might assume that the presence of an Illyadra would have one standing on their ears. But still, they spew and spew until they are breathless.*

The king's palace had towers high enough to make the surrounding mountains envious. So, it surprised Eidhin when they began down a set of stairs. He presumed that societal elevation might have translated to meeting in a high place.

Should I fetch parchment and quill, El?

"Quiet," hissed the Illyadra. "Your perceived recollection of events about to take place will be stained. I doubt I will ever need to fetch them."

Ikondu's eyes grew wide as they passed deeper into the palace. He began to walk in longer, hard-pushed strides, as if fighting against a stormy tide. But Eidhin couldn't feel a thing. He wondered, was this what weather looked like in the afterlife? If so, Eidhin found himself glad that he couldn't perceive it.

The underground grew humid. Kalyn paused outside a door for a breath. And breathe he did. He took several moments with his hand on the hellinite handle, his gaze darting around the walls as if he were collecting a madman's worth of thoughts.

He opened the door, and chatter seemed to stop abruptly as they pushed inside.

A heptagonal stone table stood at the center of the triangular-shaped room. The underbelly of the table matched the dark brick walls, as if stained by ocean. The tabletop was made of the same vibrating blue gemstone, gently illuminating the faces of the other five Illyadra with a cold dark light.

"Kalyn!" A girl's voice echoed across the room.

"At last," huffed a man nearest to the door.

"The El of Philosophy has decided to bless us with his presence," chuckled another.

Kalyn raised his palms. "I might not have been offended if you had begun without me."

"Talynguard is a day's sail away, Kalyn. How do you frequent broken punctuality each council?"

Eyes darted to the dark child in their company. "You've even went and gotten yourself a Razite! How can you be late when you have a timekeeper chasing you around, everywhere you go?"

Vylndaer laughed at that. "It's the packing. There're so many variables to the weather in Vuulguard, I never want to commit more than a forecast's worth of clothes. And the servants never get it right. They have no concept of presentability, hostility, or even perfectibility." Kalyn scraped out one of the chairs around the table.

"Indeed." Huffed the man nearest to the door.

Eidhin peered around the room. He fidgeted his fingers between clasped hands. Where should he stand? What should he say—or not say? The other servants stood silently a pace behind and to the right of each of their Els. So he did too.

Ikondu stood on Kalyn's other side. There was only one other Razite in the room, belonging to a man across the table. Eidhin watched their eyes brief past one another.

The one nearest to the door was an old man. A cluster old, by the looks of it. Which was strange because, typically a cluster was regarded as a lifetime long. But this old man looked like he had plenty of life to spare. He wore long robes of intricately woven white and gold, with a grand blue sigil adorning his upper right chest. The insignia of the Church of Rai. Eidhin nearly leapt toward him. *Grandon Delshau!* Eidhin remembered his name from school. *The Priest.* But when he opened his mouth, nothing croaked out. No stutters. Just puffs of air. As if a stone gate had sealed shut on his tongue.

Grandon turned to his servant. "We're all here, go fetch his Elness." There was a vacancy in his voice where reverence typically sat.

The other five Illyadra were shuffling through papers and parchments, sipping water and wine, readying ink and quill, stretching, and otherwise preparing themselves for a long conversation.

Eidhin picked up their names and titles as the chatter continued.

To Delshau's right was a man dressed in old clothes. His short brown hair, with strips of real silver sprinkled through, was slicked past his ears. They called him Hera'd Xen, El of History. A young woman to Hera'd's right commented on his mix-matched clothes, to which he replied, "Of all the trends from Masikus or brewed among our local name-makers, Ar'lm Lotra generation is my personal favorite. It is strange though." Hera'd lifted a parchment before him and peered at it. "I have a report on the lifespan of trends, and they're decreasing steadily. This would be a symptomatic influence if we were in the Masikonian Kortaes." He reached up and stroked his hair. "I might guess the silver-strips to fall from style quite soon."

The young woman stifled a laugh. Her dark brown hair was pinned above her head with clips of gold and rubies. She wore a dress that puffed at the shoulders and frilled down the front. Aeryn Shuvlyn, El of Medicines. "Indeed, it might be due to decreasing attention spans, which have come in since our last council." She passed a set of papers around the glowing blue table.

Grandon pointed at a spot on the paper and laughed, "Those Sigu Nii oafs can only focus on one thing for *seven* seconds?"

"Seven-point-seven seconds," corrected the next Illyadra, Porta De Laveen, the El of the Mathematics. A frail, stiff man with a beak nose and silver spectacles. His clothes were plain, and he spoke softly of demographic statistics and their continuity, saying, "Numbers are the Rai that weaves through our world, and thus must be respected so."

The El nearest to Kalyn, to whom he turned frequently to converse with, was Dronae of House Biology. He wore a doublet of ornate red-and-blue design, with a heavy black cloak draped over the back of his chair. "The population growth rates of Aylavuera have fallen recently." He passed his own set of papers around the table. "While Masikus grows—Sigu Nii has fallen, obviously; and both Ra'che and the Renovian encampments remain at their environment's equilibrium."

Eidhin wondered about their chatter. All of them spoke of numbers and foreign kingdoms, but none of them seemed to be paying attention to the other. They merely waited for their turn like a deaf person in the Aylan.

The hellinite door clicked open. Grandon's servant returned. "All rise for King Samuel Gehn."

The Illyadra pushed themselves to stand, some quicker than others.

Eidhin stared at the door. Quiet thuds approached. A man strode in with a floor-sweeping cape of blue and gold. King Samuel's face was soft, and thick spectacles adorned his bright blue eyes. He appeared to be only two generations old, though Eidhin knew he had been coronated long before. A full dark golden beard covered his pointed chin and rose up to curly hair under a heavy golden crown.

The crown seemed to glow with a sort of misty radiance. The rhythmic-glowing blue gem decorated the crown like lightning. It webbed through the gold and formed a single hieroglyphic rune of Old Vulgarhe right in its front-middle face.

"Sit," commanded the king as he took a small throne of a seat on the opposite side of the table. His voice was molten lead. Beautiful, bright, and burning.

"King Gehn, how have you been since our last council?" Grandon Delshau asked with a humble tone.

"Skip the idle small talk." The king waved a hand. "This Aylan marks four generations since the beginning of my reign over Aylavuera. The times we are in now seem especially strange. The pendulum has reached the extent of its swing and the Oscillation begins." King Samuel frowned.

Both Razites drew pendulums and swung them over their hands. Their eyes wandered over each swing, knowing what its pace meant, but Eidhin shook his head.

The other Illyadra made sounds of interest but not surprise.

"So do we skip Generation Quera once again?" asked Hera'd Xen.

"Indeed," said the king. "Cluster De'lm will conclude with the coming Niiwa. It is unfortunate: the skipping and the indefinite."

Eidhin had heard of Generation Quera. The fourth generation in a cluster. But it hasn't taken place in several lifetimes.

"It is doubly unfortunate that Renovia's marking influence united us under their calendar in the first place," interrupted Delshau, disgust heavy on his lips. "The healers no longer live, breathe, or eat with us. And we trudge through their tasks? If Masikus were to fall, honestly, would their coin still pollute our waters? At least Ra'che picks up the scraps. But these *things*," Delshau pointed at the pendulums. "Aren't perfect. They hardly even work."

"Perhaps we transition to one more reliable," agreed Dronae. "The geologists and ecologists under my employment have all written measurements of time-keeping to be relied upon, regardless of Kortaes."

"The stars tell us their age as well," said Porta De Laveen of the Mathematics.

"Quiet." The king held up a palm. His face was calm, but his voice held a hint of aggravation. "The Age of Under is breaking. I've conversed with the Chronometer Regiment of the Dii'raxis, and all our calculations align. The coming cluster of Th'lm will be the last of the age." King Gehn paused as he tapped his fingers on the table. "The Kraussing of Moments draws near."

Whispers and mutterings broke out between the other six, but Eidhin didn't know what it meant. He turned to Ikondu, and even the child made facial motions of understanding.

El Gehn continued. "We've witnessed the decline of Sigu Nii's population for several clusters now. They can no longer support their current imperialism. This is our chance to regain Kortaes, and we must capture it with precision, should it fall to the Masikonian city-states."

"It's rare for a historian to live through the turning of a Kortaes," said Hera'd with solemn excitement. "Let alone an Age."

Kalyn particularly picked up his head at that. Eidhin remembered Kalyn's talking about being the age breaker. He and his Vulgarhe. Eidhin kept his mouth shut. It seemed his El had not informed the Illyadran Council that he had discovered an entire new vuu. And still, through observations of history, trends, whatever societal factors that played, and of course—the Razite, this King Samuel Gehn had caught on.

"Perhaps my findings since our last Aylan will aid us," offered Dronae of House Biology. He looked to the king, who gestured him to continue. "In my possession are close members from each of the six in power. A servant here, a brother there, a child in some cases."

"What six?" asked Kalyn.

"All of them. The Coryndal, the Warlords, you Illyadra, even the Wardens of Ra'che. Through avid study of their minds, their memories, and their complete depiction of each El, I've found common denominators, socially evolved nuances that proclaim a higher chance of succession." Dronae let the table fall to silence.

Did this man have something to do with Tuladrna? wondered Eidhin.

It seemed Kalyn wondered the same thing. "Dronae." The name growled out of Kalyn's throat.

"Settle," said Dronae. "For the loss of each of you has brought together what I consider to be a fascinating sequel to my father's study." He paused again to let the group absorb that. Each of the Illyadra seemed to listen harder, a propped elbow here, a leaning closer there. "I have found the next evolution in our tree. A collection I call the Socialda."

"For Illians?" asked the king, deeply intrigued.

"For humanity. Regardless of subspecies," claimed Dronae.

"Does it involve vuu?" asked Kalyn.

"Indirectly. Of course, powerful vuu increases the likelihood of reproduction, but the Socialda is more a people-versus-people mentality. A step gained in our understanding of how humans interact with moral, emotional, and apperceptional ground."

"Fascinating, Dronae. It seems Kalyn here should have been the one to find this new study of yours," remarked the king with a smirk.

"But it fell to me." Dronae looked around the room, making eye contact with each Illyadra. "The factor is apathy. Apathy aids the disintegration of emotional processing, a degradation of remorse. Apathy leads to the selective culling of the weak. The Socialda is one who regards El to be nothing but himself. And the fascinating part is that it's already begun. Most of you here are, in fact, Socialda."

"Even Masikus?" Aeryn Shuvlyn of the Medicines asked. "Their whole culture is emotional. I can hardly hear the words they say, their tones range in pitch so frequently. I can see Sigu Nii in this. And I can see the relation to the Renovian demise. But surely, ours is the only kingdom that denotes expression taboo."

Dronae nodded. "My thoughts were initially the same. We smile, do we not? We laugh and chuckle, we shout when necessary. But we know that the origins of these symptoms are forbidden to us in order to save our progress as Illyadra. This gives our shouting and smiling a merely aesthetic nature. And though Masikus is polluted with it, their Coryndal have the same nature about them. They are filled with apathy for anyone save themselves."

"Well done, I say." King Gehn applauded quietly. "You never cease to bring forth worthy material, Dronae. Each of us can begin the cultivation of this finding into our taking of Kortaes within the next Aylan, whether by exploitation of those in power, or by accumulating this new Socialdan perspective.

"Kalyn, I wish to hear your findings." The king gestured a hand.

"I . . . have none, El." Kalyn dipped his head, an apologetic indication.

The table remained silent for a moment.

"This will be the sixth Aylan, you know?" Samuel's bright blue eyes squinted behind his golden spectacles. "Six in a row you have come empty handed. Have you run out of things to think of?"

"Of course not, El."

"Then perhaps you're withholding from us. Do your hands cling to what little remains of your lineage?" Samuel Gehn fiddled with the crown on his head. "Perhaps you wish to regain what was lost—the Archeodon."

He lifted the crown, glowing and misting, and set it gently on the table before them, his hand still clung between the open-topped-troughs. "Do you wish to meet Hwaerta?"

Eidhin peered around the table. Each of the Illyadra stared hungrily at the crown.

King Samuel lifted his pinky from contact with the gold. "All of our knowledge is stored in this little crown. The things you six bring forth. The accumulation of all the kings before me. Every understanding of vuu and power, miniscule or great, resides in this little ring." The king lifted his index-finger from the gold. "This crown has been in human possession since the Age of the First Kings. The first Kortaes. And I find myself indubitably curious, do you think our dear Hwaerta might remember all that she knows if I were to lose possession? We've seen how vuu-bindings break with the loss of the Renovian Archeodon." The king was smiling now. All his bright white teeth glistened in the gold and blue radiance. He lifted off his middle finger. "Do you think that you, Kalyn, could snatch this dear ring before I lifted my last finger? Do it. Take it."

Ikondu tugged silently on the hem of Kalyn's cloak.

Kalyn's right-hand twitched beneath the table. "I . . . do not wish to become king, El." He seemed to force every word.

"Good," said the king with a nod. "Then share your findings." The king retook the crown and swiveled it slightly so that it fit comfortably amid his blonde curls.

Kalyn hesitated for a moment, then said, "I call it the El Rai Ezs."

"The truth of good," translated Hera'd with an appreciative nod. "Has a tune to it."

"It is not finished. Like Dronae's Socialda, I consider it to be a continuation of my fathers' works. A sort of lid on the what-makes-a-man philosophy. It has taken me half a generation, because I have poured all my gathered vuu into it. To understand my coming El Rai Ezs is to understand systems of value and influence, how those two relate to one another, between and within cultures, on a worldwide scale down to the individual.

"This lens," offered Kalyn. "This El Rai Ezs, has suggested a key perpetrator of the Sigu Nii clasp around Kortaes."

King Samuel lowered his chin to peer at Kalyn above the rim of his spectacles.

"Sigu Nii has intentionally increased the size of their moderately vuu'd. I do not know how, or if, King Ash has learned of Dronae's father's natural selection, but he has feigned its outcome to his liking."

"How?" asked Dronae.

"The Niiwa."

"The Niiwa creates a weakness." Grandon shook his head. "Weren't you listening, Kalyn? Their declining growth rate cannot support their current spread."

"And yet, even their lowly have vuu." Kalyn paused. "Talynguard has undergone a testing of free schooling."

The Illyadra made noises of hesitation. Disbelief. Aeryn Shuvlyn asked, "You give them your insights?"

"Not mine, no." Kalyn laughed softly. "But I do give them insights. Learnings that would rival the Library of Vylandria. Their generation-time has been sped up to gather differences more quickly, but they are still several generations away from being conclusive. My hypothesis is this: With the strengthening of our weakest, we will become Kortaes. And I must admit, I've structured the schooling to reward intellect rather than knowledge. Perhaps if these findings prove worthy, our descendants will truly be the smartest among Aylavuera, rather than just those who know the most."

"You propose to usurp me?" asked Grandon Delshau, the high priest. "All of you here, save Porta, have fathers and fathers' fathers with Illyadran titles. Two of you even have the Archeodon in your heritage, which is rather a lot, considering." Grandon's fists curled into balls against the tabletop. "And you, Kalyn, propose to build what I have taken my whole life to build? I already offer schools to the lowly. And the weaving trickle of my vuu has enriched this kingdom. You propose—"

"No," said Kalyn with little enthusiasm. "I *propose* to offer them actual information. Perhaps deception is the most accessible demonstration of Illian vuu on others, but with our kingdom's current ranking in Zoë, which is barely above the barbaric courts of Ra'che and Renovia, we only deceive each other. Let us turn against the world."

"This is very . . . Sigu Nii of you, Kalyn," said Aeryn Shuvlyn.

"And Socialda," said Dronae with raised brows.

"Do you think we have the self-sufficiency to wage intellectual war?" asked Hera'd. "We still rely heavily upon Masikus for food and infrastructure."

"Three Generations, right?" asked Kalyn, laying his hands flat on the table. "We have three generations before the end of the Age of Under. Kortaes is up for grabs. The coming cluster of Th'lm is how long we have to infiltrate culture and prepare separation."

The room fell silent. One by one, the Illyadra turned to King Samuel Gehn.

"There are other ways of taking Kortaes, Kalyn," he offered with an undecided tone.

"Name them," said Kalyn Vylndaer.

The king paused. Nodded. Looked around at all the blank faces. A long silence. "Indeed. We prepare for war."

43

WESKEN

"Whoa!" Yelled Wesken. "Where did you come from?" He dragged the black bamboo staff up into a fighting grip, aimed at a newly Sigu Nii colored Kairo.

"Wesken!" Kairo slapped his own forehead.

He burst out laughing.

"Oh. It was a joke?" Kairo's voice wavered with uncertainty.

Wesken made a careless effort to keep his face from letting on. *Let the guy wonder*, smirked a mischievous voice.

In truth, he only knew Kairo because they had been together for so long. Not that Wesken could remember how long, or what they had done, or where they had been. He could only remember as far as arriving at Vasara, and even that was foggy. But he could feel it. An intimacy between them that suggested many days had passed.

He turned to the characters in his mind, some of them fictious and some of them silhouetted ghosts of previously known people, and said, *look! I have a new friend.*

Most of them didn't care.

The three of them approached the Tuidiia inside Vasara's Warlord Office. A handcrafted mountain of hellinite infused stone, gold leaf trimming on each one-ton brick, it shook somewhat consistently, and did well to tame the thunder in its halls.

What are you looking at? Wesken asked the swirling gold eye that rested in the middle, threateningly.

The place was crawling with Sigu Nii black suits, the itchy authoritarian ones. Wesken stared at them. Voices in his head mocked that he could take any of them in battle, and he hoped his gaze would spark their aggression.

One said something, voice loud, chest out.

Oooh! Here we go. Wesken gripped the dark bamboo staff tight in his hands. He leaned in. The soldier's posture spoke leagues ahead of whatever words came out. He toyed with his left-shoulder armor sleeve, his eyes moved up and down, sizing up the stoneman.

Mister Grouch ruined it by flashing his Niiwa tattoo, which Wesken admitted, was a gorgeous Sehlyian Victory, styled in the eye-straining Masikonian Colorless Coin.

The guys in black suits led all three of them past the line of people.

"Alright, boy. You first." Mister Grouch gestured Kairo to stand in an indentation along the wall.

Kairo was obviously nervous and uncertain. Wesken doubted he'd ever seen a canoe before, and now he's being thrust at the most magically advanced network of roads in the world. He stepped onto a black-metal-pad with Vulgarhe inscriptions around the edges. Dusty black sparks crawled about the plate, and with a boom, a yelping Kairo was gone.

The Vulgarhe on the pad read: "Oh, Holy Korteous, Chief-Influence of Vuulguard, the unseen and the tangible, the Great King of Life, grant us this meek passage from Vasara to Ryala."

I want one! Said Wesken.

Yeah, me too! Said another Wesken.

Can we all go? Asked a new voice.

Wesken frowned. New voices arrived at infrequent, but unsurprising intervals. Perhaps this new voice was a make-believe manifestation of Kairo within Wesken's mind. But that didn't make sense. Wesken seldom found himself cognitively intricate enough to spin three characters together in one conversation.

"Alright, you next," The stone man grumbled at Wesken.

Wesken didn't care much for his gaze. As if the Alakuel were trying to figure out which star he came from. He stared at him as he stepped onto the metal plate, wondering if the guy could hear what he was thinking. Maybe he was the third voice, using the Illian part of his Ohaer-ness to infiltrate thought.

Peanut brittle toothpaste! A voice yelled in Wesken's mind. He squinted his eyes at the stoneman, searching for even a flicker of recognition. *Ham and toes and jelly and—*

Zap! Black lightning filled Wesken's sight, and the next thing he knew, he stood in an entirely different office. It looked much the same with arched beams and ceiling, black suits everywhere, and dirty Sigu Nii peasants waiting in lines.

Look out. The new voice warned urgently.

What? He asked, scanning the room for anything out of place. His eyes rested upon a line of people, facing the plate he just came from. Arms folded, feet apart, a gaze in their eyes that itched for battle. They adorned thin, fancy beach clothing—the sort of battle suits that only utterly confident Sigu Nii would wear.

"Wesken! Over here!" Kairo called near the glass-door exit.

Something is going down, Wesken knew. *And I don't want to miss it.*

Dibs on being the one who gets to fight! Yelled Wesken.

In your subconscious dreams.

Pfft, you're the subconscious one.

Am not!

Are too!

Thunder filled the office as the stoneman joined this side of the dance with Korteous.

"Stop right there!" a girl shouted. "We are the Tamagai, acting as hands for Warlord El Rai Ezs. Masikonian, come with us peacefully."

Wesken moved his grip down a notch in the bamboo.

Her eyes were blue, and her red hair was vibrant.

She's gorgeous.

Will you wake up, you bumbling idiot?

Look at how she's staring at me.

Ooh, like she wants to fight.

Wesken lowered into a sprint-ready-stance.

A sword of black ice erupted from her palm, and she lowered into a fighting stance.

A hard calloused hand gripped Wesken before he took off at her. Wesken flinched upwards, about to whack whoever just touched him. It was the stoneman. "I got this one."

Wesken laughed. "As if."

The stoneman lifted a bright wood and silver sword from his sheath. And then the fireworks started.

It all moved too slowly. Even the lightning, which Wesken watched with amusement, struck the Masikonian's wooden sword in a spray of sparks. Before their hands could swing backward, Wesken was on their other side.

Directly behind a dog of a man—just short of two generations old, longer hair on his bare feet than his head—Wesken pulled his left hand in and pushed his right hand out, swinging the end of the black staff against the nape of his neck.

The Dog-man howled in pain.

To the left, a girl styled in Masikonian clothing, which really was just less clothing, got blasted six strides past Wesken. He watched her back scrape against the cracked tile, pulling up thick slabs of marble during her tumble.

Wesken felt his smile reach wide. He leapt and swung his staff underneath him, propelling him through the air at the ground laid woman as she began to pick herself up. His foot collided with the back of her neck and smashed her face into the ground. He could feel the small snapping of her nose through his foot.

"I called for backup!" screeched a pale, lanky Illian.

"This is no place for you!" Wesken hurtled over a confused-looking Kairo and cracked his staff against the Illian. He loved the howling sound the man made.

I haven't had so much fun since . . .

You can't even remember, dummy.

Can y'all shut up? The air is doing something funny. It was true. The air grew thick. Light drained and a strange dark-purple hue flooded in. Power radiated from somewhere, Wesken scanned the big room.

A black man, standing far back, with his eyes lit up in fiery purple, waved his hands around, and generated purple circles.

"Razite vuu!" Wesken warned. He looked to the Masikonian, who was fending off a dozen black suits. Fire rained from his hands on some, others turned to stone at the flex of his muscles.

He's strong!

Ohaer even.

I wanna fight him!

A dark-purple sphere exploded in diameter. Talons, black in color with coats of grime and sludge, slithered past the edges of the circle. Hands of a Karr ranked demon grabbed the interdimensional portal edges and drew it wider. Out crept a black beast with dirty boar's hair and thick leathery skin. The beast arched its back to stand nine reaches tall and shook its crocodile-styled head of its adorned tangible suit.

This Razite guy was strong to pull a sentient demon, not just one of Vuulguard's many beasts of the field.

"What is that thing?" Kairo's voice was creakingly hoarse.

Wesken glanced at the Masikonian. Black suits were beginning to blast holes in the Tuidiia, in attempts to flank around the soldiers that the stoneman kept at bay.

From his periphery, the demon's slitted eyes yanked at Wesken. His reptilian armored throat gurgled in contempt. "I hate this place." His Vulgarhe was heard through ears and mind, slithery and like gargled water.

When the beast stepped, dark and purple sparks burst between foot and tile, like a sword on a whetstone wheel. It arched its arm and flung a bunch of talons at Kairo.

Wesken took off toward Kairo, the beast had to cross an ocean, in comparison to pace. But reaching him, he was at a loss. He couldn't carry Kairo out of harm's way. And even a shove would not send him out of the incoming talons' area of effect.

Kairo flinched his arms over his face. The talons clashed against an invisible wall and bright-green and dark-purple sparks exploded in a flurry.

Kairo looked up, mouth hung open. "I did that?"

A wad of spit flew from the croc's mouth. Even with such an inexpressible face, Wesken knew the beast was disgusted at Kairo's Renovian vuu. It reached its grimy hands through the floor, sending tile and stone in every direction. Its arms strained, and it lifted great chunks out of the office floor.

The ground beneath Wesken began slanting, and he slid backwards. His foot caught between the cracks of the Tuidiia flooring, and he yanked upside down. Under normal circumstances, he would be able to leisurely stroll away. The demon was far too slow for him. But he was stuck. Wesken tried to claw his way from the boulder's impact. He watched as a five-step diameter burg of tile crashed down on him.

His legs crushed like grapes between the slabs. Wesken screamed. His blood pooled down the slanted slabs, coating the underside of his arms and torso. Wet. Warm. Sticky. *Stick, stick, stick.* Said one of the many voices, they all yelled within his mind, crying for attention and pleading to retreat into a daydream.

Wesken could almost hear the Wooden Prince yelling his name. But his voice was not as loud as those in his head.

A mist, green and vibrant, slithered under the boulder. Wesken cried aloud as the slab lifted from his legs and cried quietly about how this might permanently affect his speed.

The mist grabbed hold of Wesken and dragged him away from searching talons. The green soaked into his legs, stabbed them, burned them, and finally healed them. Inside and out.

Wesken wiggled his toes. He propped up on his elbows and peered at his writhing knees. They ached, but they were whole. The only remnant of the crushing was the blood soaked into his faded tie-dye white and blue tunic.

"You did it," Wesken croaked, pulling Kairo's hand to stand. "You have overtaken consequence." He toed the end of his bamboo staff and kicked it into his grip.

Thunder shook the office. And the Masikonian placed a hand on Kairo's shoulder. "Too many of them with too much vuu." Wind picked up around him. "I don't have enough left to take all three—" Dusty black-lightning exploded where he stood. He and Kairo were gone.

Like one of Wesken's many daydreams, every head in the building turned to him.

"Ope." he said with eyes wide. "That's not good." He laughed nervously and kicked off the ground with his staff fit beneath him, propelling him forward, and he sprinted for one of the office's Korteous passages. The others were still too slow—or so he was thinking as black ice erupted around his ankles.

His body continued forward after his feet locked together, and he pounded chest first into the tile floor.

The red-haired girl stood over him. "Take him," she said.

Fighting was useless, Wesken knew. They dragged him in metal chains, with ice bonds around his joints. He shivered in the cold vuu jacket.

I think you're really in a mess this time, bud.

Eh, could be worse.

Oh really, how?

I could be Illian. Wesken giggled at that.

The girl with orange hair jabbed his ribs. "What are you laughing at?"

Wesken wheezed, annoyed at his interrupted conversation. They started dragging him into some building, but Wesken forgot to pay any attention.

Kairo will come. He'll save me.

Yeah, he'll come.

You wanna bet on it?

Wesken felt his wrists clasp tightly in a new set of metal chains. They had him sat on a thick chair, bolted into the cement around the small, empty room with no windows. A single oil lantern hung across from him.

This isn't a very nice room.

I'd rather sit in the sunshine.

Me too. Can we?

The room's sole door squeaked open. Wesken strained his neck around. Periphery blurred orange blob came around at a wandering pace.

"Hi," he said in a small voice.

"The Masikonian. Who is he?"

"Who?"

A hand gloved in ice smacked his cheek. Wesken felt icicles embed themselves, and his eyes watered.

"Who is the Masikonian you were with?"

"The grumpy guy with the stone tattoos?" Wesken asked.

She slapped him again.

"I was asking!" Wesken shouted. "That's who you mean, right?"

Apologetic eyes flashed. "Yes. Who is he?"

"No idea." Wesken laughed.

Her lips parted, revealing her grinding teeth. The ice-spikes on her hand grew in size as her hand rose. Then her open palm smashed against his cheekbone.

Wesken writhed. The world began to fade. A mental retreat.

Bah-bah-booshie.

She cares not that I'm young.

That's a first.

I still want to sit in the sunshine.

Taehlish Welston.

Do you think we can extract sympathy?

Let's try.

"That really hurts." Wesken whimpered. Tears salted the gash on his cheek.

"Who is the Masikonian?" Her voice was like grinding rocks.

Wesken searched his mind for a name. "Kair-uhm, Tu-Bor- eh, Neo-r, Wes-ke. Wesken! No, that one's my name." He giggled uncontrollably.

The girl's eyebrows scrunched together. She raised her hand.

"Wait! Wait, I'm almost there. Ba-Rah-Ah-Reh-Arkk." Wesken squinted, trying to pass over some combination of letters that sounded familiar.

The girl bit her lip and lowered her hand. She breathed in, as if about hit him again. But she turned and left the room.

Heh. Well, I guess that worked. Wesken waited there, humming a small amount of forever away.

The door opened softly, and the red-haired woman entered the room and leaned against the far wall with her arms folded. Then the wimpy-looking Illian came around, wearing a dark red pelt left of his eye. His nose looked broken.

"Ah, the Illian. You should've just started with that one, save my face some skin."

"Hush," the man with glasses cooed. His voice strained to be cozy.

He's a fruity one. Wesken started laughing.

Stop being mean!

I'm not being mean, that's what he is. Look at him!

"My name is Ecanaes Raydulla. What's yours?" The Illian's voice was trained to sound how he wanted to sound. But something about his eyes spoke disdain.

"Wesken." He smiled bright and proud.

"What a lovely name. Tell me, Wesken, isn't torture so unpleasant?"

"Awh, it's the worst." His eyes fell to his lap, "I don't like it."

"I can ask my friend Ayrah here to stop hurting you."

Wesken nodded fiercely.

"Okay, I'm just going to touch your forehead here, okay?"

"Okay."

The man touched the middle of Wesken's head with a cold clammy hand. The world pulsated in rustic blue while the lantern cast piercing golden rays.

Add another to the collection!

"*Wesken, who was the Masikonian man you were with?*"

Mister Grouch! Wesken's mind instantly brought up a picture of the man with stone tattoos. Large and tall, messy dreads, and powerful.

"*You don't know his name?*"

Nope! Wesken giggled.

Yeah, me neither.

"*Who are you?*" Ecanaes asked in bewilderment.

Who am I? Who are you?

Yeah, who are you?

How did you get in here?

Tater tots!

The man with glasses collapsed backward into a squat. Wesken chuckled lightly.

"What happened?" the girl asked as she leaned forward from the wall.

"He . . . He thinks in Vulgarhe," the man stuttered. He fumbled with his glasses and winced at his uncareful touch against his nose.

"What does that mean?" she asked.

"I'm not sure. The language is practically dead, only used for writing incantations like Tuio's plates. No one *speaks* Vulgarhe, let alone *thinks* in it!" The man began a laugh, high-pitched and strained. "It's like he has an entire army of himself in his head, all fractured into tiny little characteristics. I've never seen anything like it."

"So, uhm, did you get a name or not?" the girl asked.

"Let me try again."

44

AYRAH

His lips were warm and spicy, like the magma that flowed through his veins. Errta lifted from her. "How are you feeling about tomorrow?"

Ayrah nodded slowly. "Korlaii will be easy. When's the last time a guild from the colonies won the national Kaeselwa?"

"Not since I've been alive," Errta agreed with a shrug. "But we need to practice. This chicken chase is distracting."

"From what?"

"The Kaeselwa!" He threw his hands up. The veins in his arms began a soft red glow. "He's trying to sabotage us by keeping us from practicing. I say we ditch the kid, or hand him to Rai and tell him that it's *his* problem."

"Errta. He's still a Warlord, Illian or not." Ayrah ran her fingers through his short hair until the fire in his arms settled.

"Hardly."

Errta wasn't the easiest to hold a conversation with, mainly because he was a bit dull in the head. She was content for the moment, listening to the muffled sounds of the rain.

"When are Malik and Kizmaldi getting here?"

"They'll be here in the morning," Ecanaes called across the common area.

A palm-width, deep red flame grew in Errta's hand, and he hurled it at Ecanaes.

AYRAH

The pale skinned, blonde-haired Illian squealed as it exploded off the wall behind him, but he scurried over to sit beside them anyway. "I cannot get a handle on this kid!" His voice was giddy. "His mind is fascinating. I almost feel that El Rai Ezs would want to dissect him himself."

"You've been toying with that thing for three days, and we're still not any closer to the Masikonian," Errta grumbled, "I think your time with him is over."

"Well, that's the thing! Not only does he not know who the Masikonian is, but it seems like he doesn't even know who I am. Errta, I know it is difficult for you to picture, but it's kind of hard to forget a person once they've gone digging around in your mind."

"It'll be easy to picture once I go dig around yours with my fists." Errta stretched his fingers in and out.

"I'll give it another try." Ayrah pushed herself from the couch and stepped out to the grounds of their rented-vacation manor. It was raining with tropical turmoil. Their backyard had a tool shed for the groundskeepers. Two flame-ranked guards, loyal enough to the Tamagai to stand watch in the pouring rain, opened the sliding door for her as she approached.

"Hi." His small voice peeped out at the sound of someone entering. He faced the other direction. The only visible part of him was his ear length, twisty white hair.

"Hi," Ayrah replied in a bland tone. The tool shed had been cleared of everything. They relocated rakes, shovels, manure, everything but a chair and the boy sitting on it. She strolled around to face him. His left cheek was gashed, blood had dried in rivulets down to his mouth, and down the sides of his neck. "Do you remember me?" she asked, but by the innocent look in his eyes and raised corners on his lips, she knew the answer. She wondered if the kid could even remember what caused the painful throbbing on his face.

He squinted for a moment, and then his eyes lit up in visible excitement. "Nope!"

"What a strange little creature you are. Ecanaes sure has taken a liking to you."

The kid frowned. "Is that the glasses man?" He shook his head, rather aggressively. "I don't like him."

Ayrah felt a sympathetic twitch in her heart, which unsettled her, but she had to admit that the kid was endearing. She reached out her hand, to feel the gash she had given him, but he winced away. "Don't worry. I won't let him in here anymore. But I need to know, who are you?"

"Wesken!" His face lit up in a wide smile.

Ayrah let a laugh escape her. "No, not your name. Who *are* you?"

"What?" Wesken asked, his brows coming together in a pinch. "I didn't hear you, I zoned out for a moment."

A bubble of wrath boiled out of her, "How dare you stop listening when I'm speaking!" Her palms snatched the ends of the chair on either side of him, they strained as she yelled.

An explosion went off outside, and the shack shook. A black-ice sword filled Ayrah's palm without a moment's thought.

The wooden door broke inward with a thunderous blast of wind. She had to shield her eyes from flying debris.

The Masikonian strode powerfully and silently forward.

Oh bloody El.

"The Masikonian! He's here!" she shouted as loudly as she could. The man-beast approached. He held eye contact as he ducked into the shed. He held up a hand, and the air in the room immediately grew heavy, dense, nearly visible.

"Your cries won't be heard, child." His voice was deep and raspy. His annunciation was sloppy, and he swayed in place. The man was drunk. But still, he held a hand on the hilt of his sheathed sword.

Another followed him into the room. A scrawny Sigu Nii, with tangled, unwashed, greasy black hair. His green eyes stuck out in the bland-colored shack. He stood behind and to the side of the Masikonian.

Ayrah lowered herself into a fighting stance.

"Free me!" Wesken yelled at her. "I can help! I can fight!"

She glanced sideways at the kid.

"What?" The green-eyed boy slapped his forehead in disbelief. "Wesken!"

Ayrah seized the instant and sprinted toward the opponent, while sending a weak ball of fire before her. She calculated that the Masikonian would block the cast, leaving his knees free to be amputated.

"Stop." He spoke, plain and blunt.

Ayrah screeched to a halt. The fireball crashed against his shoulder. His tunic singed, caught aflame around the edges. The matte lines of stone tattoo grew a soft, hot white, and the skin beneath his tattoos were searing.

"Kairo, heal my shoulder."

"You could've just blocked it," the boy mumbled as he reached up a hand. A thin, light green mist covered the Masikonian's shoulder. The smell of burning skin between his stone tattoos vanished, the embers cooled, and the flames extinguished with a puff.

Ayrah seethed. "What trick is this?" She tried to kick or run, to fight or flee. But she felt stuck in the place that she stood. "How did you do that?" She had never seen a flame doused by another in such a way. The healing of his skin churned her stomach in rage.

"Calm yourself," the Masikonian spoke to her strangely, like one who was tired of her presence. "I have what you seek." He unsheathed a sparring sword from his hip. It was wooden, with twisting, knotted branches for a cross guard, and a green gem on the pommel. Ayrah noticed, perhaps it could do some type of damage, there was a slight outline of sharpened silver along the blade edges. The Masikonian turned the sword in the dim light. And Ayrah felt breath drain from her.

"Wh-Where did you get that?" she asked, her voice hoarse.

The silver swirled in an intricate pattern through the flat and formed an insignia of a tree with many branches and many roots.

"What *is* that?" She asked, now desperate.

The green-eyed boy spoke up, "You know this symbol?"

"I found this engraving on swords hidden in my father's weapons factory. Brittle swords. Boxes and boxes of them hidden away. Whatever this symbol is, it got him executed for treason." She felt strange, revealing her cards so quickly, prompted by a mere question. But she ached to know the symbol's origin and meaning. She had to know why her father was dead. Everything else was secondary. "It's the insignia of the—"

"The Renovian Rebellion," the boy answered.

Wesken's chair rocked side to side, threatening to tip over as he attempted to twist his body around. "What. Is. Going. On?" he wailed, "I want to see!"

"Make your choice, girl," the Masikonian said. "Your Tamagai are coming."

"I-I—" Ayrah stuttered. She felt dizzy. *Why would my father aid the bark-eaters? Did they have something he wanted?* Movement returned to her, but she remained in place, stuck by some other spell cast within her.

I will find out. She had never wholly aligned with Sigu Nii. And the past quarter-season had been a journey of discovering. Nothing would stop her from finishing it.

Ayrah unclasped the leather straps that tied Wesken's wrists to the armrests of the wooden chair. "Follow me," she said passing them, and darted into the rain.

They nodded.

The backdoor to their manor flung open. Errta, Ecanaes, and four Tamagai guards poured out. "Ayrah!" Errta yelled. The veins in his arms glowed red, from the magma flowing in his veins.

"Run!" she yelled.

"Ayrah?" Errta yelled after her. He kept shouting, but his voice trailed away as she raced sideways along the mountain, leapt over the log fence that gated their grounds and turned south. The ground trembled ever so slightly with every pounding step of the Masikonian.

"Yoohoo!" Wesken whistled tauntingly, and laughed, "You can't catch me!"

They passed a small, wooded park along a Ryalan street, and they passed and dodged Sigu Nii peasants the whole way.

"Where are we going?" Kairo asked between breaths.

"To my father's weapons factory. We'll be safe there for the night." The chimney spires were ahead of them.

"Do they know this place?" The Masikonian asked as they approached the soot-stained brick building.

"Of it." Ayrah nodded. "But they won't chase us all this way. Only Ecanaes would care enough."

She led them through the broken-down metal door. The building was dark and eerie. Rain dripped through holes in the ceiling, and softly echoed throughout the factory.

The inkless, flee-plagued addicts had returned, now along the walls to avoid rain puddles. All of them began to scramble away.

"Wait!" called the Sigu Nii, his hands held out in peace. "Don't trouble yourselves."

Ayrah stared in wonder at the scrawny boy. He was inkless. Did the Ohaer Masikonian keep him as a pet? He and the white-haired kid, both. Ayrah nodded.

The denizens sat frozen, their pipes dangled hesitantly from mouths and hands as they looked to Ayrah for confirmational instruction. She shrugged, and they let out a collective sigh of relief.

The Masikonian looked around the building and belched. "I'm gonna look for somethin' to drink."

"My head feels squirmy," Wesken pouted.

"Let me see," answered the Sigu Nii. He knelt and put his palms on either side of Wesken's head. A radiant green mist began around his hands, it swirled and swirled. He held his hands on the boy's head for a full moment. Then the guy stood up. "All better?"

Wesken smiled and nodded vigorously.

"What is your name?" Ayrah demanded.

"Kairo." Then he pointed. "Wesken. Arden."

"Oh I *know* Wesken—"

"And I'm Wesken!"

She rolled her eyes.

Kairo turned to her, "Why are you helping us?"

Wesken wandered away. Ayrah couldn't see the child, but his distinct floppy meandering echoed somewhere overhead, among the conveyor belts.

Ayrah sized Kairo up. His skin was Sigu Nii, no doubt. But the way he walked, the way he talked, he was clearly something different. He stank of weakness and meekness. Was the boy actually a caramel-colored bark-eater? She spat. "Why does your El have a wooden sword with the same symbol as the Renovians?"

"El is a title reserved for Korteous. The Korta El Nii." When Ayrah did not respond, he continued, "Your father must have been our benefactor. We have been reusing the last supply of bronze swords he gave us, ever since they stopped coming." His eyes moved to her Niiwa. "Why did you attack us?"

"So, you are Renovian." Ayrah nodded. The Ohaer truly was powerful, and skilled in the Masikonian arts, to have done such a visibly convincing job of making the cave-man ape boy look Sigu Nii. She wasn't sure even her mutator in Pratuel was capable of that. "How is it you have vuu?"

Kairo hesitated. His eyes and mouth drifted in silent mulling, as if he could possibly have any information surprising to her. "I found the crown. The prophesied King to Come is upon us."

Ayrah shrugged. "Won't do you much."

"What do you mean?"

"With your war?" She raised her eyebrows. "Even the lost Archeodon won't win you anything."

"We're not trying to win any stupid war." The tendons in his neck tensed. "We're trying to survive! The moment you stop hunting, we'll stop rebelling!"

Ayrah hummed. "Hunt is our nature. Hunt is our vuu." She looked intensely at him. "See, what you don't understand is we don't care about your war. The warriors you fight are the weakest, scummiest, most primeval of Sigu Nii. They're nothing. *Nothing.*"

"Then the crown will free us," he growled.

They stared at each other.

"You're nothing like your father," he said.

That hurt.

Ayrah closed the space between them, and a black-ice sword fit neatly between the back of her forearm and his throat. She searched his green eyes. "My father saw something that I don't. Once I find out what that is, what he wanted from you people, then you can return to your jungle."

"I can't return to my jungle," His voice was infuriating. "You people stole my sister. I've chased her as far as here! Gone through torments you wouldn't believe."

"There are plenty of places to dispose of a Renovian along the way. Why would she be in Ryala?"

"She's an Oracle."

"The future-telling sort?" Ayrah frowned and lowered her sword.

"Aterah's probably locked in some dense cage right now, being poked and prodded by General Rai Ezs for every Renovian protocol there is!"

"Warlord," Ayrah corrected. She remembered the Renovian girl curled up on his couch. "Tell you what, if you help me find out why my father was helping you, I'll help save your sister."

"Aterah first."

"Aye," Ayrah agreed.

45

EIDHIN

A grey blanket of overcast sky illuminated all Vylandria in a meek, moldy light. Eidhin wandered the west market, inspecting carrots and potatoes, parsnips and turnips. "A copper for the sack." One of the vendors pushed a mix of vegetable farther into Eidhin's possession.

"I—" Eidhin paused for a shiver, his teeth clacked together in the harsh ocean winds. The Masikonian chef had come down with a wretched cough, so the responsibility of ingredient gathering fell to Eidhin. He was at a loss. And his speech barrier separated him and this vendor who could not communicate mind-to-mind. "I-I-I . . ." He spared himself, forked over the coin, and took the parcel.

Whitestone and limestone weaved in the collection of buildings around the courtyard. A statue of King Samuel Gehn stood at the center of a mosaic tiled pool. Water spilled from his palms.

"The chains of nuance!" A hoarse, spit-ridden, raspy voice quaked from a man that looked well over a lifetime old. He had white hair, balding in the middle, and a dirty white beard dangling in front of a ragged, open chested tunic. His legs wobbled, nearly knocking at the knees. He clutched a dark walking stick made of a strange foreign wood and strange runes spiraling around.

"Mountains and rivers move at the call." He pointed a shaky, bended finger at Eidhin, with urgency in his voice. "But mind and thought bow to the tongue. I see it. I see it. Rocks and dirt, dear farmer, dark storms wage their wrath against your open waters. I see it. I see their mists and winds and torments. You seek direction, but the needle points to the depths."

Eidhin held his free arm over his face to block projectile spit. It was like someone translated this man's thoughts through each nation's old language, literally, and spat it back out in the Common Tongue. "I-I-I d-d-don-t-t kn-know wha-t-t y-you me-mean."

"Be free!" yelled the old man. He reached out a wrinkled hand.

Eidhin winced away, before his hand would touch him.

Eidhin trudged back to the manor, vegetable sack in hand. What a strange old man. He left an even stranger feeling squirming around his mind.

El Kalyn sat straight postured in a counter chair, set in the center of the common room. "Darker here." He gestured to a section of his hair as he fiddled with a handheld mirror.

"I know how you like it, smart man," cooed a Masikonian woman standing behind him. Her hair was purple, a descending fade of dark to bright, vibrant, and sparkling with silver glitter. The woman's face was soft and young. She had been sculpted to capture the eye. With parts curving and swerving to intentionally lead attention to naught. She brushed her hand through Kalyn's hair, and the strands turned several shades darker upon contact.

The Razite child, Ikondu, sat a ways behind the two, looking bored on one of Kalyn's many leather couches.

Uhm, El?

"What?" El Kalyn jerked away from the mirror.

You told the Illyadra last night that the El Rai Ezs was still incomplete. . . . It wasn't true. Eidhin had been copying different sections of that study since he had arrived at Talynguard. Six long pieces of one very long thought. Sometimes El would instruct Eidhin to fold a copy into a charcoal-black envelope. Eidhin didn't know where it went off to, but it seemed complete to him.

Kalyn's eyes narrowed. "Mind your own," He implied a lot with tone. Eidhin prayed silently he would not end up one of the naked savants. Kalyn waved Eidhin away. "'The Rai of Ayla' is sitting on my desk."

Eidhin hurried along. He peeked into the El's quarters. The door was thick solid wood, with leather covering the seams to keep out sound. It was a spacious room, complete with a four-poster bed, bookcases lining the back wall, a desk, and a red leather chair looking over the Spar'adian Sea.

He snatched a stack of parchments and sought somewhere solitary. No sound. No El Kalyn. No servants bustling and peering about him as if he were greater or lesser than they.

The wine cellar was such a place. It was quiet, cool, and dark, save for the candle he brought with him. He curled up against a wall, cross-legged between two barrels, and began transferring the runes.

"The El of Aylavuera is knowledge."

Eidhin froze. He stared at that first line. "The El of Aylavuera is knowledge," he read it again. *I can understand this.*

Upon Eidhin fell a weight of grand turmoil. For the first time in his life, a decision wracked upon his door. To continue reading. Or to confess to El Kalyn that something was fantastically wrong.

Eidhin rubbed his hands in discomfort, they were cold and clammy. He wiped them against his pants.

"The El of Aylavuera is knowledge." He read it again. It spoke to him. There was no reasoning or cleverability. It spoke with straight, to-the-point, matter-of-factness. And it stirred longing within his very being. He ached to know. To acknowledge. To be knowledgeable.

And he read.

There was a power in the study—an Illian trick used by the highly, highly vuu'd. A cascading, gushing, pouring of understanding. When

Eidhin read, the study took his mind to perspectives of bound-servants and powerful aristocrats, to homeless wanderers, to farmers and smiths and wagon-delivery-riders. He saw slave trainers. He saw the scholarly. He saw how they thought, what caused the formation of their perspective, their culture, and the sole proponent for their system of value: the Archeodon.

By the end of the study, Eidhin had an intimate understanding of the word '*El*' in Aylavuera. How this great kingdom arrived at the forming of the word, what it meant to an Illian, how it's changed over the Ages—especially with the downfall of Kortaes-Renovia.

The study—this "El Rai Ezs" of Aylavuera—created a web in Eidhin's mind. With the Illian crown at its center, and the lowest, most forgotten people groups clutching the corners with which the web resisted collapse.

The last page of the study reported how the other kingdoms cast their influence upon Aylavuera. But instead of satisfying Eidhin, the suggestive nature created a hunger. A need to read the others. The other truths of the word good.

Eidhin peered around the wine cellar. His mind felt sharper. His senses and intuition harmonized. And there rose in him a ripping, crippling fear that Kalyn would find him, that upon contact of their thoughts, Kalyn would know that Eidhin had found a dangerous treasure. Autonomy.

In his thinking, his feeling, his intuition, conclusions from his experience, he somehow realized, and knew beyond any doubt, that this enlightenment would cost him his life.

Eidhin imagined all the possibilities. Kalyn could simply kill him— no, have him kill himself. What need would an Illyadra have to get his own hands dirty?

Kalyn could cut his arms off, gouge his eyes out, melt his ear holes over, and chop his tongue out. Strip him of any sense of being in this world and take over his mind for computational purposes.

Or the least of the three, perhaps Kalyn would just resume Eidhin's Freedom Encryption—his learned fogginess from the Church of Rai. Even this path, this route of punishment, was unacceptable. Eidhin would not lose control of his own mind again. He just couldn't.

He crept up the staircase and passed through the common room. They were no longer there. He searched each room for servant or El or the Masikonian whore from behind the corner of the last.

Ikondu sat up from the couch and looked around. He was scouring. Eidhin cursed quietly under his breath. Was there a new weight in the unseen realm, from Eidhin's gained vuu? Or was there a new lightness, from Eidhin's escaping the shackles upon his mind?

Ikondu's eyes snapped onto Eidhin's.

Eidhin darted back behind the corner. He breathed heavy. He wiped his hands on his pants. Could Ikondu sense him through the walls? He had no idea how Razite vuu worked.

If the child got to Kalyn and so much as tugged the hem of his cloak, then El would know something was horribly wrong. And that would mean re-enslavement or death.

There was a distinct ruffling on the couch. A lurch of standing up.

Eidhin reviewed his choice one last time. To receive ownership of himself, and then to lose it once more? He shook his head. He could never go back.

Eidhin burst out from around the corner, into the common room. Ikondu lurched into a sprint for Kalyn's bedchambers. Eidhin raced after him. Just before the child's dark knuckles connected with the door, Eidhin slammed into his body from the side. They crashed to the ground.

There was a sharp intake of breath, Ikondu was about to scream. Eidhin jammed his palm over his mouth. The child still yelled. The sound and breath seeped between Eidhin's fingers.

"Quiet!" Eidhin hissed.

The child ceased, suddenly still.

Eidhin's eyes widened. He didn't stutter. And he had vuu. Enough to overpower a Razite even, one who could literally *see* vuu. Eidhin awed. "Stay here. And stay quiet." Eidhin pushed himself to stand. Ikondu's eyes swept across his face. Eidhin guessed he should convince the child somehow, add a bit of information, to ensure he would remain. "The chef likes to eat children."

Eidhin cursed himself. What an obvious lie. The chef was sick, even! But to Eidhin's astonishment, Ikondu looked convinced. *That's what you get, for your absence in knowing.* Eidhin smirked.

But Kalyn was still in the way. And the Illyadra had more teachings worth consuming.

Eidhin propped the El quarter's door ajar and heard snoring. He crept in. Kalyn slept naked, curled between a feather-stuffed comforter and the purple-haired Masikonian.

Beside the bed lay Kalyn's long black cloak and his belt, with a blue-pommeled, bone-hilted, Vulgarhe engraved blade. The sword that wouldn't dull.

Eidhin stood over them.

He gently drew the sword from its scabbard.

He gripped the handle so tightly his triceps ached. A blade had cost him the freedom of thought once before, now one would restore it.

Run! yelled his instincts.

Plunge! screamed his desires.

He ripped the sword point-forward into Kalyn's back.

The Illyadra screamed.

Eidhin could feel the blade tear through muscle, nick bone, penetrate organs, and pierce out the other side. Blood spattered across the bed, his face, and the Masikonian whore.

Eidhin pulled the sword out as Kalyn swatted a hand behind him, a ball of fire igniting in the crest. Eidhin flinched and stumbled over Kalyn's clothes, barely evading the fire as he fell to the floor.

Where did the Masikonian go?

The comforter ruffled. Out of the corner of his eye, he could see the sky-blue wool and silk blended sheet raise and lower, vibrating ever so slightly. Eyes popped open, as if the blankets had grown them, and a Masikonian whore leapt at Eidhin. Her sheet-colored skin turned metallic along her arms, and her hands formed into blades. She swiped at him with a screaming cry.

Eidhin flinched backward one step at time, just out of reach from her metal hands swatting at his jugular.

"Stop!" Eidhin demanded.

The Masikonian paused for an instant. But it was enough for Eidhin to plunge the Vulgarhe blade deep into her chest. She fell backwards as her skin turned tan and pale in a leopard's design.

It worked again. Eidhin wasn't stuttering. And he had vuu enough to overpower Kalyn's personal Masikonian mutator.

Then he plunged the sword into Kalyn again, this time from the front. He moved the blade back and forth in the man's torso, to make sure that nothing could save him.

Then he stopped.

He breathed heavily. Death all around him.

He stared at the two for a moment while he caught his breath. He listened to the tremors, the shaky in and out of his breathing. There was a gloss over his eyes. A stinging perspiration mingling with absent-mindedness.

And as his mind and body slowly calmed, the hunger crept back. The thirst for more understanding. He turned from the four-poster-bed and scavenged the quarters for the other studies.

It didn't take long. Being among Kalyn's two most prized accomplishments, they didn't wander far from him. Eidhin sought the red chair by the window. He glanced out at the sea's never-ending attack on the shore.

And he read.

The evening passed as he consumed the Rai of Masikus, Sigu Nii, Renovia, and Ra'che. His bloody hands stained the first of them heavily, but it dried good and crusty by the time he reached the last.

He understood El. The word. What it meant to each kingdom and culture. How it formed. And how it oppresses the lowly.

The final suggestions of Zoë's influence on Ra'che fell from Eidhin's hands, landing softly on the floor among the rest. He felt . . . powerful. The smart kind. The kind of powerful that could glance at the stars and understand.

A shock-ridden scream let loose from across the room.

Eidhin jerked up.

Aesa Vylndaer stood with her hands clasping her mouth. She slowly crept in, croaking, "Father?" She laid tentative hands on his calves and retreated at the lifeless cool.

"He's gone," said Eidhin. His voice was dry, but it was clear. No stuttering. A channeling of vuu in his mind to tell his tongue and throat, *you will pronounce these words.*

Aesa whipped around. Her eyes fell on his. "Ei-dhin?" Sobs stained her voice. "What d-did you do?"

He rose from the chair and walked toward her. "I couldn't go back. I can understand you now, and more importantly, you can understand me."

Aesa backed away. Her butt pushed against the bed, her hands recoiled at the accidental touch on her father. "I could always understand you."

Eidhin drew near enough to peer into her blue-gem eyes. He saw the wispy strands of her blonde hair. He reached up his hand toward her forehead, palm forward. *Come.* He insisted. *Teach me . . .* "Everything."

46

WESKEN

Ayrah was pretty, but she looked like a homeless princess. Her sharp features were regal, but her head had a cluster of dirty dreadlocks. The girl wouldn't stop talking about her dead dad, and somehow that correlated with the Masikonian's wooden Archeodon.

The sun began to peak over the nearby mountain, and its golden rays fractured through the dirty, soot-stained factory windows.

The adults were talking about what to do next, and Wesken tried to pay attention. But honestly? He didn't care. He drew figures in the dust. It had been a long, cold night on the concrete floor. Even the peasants had cotton blankets.

Mister Grouch seemed especially prickly this morning. The way his purple eyes peered at Ayrah stirred discomfort in Wesken.

Words drifted through the air. But the characters running around in Wesken's mind helped to swat them away. Most times, they would battle for attention, but in the early, recent-waking hour, they were all quiet. A tiring sort of quiet. If they weren't talking, then Wesken wasn't thinking. And they didn't want someone else's external voice taking their rightful place.

"Wesken, did you hear me?" Kairo bent down to make patronizing eye contact.

"You have to say my name first. How'm I supposed to know you're talking to me, if you don't say my name first?"

"Wesken." Kairo sighed. "We're getting ready to go. Collect yourself."

Wesken glanced around the floor. There was nothing of his to pick up. "I'm ready."

They left the factory. The way Kairo looked up and down each street, the way his brows were just the slightest tense, the way he walked quicker than usual—something was wrong.

Is someone hunting us? Wesken wondered, also looking around.

I don't see anything.

"So . . . where are we going? What are we doing?" Wesken asked.

"We're headed west, toward the other edge of town. Ayrah will meet us there tonight, and we're making an attack on—"

"Best not finish that sentence, boy," the stoneman barked. "When an Illian El is in town, let alone an Illian Warlord, the streets crawl with ears."

Kairo nodded, but Wesken huffed in defiance. "But it's morning!" he whined, "We're rushing somewhere to wait *all* day?"

"It's a big city," Kairo replied. His voice held distant notes of awe. "We'll reach the ocean by nightfall."

Wesken let his arms and head visibly slump over. He kept his pace, dangling his arms from side to side, "We're walking all day? That's even worse than waiting!" He straightened his posture. "What's the girl doing?"

"She's fighting in some Sigu Nii match," Kairo answered.

"Well, let's go watch that!" Wesken's eyes lit up. Watching other people fight wouldn't be nearly as fun as fighting people himself, but certainly he could settle.

Plus, I think the Ayrah girl is really strong.

And I think she's pretty.

"Why are you laughing? I said no."

"Oh." Wesken paused. "You have to say my name—wait why?"

"I'd go," the Masikonian said. "Watching Sigu Nii weasels roll in the dirt, an ale in my hand." He hummed and nodded. "I could flash my Niiwa and catch a stagecoach to the arena."

"I don't know what a weasel is, but exactly!" Wesken bounced on the balls of his feet.

Kairo sighed. "Alright. But we must be careful. If the Tamagai see us, or if anyone sees your tattoos, we're done for. When we get there, keep them covered." His voice sank into frustrated grumbling. "We really shouldn't even be going."

Arden showed a carriage driver his colorless Niiwa rank, and they were treated like royalty as they rode up the Tuidiia mountain and descended along its spinal clutches throughout the other side of Ryala. Wesken found it humorous to hop with every bump, and even more so when the other two grumbled each time.

The fighting arena was a limestone-brick spectacle of Sigu Nii architecture, built on the backs of Masikonian vuu—made permanent by a Colorless Coin, of course. Banners hung along the walls: a snake eating its tail with five daggers driven through, for the Tamagai; a yellow sun on crimson silk, for Korlaii.

There were many open corridors around the arena, each with a long line of Sigu Nii, and gated by those black-suited soldiers. The stoneman flung his stupid Niiwa score from his arm with pride. Suddenly servants horded them and pleaded their services as they guided them around the oval to a compartment viewing on the ground floor, "Food? Ale? Anything?"

To each, the Masikonian responded, "That sounds great."

After each, Wesken raised a finger and said with a small voice, "Me too, me too."

Mr. Sun was high in the sky. He beat down on the bright yellow sand of the arena, which reflected on each powerful warrior sitting in their limestone viewing compartments around the oval.

Sigu Nii sat all around them. Some had petite Masikonian whores; others had women with matching Niiwa tattoos.

"Is this one a fight-to-the-death, too?" Groaned Kairo.

"No, no," growled the grouch. "It would be a boring match if at least one person doesn't die, but these people have proven themselves already. They're pretty much the best fighters in all Sigu Nii."

The Ryalan Kaeselwa guild, Korlaii, walked out of a corridor onto the pit. They stretched, raised voices in prayer to their ancestors, and whispered among themselves while pointing at specific positions around the arena.

"These ones here?" Kairo pointed at them in horror.

"Well, not them specifically, no," said the grouch. "Korlaii never wins the Kaeselwa. But their stature, it's the best. Everyone fights for sport, but these ones are famous for it."

"Why are they all the way out here?" Kairo frowned. "Shouldn't they be looking for outposts?"

"In the jungle?" The stoneman burst out with laughter, which sounded more like a pack of wolves fighting over food than amusement.

Wesken hummed with excitement.

I'm hungry.

I want to see a limb get chopped off.

The Tamagai exited the opposite corridor, nearest their compartment. A tall woman with flowing black hair, dressed in erotic Masikonian silver undergarments; a bulky man with horns protruding from short hair; and a young man, not much older than Wesken, with blinding red armor and red eyes. The three of them were quiet.

"I don't care about El Rai!" A gravelly voice echoed out of the corridor. "Just play well." He squinted slightly as he crossed into the sun. His hair was buzzed, his arms and legs were like sculpted brick, but he was shorter than Kairo. Wesken saw a fat bruise on the nape of his neck as he passed by.

The hobo princess trailed out after him. "I always play well." She spoke blandly, not caring if he heard her or not.

"That's her!" Wesken bounced. "I know her! What's her name?"

The stadium rustled like a forest breeze as every man, woman, child, and contestant turned their heads to the double-sized compartment on the far wall. A tall, lanky whiteman stepped into view. He smiled. His nose was long, propping golden spectacles.

Wesken leaned aggressively, curious if he could find the sun's reflection off his bald head.

A girl sat beside him. She looked soft. Her hair was dark brown. Her dress was black and red, and she wore bits of jewelry. Her head was down, like she didn't want to be seen, and her hands wrapped the backs of her arms.

Kairo leapt from his seat. He clasped the hellinite chain links that separated the compartment from the arena.

"Steady, boy," growled the stoneman.

The Warlord took his seat and whispered across the stadium, "Begin!" Though it was a whisper, Wesken heard it as if he were right next to him. His voice sounded like sand.

A man screamed. Wesken looked to the pit. An icicle spear brought the buzz-cut brick-man crashing into the wall beside them. His screaming trailed.

"Errta!" It was a concerned yell, but the contestants battled on.

"Ooh, a fight." Wesken hummed.

I wanna play!

Not just watch. He agreed.

Kairo's hand raised slowly.

"Boy," growled the stoneman. "Don't."

Kairo started climbing the chain rail.

The stoneman leapt from his seat and snatched Kairo's wrist. He clutched a mug of ale in his other hand, sloshing with the sudden motion.

"They're more than just barbarians," Kairo said. "They're people. And this one'll die if I don't do anything." He swung his other leg over the rail and landed in the pit. Green mist sprang from his palm as he approached the injured contestant, and encompassed the icicle that nailed him to the wall—it shattered. The fighter fell limp with his face in the sand. He moaned softly. His back faced them with a hole the size of a person's head, with shrimp linguine spilling halfway across the reach of his arms.

Kairo continued toward him, hand outstretched. The mist got in there. Green. Vibrant. Opaque. It sunk deep into the hole. Before their very eyes his skin began to patch. The organs lifted and returned to their place, dusted of the sand they rolled in.

He screamed again. Different this time. The last had been of desperation, life-threatening pain. This was a scream of fear. He rose to his knees, his eyes wide in horror as movement returned to him. "What is happening to me?" He looked at Kairo. "What are you doing to me?"

The battle gradually stopped. Heads all around the stadium turned to witness the event of someone being healed.

"*There you are.*" A whisper wailed through the arena.

Ohh, he's done it now! Said Wesken.

Kairo's eyes locked with the Warlord's.

47

EIDHIN

The Library of Vylandria was a mountain of courtyards and whitestone buildings with wrap-around pillared walkways. Each section of the building was distinctly square, ornate with detailed carvings in the stone, but built so elaborately together in the fashion of a tower that the building conglomerate appeared to be circular. Snow struck out from the corners and lips of the architecture, frozen into shape by the snapping ocean winds.

The library was topped with a massive brass brazier, with blue fire roaring between two rotating mirrors, making it a lighthouse of magnificent scale.

Eidhin figured the entirety of human knowledge must be stored within that structure.

The courtyard surrounding the library had a perimeter of ten-wing-high walls bordering manors and inner-city markets. On the west edge the high walls fell straight into the bay and a two-hundred-pace-wide harbor. Fishing vessels sailed to and from the snowy mists, and ships docked to unload spices and foreign goods.

Vylandria cried in Eidhin's ears. Each passerby's trudging through the snow, the delighted weight on their faces, the way their arms threw this way and that, these things spoke to him. He felt as if he could hear the tone of their thoughts. Body language and facial expressions were like paragraphs of information scribbled across the crowds. Everyone was anxious and festive.

The Aylan took place on this day. Under the watch of the Black Guard—wait, what were they doing here? Sigu Nii soldiers in black and gold armor surveyed many hundreds of people shuffling through the wide gates in the library walls and filling the massive courtyard between the gate and the pillared palaces in the middle.

Eidhin doubted he had ever seen a Sigu Nii before. Not a real one, anyhow. He had seen many during the visceral, intellectual journey that the Study had taken him on. And when he tied Aesa down in the cellar, blindfolded her, and absorbed her processing into his own, he had experienced all the important events of her life—and met a few Sigu Nii in the process.

"Aren't you scared?" It was her voice. Well, not really. It was more like, what her voice *would* say. If she were totally in charge of her own cognition, she would be fighting him every step of the way. That wouldn't be helpful at all. *"Not only are you about to take the hardest test in the world—you've killed an entire body of governance. You've murdered the Illyadra of Philosophy."*

He searched himself. And found apathy. He wasn't scared. At all. Perhaps fate drove him with a call louder than fear. Or maybe, with his new heightened intelligence, he knew that he could win the Aylan, and it would take a whole season for a servant to work up the courage to open Kalyn's bedchamber doors, in search of him. Or another possibility still, maybe emotion and Illian vuu were in combat with one another.

Most anyone could enter the walls. Most anyone could study, read, or sit in the lecture halls of the palace lowest. But Eidhin wasn't interested in this building. Now that he had consumed the direct, potent, undiluted works of an Illyadra, he knew that most of this lowest story would be full of plain lies.

It took the El Rai Ezs study for Eidhin to realize that deception was the dominant way of exercising Illian vuu. And nearly any baboon could offer their work to the lowest story of the library. The real, world-view-changing, cutthroat information was guarded in the palaces at the top. Undiluted teachings from past Illyadra. And to be granted access there, he had to prove his right by winning the Aylan.

Hundreds of wooden tables, without chairs, were spread around the courtyard. Aylan officials and attendees huddled together in the snow.

Eidhin tightened Kalyn's heavy cloak over his neck, combating the cold.

"In times recent, these written exams took place in the lowest story. But with the rise of the *De.Ae.Ar.* shipping company, and the increasing supply of outdated ships—with which people can ride, people are flocking from all over the isles," said the official to Eidhin, as he waited his time at one of the tables. The official, dressed in fur boots, and blue sashes wrapped around thick black robes, handed Eidhin parchment and quill with a number of questions.

The series of questions were rather easy assessments of intellect—propositions of pattern recognition, short-term memory, math, and words mixed together in a rather philosophical sense. A pruning of the unreasonable.

"Indeed," said the official with a frowning nod. "You've passed. What shall you be called, then?"

"E-e. . . El Rai Ezs." Eidhin stuttered out the first letter of his name and recoiled. Eidhin was hardly him any longer. Eidhin was a farm boy, talking constantly of onions and dreaming of the greats. Eidhin was a slave, constrained by mentally unfit cognitive capacities. Eidhin had killed a man. And an Illyadra at that. He decided it best to become someone new. Someone who befitted his current gulfs of understanding.

The official raised his brows. "That is not even a name." But he peered around, saw the others waiting their patience's limits, huffed, and wrote the name he was given.

"Wh-what-t—" *Stop it. You do not stutter anymore!*

Eidhin took a deep breath, trying to get used to freedom. He used his newfound vuu, his stolen knowledge of worldly congregations, and told his tongue to pronounce these words.

"H-how many people pass the entrance exam?" he asked.

The official shrugged. "About half." He gestured to move toward the library tower.

Entry parchment in hand, El Rai wiped his eyes across the beaming, magnificent Library of Vylandria while approaching its lowest level. Several buildings clutched the outside edges, hardly maintaining sameness with the library given its distance from the center mass. These buildings were probably full of books and scrolls on things that no one cared about.

How do you convince a man of something that he wouldn't give two bloody shrugs about, whether it was true or not?

He passed the pillars that wrapped around the main bulk of the lowest story, half covered in snow, and followed the crowd through the great, open double doors. His boots clacked with a hundred others against smooth marble tiles. Radiant golden light illuminated a great circular room and a hundred little stone tables holding up swords.

They were cheaply made. They were rusty. A simple leather strand wrapped around the bottom shaft for a hilt. The crossguard was a rod. El Rai Ezs' stare lingered across their edge. They were sharp. All of them.

He heard a splatter and saw a slow dripping of blood from one of the swords off to his right. He turned its direction. The blood vanished. It was just his imagination.

The irritation within him grew.

Why were all these swords around the room anyway? It was illegal to carry a blade longer than your own forearm. The king had declared them weapons of mass destruction—tools of deviance, whose only purpose is to kill or injure.

And still, they kept following him around, didn't they?

A man in thick robes took a podium at the far end of the room. His voice was mutated with Masikonian vuu to be louder, but not by much, Illians were a quiet bunch. He said, "Two to a table."

El Rai Ezs wandered around and picked a table at random. He found himself a sword away from a fat chap. You could tell he was from Isle De'tungola by his thick orange hair. He looked a lot like Tuladrna, actually.

Once the room settled, the Aylan official spoke again, "Use your vuu to convince your opponent to kill themselves. A debate to the death. All schools of thought are in bounds." There was a tense pause. "Begin."

The beginning of the Aylan, El Rai Ezs imagined, was far less explosive than the Niiwa. He assumed, in the Niiwa, vuu swelled up as far as the stands in the first half-moment of the round. Here, El Rai smirked across the table, and said, "Kill yourself."

Now, the El Rai Ezs study had so much power in it, that while everyone around him was persuading, convincing their opponent to commit suicide, a sick gleeful expression was crawling over fake Tuladrna's face. As if he wouldn't rather do anything other. He snatched the sword from between them, tossed it to the floor, and while the pommel was bouncing off the tile, cracking it, he threw his face into the point of the blade with such ferocity, that it struck out the other side. His arms and legs smacked limp against the cracked tile. Both him and the sword held each other upright and he continued to slide down the shaft by a few knuckles.

A half-amused gargle escaped El Rai's throat. He looked to the edges of the room, wondering if the officials had witnessed his victory. They had. The orientations of their faces were, surprisingly, concerned. They shared mutterings with the Black Guard. One of them, after making one final piercing contact of the eyes with El Rai, hurried out of the room, up the stairs.

El Rai Ezs waited a long time for the round to finish for everyone else. He stepped over bodies. His boots lapped in thin pools of blood. Nearly all of them climbed the stairs to the next story of the Library of Vylandria.

The next round was much the same.

His opponent, who at least had the confidence to touch foreheads, began first, *"We've found five languages predating the Common Tongue."*

El Rai Ezs scoffed. The ever elusive "we." It was a manner of establishing an *us* and a *them*, while letting your opponent's subconscious preceptors understand that whoever *us* is, you aren't apart of it.

El Rai answered, *there have been twelve different languages discovered in Masikus alone, all older than the Common Tongue—which took over Zoë as Aylavuera's marking influence in the tenth Kortaes.*

His opponent's eyes grew wide. *"A simple 'false' would suffice—"*

It's most interesting, even, that the hieroglyphics of Old Vulgarhe have been found on each continent. This seems to suggest it was a common language at one point in history.

His opponent's eyes grew wider still. *"Indeed, you've—"*

And indeed, it was. The Vuulguardians ruled Zoë in the first Age.

"Vuulguardians?"

Creatures of the afterlife. Demons. Answered El Rai Ezs.

"You're lying."

He wasn't. Deception was the dominant way of exercising Illian vuu on another, and here, he was doing it with truth. *I can prove it.* He said.

"H-how?"

Die.

His opponent's fingers had slithered up onto the table with each passing thought between them, curled around the sword's cross guard, spun the sword slowly so that it faced him, and with the final command, he pulled toward himself with all his strength. The sword launched into his chest, erupting out of his back, spraying contestants a whole table over in blood.

This was the second round of five. At this rate, El Rai would grow bored before someone had a real chance of winning intellectual combat against him—er, knowledge-based, anyhow.

He looked to the officials. Their eyes darted away, trying to appear as if they weren't solely watching him. El Rai Ezs squinted.

"I don't like this," said the cerebral ghost of Aesa Vylndaer. *"We should get out of here."*

His opponent on the next story of the tower was an old man. He had been waiting there, a sword away, before El Rai Ezs got there. He probably won the previous two rounds in a past season and had been studying the materials on the first two levels of the library for a lifetime. But now he wants more. It would be the death of him.

The Aylan official said, "Begin."

El Rai Ezs and the old man touched foreheads, and El decided to begin the offensive this time.

Begin with Vuulguard.

There is an influential realm. A place whose air, whose water, whose very dirt is made of influence. It is the afterlife.

People think that your decisions here, affect there. As if being more knowledgeable while you're alive would win you a more elegant life after death. This is ludicrous. It is the realm of influence.

Why else would we keep time, according to Vuulguard?

The soul is to Vuulguard the way your body is to Zoë. Maybe you think one comes after the other, but you have the incorrect one.

Pause on El Rai Ezs.

When you use the Old Vulgarhe word 'El,' it is not your physical self that says it. Sure, your mouth moves, and your vocal cords make the correct vibrations, but so much more so than this, it is your soul that says it.

El.

To put it in simple terms, sir, the term means 'good,' in the Common Tongue.

Your soul calls knowledge—or a more knowledgeable man than yourself, such as me, El, because of your influences. All the ways that you have been influenced, in every little moment of your life, have led you to call me El.

A Sigu Nii soul has been led to call the viciously recognized man 'El.'

A Masikonian: the trending man.

End it.

But your soul, sir, is like a droplet wandering its way down the windowpane, and instead of melding with the seams, you instead have found an ocean at the bottom. Me. Your influence in this space is overwhelmingly inconsequential.

The old man was frothing at the mouth. A grey blankness had been drawn over his eyes. He was utterly without autonomy. El Rai Ezs knew that he could have this man do whatever he wanted. Kill himself. Or the man behind him. Or maybe do a little dance.

The man probably looked a lot like El Rai had, prior to the current forecast.

El Rai Ezs' vuu was so powerful here, that it would have taken control of a much smarter man than this one. And El knew, if he were to do that, he would be in charge of their vuu as well. If this man were a Masikonian instead, then El Rai could have him turn into a monkey, or whatever he commanded. El Rai Ezs imagined then, that the Illyadra, or the king for that matter, must be in charge of entire legions of people. Whether to live their lives, or to absorb their mental capacities.

El Rai Ezs looked to the Aylan officials. One was holding his breath. The other's eyes were darting around the room. Even the Black Guard looked on edge.

What's going on? El Rai Ezs had a bad feeling creeping up his gut. His blonde hairs stood on end. The air felt thin, wispy, like before a storm. A thunderous blast boomed directly behind him. The cold touch of a blade landed on his throat.

He could see the sword out of the corner of his left eye. It was gold. A blue gem webbed through the flat like lightning.

"Did you think I would not notice the missing of my own left hand?" His voice was like lava. Burning, bright, and beautiful. It was King Samuel Gehn. "Seriously. If you cut my left hand off, would you expect me to not notice?"

Before El Rai could have the old man, who was basically a slave, come around and attack King Samuel, black electric sparks crackled in front of him, on the other side of the table. Lightning struck. And in its place stood a monster. He was taller than the room, so that he had to crouch. His skin was grey, and cracking, like dry paint. He wore a hellinite crown on his head. It was the king of the current Kortaes. Ash.

"Hold on, Sam," he said. It was casual, but it was no less a command.

"Do you know who he's killed?" His whisper felt slicing in El Rai's left ear.

"Aye," said Ash. His gaze turned. His eyes were dark iridescent. "What do you call El?"

"W-w-what?" asked El Rai Ezs.

"You said that a man's influences mold what is El to him," explained King Ash. "So, what do you call El?"

El Rai Ezs has always wanted the same thing. To be one of the greats. To be taught about, and discussed, and never forgotten. "Me," he answered.

A tormented smile sprang across King Ash's face. He turned to Samuel. "I'll have him."

The blade left El Rai's throat, and King Samuel said with an injured tone, "Indeed."

King Ash held out one of his grey, cracking skin, torso-sized hands, and El Rai Ezs grabbed it. Black lightning shot through them both. And the next moment, they stood overlooking the harbor. Thunder rang softly, as if running from them.

His voice expressed the growl of a hundred beasts. "Sigu Nii populations are falling."

It wasn't a question, but King Ash seemed to desire an answer. El Rai Ezs thought for a moment, and said, "Increase tourism. Allow immigration. Target Masikus. They are an attractive people. With their women and men walking freely among even small towns, they would undoubtedly stir pleasurable thoughts of reproduction. And perhaps, if that is not enough, I would remove vuu from the first round of the Niiwa. Sigu Nii women can be just as strong with vuu as a man, but perhaps you might scare some into becoming babymakers with just the smallest push of physical strength."

"I see your place in Sigu Nii." King Ash nodded. "You will be Lord Mayor of Vasara, in charge of the Renovian encampments. They grow restless in their prison-cities."

"The Renovians? What good are they? It might be better for all parties to just wipe them from—"

"No," growled the king. "You're to keep them alive. Keep the Renovians at bay, keep them from becoming a civilization. Wage against them just enough to keep them weak. I await the return of their Archeodon. Only then will the destruction of Vuulguard come forth."

El Rai Ezs thought on this, too. And said, "Then I will let them out. If we await the return of their Archeodon, but the Archeodon awaits a decent time to return, then let's farm it. I know a little about farming. Some nurture is what they need. Some hope. We can let them escape from the prison cities. And after a generation, maybe several, the crown will return."

48

FORST

Edrei was called The Two Half Cities because a river ran right through its center. The halves were connected by a single stone bridge, covered with moss in the ancient Renovian fashion. It was one of the high-walled cities the Sigu Nii constructed to imprison Renovians. After Adakon won it back, it fell right in the middle of the war front, making it the central hub between Renovia's untouched east, and their vast, hidden militia peoples in the west. The walls that once imprisoned them now protected them.

Forst climbed the glistening steps of the fortress in the far corner of the city. The administrative barracks of the Sigu Nii during the imprisonment, it was now the home of Commander Gaershin, and he welcomed the generals on their frequent visits.

Yet today was different. An incident had occurred, the likes none of them had seen in all their lives. Echoes of this incident rippled across all Renovia—accounts of their own soldiers demonstrating vuu.

When the Oracle made it out of the jungle, un-rescued and unfortunately alive, Baenek and Adakon had thought certainly, that was it. The rebellion was done for. Renovia has fallen. But Forst knew otherwise. The whiteman, and whatever other powers that be, were going to extract some unknown thing out of them. A resource. It hadn't arrived yet. But it would.

Was vuu that resource?

Sure, the Sigu Nii have plenty of the stuff to spare. It polluted them. But Forst had heard tales of other nations, other kingdoms and peoples that demonstrated vuu, totally foreign to Renovia and Sigu Nii alike.

So, Renovian vuu then. Was that the resource for which the whiteman kept them alive? Was this the harvest he spoke of, back near the end of the dry season?

Horns blasted in Forst's mind. Everything turned hues of blue and gold. He leaned against the wall of the spiral staircase, breathing heavy.

"You're getting old, general," chuckled Adakon, passing him. "They're just stairs."

Forst grimaced. *What do you want, El?* The Whiteman forced his blaspheme.

The Whiteman's whisper was like a slithering snake. *"Vuu has brought your people nothing but pain."*

True.

He walked as normally as he could toward the commander's war room.

Though it was deep in the fortress, the ancient ventilation did well to keep off the jungle's rigorous humidity. A slight breeze could be felt from slits in the ceiling.

The generals took seats around a table, joined by Commander Gaersh-in of Edrei, and several of his outpost's Chamberlains.

"Has it happened to any of you?" asked General Baenek, who never failed to cut through formal greetings and chit-chat.

Heads turned and eyes swept around the room. Everyone was frightfully curious. No one spoke.

"Has anyone seen it happen?" asked General Adakon. He leaned in, with his hand laid flat on the table.

"I have." One of the Chamberlains raised a tentative hand.

The seven of them turned to listen.

He continued, "It wasn't like any of the stories. It wasn't in battle. It wasn't with flesh or blood or even disease. From my balcony I watched the soldiers train near the river. They sparred. And in one particularly competitive engagement, a soldier's well-seasoned sword snapped. The bronze shattered into several pieces. His sparring opponent didn't let up. Even after the squadron's captain called off, he swung and stabbed, while the other was rolled and dodged. And then this bright flash happened. I had to shield my eyes. It was green. And when I looked next, his sword mended. Incomparably scarless."

"How?" asked General Adakon. "How has this happened?"

El Rai Ezs screeched, *"It is wicked!"*

The room turned to Forst. Had he spoken aloud?

From their eyes, their mouths, Forst knew that most of them were riddled in uncertainty. They did not know how they felt about this incident. He stuttered out quickly, "Vuu has brought us nothing but pain. Even before our great exile. It seems clear to me that the Korta Ellanii despises its wicked witchery."

There was a pause. Some shifted in their seats. Even if a chamberlain wished to disagree, Forst was a general, one of three who had founded the rebellion.

"Funny, Forst," pondered Adakon, "I would have thought you would advocate its weaponization."

"Make them fear it!" His whispers were like screams.

Forst shook his head from side to side in long sweeping motions. "No!" He held hands to his temples, to steady himself. "Green, yellow, red—vuu is bad. I would rather have three sticks and the Korta Ellanii on my side, than an army of Sigu Nii or Renovians with vuu."

"I didn't realize you were so . . . reverent," commented General Baenek.

"He has a point, though." Adakon stroked his beard, deep in thought.

"Graeynesh Law," said Forst. "We need to exile vuu, under a new Graeynesh Law entry. Immediately."

The Whiteman whispered in scowling approval, *"Yes."*

"Do any disagree?" asked Adakon.

Baenek raised his hand but there were none other.

Adakon nodded, "Alright then. Vuu is evil. Its use will be punished by exile."

Forst meandered from the war room. It seemed he was mistaken. Vuu wasn't the resource that the whiteman wanted from them—it would've been their means of escape. He climbed a bamboo-built staircase. It looked like scaffolding next to Edrei's towering walls. These giant stone bricks once kept thousands of Renovians from seeing the outside, now they helped keep the Sigu Nii out. Wind blew harsh up here. It snapped at Forst's last few strands of hair.

Finally, they were given a sword worth using, a power equatable to the vuu of Sigu Nii, and now it was illegal. Forst banged his fists on his temples and eased the balls of his feet over the edge. A hundred reaches stared up at him. He closed his eyes, held his arms wide, and tipped forward.

Wind blasted around him as he raced for the jungle floor. His arms flailed through the air. But when his eyes snapped open, sure that the ground was about to slam into him, he was still standing on the wall.

"What?" he asked.

"I've not gotten my full use out of you." screeched the Whiteman.

49

EL RAI EZS

"Little Renovian." It was a whisper. An echo of a thought. The heavily accented *t* and *le* ricocheted between Kairo's ears.

Kairo stood in the sand, near the edge of the arena. His gaze was fixed on the Warlord's. He tried to yank his eyes, his head, his attention away.

Kairo's periphery faded black. Like tendril vignette slithering across his pupils. It was like unconsciousness was grabbing hold of him.

Two melon sized palms, hard and calloused, ripped Kairo away. Arden searched his face with wide, glossy eyes. "You're ready." His breath-heavy voice reeked of ale. He unsheathed the Archeodon by its wooden hilt, turned it on its side, and thrusted it urgently at Kairo.

Kairo took a weary step back. "You said I would die."

"Aye. Ya would've. But ya 'ave vuu now." He gestured again for Kairo to take the wooden sword. "Renovian vuu is lost on me, anyways. It was always meant for you. You jus' needed to be able to wield it, withou' being consumed by He who lies inside."

Kairo hovered his hand over the hilt. Like small wooden swirling vines, a thin film of moss, and a bright green gem tucked between a bundle of roots on the pommel. He let his fingers fall in the notches.

Light blasted across Kairo's vision. His muscles convulsed. His grip around the sword tightened. He fell to his knees, arms flexing across his abdomen. He yelled and screamed; he gasped and cried. Power surged. It touched his ligaments, strengthening them. It touched his mind, freeing it. It touched his soul, deepening it.

With his free hand he wiped tears from his cheeks. "I'm king, then? *The* King?"

"Aye," said Arden, a hint of smile on his tone. "I'll be needing my silver sword back—"

Crack! Black lightning struck between them. A white ball of fire exploded in its place, blasting Arden and the injured fighter thirty steps out. The gust of blunt, firey force slammed against Kairo as well, but a white hand darted through the inferno and caught him. He slammed into the ground. Breath choked out of him in a windless cough. The fire settled and Warlord El Rai Ezs stood over him.

"Little Renovian." El Rai smiled wide, his tongue rolled over his bright white molars. Gold-rimmed spectacles glinted in the noonday sun over his rigid blue eyes.

Kairo yanked one foot beneath him, but before he could stand, a cold pair of fingers bobbed him on the forehead.

A sound like boulders smashing against one another made Kairo's ears ring. The harshly colored golden sand beneath his back slid away. He clawed through the dust, but it was falling, as if being drained from the stadium. The high arena stands melted into bouncing piles of salt. The last thing Kairo saw, before everything around him grew dark, was the Warlord's sharp blue eyes.

Even here, in this strange vuu, vibrant green lightning arched off the sword. Kairo could feel its power.

"Who are you, little Renovian, that the Archeodon has deemed you fit? Worth speaking with, mouth to mouth?" The Warlord's thoughts rang loudly. The intimacy felt cruel. Vulnerable. Advantageous to one party.

The Graey Castle's courtyard slammed up beneath Kairo. But the stone looked smooth and clean. Not as if some great-footed beast had torn through.

Faint wisps of a man drifted across the other side. *"You'll be a good king someday, better than your father."*

Kairo reached his hand out to the man. He wanted to speak, touch, feel his thoughts and ask, *"Dad?"*

"The direct son of Ivan Graeynesh?" Whispered the Warlord.

Was that true? Was that why he and Aterah grew up peerless in NeoD-erii? Everyone had a prison city of origin, like Ravid or Zetola or Edrei. But not him. This was why. He's Kairo Graeynesh.

"You're quite an old fellow, little Renovian. How are you here?"

An old man hobbled up. He leaned heavily on a dark bamboo staff and grumbled nonsense under his breath. It was him! Wesken's grandpa! When he held out his hand, black lightning shot throughout Kairo. Then, he was in the jungle.

The Warlord's finger lifted from Kairo's forehead. The arena crashed back into Kairo's perceptions. He realized that he was still lying in the sand; he grabbed his head and tried to shake the searing distortion.

So, this was Illian vuu. The Warlord gained generations of information from Kairo, that he didn't even know himself, in a matter of moments.

"It seems you've been touched by a god," remarked the Warlord, jealousy lightly hidden. "Neo Nii."

"You are *wicked*," Kairo stammered as he rose to his feet and readied the wooden sword.

"Religion is for the poor, dear boy. I would know." El Rai Ezs rolled his eyes. Slow. Deliberate. Making sure his disdain was evident. "Your value hierarchy has been tainted by oppression." He flung the claim like a fruit peel. "Before the turn of Kortaes-Renovia to Kortaes-Sigu Nii, your 'El' was obedience. A rather pompous moral, if you ask me. But now? Fear. The Sigu Nii ordinance has stained what you call good. So certainly you see now: Your meekness, your weakness, are only reverberations of a lost battle clusters and clusters ago. Little Renovian. You think me evil because I am strong when you are not. You think Sigu Nii are evil because of what they call 'El,' when theirs is the untampered definition. Even now, your precious Adakon has outlawed vuu. Your race will never evolve. They have been conditioned to fear it and call that fear 'good.' And yet, you desire power all the same. You just go about it in a pompous, paradoxical, ever out-of-reach sort of way. Indeed." He spoke with certainty, as if he had several lifetimes to ponder and articulate.

Kairo stood dazed. Each word passed like a relaxation of the muscles. A distancing of his attention. Until the end, when something clicked. He understood what the Warlord El Rai Ezs was saying and began to nod. His arms hung loose by his side.

"Fear isn't our El." Aterah's approaching voice cracked from unuse. She stood small behind the Warlord, her hands covered the backs of her arms. "Korteous, God of all spaces, Kortaes of Yeshwin and realms unseen, is our only El."

Kairo latched onto her words. He tried to nod.

"You misunderstand El," continued Aterah, looking at the Warlord. "It is not our most valued virtue. El is an entity, to whom each of us is personally encouraged to delegate the tiering of our values. El sanctions the top for himself. Then all branching, derivative matters are practiced for a lifetime."

Her words were not perfect. Spells and magic and mystical things did not ring out within them. She had not several grandfathers-to-grandkids worth of time to mull. But her point drove through Kairo. He grasped it.

An opaque green mist radiated from the wooden sword.

Kairo leapt forward. He brought the bright silver edge to the Warlord's neck. "Release her. And let us leave."

"*Kill him,*" said a powerful voice in Kairo's mind. He glanced sideways at the Archeodon, cautiously speculating.

Kairo pressed the blade in tighter but hesitated for the Warlord's response.

The Warlord's dominant hand struck up faster than Kairo could see. Black sparks dissipated in the coattails. And an explosion like thunder blasted when the Warlord's knuckles smacked the blade off his neck. "Fine," said El Rai with a shrug. "If this is how you wish to play. I have *all* of Ryala under my influence." His body turned to lightning as he teleported to Aterah, his hand on her shoulder, and with another *crack*, they were both back in the viewing compartment across the arena.

Without another word uttered, the soft song of ten-thousand drumbeats whispered from each direction. Every Sigu Nii, Masikonian, and Illian in the stands stood and marched in unison. They dropped over the arena walls and landed in the pit, billowing the sand. Some of them stumbled, groaning from twisted and sprained ankles. Others stood abruptly, uninjured, and began sprinting towards Kairo.

Kairo backed away from the arena wall and spun around in horror.

The Kaeselwa fighters native to the city dropped into fighting stances. Icy swords and rings of fire exploded in their possession.

The Tamagai let loose noises of bewilderment. Errta groaned, holding his head in one hand, "What have you gotten us into, woman?"

The red-eyed boy spat from the side of his mouth, "Illian vuu." Yet the crowd ran past them.

Men, women, and children from the stands above the corner of the arena reached Kairo first. He backed away from them initially, erratic, but quickly decided that the middle of the pit, where all the Sigu Nii would reach him simultaneously, was disadvantageous. He extended his arm, placing the silver point of the Archeodon against the neck of the closest. "Stop," he demanded.

The mindless level-two grunt swatted the point away with one hand and tried to take it in his grasp with the other.

"Stop," Kairo pleaded. The common man continued, trying to grab the sword by its edges. Kairo looked away as he thrust the point through his neck.

By then, dozens were closing in. Kairo reached out a palm, channeling energy from the wooden sword. He hoped to free their minds. Heal them. But nothing happened. No green mist radiated from the Archeodon, as if the sword had gone silent.

A wall of black ice, wind-frozen with horizontal spikes, erupted before him. The blood of three dozen commoners sprayed the arena. Organs and ligaments and torn heads splattered the sand.

Ayrah landed into a slide, one foot out and a hand up for stability. She searched Kairo's face out of the corner of her eye. "We're neck deep, now."

Kairo silently cheered. He needed her. He had been unsure that she would remain on their side when things got rough. But here she was—slaying.

A childish chant graduated in clarity as it neared them "I wanna play! I wanna play! I wanna play!" Wesken bounded up, skipping from side to side, weaving through the horde, carrying a dark bamboo staff. "So, I kinda got bored while you and the Whiteman were talking. I looked around for snacks, and look! I found this funny looking stick!"

Black lightning thundered between them. "Aye," grumbled Arden. His beaded dreadlocks swayed from his teleporting motion. He held his stone-tattooed arms out, concentration rippling across his cheeks and forehead. Five steps out from their group the sand and the stone liquidated. It turned muddy and sloshy. The groaning, mindless, approaching on-lookers slowed to a stumble as they waded waist high.

"Quicksand!" Wesken shouted. "I *love* quicksand." He bounded up to the edge of the pool, ready to dive in, but Arden snatched him back by his collar.

Ayrah threw swords into the horde that exploded into ripping spikes of black ice on impact. She aimed to thin the crowd that made it into Arden's pool.

Arden charged small flaming orbs and released them into the wading commoners.

Wesken ran around the edges of the quicksand, cracking his black staff on the forehead of any who came near.

The level-two and level-three Sigu Nii flung vuu from every direction. Little shards of ice ripping their way, or fireballs whistling overhead. Kairo could feel a drawing within him to eradicate the hostile forces. He flinched his hand in their direction, channeling power from the sword, and dispersed the incoming vuu.

"Level-five!" he called out to the group, urgency made clear in his tone. The Korlaii Kaeselwa fighters drew near. They side-stepped, ducked, and rolled around Ayrah's crowd-thinning attacks. They wouldn't be caught by chance.

"Aye," said Ayrah.

The five fighters of Korlaii circled the quicksand pit, taking cover mostly behind the peasant horde. Their veins were bright across their faces, glowing molten red and an icy neon blue.

Two of the fighters circled near each other. They turned to one another, and without a word passing between the two, one of them channeled vuu into their palms and raised the ground. The sand slid and poured out around them as rock raised where they stood. From there, one blasted a streamline of white fire while the other shot crumbling rocks from their tower with explosive speeds.

Kairo leapt in the way of the blinding white fire. He brought the Archeodon up and struggled as it connected with the sword. The skin of his forearms seared. It turned red, blistered, and cracked.

The rocks from the tower crashed into Arden. He hollered in pain as it exploded against his stone-tattoos. Another rock slammed into Ayrah and sent her flying to her back. Blood splattered across the wading commoners.

Just as Kairo finished dispersing the white-fire, two more of the Korlaii fighters ran, jumped, and kicked gusts of flame beneath them. They soared and flipped through the air and landed on their platform.

Ayrah moaned. She tried to sit up, and a squeal escaped her.

"Save her," said the crown.

Kairo reached out his hand. He could feel their wishes mingling and mixing, *save Ayrah.* Green mist blasted from his hand, it coated Ayrah, and her gashes and burns were repaired. She stood, fire dawned in her eyes.

Wesken and Ayrah leapt at the Korlaii fighters.

"Say shadowa," said the crown.

Kairo hesitated. The four of them were spread thin, fighting the four level-five fighters among them, and keeping the grunt horde at bay. Saying an unknown thing seemed amiss.

"Say shadowa," demanded the crown.

Kairo relented. "Shadowa!"

Ayrah whipped her head in his direction. Baffled turned to appalled. "You're sure, jungle boy?"

Kairo hadn't the slightest what it meant, but he nodded.

Ayrah dropped to her knees. The veins in her face, her arms, and her legs grew black. Her eyes turned black. The darkness erupted from her. That intangible mist that Verano used to slay Norly, incapacitate Kairo, and steal Aterah away. It blasted forth from Ayrah.

"To me!" Kairo yelled. Wesken and Arden leapt over the mist and took cover behind Kairo. Green exploded around them. It made like a thin bubble, shielding them from the encapsulating darkness.

Besides the faint green light around them, it was dark. Kairo breathed heavy. He could hear Wesken and Arden doing the same. The darkness waged war against their sounds, against the light, between them and the outside world.

The darkness finally swirled in on itself, fading into small tangible marbles. Every incoming attacker, many steps out, had disappeared. Stray organs and splatters of blood lay around, and the next wave of peasants slowed to a halt. Ayrah sat on her hands and knees, coughing out of weariness.

El Rai Ezs slowly approached from the middle of the arena. His lips were pursed. "I cannot have you depleting my city any longer." He shouldered off his outer robe, revealing a level-five Niiwa on his lower left shoulder. Its appearance was not like Ayrah's darkness, nor Arden's colorless tattoo. It was a blue gem. Deep and glowing in a rhythm. "How about a grash, little Renovian? The Oracle for the Archeodon."

"*Yes,*" said the crown.

Kairo nodded. When he stepped tentatively into the quicksand, the mud crusted where his steps landed, allowing him to cross casually.

They paused in the center of the stadium. Facing each other, twenty steps apart.

The Warlord threw his arms out wide and pulled them back together in a clasp. A purple shockwave rang out across the sand.

Kairo threw an arm over his brow but nothing hit him.

A dark, glowing purple sphere grew beside El Rai. Tentacles slithered out from the portal and drew the edges wider.

"I have seen the realm of influence," exclaimed the Warlord in a righteous tone. "Let its beasts reign again!"

Its tentacles slid across the sand. They were slimy with red goo. The monster that followed had no eyes, and teeth like nettles stretching across a gaping hole. It flung its tentacles in a roundabout motion, sprinting for Kairo.

"Not the pasta demon!" cried Wesken with obviously pretend fear.

The Warlord shot bursts of orange-fire at Kairo.

Kairo blocked and sliced the fire with the wooden sword. When the monster was still five steps out, a tentacle struck out with surprising reach. It punctured a hole through Kairo's abdomen. Blood gushed out. He screamed.

Green mist blasted from his own hands. It seared against the hole in his abdomen. He could feel his organs mending back together on the spot.

A slimy arm darted out again, Kairo chopped sideways, amputating one of many.

"Aim for the head," informed the Archeodon.

The monster wailed. It flung its arms, spinning around to Kairo's opposite side. Before Kairo could reach out and slice, fire blasted him from the side. He flew backwards and rolled across the sand. The Archeodon fell from his hands.

Kairo gasped for air. His head throbbed, and light danced across his vision. He could feel the Renovian vuu gone from him. With his hands throwing sand behind him, he leapt to his feet to sprint for the sword. The monster raced.

Kairo leapt onto the Archeodon, facing the blade up as the monster's teeth closed around him. Power surged through his body.

A revelation flooded his mind as the monster sizzled and fell to its side. The Sigu Nii gain proficient vuu through their ancestry. The Illians through their study. The Warlord's words rebounded between his ears, *obedience.* Kairo needed to obey the sword, align himself with it.

What would you have me do, El? Kairo asked.

Vines, dark and wooden, slithered out of the hilt and wrapped around Kairo's wrists. It wouldn't be knocked from his grip again.

Kairo approached the Warlord. He walked toward him, steady-paced. Fire and ice and neon blue lightning ripped from the Warlord's palms. Kairo dissipated each with a mere inclination of his will.

He was unstoppable. Every attack was like the manifestation of a hurt soul that needed to be healed. Where he previously feared vuu, for his life, he now marched onward, unhindered.

The Warlord cast his hands aside and tore a ravine in the ground between them. It raced between Kairo's feet, but he maintained his pace. Rocks flew above the gaping hole and he gave no second thought to whether they would hold his weight.

"An observant mind—I know what you hate, child!" the Warlord screeched.

Kairo's vision flickered off. As if someone had drawn hands over his eyes, the world grew black. He remembered what direction he was facing, toward El Rai Ezs, and took another step forward. Except, he never felt his foot land. Actually, he couldn't feel anything at all. He opened his mouth and cried aloud, but he didn't hear it. Where was his voice?

"Steady," said the crown, loud and clear in his mind.

Kairo nodded. He breathed. And the fear of vuu dispersed from him, for the moment, he wasn't afraid of senselessness. He continued forward. He couldn't even feel the push and pull of his muscles, let alone the contact of ground on his foot. He could be swimming on the ground, for all he knew. As far as he could tell, he could be dead. But he continued the motion of walking, in case it was working.

A faint whiny, "How?" drifted from the Warlord.

Just like that, the distortion lifted. Feeling returned to him, and Kairo descended upon El Rai Ezs. The Warlord slammed his pale palm against Kairo's forehead, but on contact, green mist exploded his hand away.

Kairo held the silver edge against his neck. "Aterah."

"Kill him," said the crown.

Again, Kairo hesitated. He brought the wooden sword down on the Warlord's head. But the fleeting moment of second-guessing on Kairo's behalf was enough for the Warlord to dart away. Streaks of black lightning coated him as he moved, and the Archeodon slashed through the War-lord's upper left arm.

El Rai Ezs' screaming lingered as he teleported away.

The vines retreated from Kairo's wrist. Its power receded; its voice silenced.

Kairo ran to Aterah. Sand kicked out in his wake, he reached the viewing box beneath the stands and hugged her. "You're safe now," he said. "Arden, get us out of here."

Everyone held shoulders, and black lightning surged through the five of them.

50

ATERAH

Eastern wind blew against the face of the mountain with an ocean callous. Storm clouds rolled in.

Arden rested his hands on his knees. He gasped for air. "Bloody El," He peered over his shoulder, at the Niiwa arena a day's walk down the mountain. "I'm out of vuu. Whatever Black Guard, or Illian tricked grunts we run into, it's on you."

Kairo nodded. "You did well."

He kept glancing at her. Little side-eye snatches. She understood. An age had turned since they were ununited.

"This way," said Ayrah, continuing up the flagstone streets. Her voice was like one who had just misplaced a hammock as night began to settle.

All of them were covered in blood. Even herself, who had been frozen out of the fight by the Warlord's mind tricks.

The white-haired boy wore an absent face. His eyes glossed, like he was taking a mental retreat after the day's events. His steps flopped and his bamboo staff dragged behind him.

The five of them arrived at the Tuidiia. Thunder cracked from the building nonstop, another booming before the last had finished ringing. Black Guard stood in several lines across the wide limestone steps, each in fighting stances, with vuu at the ready.

Ayrah scoffed. A tired, short, clicking of the breath. "You couldn't have put us *in* the Tuidiia?"

Neon-blue electric vuu cracked out from the row of guards closest. A dozen strands of lightning arched through the air. Kairo threw himself before the group and let the vuu connect with his wooden sword. Orange sparks blasted out from either side of the blade's flat. The vuu disappeared.

"We can't win," said Kairo.

There were too many of them. And the group was too tired.

Arden pulled Kairo and Ayrah near, shot a demanding look at her and Wesken to grab on, and screamed. His voice shattered and cracked into whispers as black lightning shot through each of them.

They were in the Tuidiia. Just near the hellinite pads that led to Vasara.

Arden looked ghostly. Sweat drenched his dreadlocks. He wobbled toward the pad and began to collapse.

"Through the cargo bay!" Ayrah indicated an indentation larger than the others. Boxes and crates piled high beside it.

Kairo caught Arden by the shoulder and channeled his green vuu. "In." Kairo glanced back at the Black Guard, who realized what had happened, and started storming the glass office doors. "In. IN!"

They piled onto the pad.

Black lightning.

The group snuck through Vasara's alleyways. Aterah stifled and silenced frequent sneezes. *Good Korteous, the city of old smells terrible.*

Arden breathed with sickly desperation the whole while. He said, "We should flee south. To the city-states."

Kairo wouldn't hear of it. "For the first time *ever*, Renovia has a hope." He gestured to the wooden sword. "We'll train the rebellion to use vuu. We can win now."

Aterah wasn't so sure. It seemed to her that powerful Sigu Nii were not delegated to the jungle, but weak ones. And now that they had the very thing that they wanted, all of that could change. Plus, the Warlord said that the rebellion had outlawed vuu. It was going to be an uphill battle, on both fronts.

By nightfall, they were half a day's walk south of Vasara.

Aterah dreamed of the Warlord.

Illian servants moved hastily, wrapping the Warlord's armless shoulder tight in a white bandage. El Rai Ezs fumed. Black Guard Officers of Ryala, the remaining Korlaii fighters, and Verano, all crowded around him in his beachside manor.

The captured Tamagai sat on their knees, bound by ankle, wrist, and mouth.

"Quiet!" the Warlord shuddered. "Take this Razite," he pointed to a dark man among the Tamagai, "and find me the nearest Renovian with vuu capable of healing my bloody arm."

El Rai Ezs closed his eyes, but Aterah could hear his thoughts.

"Your great Elness," he said.

A moment passed.

"Speak," came a voice like a thousand voices. Each wicked and snarly.

"The Archeodon has surfaced. It heads toward the Delkop."

"At last. Gather the Warlords to Sehlya. We prepare for war."

– *END* –

ACKNOWLEDGMENT

Firstly, thank you Lord Father God and your Spirit for constantly inspiring me. So many fun, cool interconnections between characters or allegories that Hannah and I have found, were not explicitly intentional on my behalf. I want to thank you, Lord, for how much you've guided my hand in this process. It warms me to bring this glory to you—please continue to grow within me an ability to boast your name.

Thank you Peter Lundell, for giving Illyadra the most attentive, detailed, developmental editing and suggestions imaginable. And thank you Adrienne Kisner, for your inspiring essay regarding Illyadra's marketability and viability in the industry, as well as your copyediting, copyediting, copyediting, and copyediting.

Thank you to the talented artists who contributed to this story: Grzegorz Wozniak and your illustration of the Delkop mountain range, Rachel Ward and your cartography of the great nations of Zoë, George Downes and your beautiful illustration and layout of the hardcover and finally, Austin Collins for helping brainstorm potential book cover ideas--can't wait to play the board game you've engineered!

Thank you John R, for helping daydream this world with me when we were in middle school. You were there when I drew the first continents of Zoë, long before they even had names. Let me know the next time you have eight consecutive hours to spare for a high round on Der Riese.

Thank you Jacob A, for being an awesome nurse and teaching me about the horrific symptoms of tetanus. You were my favorite friend to talk time travel with.

Thank you Cindy, for editing the first few chapters and encouraging me to grow as a writer. Another thank you to Ethan for listening to the first few primitive descriptions about Kairo and his world, way before he even had a name.

Thank you Kaylee and Justin, for being the first round of test readers to finish the book in its entirety. I would have a much worse story without your feedback.

Thank you Trent, for talking fantasy with me. You keep me fresh in the genre. Never stop thinking the way you do, silly, in hypotheticals.

Thank you Jake G, for being my longest standing close friend. You were the inspiration for some of Kairo's deeper characteristics—not the annoying ones, I promise.

Thank you Marie, for passing on to me an insatiable bug within my soul that requires travel. You taught me the healing power of laughter. You taught me the beauty of the foreign—a landscape, a culture, a belief system, a food—so few people know how to appreciate these, and for that, I am unimaginably grateful.

Thank you Susie, for encouraging middle school me to pursue writing this world. You were so good at providing a stable household, when church had thus far been the only consistency. The brain space that you freed up was invaluable for being able to juggle all of the characters, themes, and cultures in this series.

Thank you Mike, for being a stable, manly presence in my life. Sometimes I imagine Arden's voice like yours. You have real fight in you. Not just like Verano, or El Rai Ezs. But a chasing fight, like Kairo. A lot of men these days, me included, have been disheartened from fighting. You have a lot of wisdom on that front to speak into our hearts and minds. Read *Wild at Heart* by John Eldredge.

Thank you Sharon, for relentlessly, graciously imparting the wisdom of the Lord onto me, which is more valuable than gold. You began the conversation about value hierarchies—a theme that will continue through the rest of this series. I pray that you're able to see all of your influences on Kairo and his world and enjoy them.

Thank you John G, for being fun. The adventures we had together when I was younger are core memories. *"You's two!"* said the guy kicking us out of his restaurant. We made a time capsule when I was young containing a small bit of Kairo that stayed in the ground for ten years. You were a primary inspiration for a previous version of El Neo Nii. He's been toned down a lot in this book, but I think more of you will shine through him in later editions.

Thank you Mom, for giving birth to me. God's ability to heal brokenness is a historical, metaphorical instance of what he's able to do to our hearts, minds, and souls. He demonstrates his power of restoration through healing injuries and deformities, so that we can lean on Him with the more important parts of our existence.

Thank you also to the many other mentors that heavily influenced me during the daydreaming phase of this work, like John L, Brian, and Ms. Sherry. Another shoutout to Jack and Liz for sheltering, inspiring, and discipling me.

Thank you Kristy, for pouring into me like a mother through my middle grade years.

Thank you Dad, for loving so many people unconditionally, for being clever—I stole that eyeball question that Wesken asked straight from you, and for being daring, you taught me how necessary a daring spirit is for a man. I pray that heaven has plenty for you to explore.

And finally,

Thank you Charlee, for being an awesome sister. You're growing into such an incredible woman. I'm sorry that I haven't been able to save you from the influences of evil with Kairo's relentlessness. Even though this is a fictitious story, whose genre is of the most unbelievable kind, God *does* heal.

And thank you Hannah, for being the most supportive wife any writer could have asked for. I met you just before completing the first draft of Illyadra, an absolute nightmare of a story. But you saw what I saw. You saw where it was going. What it would be. I love you so much. Thank you for the countless hours we've spent talking about the theology behind the scenes, character motivations, or economic viability for the weird cultures. Thank you for believing in this story and my writing full time, knowing wholeheartedly that God could take any amount of time to bless this.